EXTRAORDINARY PEOPLE

Paris.

An old mystery.

As midnight strikes, a man desperately seeking sanctuary flees into a church. The next day, his sudden disappearance will make him famous throughout France.

A new science.

Forensic expert Enzo Macleod takes a wager to solve the seven most notorious French murders using modern technology — and a total disregard for the justice system.

A fresh trail.

Deep in the catacombs below the city, he unearths dark clues deliberately set — and as he draws closer to the killer, discovers that he is to be the next victim.

EXTRAORDINARY PEOPLE

PETER MAY

ISIS

LARGE
PRINT

First published in Great Britain 2014
by
Quercus Editions Ltd.

First Isis Edition
published 2015
by arrangement with
Quercus Editions Ltd.

A catalogue record for this book is available
from the British Library.

ISBN 978–1–78541–042–0 (hb)
ISBN 978–1–78541–043–7 (pb)

Published by
F. A. Thorpe (Publishing)
Anstey, Leicestershire

Set by Words & Graphics Ltd.
Anstey, Leicestershire
Printed and bound in Great Britain by
T. J. International Ltd., Padstow, Cornwall

For Ariane and Gilbert

Ordinary men have to live in submission, have no right to transgress the law, because, don't you see, they are ordinary. But extraordinary men have a right to commit any crime and to transgress the law in any way, just because they are extraordinary.

Dostoevsky, Crime and Punishment

PROLOGUE

August 1996

He finds himself in a cobbled courtyard, breath hissing back at him from buttressed walls. A rasping, gasping breath, full of fear and the certainty of death.

He knows every window by heart in this cloister of the two charnel houses. Colours embedded in the glass with affixed enamel. *Le Miracle des Billettes*, *Elijah's Sacrifice*, *The Mystic Wine-press*. Beloved images lost forever in the dark.

Moonlight glances off the shiny surface of cobbles worn smooth by the feet of holy men. His own feet slip and clatter as he scrambles through an alley between buttresses, heart squeezed by the hand of desperation. A green bin spins away in the darkness, spilling its decaying contents across the yard. The door ahead of him lies ajar, the corridor beyond bathed in the ghostly light of the moon, angling between tower and apse to slant through frosted glass arches. He sees a sign and a red arrow — *Vitraux du Cloître* — and turns the other way, past the sacristy.

The door to the church is open, and he is almost sucked through it into the vast, glowing stillness. The stained glass rises all around, its colours turned to black

1

by the dead light of the nearly full moon. His panic fills the vaulted vastness with every painful breath. To his right a statue of the virgin cradling the baby Jesus watches impassively, impervious now to the prayers he has offered her so piously over so many years. The neighbouring chapel has been given over to noticeboards pasted with announcements that he will never read.

He hears the footsteps following in his wake, and breath rasping in lungs that are not his own. He flees along the north ambulatory; past the Chapel of St. Paul, the Chapel of St. Joseph and the Souls in Purgatory. At the end of the church, ninety silvered organ pipes rise in shining columns to the figure of Christ Resuscitated, flanked by two angels. He wants to scream, help me! But he knows they cannot.

He turns beneath the nine metre span of the only remaining screen in all of Paris, a delicate tracery of stone carving and spiral staircases curling around slender columns soaring into blackness, and he stops beneath Christ on the cross, a Calvary taken from the chapel of the École Polytechnique to replace a predecessor destroyed during the Revolution. How often he has knelt here, before the altar, to receive His flesh and drink His blood.

He stops here now, and kneels again for one last time, the footsteps almost upon him. And as he rises and turns, the last thing he sees at the far end of the nave, before red turns to black, is a sign commanding him to SILENCE.

CHAPTER ONE

I

July 2006

The Rue des Deux Ponts cuts across the centre of the Île St. Louis, from the Pont Marie straddling the Seine on the north side, to the Pont de la Tournelle on the south. The island is no more than two hundred metres across and, side by side with the Île de la Cité, stands at the very heart of old Paris.

Enzo had wondered how his daughter could afford an apartment here, where four square metres of real estate could cost upwards of three hundred thousand euros. But Simon had told him that she was in a tiny sixth-floor studio up in the roof of her apartment block, and that the rental was being subsidised by her employer.

The previous night in the small hours, at home in Cahors, he had questioned the wisdom of trying to see her. He had to go to Paris, anyway. The stupid wager! But in the end, it was Sophie who had made his mind up.

It had been a hot twenty-one degrees, humid and sticky. Somewhere across the jumble of mediaeval red-tiled roofs a clock had chimed two, a deep,

3

sonorous ring that pealed across the centuries. The old quarter of this ancient town in southwest France dated back to Roman days, and in some of his lonelier moments here Enzo felt only a breath away from the beginnings of human history. His armchair reclined by the open window, his guitar laid across his chest, he stared at the ceiling and brushed his steel slider along the length of the fretboard, strings softly weeping, evoking the blues of a not so distant past. By leaving for Paris the next day he would miss the start of the annual Cahors Blues Festival.

Floorboards creaked in the hall. "Papa?"

He'd turned his head to see Sophie in her nightdress framed in the doorway, and had to blink away sudden tears, surprised sometimes by just how much he loved her. "You should be sleeping, Sophie."

"Go to bed, Papa. It's late," she'd said softly. She always spoke English to him when they were alone. English with an oddly incongruous Scottish accent, like the sweet scent of whisky drifting in the warm air of a summer's night. She'd padded across the salon and perched on the arm of his chair. He'd felt her warmth.

"Come to Paris with me."

"Why?"

"To meet your sister."

"I don't have a sister," she'd said. There was no rancour in it. Just a cold statement of fact, as she saw it.

"She's my daughter, Sophie."

"I hate her."

"How can you hate her? You've never met her."

"Because she hates you. How could I ever like anyone who hates you?" She had lifted his guitar away then, and laid it against the sill, and slid down into the seat beside her father, laying her head on his chest. "I love you, Papa."

He had found the apartment block quickly enough. Number 19 bis, on the west side of the street, next to Le Marché des Îles fruit and vegetable store. He had no idea what the entry code was for getting into the courtyard. He could have rung for the concierge, but what would he have told her? That his daughter lived here, on the top floor? And if the concierge had taken him up, what would he have said if Kirsty had shut the door in his face?

So he lunched in the L'Îlot Vache bistro on the corner of the Rue St. Louis, sitting on his own in the window, watching the faces drift past, sunlight slanting down between tall old buildings that leaned at sometimes curious angles. He sat until the restaurant was empty, his waiter hovering impatiently nearby, waiting for him to pay so that he could go home for the afternoon. Finally he settled up and walked across the street to the Louis IX Bar, and found himself a table in the doorway and nursed a beer for nearly two hours. More faces passed. More time. The angle of the sun grew more acute as it slid down the sky into early evening. And still the tourists filed by, perspiring in the July heat, and private cars and taxis belched their fumes into the fibrillating air of a long Parisian summer's day.

Then he saw her, and in spite of all the hours of anticipation still felt as if he had been punched in the gut. It was twelve years since he had last laid eyes on her, a brittle, difficult fifteen-year-old who wouldn't speak to him. She was crossing the Rue des Deux Ponts from east to west, carrying groceries in pink plastic bags dangling from both hands. She was wearing denims that cut off inches above the ankle and sat low on her hips beneath a short, white, sleeveless top that bared her belly to the world. It was the fashion, although very few girls had the figure to carry it off. Kirsty was one of them. She was tall, like her father, with square shoulders and fine, long legs. And she wore her hair long, again like her father, but not tied in a ponytail like his. It was a rich, chestnut brown, like her mother's, and flew out behind her in the warm breeze like a flag of independence.

Enzo left several coins rattling on his table, and hurried along the street to intercept her. He caught up with her as she was juggling with her shopping bags to punch in the entry code. "Here, let me take one of these," he said as the electronic lock buzzed and she pushed the door open with her foot.

She turned, startled. Whether it was the unexpected Scottish voice in the middle of Paris, or the odd familiarity of this strange male, it took her some moments to realise who he was. By which time he had taken the bags from one of her hands and was holding the door open for her. Her face flushed with confusion and embarrassment and she pushed past him into a passageway that led to the inner courtyard. The time it took for that simple act was long enough for her to find her anger. "What do you want?" she hissed, keeping her voice low as if she was frightened they might be overheard.

He hurried after her as she strode along the passage and into a tiny, paved courtyard filled with potted trees and a tangle of lush, green plants. Apartments rose dizzyingly all around them into the small square of blue Paris sky above. Ground floor windows were barred, and the door of the guardian's apartment stood at the foot of an ancient wooden staircase. "Just to talk, Kirsty. To spend a little time with you."

"Funny . . ." Her voice was coarse with bitterness. "You were never around when I wanted to spend time with you. You were too busy with your new family."

"That's not true, Kirsty. I'd have given you all the time in the world if you had only let me."

"Oh, yes!" She turned on him at the foot of the stairs. All the colour had drained from her face. "Of course. It was my fault. I should have known. It was my fault you left us. It was my fault you chose to go and live in France with some other woman and start another family. Why didn't I see it? All those nights I lay awake listening to mum crying herself to sleep in the next room, and I never realised it was my fault. All those birthdays and Christmases you weren't around. All those moments in a girl's life when she wants to know that her dad's watching, that he's proud of her. The school concert. Sports day. Graduation. Why didn't I understand then that it was my fault? After all, you always had a great reason to be somewhere else,

7

didn't you?" Her emotion finally choked off the diatribe, and she was working hard to catch her breath. The intensity in her eyes made it hard for Enzo to meet them. He had never before felt the full force of her anger. He was shocked. "Give me those!" She snatched at the bags of shopping he was holding, but he held them away from her.

"Kirsty, please. There's never a day in my life that I don't think about you, or the hurt I caused you. You've no idea how hard it is to try to explain these things to a child. But I'm still your father, and I still love you. All I want to do is talk. To tell you how it was. How it really was."

She stared at him for a moment in silence, anger turning to contempt. "I don't have a father," she said finally. "My father died a very long time ago." Her eyes dropped to the bags he was still holding. "Are you going to give me those?" But she barely gave him time to respond. "Oh, well, fuck it!" she said. "Keep them." And she turned and ran up the stairs leaving him standing in the courtyard, feeling foolish and bereft.

He had no idea how long he stood before finally laying the bags carefully on the first step. There didn't seem any point in going after her with them. He turned slowly and went back out to the street.

II

He was sitting alone at Kong's rooftop restaurant above the Kenzo building on the Rue du Pont Neuf when

8

Simon finally showed up. The place was packed with diners enjoying the Paris panorama. Enzo had hoped to dine at the Samaritaine, where the view was better, taking in all the familiar landmarks in the fading light: the Panthéon, Notre Dame, the Eiffel Tower. But it had closed down, and he'd had to make do with the more restricted view of the Tour de Saint Sulpice and the Vedettes du Pont Neuf, along with the inane babble of the Paris in-crowd. A crowd in which Enzo had rarely felt so alone. The fact that everyone else was in company seemed only to emphasise his isolation. He'd had little or no appetite, and left his main course almost untouched, preferring instead to work his way steadily through the bottle of Pinot Noir he had ordered.

Simon waved away the waiter and pulled up a seat. He'd already eaten, he said, and poured himself a glass of Enzo's wine. He turned to take in the view of the city as he sipped it, perhaps guessing the answer to his unasked question. Then he turned and said, "Why do you always look so damned miserable, Enzo?"

Enzo grinned. "Maybe because I am." He gave a little Gallic shrug, an unconscious gesture acquired over many years. "So when are you going back to London?"

"Tomorrow." Simon looked at him directly and sighed. "I don't know what your problem is. Take a good look at yourself, Magpie." It was the nickname Simon had given his friend when the white streak first grew into his dark hair during his early teens. And it had stuck. "You've got a great life here. A beautiful apartment in Cahors. A daughter most parents would die for . . ." No sooner were the words out of his mouth than he cringed at his gaffe. "Jesus, Enzo, I'm sorry."

Enzo smiled ruefully and shook his head. "Daft bastard," he said. "You're just lucky you never had any kids. Bringing home boyfriends with stupid hair and extraneous pieces of metal stuck in their faces."

"Bertrand?"

"He's too old for Sophie."

"What age is he?"

"Twenty-six."

"And Sophie's what? Eighteen?"

"Nineteen."

"So he's seven years older than her. You were what? Thirty, when you set up home in Cahors with Pascale? And what age was she?"

Enzo growled, "Twenty-three. But that was different."

"No it wasn't. Seven years is seven years."

"I didn't encourage Pascale to give up her studies. And I think I had more to offer than a lifetime pumping iron in some stupid gymnasium."

"Like what? The brilliant career in forensics you nearly had?"

Enzo glowered dangerously. He folded his arms and crossed his legs, body language drowning out what he didn't want to hear.

Simon said, "I'm not being judgmental here, Enzo. But she was just twenty-three. A kid, for Christ's sake. Have you had a conversation with a twenty-three-year-old recently?"

"Not as many as you," Enzo shot back. "Twenty-three must be about the average age of the women you're screwing these days."

"Probably. And, you know, the sex is great, but the conversation sucks. Why do you think none of the relationships lasts more than a few weeks?"

"Because you're too damned old. They tire you out."

Simon grinned. "You might be right."

They sipped in silence and listened to the animated voices of the diners at tables all around them.

Until Simon said, "So what happened?"

Enzo avoided his eye. "She wouldn't talk to me."

When he glanced up he saw Simon gazing at his glass thoughtfully and suddenly saw him looking old. For years he had only ever seen Simon as the boy he had gone to school with, played in the band with, shared girlfriends with. Now, his head slightly bowed, the once dark beard peppered with grey, the light caught the scalp beneath his thinning hair and cast shadows beneath his eyes. He looked his age — a man approaching his fiftieth birthday. Simon stopped staring at his glass and drained it instead. "I thought things might have changed."

"Why?" It was Simon who had told him that Kirsty was in Paris.

"Her mother." He signalled the waiter and ordered a brandy. "You know we've always kept in touch."

Enzo nodded. He had never been sure quite why. The three of them had grown up together in Scotland, on the south side of Glasgow. Simon had gone out with Linda before Enzo, and then all but lost contact when he went south to study law in England, returning only once to be best man at their wedding.

"Linda thought things might have changed. After all, Kirsty's a big girl, now. Nearly finished her postgrad in translation and interpretation. And you don't win a year's internship with a company in Paris unless you've got your head pretty well screwed on."

"Well, nothing's changed. Not for Kirsty, anyway."

"What did she say?"

"She told me to fuck off."

Simon's brandy arrived and he sipped on it contemplatively. "So what now?"

"I might as well just go home."

"I thought you had an appointment with Raffin?"

"I'm not sure I'll bother."

Simon cocked an eyebrow. "Two thousand euros, Enzo. You can hardly afford that on your salary."

Enzo glared at him. Simon had been instrumental in forcing the issue to a bet in the first place. And as the only lawyer present had promised to bear witness to the parties involved and keep the cash in escrow until an outcome was agreed.

The tables beneath the candy-striped awning of Le Bonaparte were nearly all full when Enzo arrived, Parisians and tourists alike indulging in the café culture that so characterised the city, sitting in serried rows sipping drinks, watching the endless ebb and flow of humanity in the Place St. Germain des Prés. It was nearly dark now, the biscuit-coloured stone of the ancient church of St. Germain floodlit starkly against a deep blue sky. Enzo took a table on the corner, beneath a No Entry sign, and ordered a brandy. He checked the time. It was after ten, and he was late. He wondered if, perhaps, Raffin might have come and gone already. He had told the journalist that he would recognise him by his hair, tied in a ponytail, a silver stripe running back from his left temple. He never thought about how other people might view him, with his baggy cargo trousers and white running shoes, and his large selection of voluminous, collarless shirts, which he rarely tucked in. And, of course, the ubiquitous canvas satchel that he slung across his shoulder. Sophie's favourite fond insult was to call him an old hippie. Which was probably how most people saw him. But he was also a big man, and kept himself fit by cycling, so he tended to stand out in a crowd. He was aware that women found him attractive, but he had always shied away from committing to another relationship after Pascale.

By twenty past he had finished his brandy and was contemplating leaving. As he searched for coins in his pocket, he became aware of a figure standing over him. He looked up to see a tall, thin man with longish brown hair swept back to the upturned collar of his white shirt. He carried a light summer jacket carelessly across his shoulder, and his trousers, belted at a slim waist, were immaculately creased, gathering in fashionable folds around neat, black-leather Italian shoes. He had a cigarette carefully held at the end of long fingers, and took a final draw before flicking it away across the cobbled street. He held out his smoking hand. "Roger Raffin," he said. "Sorry I'm late."

13

"That's okay," Enzo said, shaking his hand. He was surprised at how cool it was.

Raffin sat down in the vacant seat, and with the practised ease of a *vrai Parisien*, signalled a waiter with a black apron and white shirt who materialised almost immediately at their table. "A glass of Pouilly Fumé." He nodded towards Enzo's glass. "Cognac, is it?"

While they waited for their drinks, Raffin lit another cigarette and said, "I checked you out on the internet, Monsieur. It says you are a professor of biology at Paul Sabatier University in Toulouse. Why am I even talking to you?"

"I was with the *police scientifique* in Scotland. But it's a long time since I practised. The internet didn't even exist then."

"So what makes you think you are qualified to pass an opinion on anything today?"

"I was trained as a forensic biologist, Monsieur Raffin. Seven years with Strathclyde police in Glasgow, the last two as head of biology, covering everything from blood pattern interpretation at major crime scenes, to analysis of hairs and fibres. I was involved in early DNA databasing, interpretation of damage to clothing, as well as detailed examination of murder scenes. Oh, and did I mention? I am one of only four people in the UK to have trained as a Byford scientist — which also makes me an expert on serious serial crime analysis."

"*Made* you an expert, Monsieur Macleod. Things have changed."

"I've kept myself apprised of all the latest scientific developments in the field."

"So why aren't you still doing it?"

"Personal reasons."

Raffin looked at Enzo appraisingly, fixing him with startlingly pale green eyes. He looked no older than thirty-five or thirty-six. He had a creamy-smooth tanned complexion and pale lips. His nose was thin, and sharp, and a little too prominent, but he was a good-looking young man. He sighed as their drinks arrived and took a delicate sip from his misted glass. "Why should I co-operate with you on this?"

Enzo tipped his brandy glass to his lips and the stuff burned all the way down. He felt reckless and brave and in need of something to fill a vacant place in his life. And it seemed like a good idea not to mention the wager at this point. "Because I'm going to find out what happened to Jacques Gaillard," he said. "With or without your help."

III

Raffin's apartment was in the Rue du Tournon, on the first floor, above two art galleries. It was within a hundred metres of the floodlit splendour of the Senate building, the home of the French government's Upper House, tiers of classical pillars supporting its crowning dome at the head of a long, narrow street running all the way down to the Boulevard St. Germain, and the Seine beyond that.

Raffin tapped in his entry code, and pushed a huge, heavy green door into a cobbled corridor. At the far end, they emerged into an L-shaped courtyard dominated by a tall chestnut tree. Lights burned in windows which lay open, cooling apartments after the build-up of heat during a long, simmering day. They could hear people talking, laughing, still seated around dinner tables. Somewhere, someone was playing a piano, an uncertain rendition of Chopin.

"I'll want a guarantee of exclusivity," Raffin was saying. "No one else gets to publish the results of your investigations. I'll have sole publication rights. Perhaps we should put that in writing."

"Whatever you like," Enzo said.

Raffin pushed open a half-glazed door and they began up wooden stairs that circled a narrow lift shaft. He had made up his mind in an instant, draining his glass of Pouilly Fumé at Le Bonaparte in a single draft and getting to his feet. "Okay, let's do it. I have reams of notes made during my research. Only a fraction of the stuff ever made it into the book. Come back to my place and you can take them away to look at." He had already started across the street when he stopped, and almost as an afterthought turned back to Enzo. "And you can pay for the drinks."

On the first floor landing he fumbled in his pocket for his key and opened the main door into a square entrance hall. Pale light from streetlamps in the courtyard slanted through venetian blinds in long, narrow slats.

16

Enzo immediately sensed the journalist's tension. "What's wrong?" he said.

Raffin raised a quick hand to silence him. Double doors from the hall lay open into the dark of the main salon. Beyond, bright yellow light fell across the floorboards from an opening in mirror-glazed bedroom doors which stood ajar. They could hear someone moving around beyond them, and Raffin tensed as a shadow passed through the light.

"*Cambrioleurs*, he whispered. Burglars. He placed his jacket carefully over the back of a chair and turned to a bookcase with shelves ranged up to the ceiling. He selected a large-format, heavily bound encyclopaedia from one of the lower shelves. Clutching it above his head in both hands, he advanced into the salon. Enzo followed, thinking that the journalist looked just a little ridiculous. The *History of the World E to F* seemed an unlikely weapon. Waving an encyclopaedia around his head, he was more likely to frighten a burglar to death than do him physical damage.

Suddenly the bedroom door opened wide and electric light flooded the room. Raffin froze in mid-stride, the *History of the World* raised in readiness. A woman stood in the open doorway looking at him in astonishment. She was tall, wearing a long, black dress gathered at the waist. It was sleeveless, with a quite daring neckline. Dark hair, shot through with hints of silver, tumbled in luxuriant curls around her face and over her shoulders. Her skin was clear and lightly tanned, and large, startled black eyes held them

17

both in their gaze. Enzo thought she was quite the most beautiful woman he had seen in a very long time.

She looked up at the book above Raffin's head. "For Heaven's sake put that away, Roger," she said. "History never was your strong suit."

Slowly, Roger lowered the book. "What are you doing here?" There was no disguising his annoyance.

She half glanced back into the bedroom. "Came to get the last of my things. You weren't here, and I still have a key."

He laid the *History of the World* on the dining table and held out an open hand. "Well, I'll relieve you of that now, thank you," he said. She slipped long, elegant fingers into a pocket hidden among the pleats of her dress and produced the key on a length of leather thong. He snatched it from her. "Have you got everything?" There was still tension in his voice.

"I think so. I just need a bag to put it in."

"There are some large, plastic carriers in the dressing room."

But she made no move to go and get one. Instead she looked beyond him to Enzo. "Aren't you going to introduce us?"

Raffin glanced at Enzo, as if he had forgotten he was there. He said dismissively, "He's just come to pick up some papers."

Enzo stepped past him and held out his hand. "Enzo Macleod." He smiled. "*Je suis enchanté, Madame.*"

She shook his hand and held it in hers for just a moment longer than was necessary. Her eyes were

18

compelling, and Enzo felt trapped by their gaze. She said, "I'm Charlotte. You're not French."

"Scottish."

"Ah." A pause. "What papers?"

"That's really not any of your business, Charlotte," Roger said.

"I'm investigating the disappearance of Jacques Gaillard," Enzo told her.

Raffin sighed deeply. "Now you'll never get rid of her. Charlotte's a . . . psychologist." He spoke the word as if it made a bad taste in his mouth. "Trained in criminal profiling."

Enzo raised a dark eyebrow. "Where did you train?"

"As a profiler? The United States. I spent two years there before coming back to set up my own psychology practice. From time to time the Paris police deign to seek my advice." She glanced in Roger's direction. "But I make my living from people with everyday hang-ups. In my case, crime doesn't pay."

Roger said, "I'll get you that bag." And he headed off through a tiny door in the wall to the left of what had once been a fireplace.

Charlotte advanced towards Enzo, and he tried to put an age on her. She was a little younger than Roger. Early to mid-thirties perhaps. "What are you?" she said. "A policeman? A private detective?"

"I used to be a forensic scientist."

She nodded as if that explained everything.

Roger reappeared with two large plastic carriers. He thrust one at Charlotte and said to Enzo, "I'll get those notes for you." And he disappeared through double doors into his study.

"I suppose I should pack, then," Charlotte said, and she retreated to the bedroom.

Left on his own for a few moments, Enzo looked around Raffin's salon. Tall windows opened on to the courtyard below. Bookshelves lined the walls on two sides of the dining table at one end of the room. The remaining walls were covered in art: still-lifes, classical scenes from Greek and Roman literature, oriental tableaux, and what looked like original artwork from old French movie posters. There was an upright piano next to the window, and an old, enamel stove sat in what had been the *cheminée*. Everything seemed to have a place, and was in it. There was a marked absence of those small, personal items that clutter up people's homes providing clues to their character. Raffin had a certain style, in his deportment, the clothes he wore, the items he had chosen to furnish his apartment. But none of it gave much away, as if it were all a well-polished veneer designed to conceal what lay beneath. He reappeared, the plastic carrier now filled with heavy box files.

"Here," he said. "That should keep you busy for a while." He turned towards the bedroom. "Excuse me a moment." He closed the door behind him, and Enzo stood in the stillness of the apartment, unable to avoid hearing the voices raised in angry whispers on the other side of the mirrored panels. It didn't take long for the whispers to become shouts. Enzo focused his attention on one of the still-lifes. He did not want to be involved in other people's domestic problems. After several minutes the voices subsided again, and there was a brief period of silence before the door opened and Charlotte emerged with her plastic carrier full of clothes, her face flushed with anger and embarrassment.

"Goodbye, Monsieur Macleod," she said without looking at him, and she walked straight out of the apartment.

Raffin appeared in the doorway. He too, looked flushed. "Sorry about that." Although he didn't sound sorry at all. "Things are never easy at the end of a relationship." He tilted his head towards Enzo's bag. "When you've read through that stuff, any questions give me a call. Meanwhile, I'll get some kind of agreement drawn up on publication rights."

IV

When he reached the Boulevard St. Germain, Enzo saw her searching in vain for a taxi. There was still a lot of traffic in the street, and the cafés were doing brisk business, but there were no taxis in sight.

He joined her at the traffic lights. "Do you want me to call you one?"

Even with a sideways look her eyes had an alarmingly disarming effect. "You live nearby?"

"My studio's just down there, near the Institute. But there's no telephone there. I meant on my *portable*."

"Oh." She seemed disappointed. "I thought maybe you were going to ask me up for coffee."

21

He looked at her, caught off guard by her directness. "Sure." The green man appeared on the far side of the boulevard. "We'd better cross the road, then."

They pushed north through the crowds thronging the narrow Rue Mazarine, towards the floodlit dome of the Institute de France. The cafés and bistros were full. Voices emboldened by drink and good company, raised in laughter and argument, echoed around the canyons and mediaeval alleys of this longtime bohemian Left Bank *quartier*. Only now, it was no longer populated by bohemians, but by the nouveau riche of the *nouveau génération*, wallets bulging with euros tucked into designer pockets and bags.

A young woman laden with shopping and clutching a baby emerged in a hurry from a late-opening mini-market, colliding with Enzo and sending tins and packets clattering across the pavement.

"*Merde!*" she gasped under her breath.

"*Je suis désolé*," Enzo apologised, and he and Charlotte stooped to help her gather up her things. The baby was crying now, and the young woman was having difficulty getting everything back in the bags.

"Here," Enzo said. "Let me?" And he took the baby from her. For a moment, the mother appeared reluctant to let the child go, but something about Enzo seemed to reassure her, and she released the baby and turned to refill her bags hurriedly with Charlotte's help. In the time it took the two women to rescue the shopping, Enzo had the baby laughing. "She's a bright wee thing," he said, pulling a face and sending the infant into chuckling paroxysms. He turned to see Charlotte and the young woman looking at him, and he grew immediately self-conscious, handing the baby back to her mother and reclaiming his bag of box files.

"*Merci*." The young woman hurried away through the crowds into the night, her baby looking back over her shoulder at Enzo, a smile still sparkling in her eyes.

Charlotte stood in the roadway, caught in the light of the shop window, elegant and beautiful in her black dress, regarding Enzo thoughtfully, a half-smile on her face.

"What!" he said.

She shrugged. "Nothing. I thought you were going to make me coffee."

The studio apartment was on the first floor on the corner of the Rue Guénégaud and the Rue Mazarine, almost above the café Le Balto, and diagonally opposite the concrete monstrosity that housed the Paris Val de Seine School of Architecture. It was within sight of the magnificent Institute de France, home of the Academie Française which strove to protect the French language from the erosion of the modern world. Enzo had often thought there should be a similar institution to stop cretinous architects from ruining their cities.

From the first floor landing Enzo opened the door into the studio and Charlotte gasped. "I'd never have guessed you had such bad taste."

Enzo grinned. "Interesting, isn't it?" He closed the door behind her and followed her into the main room. The walls were lined with a padded fabric imprinted with a bold, repeating design in red, brown and cream.

"Very nineteen-sixties. Only, I'm afraid I can't claim the credit. It belongs to the very elderly uncle of friends in Cahors. He's in a retirement home, and they can't sell it until he dies. I love it. I hope he lives forever."

As he made the coffee he watched her wander about the room lightly touching the trophies and artefacts that cluttered every available space. Wood-carved African figures, a Chinese lacquered box, a green and gold porcelain dragon, a bust carved from ivory. "Apparently he was an inveterate traveller. An interesting old guy. I'd like to have met him."

Charlotte turned to watch him, a quizzical smile again lighting her face. "You live in Cahors?" He nodded. "And how many children do you have?"

He looked up, surprised. "What makes you think I have any?"

"Because I watch people," she said. "it's my job. So I can't help noticing all the little *micro signes* that give a person away. It makes my friends paranoid. They think I'm watching them all the time."

"And are you?"

She grinned. "Of course. Perhaps that's why I don't have many."

"So what *micro signes* betrayed the fact that I'm a father?"

"Your eyes. It's a simple physiological fact that when a man with children looks at a child his pupils dilate. If he doesn't have children they don't."

Enzo handed her a coffee. "It's always my eyes that give me away. I make a very bad liar. Milk or sugar?"

24

She shook her head. "And such very curious eyes. One blue, one brown. Waardenburg Syndrome?"

Enzo was surprised. "You're the first person I've ever met who knew what it was."

"A genetic disorder, characterised by a white streak in the hair. Sometimes accompanied by an arched palate and exaggerated facial features."

"And sometimes also by deafness. Fortunately I just have the eyes and the hair. And, of course, being a genetic condition, there's a fifty-fifty chance of passing it on to your children."

"And have you?"

"Fifty-fifty. One daughter has, and one daughter hasn't. Different mothers, though. So that might have something to do with it."

"You're still married, then?"

"Widowed." He sipped on his coffee to mask his discomfort. It was not a subject he liked to talk about.

"I'm sorry. Was it recent?"

"Just short of twenty years. Is the coffee okay?"

"Sure." They drank in silence for a few moments. Then she said, "So . . . what's your interest in the Jacques Gaillard case?"

"Academic." Then he smiled sheepishly and confessed, "And a rather stupid wager."

"A wager?"

"That it would be possible to solve an old case by applying new science." He paused. "Or not."

"You haven't picked the easiest of cases, then. There was never much evidence of any kind to go on. No body, no sign of a struggle. In fact, Roger took quite a bit of flak for including it among his seven most celebrated unsolved murders. No one's even been able to prove that Gaillard's dead."

"You know a bit about it, then?"

"Yes." Charlotte drank some more coffee, and Enzo had the impression that she, too, was endeavouring to conceal a discomfort. "You know that Roger was only motivated to write the book because of the unsolved murder of his own wife?"

Enzo nodded. "It's the seventh case."

Charlotte examined her coffee cup. "It's not easy, sustaining a relationship with a victim." She looked up and, as if feeling the need to explain, added, "Survivors are victims, too, you know." Then, "I was living with him while he was researching the book."

Enzo nodded. "But not any more."

"Not any more." She set down her cup. "Perhaps you could phone that taxi for me now."

"Of course." He retrieved his mobile from a pocket in his cargos and began punching in a number.

"Enzo . . ." she said after he had ordered her car. It was as if she was trying the sound of it out for size. "What kind of name is that anyway?"

"Short for Lorenzo. My mother was Italian. Married to a Scot. A lethal combination."

"It certainly is."

When the taxi arrived and peeped its horn in the street below, Enzo went down to open the door for her. They lingered for a moment on the pavement, and he felt her slipping away like sand through his fingers.

26

"Could I, you know, maybe take you to dinner sometime?" He felt foolish, like a schoolboy asking a girl on a first date.

She avoided his eye. "I've just finished with Roger. I think maybe I need a little time to myself right now." She threw her bag of clothes into the back seat of the taxi and searched through her handbag, pulling out a discreetly embossed business card. "But if you ever feel the need of some professional psychological insights into the Gaillard case, give me a call. Thanks for the coffee, Monsieur Macleod."

"Enzo," Enzo said as she shut the door. And her taxi coughed diesel fumes into the night and turned into the Rue Mazarine.

CHAPTER
TWO

I

Jacques Gaillard was dead. Enzo was certain of it.

He rubbed his eyes and looked at the clock on the mantelpiece. It was a little after three, and a party in one of the apartments opposite was still going strong. They had opened their windows wide, the musky aromatic smell of cannabis wafting its way across the narrow street, and the air was still vibrating to the monotonous rhythm of some endless Latin dance rap.

The party had begun around midnight, and Enzo had simply shut it out by reading through Raffin's notes, and allowing himself to be absorbed into the arcane world of Jacques Gaillard.

JG, as he was known to his friends, had been the eldest son of a provincial lawyer in Angoulême. Early intellectual promise resulted in his being sent to the Henry IV Lycée in Paris, one of the best secondary schools in France. There, he rose to the top of his class, and won first prize in economics at the Concours Général. By this time he already knew that he wanted to go to ENA. The École Nationale d'Administration, the crème de la crème of the French system of *grandes écôles*, accepted only the brightest intellects in the

28

country, and turned out Prime Ministers and Presidents like a shark grows new teeth.

A degree from the Institut d'Études Politiques, popularly known as Sciences-Po, would have been the normally accepted route. But his father had insisted that he take a "proper" diploma first, and so he had enrolled at the Faculté de Droit et Sciences Économiques d'Assas. But such was the young Jacques' genius, that this was not enough to keep him fully occupied. And so he had also enrolled at the Sorbonne, studying history.

By the time he graduated from both institutions, he had developed a good network of politically engaged friends. And had started his research into the history of early French cinema.

Acceptance to Sciences-Po was a formality and, given his previous academic record, his course there was reduced from four years to two. Such was his reputation for intellectual brilliance that by the time he sat the competitive exam for entry to ENA, he was already known to nearly half the members of the examination board. He sailed through the gruelling forty-five minute *Grand Oral*, during which prospective students are grilled, in public, on any subject chosen by a panel of five experts.

According to memoirs published later by some of that panel, and others who were there that day, Gaillard barely allowed them to get a word in.

Finishing in the top ten of his twenty-seven month course guaranteed him a pick of the top jobs in the Civil Service. Over the next twelve years his career went

29

from strength to strength, and after a highly successful stint as principal advisor to the Minister of Finance, he was actively pursued by the Prime Minister's office, eventually being appointed an advisor to the Prime Minister himself.

Which is when he published his book, *The History of French Cinema*, and his spectacular rise to prominence hit a brick wall.

Satirical cartoonists in the French media used him as a club with which to beat the Prime Minister. He was variously depicted as whispering advice into the premier's ear on which of that week's movie releases he should watch, or offering him tips on the most likely winner of best actress at the César Awards, or which film would take the Palme d'Or at Cannes. One particularly cruel cartoon in the satirical journal *Le Canard Enchaîné* conjured up an exceptionally gross-featured Prime Minister slipping JG a thick wad of two-hundred franc notes and asking if he could fix him up for the night with Sophie Marceau.

It seemed, however, that Jacques Gaillard was enjoying his new-found celebrity, and positively thrived on his increasingly frequent television appearances.

Then, between 1994 and 1996 he was "invited" — a clear euphemism for "instructed" — to direct students at ENA in an investigation into the history of French financial policies since the war. Perhaps an attempt by the government to lower his profile. But if that were the case, then it failed. For it was during that same period that Gaillard was asked by the French broadcaster TF1 to host his own cinema review show on television once a month, a chance he jumped at.

And then, that August, he vanished off the face of the earth. Enzo re-read Raffin's account of it in the book.

He failed to return to his desk at the end of the August holidays. It caused a huge stir at the time. The papers were full of it for weeks. But the police made no progress at all. And, as always happens with these matters, the press found other things to write about, and the curious case of the disappearing Jacques Gaillard gradually slipped from public view. That was ten years ago. It still crops up from time to time. An article here, a feature piece there. But no one has ever shed new light on what happened to him.

Enzo had never seen Gaillard's show, but when he looked through the various photographs in Raffin's file, his face was very familiar. A cartoonist's gift. Aged forty-nine when he disappeared, Gaillard had disguised his encroaching baldness by contriving an extraordinary bird's nest of dyed and lacquered curls. He had also cultivated one of those excessive French moustaches which, after an initial droop, curled extravagantly up around his cheeks.

Also in the file was a copy of the page beneath the final entry in the desk diary found in Gaillard's study. Enzo reflected that Raffin must have had good sources to get hold of material like this. The page containing the final entry itself had been torn out. But because of the impression it had left on the page below, the *police scientifique* had been able to treat the paper in the lab with electrostatic detection equipment to find and then visualise the fibres damaged by the abrasive pressure of the pen. Enzo looked at it carefully. *Mad à minuit*, it read. Evidently, Gaillard had spent some time on the entry, for he had gone over the letters several times, and then surrounded them with idle doodles and curlicues. The kind of doodles he might have engaged in absently during a lengthy telephone conversation. The police had secured phone records for the night before the date of the entry. They showed that there had been a phone call — about fifteen minutes long — shortly before ten o'clock. It was the last call registered to Gaillard's phone, and it had been made from a public call box. In spite of extensive publicity, no one had ever admitted to making the call.

Enzo frowned and read and re-read the entry. *Mad à minuit*. Many before him had puzzled over it and, in the end, failed to make sense of it. *Mad* at midnight. Except that there was no such word as mad in the French language. And why would he have mixed English and French? It had to be a shortening of another word. Enzo pulled a French dictionary from the bookcase and looked up words beginning with *mad*. There were not many. *Madame, mademoiselle,* and *Madeleine*, the French for Magdalene. Madagascar and Madeira, Madras and Madrid. *Madalopam*, a strong calico. *Madéfier*, the verb to wet or moisten. *Madone*, the Madonna. *Madrier*, a thick plank of wood. *Madrure*, a mottle on wood or porcelain. A few others. But nothing that chimed.

The date of the entry was Friday 23 August, 1996. So presumably it referred to a rendezvous somewhere at midnight that night. The speculation was that the entry had been made in the course of that final phone call registered to his number the night before. But there was no way to prove it.

Enzo turned his attention, then, to photographs taken of Gaillard's apartment, and wondered again how Raffin had managed to get copies. Then he noticed a tiny sequence of figures printed in red in the bottom corner of the prints. 29.03.06. A date. These pictures had been taken just a little over three years ago. He frowned. How was that possible? It was ten years since Gaillard had disappeared. He dug into the thigh pocket of his cargos and found his mobile. He tracked down Raffin's number and pressed dial.

Raffin managed to convey sleepy and irritated in a single word. "*Oui?*"

"Roger, it's Enzo."

There was a splutter of indignation from the other end. "Jesus Christ, Macleod, do you have any idea what time it is?"

"How did you manage to take photographs of Gaillard's apartment seven years after he'd disappeared?"

"What?" Raffin was now transmitting a mixture of incomprehension and anger.

"Did you take these photographs of Gaillard's apartment?"

"Yes."

"How?"

"Because the place hasn't been touched since he vanished. His mother has preserved it. Like a shrine.

Except that she refuses to believe he's dead. She wants it to be there for him, just as he left it, the day he returns."

Enzo could hardly believe his luck. A potential crime scene, preserved as in aspic, available for re-examination after ten years. "I want to see it."

"Talk to me tomorrow."

"No, I want to see it tomorrow. As early as possible. Can you arrange it?"

He heard Raffin sigh. "Call me in the morning." He paused. "At a civilised hour." And he hung up.

Enzo sat for several minutes contemplating the prospect of being able to revisit Gaillard's apartment after all these years. No doubt it had been cleaned after forensics had finished with it. But there was so much you could learn about a man from the space he inhabited. And there was always the possibility that Enzo might see something others had missed.

The party across the street continued relentlessly. God, did these people not have homes to go to? Enzo adjusted the desk lamp and rubbed his eyes again in the bright light it spilled across the papers strewn over the desktop. He stretched and thought about bed. But his mind was still full of Gaillard, and his eye lighted again on the photocopy of the diary page treated by forensics. He stared at it for a long time, and then screwed up his eyes, inclining his head, and became aware that his heart-rate had suddenly increased. He looked around the apartment, frustrated that it was unlikely to provide the tracing paper he needed. And then he had a thought and crossed to the small, open-plan kitchen where he began going through the drawers. The third one turned up what he was looking for. A roll of greaseproof paper. He tore off a good twelve inches, and took it back to the desk, smoothing it out over the top of the photocopy. Crisp, opaque paper, but thin enough for the lines beneath to show through. Ideal. He reached for a pencil and immediately began the careful process of retracing Gaillard's final doodles.

CHAPTER
THREE

I

Passy is on the green métro line No. 6, which loops right across Paris from Nation in the east to Place Charles de Gaulle and the Arc de Triomphe in the west. It is a short walk up a steep hill from the station to the Place Costa Rica.

It was a misty morning, cool after the heat of the night before, and Raffin had the collar of his jacket turned up as if he were cold. But he had chosen to sit at a table on the pavement outside the Brasserie Le Franklin. The dregs of a *grande crème* stained his cup, and the crumbs of a croissant littered the tiny table in front of him. He was reading that day's edition of *Libération*, the left-wing daily to which he most often contributed as a freelance. He looked up and frowned as Enzo slumped into the seat beside him. From here they had a view back down the Rue de l'Alboni to where the métro line stretched away above ground, disappearing into the mist over the Pont de Bir-Hakeim.

"You're late," Raffin said. It was all of five minutes beyond their agreed meeting time.

"It happens," Enzo said without guilt, remembering the more than twenty minutes Raffin had kept him waiting the night before. "Is it all fixed?"

"Of course. She's waiting for us in the apartment."

The elegant stone façade of Gaillard's five-storey apartment block was in the Rue Vineuse. Raffin entered the code that unlocked the wrought-iron gate and pushed it open. Through a passage they walked into a small courtyard, glass doors leading to a wood-panelled lobby, where polished brass stair-rods held in place a thick-piled red carpet dressing a marble staircase. Beyond, Enzo could see another, bigger, courtyard, a garden with manicured lawn and shady trees. Everything about the place reeked of wealth.

Raffin said, "Gaillard achieved the aspiration of every ambitious Parisian to be *entre court et jardin*." Enzo had heard the phrase before. To be between the courtyard and the garden was Paris-speak for having made it. To live almost anywhere in this prestigious sixteenth *arrondissement* was to have made it. It was an area populated by politicians and film stars, TV celebrities and pop idols.

They took the lift to the fifth floor, and Madame Gaillard opened tall mahogany doors to let them into her son's long-empty apartment. She was a surprisingly small woman, shrunken by age, a little unsteady on her feet. Raffin had told Enzo on the way up that she was nearly ninety. As they shook hands, Enzo's big fingers enveloped hers, and he was afraid to grasp her hand too firmly in case it broke.

"Monsieur Raffin tells me you're going to find my son," she said. And suddenly Enzo felt burdened by that responsibility. This was about more than just a bet entered into lightly over dinner. It was about a man's life, a woman's son. An almost certain tragedy.

"I'm going to do my best."

The old lady left them to wander through the apartment as they wished, while she went and sat by the window in the front room, staring out across the sea of mist that washed over the city below. Beautifully polished parquet flooring, liberally littered with expensive oriental rugs, led them from room to room. Antique furniture stood against cream-painted walls. A Louis Quinze armoire, a nineteenth-century chaise longue, an ancient, carved wooden trunk inlaid with silver and mother of pearl. All the furniture seemed to have been bought for effect. Chairs looked stiff and uncomfortable, the four-poster bed in Gaillard's bedroom was unyieldingly hard. Heavy curtains were draped around all the windows, tied back by gold silk cord but still obscuring much of the light. There was an oddly gloomy feel to this top-floor apartment with its large French windows leading to ornate wrought-iron balconies. Enzo had an urge to throw back all the curtains and let the light in. But this was how Gaillard had lived. This was how he liked it.

Rows of dark suits hung in his wardrobe, polished shoes in a line along the rail beneath them. Dresser drawers were filled with neatly pressed shirts, socks, underwear. A silk dressing gown hung on the back of the door, as if Gaillard had left it there just moments earlier. A simple cross, adorned by the figure of Christ, hung on the wall above the bed. Enzo found his reflection looking back at him from a large, gold-framed mirror above the dresser. He saw Raffin behind him, hands thrust deep in his pockets, staring gloomily out of the window. On the dresser, a carved ivory box held tie-clips and cufflinks engraved with the initials JG. There was a clothes brush, a gilt hairbrush with two combs wedged in the bristles. There were traces of Gaillard's hair still trapped between the roots of the teeth. Enzo glanced back through the open door, across the hall to the sitting room. Madame Gaillard had not moved from her seat by the window. He pulled one of the combs from the brush and carefully teased out a pinch of thick dark hair, two to three inches long. He took a small, clear plastic ziplock bag from his pocket, dropped in the hair sample and resealed it. Then he turned to find Raffin watching him. Neither man said anything.

They crossed the hall to the study, which adjoined the sitting room. Half-glazed double doors stood open between the two rooms, and Enzo could see through to the marble fireplace in the *séjour*, and the tall mirror set into the wall above. While the rest of the apartment seemed almost for show, Enzo felt he was meeting Gaillard for the first time when he entered the study. Here, the man was everywhere in evidence. A glazed bookcase against the far wall held his collection of literary classics. Something to be prized and kept safe behind glass. No doubt there would be first editions amongst them, but Enzo had the feeling that many of them had probably remained unread. His "living" bookcase faced it on the opposite wall. Open shelves on either side of the door were untidily crammed with well-thumbed tomes. There were books and magazines on French and American cinema, rows of popular fiction with creased spines and dog-eared fly-leafs, whole series of works on politics and finance. An entire shelf was devoted to a collection of comic books — *bandes dessinées* as the French called them.

Enzo whispered to Raffin, "He never married, did he?" Raffin shook his head. "Was he gay?"

Raffin shrugged. "Not that I know of."

"But no women in his life?"

Again, Raffin shrugged and shook his head, and Enzo wondered if they were to believe that Gaillard had practised an odd kind of celibacy. He looked around the walls at the dozens of framed photographs of Gaillard pictured with well-known faces of the day. Président Jacques Chirac, Prime Minister Alain Juppé. Movie stars and pop icons. Gérard Depardieu, Johnny Halliday, Vanessa Paradis, Jean-Paul Belmondo. And others whom Enzo did not recognise. There were several portraits of Gaillard on his own, posing for the camera with an imperious self-confidence. And a portrait-painting which caught that same expression. And Enzo began to wonder if the reason there were no women, or men, in Gaillard's life, was because his ego had allowed no space for anyone or anything else.

Behind a large desk with a deep maroon leather-tooled top, more shelves groaned under the weight of literally hundreds of videos. French movies, American movies, Japanese films, South American, European, Chinese. More films than you could conceive of watching in a lifetime. In the far corner of the study there was a wide-screen television set, a mid-nineties state-of-the-art sound system. Opposite was the only comfortable chair in the apartment, a soft leather recliner with a drinks table placed at the right hand. It was not hard to imagine how Gaillard had passed all his solitary hours in this study.

"The films are all catalogued." Enzo was startled by Madame Gaillard's birdlike voice. She had left her chair and was standing in the doorway. "He has notes on every one of them."

"Did you watch them with him?"

"Oh, no. I was very rarely here. He always came to me. After my husband died, he brought me to Paris and bought an apartment just a few streets away. He came every day." She wandered across the polished floor, supporting herself on a rubber-tipped stick, and gazed up at the collection of movies. "He loves his films." A tiny smile creased her face, and she stepped forward to slide one out from its place on a shelf a little above head-height. "His favourite. He says he has watched it nearly thirty times. He says it is the absolute true essence of Paris."

Enzo took the box from her and looked at the black-and-white still on the cover. The title was blazed across it in yellow: *La Traversée de Paris*. A film by Claude Autant-Lara, starring Bourvil and Jean Gabin. Enzo vaguely remembered having seen it on television. Made in the nineteen-fifties, it was set during wartime Paris. Under the noses of the Nazi occupiers, two unlikely compatriots try to smuggle the dismembered pieces of a pig across the city to sell on the black market. Enzo was not sure why Gaillard had thought it so remarkable. Madame Gaillard took it back from him and returned it to its place on the shelf. "It's the first one he'll want to watch when he gets back, I'm sure."

Enzo wondered how she could possibly imagine that he was not dead. Perhaps that belief was all that kept her alive. She gave him a wan smile and shuffled back through to the sitting room.

Enzo turned to Raffin. "Where's the diary?"

"On the desk."

It lay open, beside the telephone, at the page which had been treated by the police forensics lab to reveal Gaillard's final entry. Enzo could see where the page before it had been carefully torn out. By Gaillard? Or by someone else? Only Gaillard's fingerprints had been found. Enzo flipped back through the diary. There was no evidence of other pages being removed. So it was not something Gaillard was in the habit of doing. From his pocket Enzo took the forensically treated copy of the last entry and spread it out on the desk. *Mad à minuit.* "Obviously you're familiar with this," he said.

Raffin peered at it over his shoulder. "I've nearly gone blind looking at the damned thing."

"But sometimes it's possible to look and not see."

"What do you mean?"

"All these doodles next to the words, what do they look like to you?"

"Well, nothing." Raffin squinted at them. "Just doodles."

"Have you ever doodled while talking on the telephone?"

42

"Of course."

"So you start off with some basic design. You're not even necessarily conscious of what it is. But the longer the call goes on, the more elaborate it becomes, until that first image gets lost. You might be hard-pushed yourself to remember how it started out."

"So?"

"So, supposing we were able to take this back to that first, unconscious image, maybe it would tell us something about what was in his mind."

"How would we do that?"

Enzo said, "The early lines of a doodle tend to be gone over several times before you start expanding on it. So if we look for the heavier lines . . ." He went into his pocket and took out the folded greaseproof paper he had used to trace the doodle the night before, and smoothed it over the copy of the diary page.

Raffin peered at it. He could see the lines Enzo had traced, and the ones he had not still showed through, but it wasn't until Enzo lifted the tracing paper away again, that he saw what it was Enzo had drawn. "Good God! It's a cross."

"There's even the suggestion of the figure of Christ on it." Enzo traced his finger around the outline.

Raffin stood upright. He seemed startled. "Well, what does it mean?"

"I don't know," Enzo said. "There's a cross on the wall above his bed. Was he a religious man?"

Gaillard's mother looked up at them from her chair at the window when they came through to ask, and seemed puzzled by the question. "Of course," she said. "He went to mass several times a week. He was absolutely devoted."

"What church did he go to?"

"St. Étienne du Mont," she replied without hesitation. "It is the parish church of the Sorbonne. He began going there when he was still a student."

II

St. Étienne du Mont, not unnaturally, stood at the top of a hill at the end of the Rue de la Montagne de Ste. Geneviève. It dominated the skyline as Enzo and Raffin walked up the steep incline from the métro station at Maubert Mutualité. The mist had lifted, and the sun was burning its way through a hazy sky. It was a warm climb.

The clock beneath the lantern on the oddly turreted bell tower of the church showed nearly ten-thirty. Below, in the Place de l'Abbé Basset, young artists sat sketching on semi-circular steps leading up to an arched doorway. Raffin led them around to the Place Ste. Geneviève, past the rear of the Panthéon, and along the Rue Clovis to a side entrance leading to the priest's house beyond.

The priest was an elderly man, bald, with a wispy fringe of thin silver hair. He walked them through the cloisters, his gowns flowing impressively in his wake. Sunlight streamed through the stained-glass windows. There were twelve of them, vividly coloured images of the Prophet triumphing over the priests of Baal, the miracle of the Manna in the Wilderness, the Last Supper.

"I remember him well," the priest was saying, his voice reverberating through the apsidal Chapel. "He came to mass several times a week. He was a regular at confession." They passed along a short corridor, bypassing the sacristy, and through a door into the church itself. Enzo gazed up into its towering vaulted roof in awe. Light flooded in through stained glass in the apse and in the chapels all along each ambulatory, on to the organ pipes rising up at the far end in tiers of shining elegance. Somewhere unseen, the organist was practising, and the sonorous resonance of Bach's Toccata and Fugue in D minor cascaded down from the roof in a waterfall of sound. The priest had to raise his voice to be heard above it. "Of course, like everyone else, we had no idea he'd gone missing until after La Rentrée. It was August, after all, and most of Paris had left on holiday."

"I know that you cannot breach the confidentiality of the confessional, father," Enzo said, "but had Monsieur Gaillard given you any reason to think that he might have been depressed, or under stress in any way?"

"To be honest, I really don't recall. I'm sure the police must have asked me at the time. But there's nothing that sticks in my mind. I do remember I was far more distracted that month by the defiling of the church. We're just coming up to the tenth anniversary of it. I do hope the culprits don't feel the need to deliver any reminders. I've asked for a police guard just in case."

"Defiling of the church?" Enzo was intrigued. "What happened?"

"I remember something about that," Raffin said suddenly. "It was in all the papers at the time. Someone broke in and sacrificed an animal in front of the altar."

The priest said, "It was a pig. They butchered it. Dismembered the poor creature. Blood and bits were everywhere."

"Why would anyone do something like that?" Enzo asked.

"God only knows." The priest raised his eyes to Heaven as if searching for belated enlightenment. "Some Pagan rite perhaps. Some Black ceremony, a sacrifice to the Antichrist. Who knows? No one ever owned up to it. But no matter how much we rubbed and scrubbed, we never could get the blood out of the stone. Here, see for yourselves . . ." He walked briskly along the north ambulatory, past several of the chapels, to an altar beneath a delicately woven stone screen dominated by the figure of Christ on a large cross overhead. The area immediately in front of the altar was roped off at each side to keep tourists away. Rows of wicker chairs ranged off towards the back of the church. "There, you see." The priest pointed to the ancient stone flags and two steps leading up to the raised altar. "It's faded over the years, but still quite visible." A large area covering the flags and the steps was discoloured. It would have been impossible to guess that it was blood. It was just darker where the blood had pooled and splashed and lain undisturbed long enough to be absorbed into the stone.

"This happened during the night, then?" Enzo said.

"I discovered it myself the following morning. It made me physically sick."

"Can you remember what date that was?"

"Monsieur," the priest puffed himself up indignantly, "it is a date burned into my memory for eternity. It was the night of the twenty-third to the twenty-fourth of August 1996."

Enzo glanced at Raffin. The significance of the day was not lost on either of them.

The shrill warble of a phone was just audible above the reverberating roar of the organ, and the priest reached beneath his cassock to retrieve the latest Samsung flip-open model. God's work, it seemed, could now be done by mobile. "Excuse me." The priest hurried away.

Enzo gazed thoughtfully at the dark-stained flagstones. A group of tourists stood opposite, beyond the rope on the south ambulatory, staring up at the stone screen beneath the cross. They became distracted when suddenly Enzo stepped over the rope on the north side, walked to the centre of the church, and crouched down in front of the altar as if praying. But if he said a prayer at all, it was to the God of Science. He searched in his satchel and produced a sturdy, bone-handled knife, folding out its well-sharpened steel blade. He began scraping along the edge of one of the flagstones, breaking off splinters and flakes of crumbling stone, and digging out the dirt of centuries from the cracks between them. He very quickly accumulated a small pile of stone flakes and dirt, which he gathered together with his knife and dragged on to a sheet of clean paper torn from a notebook. He carefully folded the paper to seal in the scrapings, and slipped it into a plastic ziplock bag.

Raffin was embarrassed. "What are you doing?" he hissed, his voice almost drowned by the organ.

Enzo looked round. "What?"

"What the hell are you doing?" he shouted, just as the organist finished his piece. Raffin's voice reverberated around the church, chasing the dying echoes of the fugue. Tourists all along each ambulatory turned to look.

Enzo returned the plastic bag to his satchel and walked back to the north ambulatory, stepping over the rope to rejoin Raffin. "No need to shout."

Raffin lowered his voice self-consciously. "What are you playing at, Macleod? You can't just go digging up the floor of a fifteenth-century church."

Enzo steered the journalist towards the back of St. Étienne du Mont and the small door to the left of the main entrance. "I don't know if you're familiar with idiomatic English. But we have an expression in which we describe the process of trying to get information out of someone who refuses to talk, or even money out of a Scotsman, as like trying to get blood out of a stone. It's another way of saying that it's impossible."

Raffin shrugged. "We have a similar expression, except that it's oil from a wall — *on ne saurait tirer de l'huile d'un mur.* I'm surprised you haven't heard it."

48

"Well, I don't know about oil and walls, but these days it's perfectly possible to get blood out of a stone."

Raffin frowned. "Even blood that's ten years old?"

Enzo nodded. "And even from the floor of a fifteenth-century church." He smiled. "The wonders of modern forensic science. It will be a fairly straightforward matter to extract DNA from the sample scrapings I've taken and subject it to some basic precipitin tests."

"Precipitin?"

"You mix the DNA on a glass slide with some anti-pig globulin. If there's a positive reaction, there will be a visible clot, or clump — or 'precipitate' form — and we'll know whether or not it was pig's blood."

"But we already know that it's pig's blood. You heard the priest. They left the butchered beast behind."

"That's right. And I confidently predict that we will indeed confirm the presence of pig's blood. But we'll also mix the DNA with some anti-human globulin, which will tell us if there is any human blood amongst it."

Raffin's face darkened, and he glanced around self-consciously. A sign on a stand next to them urged them to SILENCE. He lowered his voice. "Gaillard's blood?"

"Well, we'll be able to tell that, too, from the DNA."

"You think Gaillard was murdered here?"

"I don't know." Enzo paused. "Yet. But this was his church. Even although it was another ten days before he was actually reported missing, he made a rendezvous to meet someone the same night that intruders broke in here and slaughtered a pig. He drew a cross next to the rendezvous in his diary. A lot of coincidences there."

"It's a bit of a leap, though."

"Perhaps. But sometimes you have to make those kinds of leaps." Enzo paused for reflection. "And think back to earlier this morning. His mother told us that his favourite film was *La Traversée de Paris*. Two men smuggling the pieces of a dismembered pig across Paris. Another coincidence?"

"What are you suggesting?"

"Suppose that someone lured Gaillard here and murdered him in front of the altar."

"Why?" Raffin frowned. "Why would they?"

Enzo raised his hands. "That's another question altogether. But make the leap with me. Suppose that's what happened. Suppose he was murdered right there . . ." He turned and looked back down the church towards the cross and the screen and the bloodstained flags. "Suppose he was hacked to pieces in front of that altar, some bizarre, ritualistic killing, and then the pieces of a pig and its blood strewn about to disguise the fact that it was a human being who had been murdered. Who would ever think to check that there was human blood with the pig's? You heard the priest. They were shocked, horrified by the thought of an animal sacrifice being performed in their church. They called the police, yes, but I'll bet you it was all cleaned up before anyone would even have thought to question it."

The notion seemed to shock Raffin. "What makes you think he might have been dismembered?"

"Ah, now that's more difficult to quantify. But in my head I keep coming back to *La Traversée de Paris*. A dismembered pig in the film, a dismembered pig in the

50

church. Only, they left the pig behind. So what happened to Gaillard? Wouldn't it be easier to take him away in pieces? And might that not also be like some kind of strange homage to *La Traversée?* Instead of the pig, it was the dismembered pieces of Gaillard which were smuggled away across the city."

Suddenly the organ burst into life again, and the dramatic opening notes of Bach's Trio Sonata for Organ No. 2 in C minor filled the church.

The world outside, awash with sunshine and filled with tourists, seemed strangely unreal. Only the strains of the organ from within carried with them the reminder of the dark theories that Enzo had conjured out of the bloodstained flags. The two men stood on the steps, blinking in the sunlight, gazing out beyond the Panthéon and the arcaded arches of the Ste. Geneviève Bibliotheque towards the ancient Faculté de Droit and the Mairie of the sixth *arrondissement.*

"What now?" Raffin asked.

"First of all, I have to call in a favour from the director of a laboratory here in Paris. Then we need to find out how many unidentified body parts have turned up over the last ten years."

Raffin raised a sceptical eyebrow. "Well, that should be easy. Where do you propose we start?"

Enzo pulled the folded newspaper from Raffin's jacket pocket. "I take it you have access to the cuttings library at *Libération.*"

"Of course." Raffin snatched the journal back.

"Then that's where we'll begin."

CHAPTER
FOUR

I

The offices of *Libération* were tucked away in the narrow Rue Béranger in the third *arrondissement*, where the city's rag-trade conducts its wholesale and retail activities.

The newspaper archives were reached by a rickety lift which took them to the fourth floor, glass-walled offices lined with shelf upon shelf of box files and bound copies tracing the history of the newspaper back to its first edition in 1973. Large windows looked out on Le Petit Béranger brasserie in the street below.

Raffin and Enzo spent nearly twenty minutes flicking through drums of index cards and fetching corresponding boxes from shelves that groaned with numbered files. A row of filing cabinets had drawers labelled with everything from *Accidents du Travail* to *Vietnam*, but their contents held nothing of any interest. They had been unable to find a single cutting referring to unexplained or unidentified body parts.

"Isn't there microfilm we can look at?" Enzo was frustrated by their lack of progress.

"They started to put everything on to microfiche a few years ago," Raffin told him, "but somehow it all got scratched and ruined in the reader."

"Well, aren't there internet archives?"

"Oh, yes. Everything from 1994 on. But you have to subscribe to get access to it."

"And don't you subscribe?"

"Well, no," Raffin confessed. "Why would I? I've got access to this place."

"Where you can't find anything!" Enzo was losing patience. "Can't the newspaper access the internet for you from here?"

"I suppose they could. Only I don't think they have a computer here in the cuttings library."

There had been an odd sense of old-fashioned informality about the whole place. The lack of security, the worn carpet in the lobby, the unfinished renovation work which greeted them when they stepped out of the lift, the tables of apparently randomly stacked boxes of cuttings lining the hallway. It was a sense which only increased with the arrival of a middle-aged man with dark, thinning hair and a close-cropped beard. He wore black, corduroy trousers and a grey tee shirt, and Raffin introduced him to Enzo as *La Mémoire du Journal*. The memory of the newspaper. "He's been with *Libé* since the first edition hit the streets more than thirty years ago." It seemed that the most reliable archive the paper possessed was filed in the head of *La Mémoire du Journal*.

"What exactly is it you're looking for?" he asked. When Enzo told him he frowned. "I don't think we have a separate category for that. We would only file what was reported, and we would only report something particularly unusual. There's nothing that immediately springs to mind."

Enzo sighed. This had been a complete waste of time. "Thank you anyway." He and Raffin turned towards the lift.

"Except, of course, for the skull in the trunk."

Enzo turned back. "A skull in a trunk?"

"Yes . . ." *La Mémoire* began flipping through file cards, every one meticulously handwritten by himself. "Yes, here we are. I filed it under *Catacombes*."

Which pricked Raffin's interest. "Why?"

"Because that's where it was found." He crossed the room and ran his finger along a row of box files until he identified the one he was looking for. He pulled it out and laid it on the desk to open it, and then flipped back the spring to release its cuttings. "There was quite a bit of coverage at the time, just because it was so unusual. But it was a one-day wonder, really. Nothing ever came of it as far as I remember."

Enzo sat down and started spreading the cuttings out in front of him. "What do you remember exactly?"

"Just that it was discovered somewhere in the tunnels below Place d'Italie. About five years ago. A surveyor, I think, working for the Inspection Générale des Carrières. There had been some kind of collapse beneath the Avenue de Choisy, and that's how the trunk came to light."

Raffin peered over Enzo's shoulder at the cuttings. "And it had a skull in it?" There were photographs of a skull with the mouth and teeth smashed.

54

"Yes, the skull of a middle-aged male, I believe. Quite recently deceased, they thought. Five, ten years, something like that. But it wasn't so much the skull which created the interest, as the items found with it." Even as *La Mémoire* spoke, Enzo turned over one of the cuttings to reveal a grainy photograph of an odd collection of apparently unrelated items. "Ah, yes," said *La Mémoire*. "I remember now. Very strange stuff. A scallop shell. An antique stethoscope. A thigh bone — I think there were tiny holes drilled through either end of it. A gold insect on a chain. A pendant, I think." He shuffled through the cuttings. "Yes, it was a bee."

Raffin lifted one of the clippings, squinting at its picture and caption. "And a copy of an *Ordre de la Libération* with 12 May 1943, engraved on the back of it."

"What's an *Ordre de la Libération*?" Enzo asked.

"They were medals given out by de Gaulle to men and women who helped in the Libération of France," *La Mémoire* said.

Enzo let his eyes drift over the cuttings in front of him. "How bizarre. And they never figured out what it was all about?"

"Apparently not."

II

Place Dauphine, at the west end of the Île de la Cité, was where officers from the Brigade Criminelle on the Quai des Orfèvres sometimes grabbed a bite of lunch.

It was a dusty, tree-filled square lined with apartments and restaurants, once the home of Yves Montand. And because of the proximity of the Palais de Justice, it was also home to the Paris Bar, *le Barreau* de Paris, from which the city's advocates practised their black arts from beneath a grinning Cheshire cat painted on a rooftop gable. The pavement tables under the twin awnings of Le Caveau de Palais restaurant had been full just a little earlier. But Inspecteur Georges Thomas was having a late lunch, and so some of the seats around him had already emptied. Enzo and Raffin pulled chairs up at his table and ordered a couple of glasses of chilled white wine and watched as he used fat fingers to tear off chunks of bread and mop up the juices on his plate. His hair was cropped short, shiny steel bristles above a round tanned face with a day's growth of silvered whiskers. His lips shone with the grease from his meal. He dragged a crumpled napkin across them and then wiped his fingers one by one. He cleansed his palate with a last mouthful of red wine and belched loudly, nodding his satisfaction.

A quick call to Raffin's contact at the Préfecture de Police had established that Thomas had been in charge of the unsuccessful investigation to identify the skull found below Place d'Italie. He was in his mid-fifties now, treading water until retirement, and was in the habit of treating himself to long lunches in the Place Dauphine. "The skull? Yeah. Fucking weird one that," he said. "The local cops passed it on to us. But, you know, there was fuck all to go on. No fingerprints on the trunk, or on any of that strange shit that was in it."

He waved the waiter over and said he would have an *île flottante* and a coffee.

"What happened to it?" Enzo asked.

Thomas looked at him as if he had two heads. "What kind of fucking accent is that?"

"He's Scottish," Raffin said.

Thomas made a slight forward thrusting movement of his jaw to indicate his contempt for anyone who wasn't Parisian. "What happened to what?"

"The trunk and the stuff that was in it."

"They'll still be in the *greffe*."

"*Greffe?*"

"The evidence depository," Raffin explained. He looked towards Thomas for confirmation. "In the Palais de Justice?"

Thomas nodded. The waiter arrived with his dessert, and the detective chased frothy lumps of egg white around a pale, watery custard which he managed to dribble down his chin. "I gotta blizzard of paperwork on my desk gonna make me go blind." He wiped his face again with his napkin. "But if you guys want to see the stuff, then I guess I could always take time out to show you."

Le greffe was a large subterranean room in the bowels of the Palais de Justice, rows of metal staging supporting lines of shelves filled with the accumulated evidence of investigations past and present. Each item was bagged and labelled and tracked by a computerised index held by the *Gardien du Greffe* — the Keeper. It

57

was less than five minutes' walk from Le Caveau de Palais.

The Keeper was a man who looked as if he rarely saw daylight. His skin was pale, almost grey, and his oiled black hair was scraped back across a shrunken head. He displayed no interest when Thomas asked to see the trunk. He searched through the index on his screen and gave the detective instructions on where to find it — Row 15, Shelf C, Production Number 53974/S.

Row 15 was at the bottom end of the room, and Shelf C was near the ceiling. Thomas required stepladders to reach it. He located the bag, wrapped his arms around the trunk and lifted it down, carrying it to a table at the end of the aisle. He untied the bag and removed it to reveal a battered tin trunk, about the same size as an average suitcase, but deeper. It was a dark, military green, scraped and scored and a little rusted. "There were no distinguishing markings on it," Thomas said. "No manufacturer's label. And it was probably damaged in the tunnel collapse." He released the catches on either side and the lid creaked as it opened. "*Et voilà.*"

Enzo and Raffin peered inside. There were the items described in the newspaper articles: the scallop shell; the antique stethoscope, looking for all the world like an elongated horn from a vintage car; the thigh bone with its tiny holes drilled at either end; a bee, elaborately fashioned in gold and attached to a fine neck chain; the *Ordre de la Libération* with its green and black strip of cloth, the medal itself engraved in

58

black with the double cross of Lorraine. "Where's the skull?" Enzo asked, disappointed.

"The pathologist's still got it." Thomas snorted. "Fucking weirdo. He does these facial reconstructions in clay. It's a hobby. Like, you know, he enjoys it or something."

"He did a facial reconstruction from the skull found in the trunk?"

"Sure."

"And?"

"And what?"

"You circulated photographs of it?"

"Sure we did. It was pretty distinctive. Completely bald. But no one recognised it."

Enzo felt a wave of disappointment. 'Bald' was not a word he would have used to describe Gaillard. "Was the face cleanshaven?"

"Completely hairless."

"Would it be possible to see it?"

"You'll need to ask him that."

Enzo looked at the items in the trunk again. He put a hand inside. "May I?"

"Allez-y."

Enzo lifted them out one by one and laid them on the table. They were an odd collection of articles to find together at any time. But buried in a trunk with an unidentified skull, made them notably peculiar. "What about the thigh bone? Was it related to the skull?"

Thomas shook his head. "The experts said it was much older. They figured it was probably part of an anatomical skeleton. You know, the kind of thing a bone specialist would have in his office." He lifted up the femur. "And these tiny holes . . . They figured that's where the bones were wired together."

Raffin said, "And you never worked out what these things were doing in there with the skull?"

The detective shook his head. "A complete fucking mystery. Take a better man than me to work it out." Enzo and Raffin made fleeting eye contact.

"What about the date on the back of the medal? 12th May 1943. Does it have any significance?"

"Not that we could figure."

Enzo reached into his satchel and produced a small, square digital camera. He held it up between thumb and forefinger. "Would it be okay if I took some photographs?"

Thomas thought about it for a moment, running a chubby hand over his bristled jaw. "Yeah, I guess . . ." And as Enzo lined up the items one by one to snap them, the detective said, "So when's this piece going to be in the papers?"

Enzo felt his face colouring, and concentrated on the photographs. They had required a cover story. But Raffin was not in the least uncomfortable with their subterfuge. "Depends what progress we make," he said.

"As long as you don't quote me," Thomas growled. "I'm retiring at Christmas. I don't need the hassle."

"Any quotes will be strictly unattributable," Raffin reassured him.

Enzo finished taking his photographs. "And the trunk was found in the . . . the catacombs?"

The detective nodded. "That's right."

"I didn't know there were catacombs in Paris."

Thomas spluttered and laughed. "You're kidding me! Jesus, there's nearly three hundred kilometres of tunnels under the city."

"You mean the sewers?"

"No, no, no. The catacombs are way below that. Way below the métro, too."

Raffin said, "The catacombs are twenty to thirty metres down. Hacked out of solid rock by quarriers over centuries."

Enzo was astonished. "What for?"

"For the stone. The whole of Paris was built with rock dug out from beneath it. There's a few kilometres of catacomb that you can visit officially, but the rest of it's dangerous, and strictly off limits."

Thomas snorted. "Which makes it a magnet for every freak and weirdo in the city. There's all sorts of shit goes on down there. Drug dealing, illicit sex, you name it."

Raffin said, "They recently discovered an underground cinema, and a nightclub. All powered from lines tapped illegally into the power grid. There's a whole subculture that exists down there. Tunnel rats, they call them. People who just love to explore the dark and the unknown. And there are extreme tourists who pay illicit guides to take them down for a good time. I wrote a piece about it a few years ago. I went down officially . . ." He glanced at Thomas. "And unofficially. My unofficial guide had better maps. He'd spent years exploring the tunnels and charted them meticulously."

Thomas sighed and looked ostentatiously at his watch.

Raffin took what he thought was his cue. "Well, thank you, Inspecteur. We'd better not keep you."

Thomas scratched his jaw again. "No, I'm just thinking. Maybe you guys would like to see where the trunk was found. My paperwork can wait. And, anyway, this case has never been officially closed. So any publicity's good publicity."

Raffin looked to Enzo for a response. Enzo nodded. "That would be very helpful, Inspecteur."

III

Enzo felt the temperature falling as they went down rung by rung, hand below hand, foot below foot. Until they reached a small, stone-clad chamber. The manhole cover thirty feet above them had slipped back into place with a deep thud, shutting out the daylight. All that lit the thick, velvet blackness that wrapped itself around them now were the battery-powered lamps mounted on the helmets that the tunnel cop had insisted they wear. Their beams raked back and forth in the damp air as they turned their heads, and Enzo saw a stone staircase arcing down into deeper darkness. The distant rumble of traffic from the Place d'Italie overhead was still audible. Just.

The tunnel cop had met them in front of the soaring glass frontage of the Gaumont Grand Écran opposite the nineteenth century splendour of the thirteenth

62

arrondissement's town hall, and led them down a side street to where a temporary canvas awning had been raised around a circular manhole cover in the pavement. The metal-framed letters IDC were embedded in the cover, above a slot into which the cop inserted a sturdy iron key to lift the lid. Thomas had introduced him simply as Franck, and then announced that he would wait for them in the café on the corner of the Rue Bobillot.

"Be careful, these steps are uneven." Franck led them down in what felt like an unending spiral, dizzying and disorientating. They heard a far-off growling, the air around them vibrated and the ground shook. "It's just the métro," Franck shouted back to them. "Don't worry about it."

And still they went down. Enzo felt his ears popping with the pressure, and he shivered. The temperature had dropped by more than fifteen degrees. Finally, they seemed to reach the foot of the staircase, and bowed their heads to pass through an arched entryway into a narrow tunnel. The walls and ceiling were constructed entirely from masonry and led them into a section of tunnel hacked from pure limestone. It ran off to left and right. Franck turned right, taking them past columns and arches to a junction where a long gallery led to another arched doorway opening into a square room lined by stone benches. There were niches set into the walls, charred by candles, and layered with the solid coloured pools of once molten wax. There was a stone table set in the centre of the room. There was, too, evidence of recent habitation: food wrappers and

63

empty beer cans and cigarette ends. It smelled of grease and stale smoke.

"I thought since we were down here anyway you might be interested in seeing this place," Franck said. "The quarriers built it for their own recreation. It was originally called the *salle des carriers*, but it's more popularly known these days as the *salle de repos*. It's a favourite meeting place for tunnel rats. We raid it from time to time, but they usually have a pretty good early warning system."

Enzo wandered around this perfectly constructed stone room more than thirty metres below an unsuspecting world above and ran his fingers lightly over the cool, smooth stone. Beneath an arched niche in the back wall, the date 1904 had been carved into the stone. It was just over a hundred years since men had created this room as a place of rest. He could not imagine what life must have been like down here for the generations of quarriers who had hacked tens of thousands of tons of stone from limestone bedrock to build their city. What kind of existence had they eked out in this dark, choking, subterranean world?

Franck was watching him with mild amusement. "You should visit the ossuary sometime."

"Ossuary?"

Raffin said, "In the eighteenth and nineteenth centuries, the Paris authorities started clearing city centre cemetreies which had become a health hazard. They allocated about eleven thousand square metres of the catacombs out at Denfert as a dumping ground for the bones. There are something like six million people stacked up in those tunnels, floor to ceiling. The bones and skulls are arranged in macabre patterns." He chuckled. "I suppose the men who transferred them from the cemetreies had reason enough to find ways of amusing themselves."

It occurred to Enzo that there was irony in the discovery of a single skull in tunnels which concealed six million.

"Anyway," Raffin said, "this isn't what we came to see, is it?"

"No." Franck turned and led them back along the gallery and through a rabbit warren of tunnels. They passed street names beautifully carved into blocks of stone corresponding to the names of the streets above — BOULEVARD VINCENT, RUE ALBERT BAYET — and surrounded by the scratched and spray-painted graffiti of a less elegant generation.

They carried on until they reached a stone marked ROUTE DE PARIS À CHOISY CÔTÉ EST, and they turned left into a narrower transverse tunnel that took them to the other side of the street overhead.

"We're under the Avenue Choisy here," Franck said. "Right below Chinatown."

On the other side, a marker stone was inscribed ROUTE DE PARIS À CHOISY CÔTÉ OUEST. But here, the way was blocked. The roof and part of the wall had caved in, piles of stone and rubble and earth preventing their further progress.

"Well, this is it." Franck turned around and his lamp nearly blinded them. "For what it's worth." Both Enzo and Raffin raised their hands to shade their eyes. "The

Inspection Générale des Carrières send surveyors down regularly to check below the sites of possible new buildings. No point in throwing up skyscrapers if they're just going to fall down again. It was a surveyor who came across this tunnel collapse. It seems the tin trunk had somehow been concealed in the wall, bricked into a recess. If the roof hadn't come down it would still be there."

The world above ground was a burned-out white, blinding and hot. Enzo's eyes adjusted quickly, but he knew that it would take the sun longer to warm through to the chill deep in his bones. The Place d'Italie was jammed with traffic and late afternoon shoppers. White flags emblazoned with red Chinese characters fluttered on either side of lamp posts around the small park which created a roundabout for the traffic, and Enzo noticed for the first time that half the population seemed to be oriental. Ethnic Chinese from French Indochina. He looked down the length of Avenue Choisy and saw the red lanterns and flashing neon characters delineating Chinatown and wondered just where exactly they had been below ground.

Franck had gone to find detective Thomas from the Quai des Orfèvres. Raffin was still brushing the dirt from his trousers. "What now?"

"I want to talk to the pathologist."

Raffin checked his watch and shook his head. "Then you'll have to go on your own. I still have to earn a living — and I'm going to have to change out of these clothes."

IV

It was only four stops on the métro from Place d'Italie to the Quai de la Rapée in the neighbouring twelfth *arrondissement*. Enzo sat gloomily in the crowded carriage, sunlight streaming through windows as the train rattled beneath the girdered arch that spanned the Seine. With all these bodies pressed around him, the heat was stifling. He looked down to his left and saw the square redbrick building that housed the Institut Médico-Légal on the west bank of the river. The bodies stored there, in tiered drawers, would be kept at a somewhat cooler temperature.

Enzo was not optimistic. What had seemed like an interesting development, the skull in the trunk, was probably no more than an eccentric diversion. If the pathologist had reconstructed a head from it without facial or scalp hair, then it couldn't be Gaillard. Even if the flesh and brain of the head had rotted away to nothing, the evidence of hair would still have remained. It took hair much longer than five years to decompose. King Tutankhamun had still had hair.

So what was left? Nothing but a theory constructed from a bloodstained floor, a doodle in a diary, and a fifty-year-old French movie.

He got off at the Quai de la Rapée and walked back along the river bank, traffic roaring past on the expressway below. On the far side of the water, the boats of the River Police were tied up at the Quai St. Bernard. A small park beside the morgue was deserted. Cars and trucks thundered across the Pont d'Austerlitz, and the clatter of the métro trains was only slightly muted by their rubber wheels. It was a noisy corner of the city, but Enzo supposed that the morgue's present tenants would not be too troubled.

The bodies were kept downstairs, behind the thick stone walls of the basement, and there cut open in tiled rooms devoid of daylight by pathologists in pursuit of death's dark secrets. There was disabled access to the main entrance one floor up, but it occurred to Enzo that the real disabled access was one floor down, via the back door. He climbed steps to the front door and walked into an airy reception hall lined by the busts of famous physicians and asked for Docteur Henri Bellin.

Bellin's office was up a narrow staircase on the first floor. The pathologist was a man in his sixties, and gave the impression of being possessed by a nervous energy he found difficult to contain. A tweed suit hung on a tall, angular frame that Enzo was sure carried less flesh than some of the cadavers downstairs. He had a pathologist's pallor, and strong, bony hands scrubbed so clean they were almost painful to look at. He was in the process of clearing his desk for the day. Like most pathologists, he was meticulously tidy.

"Yes, yes, yes," he said. "I remember it well. Odd, very odd. All those strange items in the trunk. Still, that wasn't my brief. My only interest was the skull."

"You carried out a forensic examination?"

"Yes, yes I did. Nothing very remarkable about it as I recall. A middle-aged male, aged somewhere between forty-five and fifty-five."

"How could you tell?"

"Females have more delicate mandibles, and much more gently sloping foreheads." He laughed nervously. "And I never like to discuss the fact that there is roughly two hundred cubic centimetres less space in a female skull to house the brain. Women don't like to hear it." He slipped some papers into a briefcase. "I was able to determine the age because the sutures — that's the joints between the bones — were completely ossified. There were also some deep furrows on the inside of the skull, something usually caused by blood vessels in an older person."

"I believe the teeth had been smashed."

"That's correct. Someone had taken a cylindrical instrument of some sort and done considerable damage. To the mandible as well. I had to do quite a bit of reconstruction work around the mouth."

"Presumably the teeth were smashed to prevent identification from dental records."

"Yes, of course. There were a number left intact, though. Not enough to facilitate positive identification — assuming that we'd had something to compare them to — but enough for me to recast and recreate a mouthful of teeth for the facial approximation."

"The reconstruction?"

"Forensic facial approximation is what I prefer to call it. I have evolved my own technique. A blend of the Russian and American methods. You know, Gerasimov claims one hundred percent success. Even Gatliff claims seventy percent."

"And what is your success rate?"

"Oh, I think probably around eighty. The skull from the catacombs is one of my notable failures." But it was not a failure with which he seemed too concerned. His present preoccupation seemed to be with leaving. "Was there anything else?"

"Do you still have it?"

"Do I still have what?"

"Your forensic facial approximation."

"Well, yes, of course."

"Could I see it?"

Bellin sighed his irritation and glanced at his watch. "I suppose so." He crossed his office and threw open the doors of a tall wall cabinet. The shelves inside were lined with heads, strange lifeless eyes staring out from the darkness of their odd final resting place. Nearly thirty human faces sculpted in plasticine. Likenesses of the dead. Hair, too, was represented by interwoven layers of plasticine, making it easy for Enzo to recognize the skull in question. It was the only one without any. Enzo stared at it curiously. It did not appear to bear much resemblance to Gaillard, except for a similar fleshiness about the lips and a slight droop at the corners of the eyes. The nose was, like Gaillard's, unremarkable. Enzo was disappointed that the face did not seem more familiar. He had spent hours the previous night staring at photographs of Gaillard. But he knew that facial and head hair can dramatically change the way a person looks.

Enzo reached up and touched the recreated face, almost as if he were hoping to feel the bristles where the flamboyant Gaillard moustaches had been shaved.

"You recognise him?" Bellin seemed surprised.

"Only because I'd been told you'd made the face and scalp hairless. Why did you do that?"

"Because there was no hair with the skull."

"Isn't that unusual?"

Bellin shrugged his indifference. Lack of success had bred lack of interest. "Sometimes mice take hair away from decomposing heads to build nests."

"But the head was locked in a trunk. It wasn't airtight, so no doubt insects got access to accelerate the process of decomposition. But there was no way mice could have got into that trunk."

"That's true," Bellin conceded.

"So didn't it strike you as odd that there was no hair at all?"

"It was impossible for me to determine why there was no hair. He might have suffered from alopecia. His head might have been shaved."

"And if his head and his face had been shaved, might someone not have done that for the same reason they smashed his teeth — to prevent recognition, to stop identification?"

"Of course, anything is possible."

Enzo reached into his satchel and searched for a photograph of Gaillard from Raffin's file. He held it out towards Bellin. "Whiskers and a coiffure like this might have been somewhat recognisable, don't you think?"

Bellin took the photograph. "Good God! It's Jacques Gaillard."

"Like I said. Somewhat recognisable."

Bellin lifted his reconstruction off the shelf and carried it through to a small adjoining room. There were computers here, and facial and cranial charts on the walls, and a table in the centre of the room with a half-completed facial approximation on it, tiny wooden dowels inserted at thirty-four different reference points around the head. The skull had been cast in plaster, and the mandible in cold cure resin, before being rearticulated with the cranium. Both were visible down one half of a face criss-crossed with a complex of plasticine strands representing the musculature. Bellin placed the finished head next to it and switched on a bank of overhead lamps which bathed the table in soft, bright light. He looked at the photograph, examined the head, and then re-examined the photograph. Suddenly he had rediscovered all his lost enthusiasm.

"There are umpteen points of correlation here."

"Can you put hair on the head? And a moustache?"

"I can do better than that. The danger is, of course, that one is influenced by the original. But I can photograph my approximation, front, side and back, and digitise the images into the computer. And with the help of an interesting piece of software called Face, as well as Adobe Photoshop, I can recreate Monsieur Gaillard's unusual whiskers and coiffure and superimpose them on to a 3D image of the head." He removed his jacket, draping it over the back of a tall stool at the table, and lifted a white overall from the back of the door. His earlier impatience to leave for the day was quite forgotten.

"How long will it take?" Enzo asked.

"Hmmm?" Bellin seemed almost unaware that Enzo was still there. He had already begun setting up his camera.

"How long?"

"Come back tomorrow morning, Monsieur."

CHAPTER
FIVE

I

Enzo sat in the window of Le Balto, below his studio, dipping his croissant in a large, milky coffee, and absently watching the regulars lining up along the bar drinking small, black coffees which they washed down with cold water. The morning was sticky and overcast. Across the street, people were breakfasting under the green awnings of the Bistro Mazarin, and the street cleaners had opened sluice gates to let water wash down the gutters of the Rue Jacques Callot before draining back into the sewers below.

"*Salut.*" Her voice startled him out of his reverie, and he turned to find Charlotte standing by his table. She wore jeans, and a knee-length, black cotton waistcoat open over a white tee shirt. "May I join you?"

He stood up. "Of course." They shook hands formally.

She turned towards the small, ginger-haired woman behind the bar. "*Un petit café.*" They sat facing each other. "Do you want another?" she asked as an afterthought.

He shook his head. "What are you doing here?" And, then, before she had time to answer, "Looking for me, I hope."

A smile split her face and crinkled around her eyes. "Naturally." When her coffee arrived Enzo waited while she stirred in the sugar. She took a sip and looked up. "Roger tells me you have come up with a theory about what might have happened to Jacques Gaillard."

Enzo shrugged. "It's just a theory." He tipped his head quizzically. "Why would that interest you?"

She shrugged. "I'm always interested in the psychology of murder." Then paused. "And, as you know, I was around when Roger was doing his research." She took another sip of her coffee. "And . . . maybe it seemed like a good excuse for seeing you." She examined the table for a moment, as if reluctant to meet his eye. Then she looked up boldly. "So?"

"So what?" It made him feel good that he might have been the real reason she was here.

"So what's your theory?"

"Didn't Roger tell you?"

"No, he didn't, actually."

Enzo regarded her thoughtfully. "Tell you what. I've had analysis done on some hard evidence I collected. The lab should have the results for me in . . ." He looked at his watch. ". . . About half-an-hour. Why don't you come with me? And then we'll know whether or not it's more than just a theory."

She held him in the gaze of her dark eyes for several moments, and he felt his stomach flip over. She was having a disproportionately disconcerting effect on him. "Okay."

As he made his way down towards the Seine from the Rue de l'Université Enzo saw her rise in expectation from the bench where she had waited for him. Barges ploughed their way up river. A private motor boat passed in the other direction. The long, glass-topped boats of the *bateaux mouches* below the Pont de l'Alma opposite rose and fell gently on the wash. A little further east, along the leftbank, tourists queued for tickets for a tour of *les égouts* — the Paris sewers. They were not yet open. Enzo was holding the large manila envelope they had given him at the lab, and seemed a million miles away.

"What happened?" Charlotte asked.

Enzo forced himself to focus on her. "The night Gaillard disappeared, a person or persons unknown broke into the church of St. Étienne du Mont. St. Étienne's had been Gaillard's church for nearly thirty years. The intruders slaughtered a pig in front of the altar."

"Why?"

"To cover the fact that they had just murdered Jacques Gaillard on the same spot."

Charlotte's eyes opened wide. She had turned quite pale. "How can you know that?"

"Because I took a sample of the bloodstains left in the stone. And the laboratory analysis shows that there were two types of blood staining the flagstones in the church. Pig. And human."

"That doesn't prove it was Gaillard's."

"No. But the DNA does. The DNA extracted from the human blood in the church matches the DNA in a sample of hair that I provided for the lab. I took that hair from a comb in Gaillard's apartment." Enzo paused. "Gaillard was butchered — very possibly dismembered — right there in front of the altar where he normally worshipped."

For a moment he thought that she was going to faint. She grabbed his arm and half-staggered.

"Are you all right?" He put an arm around her and felt that she was trembling.

She pushed him away. "I'm fine." She seemed embarrassed. "It's just . . . well, it's horrible." She took a deep breath. "In my job, you deal with everything in the abstract. In the mind. It's a shock to be confronted with the reality."

The sun broke through the mist above the city for the first time, sending light coruscating across the broken surface of the river. Somewhere a tug sounded its horn, and they heard laughter coming from the queue for *les égouts*.

"One more shock, then. If you can take it," Enzo said, and she looked up into his face, brows deeply furrowed. He preferred her eyes when they were smiling.

"What?"

"A visit to the morgue."

II

Docteur Bellin was involved in an autopsy when they arrived at the Institut Médico-Légal, and so they waited in the tiny park next door. It was named after an architect, Albert Tournaire, and was little more than a central flowerbed ringed by a path and flanked by tiny lawns and a handful of trees. They sat on one of the benches, with their backs to the dead, and looked along the river instead towards the Pont Sully and the twin towers of Notre Dame beyond. A hot July sun had burned off the early morning cloud, and the sky was the clearest summer blue. A dusty white heat was already beginning to settle on the city.

Charlotte had barely spoken two words on the métro, and now she sat in contemplative silence, before turning to look thoughtfully at Enzo. "I saw him on television, you know. Never missed his show. I was a student then, and movies were important." A pale smile flickered briefly across her face, reflecting some thought that came and went. "I suppose he must have been more than twice my age, but I had quite a crush on him at the time."

Enzo was surprised. "He was a strange looking guy."

"He had charm and personality and wit. You don't find much of any of that in today's crop of celebs." She almost spat the word "celeb" on to the path, a clear enough indication of the contempt with which she regarded contemporary French celebrities. She turned to gaze earnestly at Enzo. "Why would anyone want to murder him like that?"

"You're the psychologist. You tell me."

She didn't seem to like that much and looked away again, and Enzo regretted his bluntness. But she changed the subject before he could try to soften it. "You said your daughters had different mothers. What happened?"

78

He wasn't sure if she was genuinely interested, or simply finding an excuse to talk about something else. "I got married when I was twenty."

"Ouch! Too young."

"It was. We were still students. At our hometown university. We did it to get away from home, really. Get a place of our own." He shook his head at the memory. "A damp, grotty, one-bedroomed tenement flat in Partick with a shared lavatory on the landing. By the time we graduated, the relationship had probably run its course. But then she got pregnant."

Charlotte looked at him. "Women don't just get pregnant, Enzo. Men make them pregnant."

Enzo nodded his acknowledgement. "Okay, we got pregnant — and spent the next seven years regretting it. Not the kid, not Kirsty. Us. The fact that we'd tied ourselves to one another when it wasn't really what either of us wanted. And, you know, you do that thing, stay together for the kid. And I'm not sure it's the right thing."

"Sounds like you're building up to a justification for leaving them."

Enzo looked at her. "I forgot. I'm talking to a psychologist." And, after a moment, "Are you going to bill me for this?"

"So you met someone else?"

Enzo looked away. None of it had seemed predictable to him then. But no doubt Charlotte had heard the same story a thousand times. "At a conference of the International Association of Forensic Scientists in Nice."

Charlotte smiled. "I suppose they picked Nice because of its importance to forensic science."

Enzo laughed. "It's true. Sunshine and seafood are very important to forensic scientists."

"Was she a forensic scientist?"

"She'd just graduated. She was twenty-three. I was thirty. And I knew she was the one. From the minute she spilled her drink in my lap."

Across the Seine a police boat gunned its engine and set off up river at speed, blue light flashing, siren wailing.

"So you left your wife and kid and came to France?"

"It wasn't just my family I gave up. It was my career. In those days my French wasn't that great, and I'd never have got a job in the *police scientifique*. And, of course, by then Pascale was pregnant." And before Charlotte could say anything he corrected himself. "I'd got her pregnant."

"Good God," Charlotte said, "have you never heard of condoms?" He smiled. "So what happened?"

Enzo's jaw set and he stared silently towards the Île St. Louis. "She died in childbirth. Left me a beautiful daughter to remind me of her every day of the rest of my life." He stood up quickly, thrusting his hands in his pockets to hide the emotion he felt welling up inside. "But Sophie was also her gift. The best thing that ever happened to me."

After a long moment, Charlotte asked, "What about your other daughter?"

Enzo's lips tightened. "Kirsty won't even speak to me. And do you know what's ironic?" He turned to find

Charlotte looking up at him. "She's here, in Paris. Living on the Île St. Louis. Not half a mile from here." He gazed back down river. "And it's as if I don't even exist."

Bellin had the smell of death about him. No doubt he had showered after changing out of his surgical pyjamas, but still he brought the perfume of the autopsy room with him into his office. He was clearly excited, dark eyes shining with anticipation. He took them through to his tiny studio. The head he had taken down from the shelf the day before was still on the table. Charlotte looked at it curiously.

"Is this it?" she asked. Enzo nodded and watched her closely. She had been a fan of Gaillard. Watched his TV show. Had a crush on him. But she just shrugged and frowned. "Doesn't look like anyone I know," she said.

"Wait," said Bellin, and he sat down in front of the twenty-inch cinema screen of his Macintosh G5 and shuffled the mouse. His screensaver vanished and a photograph of Gaillard appeared in its place. He turned and looked triumphantly at Enzo.

Enzo was confused, uncertain of what he was supposed to be seeing. "Where's the head?"

Bellin smiled. "You're looking at it. Digital photographs of it manipulated by software, hair and whiskers superimposed and morphed on to the image." He hit a key, and an extraordinarily lifelike 3D image of the head began slowly revolving on the screen.

Enzo heard Charlotte gasp and glanced at her across the room. Her eyes were fixed on the image. "It's him," she whispered.

Enzo looked back to the screen. "It certainly looks like him. But it's not proof."

"How can you prove it, then?" she asked.

"DNA," Bellin said.

Enzo asked him, "Do you still have the skull?"

"Of course." Bellin stooped to open a cupboard door. A row of seven or eight skulls sat side by side on the bottom shelf. He checked the labels, and then lifted one of them out and placed it on the table. The repair work around the lower mandible, where it had been smashed, was evident.

Enzo gazed at it curiously and felt the hairs lift up on the back of his neck. He had no doubt he was looking at Jacques Gaillard's skull. He said to Charlotte, "When the Americans sent forensic pathologists to Bosnia in the nineties to try to identify bodies found in mass graves, they employed a new technique which allowed them to extract a DNA profile from old bones by, literally, grinding them down. It's a technique more recently employed in Iraq." He looked at Bellin. "Your people can do this by grinding down a piece of the skull, can't they?"

Bellin inclined his head in acknowledgement. "We can have a result in twenty-four hours."

CHAPTER
SIX

I

A large white swan left a gentle V-shaped ripple in its wake as it glided effortlessly up to their window and peered in jealously at the food on the table. Beyond, the shimmering red-tiled roofs of the old town rose up from Port Bullier to the imposing stone tower of the mediaeval prison and the painfully blue Lotois sky behind it.

Enzo was pleased to be back in Cahors, an escape from the noise and pollution of Paris, oppressive high buildings crowding narrow streets. Here, he could breathe again. He had missed the tree-covered hills rising all around from the banks of the river, the purity of the air, the simple sound of a church bell pealing out across ancient rooftops, calling the faithful to prayer. Life seemed so much less complicated here.

He was pleased, too, by the discomfort of Préfet Verne and his chief of police, Madame Taillard, who were sitting opposite. A copy of *Libération* lay on the table between them. The headline the sub-editors had given Raffin's story was: GAILLARD ASSASSINÉ. A subheading read: *La Vérité Après Dix Ans*. There was a large reproduction of Bellin's digitally treated forensic facial approximation of Gaillard's head, full-face and profile.

The police chief was fixing Enzo with a hard stare, colour high on her cheeks. Enzo reminded himself that Hélène Taillard had once been attracted to him. There was a time when he might have felt something reciprocal, but that had long since passed. He suspected that she sensed this, and that it was fuelling her hostility now — a woman scorned. "It proves nothing," she said dismissively.

"It proves that he was murdered," Enzo said.

"Which is no more than everyone suspected," said the Préfet. He tore off a piece of bread and mopped some Roquefort sauce from his plate. He was handling the situation with more dignity than his chief of police.

Enzo liked Jean-Luc Verne. He was one of more than a hundred regional administrators, state-appointed and hugely powerful. A man several years Enzo's senior, he had been running the Département du Lot for the past two years. They had met at a party and found they shared the same ironic sense of humour.

"Suspected perhaps," Enzo said. "But in ten years the Paris police failed to find a single piece of evidence to prove it."

Madame Taillard said, "Policing techniques have changed radically in ten years."

"Which, I think, was Monsieur Macleod's point in the first place," the Préfet said. "And he is to be congratulated on his achievement. The political repercussions of Gaillard's murder are, as we speak, reverberating around the corridors of power in Paris."

84

He sipped appreciatively on a Château Lagrézette, which he had selected himself from the Carte des Vins, and turned back towards Enzo. "However, proving that he was murdered is one thing. To win our little wager you'll need to determine who murdered him, and why. And that is quite another."

There had been four of them at the dinner table the night they made the bet. Enzo, Simon on one of his unannounced visits from London, Préfet Verne, and police chief Taillard.

"Which, I think, was my point," she said now, clearly piqued. "The trail is ten years old, as cold as the stone upon which Monsieur Gaillard was apparently murdered."

"But not as cold as it was," Enzo pointed out.

"Ah, yes," said Préfet Verne. "The items in the trunk."

They were all startled by a sharp rap at the window, and turned to see the swan glaring at them. It was not pleased at being ignored.

The Préfet said, "I think perhaps diners on the top deck are in the habit of throwing it titbits. It's probably wondering why we're not doing the same." Which would have been impossible since the air-conditioned lower salon of the Bateau au Fil Douceurs restaurant was almost at river level, its windows sealed against the summer heat. And the water. The boat was berthed on the east side of the river, beyond the Pont de Cabessut, a chunky, white-painted vessel which looked as if it might topple over if ever it were to set sail. It had been Préfet

Verne's suggestion that they lunch there. He had expensive tastes. He turned his attention away again from the swan. "Where were we? Ah, yes, the items in the trunk. What on earth do they mean?"

"Well, that's just it," Enzo said. "They must mean something."

"Why?" asked chief Taillard.

"Because you wouldn't cut off a man's head and bury it in a trunk with five seemingly unrelated items unless you had a reason. And if there's a reason, then there must be a way of working out what it was."

"And you intend to use forensic science to find out?" said the Préfet.

"No, I intend to use my brain."

II

Madame Taillard drove back on her own to the Caserne Bessières at the north end of town. Enzo walked across the Pont de Cabessut with Préfet Verne, who was puffing gently on his postprandial cigar. Bright southern sunlight spilled across the rooftops to the old city wall and the Tour des Pendus, where lawbreakers were once hanged in full public view. They turned south towards the Place Champollion. "I know we all believed that something awful had happened to him," the Préfet said, "but one is never really prepared for the truth. Somehow it's always worse than you could possibly have imagined. Poor Jacques."

"You knew him?"

"Yes, but not well. We were at ENA together. There were nearly a hundred and thirty of us in our *promotion*, but everyone knew Jacques Gaillard. He was a character. Not necessarily a likeable one — he was somewhat full of himself. But he certainly brought a little colour into our dull academic lives. Ironic that he should have spent his last year back there teaching."

"It must have been something of a comedown for him. From Prime Ministerial advisor to teacher."

"No, not really. He wasn't a teacher, exactly. There are no full-time professors at ENA — except for sport. The brightest pupils are taught only by the best brains. Top civil servants, captains of industry, former cabinet ministers, all invited to take time out of busy lives to pass on their experience to the next generation. It was George Bernard Shaw, wasn't it, who said that those who can, do, and those who can't, teach? Well, it was de Gaulle's vision that those who do exceptionally well should teach their successors how to do likewise. Which is why he created ENA." They turned west and began the climb up the narrow Rue Maréchal Foch at the back of the cathedral towards the Hôtel du Département, and the offices of the Préfet. "So it wasn't really a demotion, as such," he added. "More a sideways shuffle to move his celebrity spotlight away from the Prime Minister."

They stopped at the gate of the Conseil Général and shook hands, and Préfet Verne pushed through wrought iron into the cobbled courtyard beyond, to vanish into his own administrative empire. Enzo crossed the square opposite the cathedral with a lightness in his step. The

Saturday market was over, and a truck with large rotating brushes was cleaning away the debris. He reached the brick arches of La Halle at the foot of the Place Jean-Jacques Chapou and strolled in through the back entrance of the covered market with his hands in his pockets. Past the *poissonerie*, with all its fresh fish laid out on crushed ice; Le Chai the wine seller, where you could fill your own container from huge stainless steel vats; Monsieur Chevaline, the butcher; the *charcuterie* where Enzo sometimes bought pre-cooked *plats asiatiques* to carry out. The wine seller waved and shouted *salut*. The butcher called that he had some very tender filet mignon just in. But Enzo wasn't buying. He was just revelling in being back. Where everything was a known quantity and everyone was familiar. Such a contrast with the hostile anonymity of Paris.

His good mood lasted for as long as it took him to open the door of his apartment and trip over something lurking in the shadows of the hall. It was hard and unyielding and caught him squarely on the shin. He cursed, and saw that it was Bertrand's metal detector.

It had been there since before his trip to Paris, arriving unexpectedly one night as Enzo was heading down for a nightcap at the Café Le Forum. He had been confronted by Bertrand out on the landing, cradling the long-necked creature with its disc-like head in strong, muscular arms.

Enzo had never made any attempt to disguise his disapproval of this young man with his spiky, blond-tipped brown hair, and pointless pieces of metal piercing eyebrow, nose and lip. "What the hell . . ."

"Hi, Papa." Sophie's bright, smiling face, appearing at Bertrand's shoulder, had made Enzo momentarily forget his irritation. It happened almost every time. Whenever he wasn't expecting to see her, and she caught him unawares, he always saw her mother in her. Those bright, dark eyes, her elfin face, long blue-black hair fanning out across her shoulders. And the memory of Pascale would wash over him, powerful and melancholic. The only part of Sophie which was identifiably him was the pale streak in her hair which ran back through it from her left temple, not as pronounced as his own, although there was no mistaking the stubborn streak they both shared with equal vigour. "You don't mind if we leave it here for a couple of days?" she'd said. "There's no room at Bertrand's mum's, and the health and safety people would object if he left it lying around the gym."

In spite of his antipathy towards Bertrand, Enzo could never bring himself to be angry with his daughter for long. "What on earth is it?" he had asked.

"A metal detector. Bertrand got it cheap at a *brocante*. Lots of the kids have got them now. Ever since they found those old Roman coins along the riverside above the Pont Louis-Philippe. They're worth a fortune, you know."

"It wouldn't be for long, Monsieur Macleod," Bertrand had promised. "Just until I can clear a space in my mother's attic."

But as the pain on his shin testified, it was still there. Enzo glanced at his watch. It was well into the afternoon now, but Sophie's bedroom door was shut tight, and he figured she was probably still asleep. Kids! They thought nothing of sleeping their lives away. It seemed criminal, somehow, when you had lived longer than you had left, to think of wasting a single moment of your youth. It was gone before you knew it. He thought of that most famous of verses from the *Rubaiyat of Omar Khayyam*:

The moving finger writes: and, having writ,
Moves on: nor all thy Piety nor Wit
Shall lure it back to cancel half a line,
Nor all your Tears wash out a word of it.

It seemed, too, particularly appropriate to Jacques Gaillard. Although not a young man, he'd had, from all accounts, an abundance of both piety and wit. And neither tears nor time had washed away his blood, spilled on the steps of the altar of St. Étienne du Mont. It made Enzo all the more determined to find his killer. He pushed open the door into the front room to see if the workmen had finished.

The *séjour* was in chaos. The *ouvriers* had removed the bookshelves along the far wall, and piled the hundreds of displaced books untidily on tables and chairs, and on most of the available floor space. Mounted in their place was a huge whiteboard, three metres by two. Enzo looked at it with satisfaction and began clearing a way to get to it. He would need to make some space on the table to set up his computer.

There was a knock at the open door from the landing, and a girl's voice called, "Monsieur Macleod?"

"Through here."

A young girl, about Sophie's age, appeared in the doorway. As soon as Enzo saw her he knew why she was there, and cursed inwardly at his forgetfulness. She was not an ugly girl, but physically awkward, big without being tall. She had what in Scotland would have been called good childbearing hips. She wore jeans stretched tightly across them, and a V-necked tee shirt which strained to contain breasts which one of Enzo's fellow lecturers had once lasciviously described as being like cantaloupe melons. They had a tendency to draw the eye, and to his shame Enzo had found his eyes drawn to them on more than one occasion. She had a pretty face, and very long, dark, wavy hair which she often tied back in a loose ponytail. Her cheeks burned with the pink bloom of embarrassment.

"I'm sorry, Monsieur Macleod . . . I hope I'm not disturbing you."

"Nicole." Enzo raised both hands in surrender. "I'm sorry, I completely forgot. You know, things have been . . . well . . ." He gave up trying to find excuses. "I just forgot, that's all."

"I know. I've been to the hospital. They didn't know anything about it."

"Well, they wouldn't. Because I never got around to speaking to Docteur du Coq."

"They said that I was too late and they'd already taken their complement of students for the summer."

"Shit," Enzo muttered under his breath.

"Only, I'd been kind of counting on it. You know, for the money." She dropped her eyes to the floor, too self-conscious to meet his. "I'm sorry, I didn't know what else to do, or where else to go."

"Oh, God. Nicole, I'm sorry." He wanted to give her a hug and tell her everything would be all right. But he wasn't sure how close those breasts would let him get, and in any case he knew that everything wouldn't be all right. Student jobs everywhere had been filled by now. He had let her down badly. And then he had an inspiration and said impulsively, "Look . . . why don't you come and work for me here?" Almost as soon as the words were out of his mouth he regretted them. How could he pay her? He supposed that if he won the bet — a thousand euros each from the Préfet and the chief of police — then he could afford to pay her handsomely. If not . . . well, that was something he would face up to later.

She looked up in astonishment, embarrassment replaced suddenly by a flush of slow-burning pleasure. "For you?"

"I have a sort of project I'm working on this summer. I could do with an assistant. Someone smart. Someone good on computers, and the internet."

"Well, that's me," she said eagerly.

"I know."

"I've been online ever since I can remember. You know, 'Nicole calling the world.' "

Enzo nodded, thinking that this was definitely a mistake. She might be his brightest student, and there was no doubting her academic brilliance. But there was no doubting, also, that she lacked certain social skills. Her upbringing as a single child on a remote hill farm in the Aveyron had not prepared her for sophisticated student life in France's fourth-largest city. Her first year in Toulouse had been hard, not least because of the cruelty of some of her fellow students.

"Oh," she said, suddenly downcast. "But where will I stay? It's too far to travel."

Perhaps, Enzo thought, this was a way out. "There's a spare room here," he said, hardly believing he'd said it out loud. But, after all, he had let her down.

Her spirits lifted again. "I won't disappoint you, Monsieur Macleod. I promise." And then she said, "What's the project?"

Enzo sighed. "It's difficult to explain, Nicole. Why don't you go home and pack a suitcase tonight and come back tomorrow? I'll explain in the morning."

As he was seeing her out, a sleepy Sophie emerged from her bedroom wrapped in a towelling robe. She craned up to kiss Enzo on the cheek. "What's happening?" she said, looking at Nicole and blinking the sleep out of her eyes.

Enzo said, "Sophie, this is Nicole. She's a student at Paul Sabatier." And to Nicole, "Sophie's my daughter."

Nicole put her hand over her mouth to stifle a giggle. "Well that's a relief." And then she thrust her hand out to shake Enzo's. "See you tomorrow, Monsieur Macleod."

When Nicole had gone, Enzo turned back to the *séjour* and caught his shin for a second time on Bertrand's metal detector. "Jesus Christ, Sophie! Will you get rid of that damned thing?"

"I'm sorry, Papa, I meant to put it in the spare room. I'll do it now."

"No," Enzo said quickly. "Nicole's going to be in there."

Sophie looked at him as if he had two heads. "That girl?" Enzo nodded uncomfortably. "Papa, what's going on?" She pursued him into the front room. The French windows were open and hot air wafted in from the square below.

"It's just for a few weeks."

"Weeks!"

"I promised to get her a summer job at the hospital, and I forgot. Now she's too late to get anything else."

"So she says." Sophie was highly sceptical. "Papa, I saw the way she was gazing up at you. She's infatuated."

"Don't be silly, Sophie. Of course she isn't." Enzo was indignant. "She comes from a tiny hill farm in the Aveyron, and her folks have been struggling to put her through university. She needed that job. I owe her. So she's going to help me with the Jacques Gaillard thing."

Sophie relented and took his arm and squeezed it. "Papa, you're too soft for your own good." She looked up at him with her mother's eyes. "How are you going to pay her?"

"I'm just going to have to win the bet, that's all."

94

For the first time Sophie became aware of the chaos in the *séjour*. She untangled herself from her father and looked around. "What's going on in here?"

Enzo cast his eyes over the piles of books and glanced across at the whiteboard. "This is my war room," he said. "It's where I'm going to do battle with Gaillard's killer."

III

Sophie had gone to the gym, where Bertrand ran courses in everything from dance to weightlifting, and Enzo had the apartment to himself again. The computer was set up on the table, wires trailing everywhere — to the wall socket, the telephone, the printer. He had downloaded the photographs from his digital camera and printed them out one by one. All five items found in the trunk below the Place d'Italie with Gaillard's skull. Now he was sticking them up on his newly mounted whiteboard. Bellin's approximation, cut from the front page of *Libération*, was taped to the top left-hand corner. Top-centre he placed the thigh bone, top-right the bee. He taped the shell, the antique stethoscope and the *Ordre de la Libération* along the bottom of the board, cleared a space in his favourite recliner and sat back staring at them. A pack of marker pens sat on top of a pile of books below the board, ready for writing up his initial thoughts. But he didn't want to rush it. He wanted to clear his mind first. He needed to wash away all preconceptions and let these five puzzling pieces find their own place in his thoughts. This was going to be a long road, and he wanted to make as few wrong turns as possible. He reached for his guitar and began picking out a slow, mournful twelve-bar blues, and closed his eyes to find Gaillard staring back at him from the haunted shadows of his dead skull.

CHAPTER
SEVEN

I

Nicole was waiting among the deserted Sunday morning tables of the pizzeria when he returned from breakfast at the Café Le Forum. She was pleased to see him. "Hi, Monsieur Macleod." She ignored his outstretched hand and leaned up to kiss him three times, alternating cheeks. He was taken aback. It was a customary French greeting between men and women familiar with each other, but not usual between lecturer and student. He wondered if, perhaps, Sophie was right about Nicole.

Her suitcase was huge, and very heavy, and she allowed Enzo to carry it up to the second floor. Circumventing the metal detector, he put the case in her room. She looked from the window over the jumble of rooftops behind the apartment. "This is lovely. Better than any job at the hospital."

While she unpacked, Enzo explained the background to the Gaillard case. For her further enlightenment he had left, on the bedside table, a copy of Raffin's book, as well as his front-page piece in *Libération* about the identification of the skull. Nicole's eyes opened wide. "So we're going to be kind of, like, detectives?"

"Exactly."

"Oh, wow. That's amazing."

"It's serious work, Nicole. We're talking about a man's murder here. And a killer, or killers, who are still at large."

"Okay," she said, eager to get started. "Let's get them, then."

He ensconced her at the computer in the *séjour* and she said, "Are we broadband?" Enzo nodded. "Good. I don't know how anyone can work with dial-up any more. It's so-oo slow. What search engine do you use?"

"Google."

"Good, so do I."

Enzo picked his way through the books littering the floor to the whiteboard. "This is how I'm going to work it," he said. "Around the board I've taped up photographs of the items found with the skull. As you can see, I've already started making notes under each of them. Each time we come up with a valid line of thinking on any of them, we'll note that somewhere in the centre of the board, circle it, and draw a line to it from the item which has sparked the thought. Then we'll be looking for connections, either between the thoughts or between the items, and we'll draw more arrows and more circles. The theory is, that the thought which ends up with most arrows pointing to it is the key to the puzzle."

Nicole stared at the board thoughtfully, and her intelligence kicked in over her immaturity. "What makes you think it's a puzzle?"

"Because there has to be a reason for these things being there. Some kind of message. It must be. Each item kind of like a cryptic clue."

"Why would the killer want to leave a message?"

"I haven't the least idea. But I'm not concerned with that for the moment. The first thing is to decipher the message. You can see I've started making notes on my first thoughts."

"You'd better take me through them, then."

"Okay, let's start with the femur, the thigh bone." Underneath it he had written *Anatomical Skeleton*. "The police had already figured out that this was probably taken from the kind of anatomical skeleton used for demonstration purposes in medical schools. The small holes drilled at either end would have been for wiring the bones together. So now I'm thinking, why? What's the point of this bone? Sometimes, in primitive societies, bones like this were used as weapons. Which is why I've written up *Club* with *Murder weapon?* in brackets." He held up his hand. "But don't pay too much attention to that. There was no sign of cranial damage to the skull. It was just an initial thought. And there's no particular reason I started with the bone." He moved along the board. "But it was after that I had my first revelation."

"Good," Nicole said. "I like revelations."

Enzo pointed first at the scallop shell, and then to the bee. "Do either of these things mean anything to you?"

Nicole thought for a moment. "Didn't Napoléon use the bee as his emblem? I can see golden bees embroidered on blue velvet. Something like that."

"Good girl. And what about the shell?"

"A *Coquille St. Jacques* . . ." Nicole said thoughtfully.

"Okay, I'll stop you right there. Why's it called a *Coquille St. Jacques?*"

Nicole frowned. "Something to do with pilgrims, wasn't it?"

"Exactly. Since the early middle ages, pilgrims from all over Europe have been following trails through south-west France to Galicia on the northern Spanish coast, to a place called Compostela. It's where the saint we call James in English, and you call Jacques in French, was supposed to have landed not long after the death of Christ. Saint-Jacques de Compostelle."

Nicole was tapping away furiously at the keyboard. "Yeah, here we are." She had come up with a page on a website about routes to Compostela. "Compostela's from campo stella, field of stars. Apparently the decapitated body of Saint-Jacques the Elder was landed there in 44 AD." She looked up, eyes shining. "Decapitated! Is that another clue?"

Enzo tipped his head thoughtfully. They were certainly looking for a body without a head. "Perhaps."

She turned back to the screen. "Wow, this guy's shown close to Christ in most of the paintings of the Last Supper. It says the body got floated ashore from a stone boat to a beach covered with scallop shells, and

100

that's how the shell became symbolic of the pilgrimage."

Enzo said, "There are arguments about that. Some people say that the pilgrims brought shells back with them to show that they had reached the sea. You must have seen scallop shells carved in the stone lintels of houses in villages all over this area."

Nicole nodded. "Yeah, we've got one above our door. I never knew why."

"They say that the pilgrims begged for water as they passed, and that it was given to them in the shells they brought back with them. If you had a shell carved above your door, it meant that you were willing to provide pilgrims with food and drink, even a bed for the night."

She had been tapping away again as he spoke and abruptly changed the subject. "Okay . . . Here's some stuff about Napoléon and the bees." She grinned. "I was right." And she read, "At his coronation as Emperor in 1804, Napoléon adorned his imperial robe with the gold bee figurines which had been discovered in the tomb of Childeric the First. And his throne room at Fontainebleau is filled with silks and brocades enriched with precious gold bee decorations." She looked up from the screen and screwed up her nose. "Why did he have a thing about bees?"

"There is a legend that Bonaparte was advised to marry Josephine and adopt her two children, because they were supposed to be of Merovingean lineage — descendants of Christ. He was told it would make him part of that lineage. Childeric was the son of King

Merovee of the Franks, the first of the lineage, and supposedly a direct descendent of Mary Magdalene. When Childeric's tomb was opened in the middle ages, more than eleven hundred years after his death, it contained three hundred solid gold replicas of honeybees." He shrugged. "That's one story, but who knows. The bee also has certain royal connotations. The Queen served by drones. Royal jelly. Maybe that's what appealed to him." He turned back to the board. "Anyway, hold on to those thoughts." He lifted his marker and wrote *Napoléon* below the bee, and *Saint-Jacques* and *Pilgrims* below the scallop shell. Then he turned to Nicole again. "So the shell and the bee are both what?"

"Symbols," she said simply.

"Exactly. So, if those two are symbols, it would be reasonable to assume that the other items are also symbols, or at least symbolic of something, rather than being important in their own right."

"I see what you mean." She stared at the board where he had written *Old Medicine* next to the antique stethoscope. "So the stethoscope doesn't have any meaning in itself. It's symbolic of something like early medicine." She frowned. "When was the stethoscope invented?"

"I have no idea."

"Well, let's see if we can find out."

Enzo picked his way back across the room to stand behind her as she put Google to work. She entered *Antique Stethoscopes* into the search window and hit the return key. The search brought up one hundred and four results, the first one of which was a site called ANTIQUE MEDICAL INSTRUMENTS. Nicole selected it and brought up a website headed ALEX PECK — MEDICAL ANTIQUES. She scrolled quickly down the page to find the first mention of antique stethoscopes, but it was just a list of early types and manufacturers. She scrolled further down to the second mention, and here found a link to two specific types of stethoscope. She clicked on the first, and up came a page on the Laennec stethoscope. She read out the entry. "A circa 1820s Laennec monaural stethoscope turned in three parts from cedar. Blah, blah . . ." She skimmed through the rest, then, "René Theophile Hyacinthe Laennec — 1781 to 1826 — invented the stethoscope around 1816." She paused. "Just what I've always wanted to know. It doesn't really tell us much, though."

"It's a date," Enzo said. "1816." And he went to mark it up on the board beside the stethoscope. He heard Nicole tapping away at the keyboard behind him. And then an exclamation.

"Oh, my God!"

Enzo turned, alarmed. "What is it?"

Her face was flushed with excitement. "I put Laennec's full name into the search engine, and the first of about a thousand links that came up was for the Catholic Encyclopaedia. You're not going to believe this. The entry for Laennec says that while studying in Paris he became a pupil of a Doctor Corvisart, who is described here as Napoléon's great physician." She looked up, eyes shining. "Napoléon!"

Enzo grinned. "Clever girl." He immediately turned and, in the centre of the whiteboard, wrote in bold letters, *Napoléon's Doctor*. Underneath it, the name *Corvisart*. He drew a circle around the names and pointed arrows to the circle from both the stethoscope and the bee.

"What about the thigh bone?" Nicole said. "If it's really a piece from an anatomical skeleton, then that's a medical allusion, too, isn't it?"

"You're right," Enzo said, and he drew another arrow from the femur to the circle in the centre of the board. So there were now three arrows pointing to it. "It's working," he said. "This is what's supposed to happen."

And then they hit a dead end.

Nicole spent the next hour chasing down dozens of websites about the physician. In the space of that hour they learned nearly everything about the man there was to know, but nothing that brought enlightenment. Napoléon was quoted as saying of him: "I do not believe in medicine, but I believe in Corvisart."

"I think I remember reading somewhere that Napoléon had an ulcer, and suffered terribly from piles," Enzo said.

Nicole made a face. "Monsieur Macleod! Too much information!"

Enzo retired to his recliner and stared at the whiteboard, listening to the clackety-clack of Nicole's keyboard tapping away the seconds of his life. What possible relevance could Napoléon's doctor have? He let his eyes wander to the *Ordre de la Libération*. Perhaps it had a website. He made a mental note to ask

Nicole to check when she had finished with Corvisart. And then he thought about the date engraved on the back of the medal. 12 May, 1943. Perhaps it was a famous date in French history. He'd ask Nicole to check that as well. Sometimes streets or squares in France were named after important dates. He went in search of his Paris street planner among the clutter of books, eventually finding it and scanning through it for a street named 12 May, 1943. But without success.

Sophie emerged from her room late morning, bleary-faced and puffy-eyed. She barely acknowledged Nicole. "I'm off to Bertrand's," she said. "I'll see you later, Papa." And she was gone before Enzo could tell her to take the metal detector with her.

"There's a Rue Corvisart in Paris," Nicole said suddenly, as if her thoughts had been running along the same lines as Enzo's. She was staring at the screen. "And a Hotel Corvisart. And a Lycée Corvisart, all in the same street. Oh, and there's a métro stop called Corvisart. On the Green Line. Just one stop away from Place d'Italie."

Enzo sat up. "Place d'Italie?" He jumped out of the recliner and crossed to the whiteboard and wrote up, *Street, Hotel, School, Métro*, one below the other, and circled them. Then he pointed an arrow to them from *Corvisart*. "We're getting somewhere, Nicole. If the head was buried in the catacombs beneath Place d'Italie, maybe the rest of him is also somewhere down there. Is there any way we can find out if there are tunnels below the Rue Corvisart?"

"Let's see . . ." Nicole called up Google and entered Catacombs and then *info*, bringing up a list of around two-and-a-half-thousand links. Top of the list was a site advertising the official catacomb tour at Denfert-Rochereau. But they struck gold with the one below it. The link took them to *www.catacombes.info*, and eerie music immediately began to fill the room.

"What the hell's that?" Enzo asked.

"They've put a soundtrack on the website for a bit of atmosphere," she said.

Enzo came around to have a look at it. The site displayed vivid orange and white lettering on a black background. Nicole moved her cursor over a photograph of a manhole cover with a circle of blue around the letters IDF. She clicked on it, and the manhole cover slid aside, prompting a fresh page to appear with links to a welcome page, a history page, a page of photographs, and several others.

"Try the photos page," Enzo said. Nicole clicked on the link, which took them to a page with a map tracing the peripheral boundaries of Paris and the route of the Seine through the city. It also delineated areas where the largest number of tunnel networks were to be found. Enzo pointed to the thirteenth *arrondissement*. "That's where the Place d'Italie is." Nicole moved her cursor over it, and the area of tunnels on the map was immediately highlighted in green. She clicked, and they were taken to another page with a detailed map of the tunnel network below. Enzo gasped. "*Salle des carriers!* I was there."

Nicole moved her cursor over the *salle des carriers*, clicked on it, and they were taken to another page filled with photographs of tunnels leading to the room, all spookily lit by strategically placed candles.

"This is extraordinary," Enzo said. "Someone's gone to a huge amount of work to put this site together."

Nicole took them back to the map and located Place d'Italie on it. Almost all of the network was immediately north or east of it. None of the tunnels extended far enough west to take in the Rue Corvisart. "It doesn't look like there are any tunnels under Corvisart," she said. "At least, not if this map's to be believed."

Enzo was disappointed. "Maybe I'm going to have to go back to Paris and look at this Rue Corvisart myself."

"It's a pretty long street." Nicole looked at the map. "And anyway, aren't you getting a bit ahead of yourself? I mean, we still don't know the relevance of the scallop shell, or the *Ordre de la Libération*, or the date on the back of it."

Enzo nodded. "No, you're right." It was good to have someone else there to keep him focused. He felt his stomach growling and checked the time. It was midday. After twenty years in France he had acquired that quintessentially French biological clock which told him when it was time for lunch. "I'm going downstairs for some pizza. Are you coming?"

But Nicole's attention was still riveted on the screen in front of her. "Um . . . no, thanks. I'm on a diet."

"Oh. Okay. Well, there's stuff in the fridge if you get hungry."

II

Enzo had a simple Margarita at La Lampara restaurant below the apartment. He washed it down with a *quart de vin rouge* and a half bottle of Badoit and stared through the trees opposite, past the cars in the square, to the arches of La Halle, closed now for lunch. Tables at all the restaurants and cafés were filled, groups and couples, locals and holidaymakers enjoying the food and the company. Even after all these years Enzo had never quite got used to eating alone, and he had developed the habit of eating quickly and settling up. There was never any reason to linger. But today he had a more pressing reason for speeding up the process. He had a sense that they were almost within touching distance of Gaillard's killer.

When he got back to the apartment he found Nicole in a state of excitement, her breasts heaving hypnotically as she told him that she thought Corvisart had taken them up a blind alley.

"Why?" Enzo asked.

"Because we thought all this medical stuff leading us to Napoléon was supposed to take us to Corvisart, because he was Napoléon's personal physician."

"So?"

"So Napoléon had another doctor. A much more famous one." She scrolled through the history of recently visited websites and recalled a page she had found during lunch. "Doctor Dominique Larrey."

"What's so remarkable about Larrey?"

"He revolutionised medical treatment on the battlefield. He pioneered amputation surgery, introduced ambulances to remove the wounded from the field, and the concept of triage in their treatment. Napoléon appointed him Surgeon-in-Chief to the French army, and he accompanied Napoléon on his expeditions to Egypt, Palestine, Syria, Germany, Poland, and Moscow. He was made a baron in 1810."

Enzo shrugged. "Why do you think he's more relevant than Corvisart?"

"Okay, just listen." And she started reading. "Larrey's name remains associated with an amputation of the shoulder joint, Mediterranean yellow fever, and ligation of the femoral artery below the inguinal ligament." She looked up, her face shining. "Femoral artery. That's what you called the thigh bone, wasn't it? The femur."

Enzo inclined his head in doubtful acknowledgement. "Well, yes. But that seems a bit thin, Nicole."

"Ah, but wait, that's not all. Here's the best bit. He was born in the Pyrénées, and studied medicine under an uncle who was a surgeon in Toulouse."

For the first time, Enzo's interest was aroused. "Toulouse?"

Nicole grinned at him. "I thought that might get you. I checked. Toulouse was one of the most important stopping places on the pilgrim's route to Compostela." She left the computer and brushed past Enzo to the whiteboard. She took a different coloured marker, scored out *Corvisart* under *Napoléon's Doctor*. "If we make that Larrey instead . . ." and she wrote up the name, ". . . we can point arrows to it from the femur, the bee, the stethoscope and the scallop shell." She drew in the arrows.

Enzo took the pen from her. "And we can add something else." He wrote *Toulouse* up on the board, circled it, and drew arrows to it from Larrey and from the scallop shell. "So now we have four arrows pointing through Larrey and a second from the shell, all going to Toulouse." Which was much closer to home than Enzo could ever have imagined — just an hour south of Cahors. Was it possible that Gaillard's remains had been brought all the way to Toulouse? And if so, why? He stood back and examined the board afresh. "We haven't looked at the *Ordre de la Libération* yet."

"They've got a website," Nicole said, and she started back to the computer. "I found it while you were out." She began tapping at the keyboard. "It didn't seem very interesting, though." She brought the site up on screen, and read, "The *Ordre de la Libération* is France's second national Order after the Legion of Honour, and was instituted by Général de Gaulle, Leader of the Free French movement, with Edict Number Seven, signed in Brazzaville on 16 November, 1940. Admission to the Order is meant to reward individuals, military, and civil organisations for outstanding service in the effort to procure the Libération of France and the French Empire." She sighed and clicked on a link to the site map, which brought up dozens more links. "There are links to all sorts of pages about the history of the Order, the chronology, official texts . . . You can download a PDF file with the names of all one

110

thousand and thirty-eight recipients of the Order. There's even a list of only those recipients who are still alive. Which no doubt needs regular updating."

Enzo thought about it. "And the date? 12th May, 1943?"

"There's no reference to it on the site."

"Can you search Google just for the date?"

"Sure." She tapped the date into the search window and hit the return key.

Enzo stood by her shoulder as the first ten results of three hundred and fifty-nine appeared on the screen. He groaned. "That's a lot of links to wade through."

"We only need to look at ones that seem interesting." She began scrolling quickly through them, seemingly able to read them much more quickly than Enzo. The first site she brought up was about the capitulation of German and Italian forces in Tunisia on 12 May 1943. Many of the other sites also related to the same event. But Enzo couldn't see any connection. Nicole carried on scrolling. There was some Nazi documentation on anti-semitism issued on that day, an Italian army commander who received his promotion, a Swiss composer whose date of birth it was. Nicole moved on to the second page. Several of the links led to German websites which neither of them could read. Nothing seemed relevant until Nicole moved on to the third page. And it leapt off the screen at them — the penultimate link. ORDRE DE LA LIBÉRATION. Nicole let out a tiny shriek and clicked on the link.

They found themselves back on the website of the Ordre, on the biography page of one of the medal's recipients. A soldier in the French army called Édouard Méric. There was a black and white photograph of him, wearing what looked like an old sackcloth coat over his uniform. He had a cigarette burning between his fingers, and a slight, enigmatic smile below a thick mop of untidy hair. Nicole scrolled quickly through his life. He had been trained at Saint-Cyr military school in the nineteen twenties. He had spent two years in Germany before being transferred to Morocco, where he was wounded in action in 1926. He seemed to have remained, then, in North Africa, in various capacities, until the Second World War when he led a Moroccan unit of the French army to victory over the Germans in Tunisia. On 11 May and 12th, 1943, he and his men crushed the final resistance of German and Italian troops, capturing a large number of prisoners and a significant amount of equipment.

Both Enzo and Nicole were disappointed. "Is that it?" Nicole asked.

"It looks like it." Enzo scratched his head. "It's not even very specific about the date. It's May 11th and 12th. And I'm not sure what Tunisia has to do with anything else we've come up with." He drew a deep breath. "I'll mark the name up anyway, since we've not come up with anything else." And he went to the board and wrote *Édouard Méric* next to the medal. He heard Nicole still tapping away at her keyboard.

"Do you know what's odd?" she said, and then answered her own question. "You can get back to the main website from Méric's page, but there doesn't seem to be a link to it from the site. Which is very strange. I mean, I'm assuming that if there's a biog page for Méric, there must be pages for all the others. But I can't see any way of accessing them."

"Maybe we're both tired, Nicole," Enzo said. "My brain hurts, so maybe I'm not thinking too clearly. And maybe you're not either. Why don't we take a break?"

"Good idea." Nicole seemed to brighten. She put the computer to sleep. "What do you want to do?"

"I don't want to do anything. That's the point." Enzo slumped into his recliner. A couple of glasses of red wine with lunch always made him sleepy in the afternoon. "I'm going to close my eyes for a bit. Maybe you want to go shopping or something."

Nicole shook her head gloomily. "Haven't got any money." And Enzo felt a stab of guilt.

"Maybe I'll go and see Audeline. You remember Audeline, don't you?"

Enzo was already starting to drift. "No."

"She's in your first year biology class. We always sit together. Her parents live here. She's got a summer job at a filling station . . ."

He felt soft breath in his face, and the back of a hand gently running down his cheek. He opened his eyes and saw her just as she had been all those years before. Just as he remembered her.

"Pascale," he whispered, and she kissed him gently on the forehead.

"It's Sophie, Papa," he heard her say, and he sat up with a start. Sophie was sitting on the arm of his recliner. The air was very warm, the square below still crowded, although the shadows of the trees were lengthening towards the east. "How long have you been asleep?" she asked.

He blinked, still groggy. "What time is it?"

"After six."

And he realised with a shock that he had been asleep in the chair for nearly four hours. His trip to Paris had taken more out of him than he thought. "Too long."

"Where's the Amazon?"

"What?"

"Nicole."

"She's not an Amazon."

"She looks like one."

"She can't help the way she's built. And, anyway, Amazon women cut off their right breasts so as not to hinder the action of drawing back their bow strings."

"Right enough," said Sophie. "She's not lacking anything in that department."

"She's gone to visit a friend." He heaved himself out of his chair.

"Are you two planning a cosy evening in together, then?"

"Don't be ridiculous, Sophie." His sleep had done nothing to improve his mood. "And I don't suppose you'll be gracing us with your company tonight?"

"I'm going to a concert with Bertrand."

"Of course you are." His voice was laden with sarcasm. He picked up a crumpled linen jacket and pulled it on over his tee shirt, and headed out to the hall.

Sophie followed him. "Papa, why are you so down on Bertrand?"

But he didn't want to get into that right now. He spotted the metal detector and poked it with his foot. "Because he leaves booby-traps for me in my own house." He turned to face her. "Sophie, if that thing is not out of here by the time I get back, I'm going to throw it out of the window." He opened the door to the landing.

"Aw, Papa —"

"I mean it." And he headed off down the stairs.

III

The night could hardly have been clearer. The Milky Way was like smoke smeared across the sky. Pinpricks of light burned through the darkness, encrusting it like jewels, each one a sun with its own solar system. Millions of them. The possibilities of other life forms existing somewhere out there in the universe seemed infinite. And yet Enzo's sense of being alone in it was almost crushing.

Mont St. Cyr was not so much a mountain as the highest hill around. It was on the south side of the River Lot, at the bottom end of the loop which defined and contained Cahors. And from here, the town lay spread out below, almost at Enzo's feet, its lights washing the darkness and reflecting in the water. On the far side of the loop he could see the floodlit towers of the Pont Valentré, and far beyond it, cutting through the hills, headlights on the autoroute heading south towards Toulouse.

There was a huge radio mast here, clustered with antennae and satellite dishes, and a telescope for daytime tourists to view Cahors more closely from on high. Enzo perched on a bench below the balustrade, and Mont St. Cyr fell away sheer beneath him. He had come here the night she died. There had seemed no reason, then, to go on living. He had been consumed by grief and self-pity, drawn to the precipice. He had given up everything for her, and now she was gone. But almost as if she knew he would need a reason, she had left him one. A tiny part of herself. A little pink-faced, crusty-eyed screaming bundle wrapped in swaddling blankets that he had hardly been able to bring himself to hold. And as he sat here that night, wrestling with his darkest demons, she had been the only light in a very black place. A light drawing him back to sanity, to responsibility, to life.

He had come here often since then. It was a place that symbolised hope, a place where he knew that however lonely he might feel, he was not alone.

Tonight he had drunk too much at Le Forum, and then eaten alone in a tiny bistro off the Place de la Libération. He had not wanted to go back to the apartment, to face an evening alone with Nicole, the conversation of a nineteen-year-old, the awful temptation of those cantaloupe breasts. Alcohol had a habit of weakening the resolve. And that was not something he would have been able to live with in the cold light of day. And, so, here he was, on this hot summer's night,

116

in the same place he had been almost twenty years before. Nothing much had changed, except that he was almost twenty years older, the pink-faced bundle was on the verge of womanhood, and he was still alone.

Tonight, though, he was wrestling with different demons. A man's murder. His killer, or killers. He had a sense that there must have been more than one of them. To have carried the dismembered corpse of a pig into the church and then taken away Gaillard's body on his own seemed a monumental task for one man. And if there were more than one, then this was not just murder, but conspiracy to murder. For which there had to be some compelling reason. Something, perhaps, which Gaillard knew, that his killers did not want him to reveal. They had successfully made him disappear, concealing for ten years the fact that he had been murdered, so nobody had ever looked for a reason. Until now.

The most puzzling things were the clues left with the skull. For Enzo had no doubt that that's what they were. But what possible reason could they have had for leaving them in the trunk — a trunk which, clearly, they had hoped would never be found? And where on earth would they lead, if indeed Enzo was capable of ever deciphering their meaning?

He heard a car coming up the drive through the trees behind him and sighed. He was no longer alone. In recent years the viewpoint had become a popular place for young men to bring their girlfriends. A romantic spot for back seat seduction. Reluctantly, Enzo rose from the bench and took the footpath back through the trees to where he had left his car by the basketball courts. He did not want to be accused of spying on courting couples. He saw the headlights of the car rake past the radio mast and draw to a stop at the balustrade. The engine was cut and the lights went out, and looking back Enzo could see the silhouettes of the young couple through the rear windscreen as their heads came together in a kiss. And he wondered if Sophie had ever been up here. Which led his thoughts to Bertrand, and he felt a stab of anger that his daughter should be taken from him by such a wastrel. Surely to God she deserved better?

He got into his car and started the engine, turning in the moonlight and driving several hundred metres downhill before putting on his lights. There was no point in spooking the young lovers.

The apartment was in darkness when he got back. It was after midnight. Sophie was not yet home. Her bedroom door stood ajar, and he could see moonlight slanting across the crumpled sheets of her empty bed. Nicole's door was closed. He listened outside it for a moment and could hear her gentle breathing, almost a purr. She was asleep. He went quietly to his own room and eased the door shut. He undressed quickly in the moonlight which washed across the rooftops and through his open window, and slipped into bed.

For a long time he lay thinking of French medals and gold bees and stethoscopes. Of Napoléon and doctors. Before slipping into a shallow, restless sleep. He surfaced again, when he heard Sophie come in, and he glanced at the digital bedside clock. It was a quarter past two. He could never really sleep until he knew she was home. She went into her room, closing the door softly, and he heard her moving about, undressing, and then the creak of her bed as she climbed into it. What did she see in Bertrand?

And then he was dreaming of blood on a darkened altar. Great pools of it, blackened by the dark. He looked up and saw that it was dripping from the cross overhead, which toppled suddenly forward, landing with a crash on the altar. And he sat up with a start. His heart was pounding. He had heard something. Not the falling cross in his dream. Something real. Something that had wakened him. He looked at the clock. Nearly an hour had passed since he heard Sophie come in. Then there it was again. It sounded like something falling to the floor. And it was in the apartment.

Enzo slipped out of bed and crossed to the door, very slowly easing it open. He could see across the landing that Sophie's door was shut. As was Nicole's. And then a floorboard creaked in the front room, and Enzo saw a shadow cross the door frame. There was someone moving about in the *séjour*.

CHAPTER
EIGHT

I

Enzo looked around his room for something that he might use as a weapon. But there was nothing immediately apparent. He thought of Raffin and his *History of the World*, and would have been grateful even for that. In the end he settled for one of his heavy winter brogues which he snatched from the bottom of the wardrobe. He clutched it in his right hand, level with his head, and made his way cautiously into the hall, dressed only in his boxer shorts.

He never bothered to lock the front door, and had been meaning for some time to fix the door-entry system downstairs. Now he cursed himself silently on both counts. The moon was at the back of the apartment, and so it was the light of the streetlamps from the square that fell in wedges through the French windows. They lay unevenly across the book-littered floor of the *séjour*, reaching towards the open double doors leading to the hall.

Enzo could hear the blood rushing in his ears. It was so loud he was convinced the intruder would be able to hear it too. He saw a shadow move across his line of vision, and he knew he had to strike while he still had surprise on his side. He moved swiftly through the hall and caught his shin on something hard and sharp, and called out in pain as he pitched forward, headlong into the *séjour*. His head sank into something soft and giving, and he heard a loud grunt. Both he and the intruder went sprawling across the floor. Enzo found himself lying on top of a large man breathing stertorously into his face. The smell of garlic and stale alcohol was almost overpowering.

Enzo was a big man himself, fit from years of cycling, but bigger hands grabbed his shoulders and lifted him bodily aside. The intruder roared, and before Enzo could move was on top of him. A huge, crushing weight. Now Enzo smelled body odour, the rank stink of stale sweat, and he had no choice but to breath it in as he gasped for breath. He felt hands at his throat, coarse digits like rusted steel, and he reached up in desperation to dig fingers into the man's face, searching for his eyes, and finding a great thatch of wiry hair. He grasped two handfuls and pulled with all his might. His attacker howled and released his stranglehold on Enzo's neck and tried to free himself from the grip on his hair.

Light flooded the room suddenly. Bright, yellow, electric light, and both men froze, mid-struggle.

"Papa!" a girl's voice screamed in distress. They both looked around to see Nicole standing in the doorway. She was wearing a short, almost see-through nightie, the line of her breasts and hips clearly visible beneath it.

The man on top of Enzo issued an almost feral howl of anguish. "*Putain!*" he screamed, spittle gathering all around his lips, and he took a swing at the face immediately beneath him. Enzo turned his head to try to avoid it, but the fist caught him a glancing blow on the cheekbone, high up, just below the left eye. Lights flashed in his head.

"Papa!"

The man looked round again. This time Sophie stood next to Nicole, naked beneath the towelling robe she held closed across herself. The man's eyes nearly popped out of his head.

"Two of them! You filthy *salaud*!" And he swung again, this time with his left hand, catching Enzo just below the ear. Sound, as well as light, exploded inside Enzo's head.

But it wasn't enough to drown out Sophie's scream as she struck her father's attacker full in the eye with a tightly clenched fist, following up with a left hook which caught him squarely on the nose. The man bellowed and blood spurted from his face. Enzo took the chance to heave him off, and he scrambled to his knees. The room was spinning, and he was unable to stand up.

"Papa, what in God's name are you doing?" Nicole screamed at the man.

"I knew he was up to no good!" He was clutching his nose, blood trickling through his fingers, tears streaming from both eyes.

"You're Nicole's father?" Enzo was slower than he might have been in other circumstances. But still incredulous. "And you thought . . ." He waved a hand wildly at Sophie, who was standing breathing hard, and ready to inflict more damage if necessary. "Jesus Christ,

122

man! This is my daughter. Do you really think I'd be setting up some kind of love nest with Nicole right under the nose of my own daughter?"

Nicole's father blinked at him in confusion, sitting on the floor amongst Enzo's books, bleeding and gasping for breath.

"You can check the sleeping arrangements if you want. Christ Almighty! What kind of pervert do you think I am?"

Nicole strode across the room, her face beetroot red with humiliation. She took her hand hard across the side of her father's face. Enzo could see the force in it, and winced. He would not like to be on the receiving end of Nicole's ire. "How dare you!" she screamed at her father. "How dare you humiliate me like this! I hate you!" And she turned and fled back to her room, deep sobs catching in her throat as she went.

Sophie knelt in front of Enzo and cupped his face in her hands. "Are you okay, Papa?"

Enzo put his hands over hers and gazed into her face. "I'm fine, Sophie." And he squeezed her wrists. "Thank you." Beyond her he saw, in the hall, Bertrand's metal detector. It's what had tripped him in the dark and sent him careening into the intruder. Bertrand! That stab of anger again. But he couldn't be angry with Sophie. Without her intervention, God knows what damage Nicole's father might have done him. "Go to bed, pet. I'll deal with this."

"Are you sure?"

Enzo nodded. "On you go."

Reluctantly, Sophie stood up. She glowered at the man whose nose she had very probably broken, and marched back through the hall to her bedroom.

Enzo leaned on a pile of books and pulled himself to his feet. He was giddy, and his face felt swollen and bruised. His shoulder-length hair was a tousled mess. He ran his hands through it, drawing it back from his face. With an effort, the farmer, too, heaved himself off the floor. The two men stood unsteadily glaring at each other.

Nicole's father wiped his bloody hand on his trousers and held it out for Enzo to shake. "Pierre Lafeuille."

Enzo hesitated a moment, then shook the proffered hand. What else was there to do? "Enzo Macleod."

Lafeuille nodded, his eyes darting aimlessly around the room, anxious to avoid Enzo's. "I thought —"

"I know what you thought," Enzo interrupted him. "You were wrong." And he felt a momentary pang of guilt, recalling the fleeting temptation of the cantaloupe breasts. He looked at the farmer's bloody face. "You're still bleeding. We'd better clean you up."

Lafeuille followed him across the *séjour*, through an archway and into the dining room. A breakfast bar separated the dining room from the kitchen area, and Enzo put a large bowl on it and boiled a kettle. When it had come to the boil he poured water and disinfectant into the bowl and handed Nicole's father a wad of gauze dressing. The farmer dipped the gauze into the water with filthy hands and smeared the blood all over his face. Enzo threw him a towel. "Whisky?" he asked.

"Never tried it," Lafeuille said.

"What?" Enzo couldn't believe it.

"We make our own *vieille prune* on the farm. And *poire*. No need to go buying the commercial stuff."

"Well, now seems as good a time as any to have a go. I could certainly do with a drink." Lafeuille nodded, dried his face and watched as Enzo poured two generous measures of amber Glenlivet into short, chunky glasses, and added a splash of water. Enzo took the bottle and lifted his glass and picked his way back through the *séjour* to his recliner. Lafeuille followed, clutching his glass in one hand, and his nose in the other. "Push those books off that chair and take a seat," Enzo said. Both men sat and Enzo raised his glass. "To daughters." And for the first time, Lafeuille cracked a smile.

"To daughters."

And they drank deeply from their whisky glasses, so that Enzo very quickly had to refill them. "You like it?"

Lafeuille nodded. Then, "I'm sorry. She's my little girl. She's very precious."

Enzo was touched. It seemed incongruous that a big bull of a man like Lafeuille should express such tender emotions. "They all are."

"I've never been to Cahors before." Lafeuille lived no more than a hundred kilometres away. "Never been anywhere. Missed my national service, because my father died and there was no one else to run the farm. This is the furthest I've ever been from home." Enzo looked at him with fresh eyes. He wore thick, blue working trousers and a crumpled cotton jacket over an open-necked checked shirt. His flat cap was folded into one of the pockets of his jacket. His hands were huge, scarred shovels, and he looked strong enough to pull a plough on his own.

"I was scared when Nicole went to Toulouse," he said. "Her mother went with her to look for accommodation. I didn't want to, because I was afraid if I saw what kind of a place it was I wouldn't let her go." He seemed compelled to unburden himself. Perhaps, Enzo thought, he felt he owed an explanation to the man he had just tried to throttle. "When she told me she was moving in with you for the summer because you wanted her to work for you, I knew she believed that to be true. But I didn't."

Enzo ran a hand ruefully down the side of his face. He could feel a swelling on his left cheek, and it was painful to the touch. "No, I probably wouldn't have either. To be honest, Monsieur Lafeuille, I only offered her the work because I'd promised to get her a job at the hospital and forgot. And I knew she needed the money."

Lafeuille flushed deeply and got immediately to his feet. "Then I'll take her home with me right now."

"No, no," Enzo said quickly. "She's doing a great job. I really do need someone with her kind of skills. She's a smart kid."

"We don't need charity."

"Of course you don't. But I do need Nicole. Even after just one day, I realise how difficult this project would be without her. Here, let me refill your glass . . ."

The big farmer hesitated for a moment, then sat down again, reluctantly, and held out his glass. Enzo

126

filled it liberally, and the two men drank in silence for several minutes.

"It's hard being a father," Enzo said finally.

"That's true," Lafeuille agreed. "What's your girl's name?"

"Sophie."

"Where's her mother?"

"She's dead."

Lafeuille looked at him, reappraisal in his eyes. "You raised her yourself?" Enzo nodded. "*Mon dieu*, I could never have raised Nicole without her mother."

Enzo shrugged. "You learn how. Sometimes the hard way." And a slight smile flickered briefly in his eyes. "She was about twelve years old," he said, "getting ready for school one morning, and her face was all flushed and pink. She told me she had cramps and felt sick. And I thought, oh my God, she's starting her period. I guess that's the sort of thing mothers usually deal with."

Lafeuille chuckled. "Not if you grow up on a farm. You know about these things before you can walk."

Enzo grinned. "Aye, well, it's different for us townies."

"So what did you do?"

"I sat her down and started to explain it to her in terms I thought she might understand. Nothing too explicit. And she listened and nodded solemnly as I talked round and round the houses. And when, eventually, I'd finished, she said, 'Are you talking about menstruation? Because I started my periods last year.' "

127

Lafeuille laughed and his nose began bleeding again. He dabbed at it with the gauze. "*Putain*! That's priceless!"

And so they sat and drank whisky until the bottle was finished, talking about their girls. And when the first light appeared in the sky, Lafeuille got unsteadily to his feet. "I've got to get back and milk the cows."

"You can't drive in that state."

"I've driven in worse. Anyway, there's no one on the roads at this hour. It's just myself I'll kill."

"Let me at least make you a coffee."

Reluctantly, Pierre Lafeuille stayed another half an hour while Enzo poured hot, black coffee into him and tried to sober him up. Finally, there was no keeping him any longer. Enzo walked him down into the square. The sky was a pale yellow glow in the east, but the town was still asleep. Lafeuille shook his hand. "It's been a privilege, Monsieur Macleod."

"It's been an experience, Monsieur Lafeuille."

Lafeuille grinned and got into his battered 2CV. It coughed unhealthily as he turned the key, but roared into life and the sound of it echoed around the square. Enzo watched as it weaved away down the Rue Georges Clemenceau towards the church of St. Urcisse. It would be a long hundred kilometres.

CHAPTER
NINE

I

Outside, the town was starting to come alive. He heard the street sweepers and the bin men, the growling motor of the machine that washed down the pavements, great circular brushes spinning along the gutters. He heard bakers' vans heading off on their first deliveries, and the smell of fresh bread wafted warm and yeasty on the cool morning air. *Commerçants* were arriving to open up cafés and bars, the first cars were laying claim to their parking places in the square, and rising above it all, the frenetic chatter of birds concealed among the leaves of the plane trees.

Enzo leaned on the rail at the open French windows and looked down into the square. The sun was beginning to squint over rooftops to the east. His head was pounding, and his face was sore. The smell of coffee came to him now, and cigarette smoke, and he turned back into the *séjour*. The moment when he might have gone back to bed had come and gone. Sleep had seemed unlikely in the aftermath of an eventful night, and the *Ordre de la Libération* had begun nagging at him again. He gazed thoughtfully at the board, and the name of Édouard Méric, which he had written up beside the photograph of the medal. And he remembered Nicole complaining that although she had been able to get back to the main website from Méric's biography page, there didn't seem to be a link to it from the site itself. Or to any of the other biographies, which surely existed.

He sat down at the computer and hit the space bar. The screen lit up. At least one of them had enjoyed a good sleep. He found the home page of the *Ordre de la Libération*, and a menu on the left side of the page offered him a link to *Les Compagnons de la Libération*. He clicked on it, and a fifteen page document downloaded and opened up on his screen. It consisted of three columns. The left-hand column listed the forenames of the medal's one thousand and thirty-eight recipients. The middle column gave their surnames, and the right-hand column the date when the medal was awarded. But the list was alphabetical, rather than chronological. So Enzo asked his computer to search for the date 12/05/43. A message came up which read, *No occurrences were found in the document*. His heart sank. Another dead-end. Then he realised that the dates in the right-hand column gave the year in full. So he made another search, this time asking for 12/05/1943. Up came the name André Mounier. Enzo was getting excited. He was given the option to search again. He took it. And another name appeared. Philippe Roques. He searched again. There were no further names. So, both André Mounier and Philippe Roques had been awarded the *Ordre de la Libération* on the same day — 12th May, 1943.

Enzo returned to the home page and found what Nicole had missed the previous day — a sub-list of links under *Les Compagnons de la Libération* which led to individual biographies. He clicked on it. A long page listed all the names in alphabetic groupings. Enzo selected the letter M and immediately jumped to the list of names starting with that letter. There were dozens of them. He searched through them several times, with a growing sense of frustration. For some reason André Mounier did not appear on the list. He returned to Google and asked it to search the internet for André Mounier and *Ordre de la Libération* in the same sweep. They came up together at the top of a very short list, and the link took Enzo to an empty biography page on the website of the *Ordre*. A message told him that this biography was currently unavailable.

He cursed his bad luck and went back to the page with the list of alphabetic groupings, and hit the letter R. There were six lines of names. Philippe Roques appeared in the middle of the fourth line. He clicked on the name, and Roques' biography materialised in front of him, along with a photograph. Roques had an old-fashioned, square-jawed face with neatly parted dark hair and round, tortoiseshell glasses. He had the faintest smile on his face, gazing off to camera left, lights reflecting in both eyes. He looked like an intelligent man, and his biography confirmed that impression.

Born in Paris in 1910, Roques studied political science before going on to become a parliamentary correspondent. He was called up as a reservist in 1939, then spoke out fiercely against Pétain and the Vichy government after the armistice, going on the run to try to establish contact with the Free French. He was successfully involved in the creation of resistance networks in the Cantal, and eventually airlifted out to London where de Gaulle entrusted him with an important mission. He was to return to France and hand-deliver letters to key political figures. He succeeded in his mission and, after helping to establish the National Council of Resistance, was called back to London. His plane, however, was unable to land, and he was forced to take the circuitous route to England via Spain. Which was when disaster struck.

At Argelès railway station on the Mediterranean coast, almost within sight of Spain, he was arrested by the Gestapo and taken to Perpignan. Outside the Gestapo headquarters he attempted to escape and was shot twice.

Enzo looked again at the photograph of Roques. A man who had loved his country and done everything in his power to secure its freedom, shot down in the street by brutish occupiers who shared neither his intelligence nor his culture. His smile seemed sad now. He had not lived to see his country freed from Nazi tyranny.

Enzo's eyes drifted back to the final paragraphs of Roques' story and he felt a wave of pins and needles prickle across his scalp.

A loud thump made him turn, and his excitement was momentarily interrupted by the sight of Nicole, fully dressed, standing in the doorway with her large suitcase beside her. She was very pale and avoided meeting his eye. "I'll need a hand down the stairs with my case."

Enzo was nonplussed. "Where are you going?"

"Home, of course. I can hardly stay after what happened last night."

Enzo waved a dismissive hand. "Oh, forget about that. Your dad and I sorted everything out. He's a nice guy."

Nicole gazed at him in astonishment. "He was beating you up."

"Yeah, well, understandable. I'd probably have done the same thing." Nicole was shaking her head in disbelief, and Enzo said, "Look at it this way. It shows how much he loves you."

Nicole blushed. "Well, I wish he would show it some other way." She tilted her head and looked at Enzo as if for the first time. "Oh, your poor face. You need a cold compress on those bruises."

"It's too late for that."

But she was already heading for the kitchen, and spotted the empty whisky bottle and the two glasses. "Were you two drinking?"

"We had a couple."

"A couple? The bottle's empty!"

"Well, it wasn't exactly full to begin with." Enzo wondered why he felt the need to defend himself.

Nicole returned, with ice cubes wrapped in a dish towel. "Here." She pressed it on to his bruised cheek.

He winced. "Ow! That's sore!" Her large, trembling breasts were level with his eyes, and he was momentarily distracted from his pain.

"I can still smell the alcohol off you," she said. "You need a coffee and something to eat." And then a thought occurred to her. "Have you even been back to bed?"

"Look . . ." Enzo pushed the ice from his face. "Never mind all that." He nodded towards the computer. "I've made a breakthrough here." The Roques biography and his photograph were still up on the screen.

Nicole glanced at it, her interest piqued. "Who's that?"

"Philippe Roques. Awarded the *Ordre de la Libération* on 12th May, 1943. He was working for the Resistance until the Gestapo caught him on the south coast. He was shot trying to escape outside the Gestapo building in Perpignan."

Nicole shrugged and pushed the ice back into Enzo's face. "So what's that got to do with anything?"

"Well, the thing is, he didn't die immediately. They rushed him to hospital, where he died in the early hours of the morning."

"I still don't understand."

"Guess what the hospital was called?"

She frowned, and thought. And then her face lit up. "St. Jacques?"

Enzo grinned. "I knew you were smart." He drew a deep breath. "Philippe Roques died in the Hospital St. Jacques in Perpignan. And apart from the connection with our scallop shell, do you know why else that's important?"

134

She shook her head and shrugged. "I don't know . . . Is there a hospital called St. Jacques in Toulouse?"

"*Et voilà!*"

"You're kidding?"

"I'm not. And I bet you know it, even if you don't know you do. The Hôtel-Dieu St-Jacques. It's the large, pink-brick building on the west side of the Pont Neuf, right on the river. Only it's not a hospital any more. Parts of it are open to the public now, and I think there's a museum there. But originally it was the first big hospital in Toulouse, built sometime in the middle ages, and used as a shelter for centuries by pilgrims on their way to Compostelle." In spite of being assaulted by Nicole's father, his excess of whisky, and his lack of sleep, Enzo's eyes were shining.

He stood up and hobbled across the room to the whiteboard. All his muscles from the night's exertions were beginning to stiffen up. He lifted an eraser, wiped out *Édouard Méric* and wrote *Philippe Roques* in his place, next to the photograph of the medal. Then he drew an arrow directly to the circle he had made around *Toulouse* and wrote *Hôtel-Dieu St-Jacques* underneath it.

"Everything leads here," he said. "Everything. Either directly, or indirectly." He turned around to see Nicole in his seat at the computer, concentratedly tapping at the keyboard and staring at the screen.

"Here we are." She was triumphant. "You were right, there is a museum there now. La Musée d'Histoire de la Médicine de Toulouse. And that makes absolute sense of the antique stethoscope, too. There's some background about the place on the website." She scanned through it. "Ah-ha!" She looked up, her face glowing, all memories of the night before long forgotten. "On the 1st of May, 1806, the hospital became the Imperial School of Medicine. And it's first director?" She didn't wait for Enzo to guess. "Alexis Larrey — Dominique Larrey's uncle — who was also appointed professor of anatomy." She nodded knowingly. "The femur. There's even a painting of Dominique Larrey here . . . sorry, Baron Dominique Larrey." She pulled a face. "Weird-looking guy." She tapped some more. "And this is interesting. One of the exhibition rooms in the museum has got lots of stuff about him in it."

"Then it's got to be there," Enzo said.

"What has?"

He waved his hand vaguely. "I don't know . . . A clue. Something that's going to lead us to Gaillard's remains."

Nicole looked horrified. "You mean, you think the rest of his body's there?"

"Maybe."

"How? I mean, how would they get it into the place? Where would they put it? It wouldn't exactly be easy to hide a body in a museum."

But Enzo had an inspiration. "Wait a minute. The whole place was closed down for several years during the nineties, while it was being renovated. I can remember passing it. It was just like a building site. What better place to hide a body?" He dropped his ice pack on the table and lifted his satchel. "Come on."

"Where are we going?"

"Toulouse."

"Now?"

"Right now."

"How?"

"In my car."

"You're in no condition to drive."

"Neither was your father."

"He never is. I won't get in the car with you, Monsieur Macleod."

Enzo sighed. "Well, do you drive?"

"Of course."

"Okay, then I'll get in the car with you."

II

It was not yet ten when Enzo and Nicole stepped off the métro at St. Cyprien and began back along the Rue de la République towards the river. They had parked two levels below the Place du Capitole, emerging into the vast paved, pedestrian square, with its magnificent Hôtel de Ville at the east side facing a long gallery of arcaded shops on the west. Even though the universities were on summer break, Toulouse was still a young person's town, brimming with life. There were bistros and cafés and boutiques on every corner. Kids on bikes and roller blades. *La Ville Rose*, it was called, because of its distinctive pink brick. The roofs of the buildings were shallow-pitched and Roman-tiled in the Mediterranean style. The Mediterranean itself was less than two hours away. Enzo disliked cities. But if he was forced to live in one, he would probably pick Toulouse.

The Rue de la République was a long, narrow street. Some of the brick buildings had been rendered and painted. Green and pink and peach, with grey and maroon and pale green shutters. It was the heart of the city's Latin Quarter, which was really just an area with a large immigrant population, mostly from the former colonies.

The Hôtel-Dieu St-Jacques stood on the very edge of the Garonne, the walls of its basement cellars plunging down into the river's slow-moving green water. Essentially, it comprised four-storey buildings around three sides of a long, rectangular garden. The entrance was on the corner of the Rue Viguerie and the Rue de la République, leading to the west wing of the mediaeval former hospital, and a small car park in front of the gardens. On the wall beside an open, glass-paned door, two large scallop shells flanked a sign which read, HÔTEL-DIEU SAINT-JACQUES. A large poster was pasted to a hoarding advertising the museum, and featured the face of a man who looked to Enzo like the Scottish Bard, Rabbie Burns. In fact, it was Dominique Larrey.

A man in uniform sat on the ledge of an open window next to the door and watched them approach.

"We're looking for the museum," Enzo said.

"Closed," said the man.

"What?" Enzo couldn't believe it. He looked at his watch. Surely it must be open by this time.

"Closed Mondays and Tuesdays. Open every other day from one till six."

Enzo cursed. It was still only Monday. And they had never thought to check the opening hours. How could they possibly wait another two days to get into the museum?

Nicole flicked her long hair back off her shoulder and did a flirty thing that Enzo had never seen her do before. He wouldn't have believed her capable of it. Her father would have been mortified. "We've come a long way." She made big eyes at the man in uniform. "You couldn't open up just for us, could you?"

The man let his eyes wander lasciviously down to her quivering breasts. And then he looked up. "Sorry." Apparently the pleasure of exercising his power outweighed the allure of the girl from the farm.

"Come on." Enzo led a disappointed Nicole back through the gate. Someday, he was sure, her charms would work on someone.

They decided to walk back to the Capitole, and turned left across the Pont Neuf. Over the river they could see the roofs of the ancient city centre rising above apartment blocks and government buildings, a jumble of turrets and bell-towers, an odd blend of European and North African architecture that sat somehow comfortably together in this cosmopolitan old town. On the far river bank, tourist cruise boats were berthed at the quayside, and a Rastafarian in a black tee-shirt and sweat pants practised karate on a strip of grass, watched indifferently by his old Alsatian dog. Joggers trundled laboriously along the towpath before the heat of the day set in.

The Hôtel-Dieu St-Jacques was below them now, on their left. The garden at its centre was ringed by carefully pruned lime trees. The lawn was divided into classical patterns by a low, manicured hedge, and two columns of bushes in the shape of egg cosies created a grassy avenue running from front to back. Enzo barely glanced at it. His mind was stewing over their misfortune. To have come so far in decoding the clues, to be within touching distance of a solution, and yet be denied by a quirk of opening times, was infuriating. He had no idea how he was going to fill the next forty-eight hours. He wasn't even listening to Nicole. She had begun a diatribe on how he needed to take better care of himself. He still hadn't had breakfast, she pointed out. He drank too much. He was too old to be getting into fights with her father. It wasn't easy to shut out the voice. God help the poor soul who married her! There would, of course, be a couple of consolations. Although he doubted if that would be quite enough to make up for the rest. Then he felt her tugging on his sleeve. "What?" he said tetchily, pulling his arm away.

"What's that?" She pointed down to the gardens.

Enzo glanced with irritation towards the expanse of meticulous greenery. Some anal gardener's *raison d'être*. "It's a bloody garden!"

"No, at the far end, beyond the line of bushes."

Enzo peered in the direction she was pointing and saw what looked like a giant white saucer at the very apex of the lawn. He felt in his pockets for his glasses, but in their hurry to leave he had left them lying on the table in the *séjour*. "I've no idea. Why?"

"Well, it looks to me very much like a giant scallop shell."

"What?" Enzo struggled to try to bring the thing into focus. "Let's go and see."

And they turned around and went back down to the gate. The man in uniform watched them approach and his eyes narrowed with suspicion. "It's still not open."

They walked straight past.

"Hey, where are you going?"

"A walk in the garden. Any objections?"

Rose bushes in full bloom lined the gravel path which led them around the perimetre of the lawn and, as they approached the far end, it became apparent that Nicole's eyes had not deceived her. A huge concrete scallop shell, around two metres across, was set in a circle of lawn, and half filled with brackish green water. A rusting pipe poked up through the slime.

"It's a fountain!" Nicole said. "A fountain in the shape of a *coquille St. Jacques*." Although it appeared that the fountain had not been in working order for some time.

Enzo stared at it. A perfect scallop shell, ribbed and cupped to hold water, the function for which hundreds of thousands of pilgrims over the centuries had used it. "That's it." His voice was little more than a hoarse whisper, and he had to clear his throat.

"That's what?"

"He's got to be here. Under the shell."

Nicole screwed up her nose. "You really think so?"

"He must be. Everything has led us to this spot, Nicole. Every one of those clues. Why else are we standing here? The killer must have had access to the renovation plans. They were probably available to the public at the planning office. He'd have known where the scallop shell fountain was to be sited, and he buried the body right underneath it. The place was a building site at the time. The whole area around here had probably already been dug up."

She surveyed the shell thoughtfully. "Well, how are we going to find out?"

"The police will have to excavate it."

Traffic thundered along the boulevards on either side of the Canal du Midi, shaded from the heat of the sun by lines of dusty-leafed trees. The Hôtel de Police, headquarters of the Police Nationale, stood on the corner of the Boulevard de l'Embouchure and the Rue de Chaussas. Nicole had barely settled herself on the *terrasse* of the Café Les Zazous around the corner in the Avenue des Minimes, when she saw Enzo storming across the road towards her. His face was red. It would have been difficult to tell if it was from heat or exertion. But, in fact, it was anger. He threw himself into the seat beside her. "Bastards!"

"What happened?"

"They thought I was some kind of nutter. I never even got beyond the duty officer."

"What are you going to do?"

"Have a drink." He waved the waiter over.

Nicole lowered her voice. "Do you not think you've had enough alcohol already, Monsieur Macleod. You'll be dehydrated."

142

The waiter stood over them. "Monsieur?"

"Two *Perriers citron*," Nicole said firmly before Enzo could open his mouth.

Enzo glared at her. "What are you, my mother?"

"Don't take it out on me," she said evenly. "It's not my fault they won't take you seriously." She cast a critical eye over him. "Although it might help if you didn't look like a tramp."

Enzo stared sullenly at the ancient brickwork of the Église des Minimes opposite. The waiter arrived with their drinks, and left the bill under Enzo's glass. He glanced at it and grunted. "Huh! Alcohol would have been cheaper."

Nicole poured sparkling water into both of their glasses. "So what are you going to do?"

He took a drink of his *Perrier citron*, felt the bubbles tickling his nostrils and had a sudden inspiration. "I'm going to call on the old school tie."

"What do you mean?"

He took a long draft from his glass and stood up, dropping several coins on the table. "Come on, drink up. We're going back to Cahors."

III

Enzo pushed open the heavy wrought iron gate and walked across the cobbled courtyard. The administrative buildings of the Hotel du Département rose up around him on three sides to steeply pitched, grey slate roofs. He went through an archway and followed the *accueil* sign to the reception desk.

"I'd like to see the Préfet," he told the young woman behind the counter.

"Do you have an appointment, Monsieur?"

"Just tell him that Monsieur Enzo Macleod needs to see him as a matter of urgency."

Préfet Verne's office was on the first floor, a large room with three tall windows overlooking the courtyard. The wall behind his desk was draped with crossed Tricolours. There were photographs of him with the President, the Prime Minister, the Foreign Minister, the *Garde des Sceaux*. His desk was enormous, and the Préfet himself seemed almost small behind it. Sunlight slanted golden across a floor of polished parquet, and draped itself over two Louis Quatorze armchairs and a chaise longue set around a low antique table.

The Préfet rose to shake Enzo's hand. "My staff is not used to my receiving visits from such disreputable characters." He smiled. "What can possibly be so urgent?" He waved a hand towards one of the Louis Quatorze armchair and sat in the other one himself, folding his hands in his lap. Enzo remained standing.

"I know where the rest of Gaillard's body is buried."

Préfet Verne tilted his head and raised an eyebrow. "Really?

"But I need your help to prove it."

"Curiouser and curiouser."

"I need the police in Toulouse to excavate beneath a fountain at the old Hospital St. Jacques. But I can't get them to take me seriously."

144

"I'm not surprised."

"But if the Préfet at Toulouse ordered them to, they'd have to, wouldn't they?"

"And why would he do that?"

"Because you'd asked him to."

The Préfet regarded him thoughtfully. "And why would he listen to me?"

"Because he's almost certainly another *énarque*, and you ENA old boys stick together, don't you? A favour here reciprocated there. I take it you do know your counterpart in the Garonne?"

"Naturally." His hands were still folded in his lap, and he began tapping his thumbs together. "I'm just wondering why I would ask him to do that?"

"Because I'm asking you."

"And that would make me ask him, because?"

"Because we have a bet," Enzo said, "that I can't find out what happened to Jacques Gaillard and why. I imagine that's probably pretty common knowledge by now."

Préfet Verne gave a tiny shrug. "These things have a habit of getting around."

"So if you were to refuse to help me, that could be construed by some people, not to mention the press, as . . . well, not to put too fine a point on it, welching on a bet."

The smile faded just a little from the Préfet's eyes and he pursed his lips in quiet contemplation. "There's Italian blood in your family, Macleod, isn't there?"

"My mother was Italian."

"Hmmm. Any relation to the Machiavellis?"

Arc lamps flooded the garden with light, and the pink of the ancient hospital building stood bold against the black of the midnight sky. A crowd gathered on the bridge in the warm night air, idly exercising their curiosity. They had no idea why there were police cars filling the tiny car park below, or that the white vans they saw belonged to the *police scientifique*. And they could not see what was happening behind the canvas barrier erected around the fountain. But they knew that something was going on.

The caterpillar tracks of the crane had chewed up the once pristine lawn, and it swung high above the Toulouse skyline as its cable strained and pulled, lifting the great concrete coquille St. Jacques clear of the barrier. A municipal plumber had disconnected the pipes and turned off the water.

Men in white Tyvek suits drifted around the site like ghosts, directing a digger in its painfully slow process of excavation, ready to take over at the first hint of discovery, prepared if necessary to remove the dry, crumbling earth one grain at a time.

Behind the barrier, Raffin stood next to Enzo, the collar of his jacket turned up as if the evening were cold. His hands were thrust deep in his pockets, and he was watching the proceedings with an odd sense of professional detachment. He had caught the first flight from Paris after Enzo's phone call. All he had said was, "Are you certain?" And when Enzo replied, "Ninety-nine percent," he'd said, "I'm on my way." He had cast a curious eye over Nicole when Enzo introduced them, but refrained from comment.

Enzo looked up at the concrete shell hanging overhead. It seemed almost surreal, caught in the arc lights, as if it were floating. He was tense with anticipation, and misgivings. What if he was wrong? What if there was nothing there? His disquiet was heightened by the approach of the city's chief of police, a squat, tough-looking man, uniform stretched tightly across broad shoulders. He had long sideburns and was chewing a match in the corner of his mouth. His peaked hat cast a shadow across his eyes. He pulled Enzo to one side and lowered his voice. He moved close to his ear to be heard above the roar of the engines. "If this turns out to be a wild goose chase, Monsieur, I'll have your fucking hide. Friends in high places or not." Evidently he had not taken kindly to receiving his orders from on high.

Enzo watched him saunter away again towards a group of officers who were standing watching. His mouth was dry, and he wished he had brought a bottle of water.

Then a shout cut across the revving of the digger. One of the ghosts raised an arm and the articulated claw stopped scooping. It jerked and twisted away from the hole, spilling sandy soil as it went. The other ghosts moved in, climbing carefully into a pit which was now more than two metres deep. Enzo, Raffin and Nicole moved closer as the forensic scientists began scraping away the earth, one trowel at a time, from the corner of a metal object lying at an angle in the ground. Lights

147

were moved in so that they could better see what they were doing. The digger cut its motor, and a strange silence fell across the site. Only the sound of men breathing, and the scraping of trowels, could be heard in the night air.

It took nearly fifteen minutes to uncover the tin trunk. It was the same military green as the one Enzo and Raffin had seen at the *greffe* in Paris. Battered and scored, and more rusted than its twin. There was a sense of everyone around the hole holding their breath as one of the *police scientifique* carefully released the clips and opened the lid. He swung a light to shine inside the trunk to reveal the skeletal remains of two arms lying side by side. But there were other items, too, loose in the bottom of the trunk.

A forensic photographer was lowered carefully into the hole to make a photographic record of the trunk and its contents, before the head ghost crouched down to examine them more closely with delicate, latexed fingers. "Definitely looks like two arms," he called up. "The radius and the ulna of both forearms seem damaged. Scarred or scored in someway. Each of the arms appears to have been cleanly jointed from the shoulder at the head of the humerus, although there is also damage to the bone here, too." He turned his attention, then, to what looked like a rectangular wooden box. "It's a Moët et Chandon presentation box." A quality in his voice reflected the bizarre nature of his words. He slid off the front cover to reveal that it was filled with wood wool, finely curled wood shavings packed around a Champagne bottle. "Dom Perignon,

148

1990. It's never been opened." Now his voice carried a hint of disbelief.

He replaced the lid and lifted up a moulded pewter crucifix, adorned with the figure of Christ. It was about fifteen centimetres long. He turned it over, examining it minutely. "There's something engraved on the back." He produced a small eye-piece to magnify it. "It's a date. April 1st." He looked up at all the faces looking down at him from around the edge of the pit. "Is it a joke?"

"Do you hear us laughing?" the police chief said grimly.

The forensics officer laid the crucifix back in the bottom of the trunk and lifted a small disk which looked like a bronze coin. "It's a lapel pin." He examined it. "Two men on a single horse in relief on the front. An inscription around the perimetre." He used his eyeglass again. "*Sigilum Militum Xpisti*," he read. Then, "Latin, I think. No idea what it means." He put it back in the trunk and picked up what seemed to be another coin. But it turned out to be a simple metal disk engraved with the word Utopique. "Looks like a name tag for a dog."

The officer laid it down and picked up the final item in the trunk. Another bone. "Doesn't belong to the arms," he called. "Too short to be from a leg. I don't know what it is." He looked up again, his face a mask of confusion. "Jesus Christ," he said. "What's all this stuff supposed to mean?"

But Enzo knew what it meant. He stared into the pit, focused on the contents of the trunk. The sickening realisation had already dawned on him that these body parts, and the things found with them, were just more pieces of a much bigger puzzle. And only the beginning of some kind of macabre treasure hunt for the remaining bits of the murdered man.

CHAPTER
TEN

They drove up Avenue President Wilson to the Place du Trocadéro. Across the river the Left Bank fell away below them, still dominated by the Eiffel Tower. This close, it was a massive presence, its unmistakable girdered steel structure piercing the evening sky. On the concourse of the Place des Droits de l'Homme, crowds had gathered to watch an anti-China demonstration by the extreme religious group Falun Gong, whose leader claimed to be a visitor from outer space. Enzo wondered where he had parked his flying saucer.

The cafés around the Place du Trocadéro were doing brisk business. There were queues standing outside Carette, people desperate for seats on the *terrasse*. They were in the sixteenth *arrondissement*, after all, and this was the place to be seen. Worth standing in line for twenty minutes with your Shih Tzu tucked under your arm.

Enzo felt as if all his faculties of perception had deserted him. The items found in the trunk under the shell in Toulouse made not the least sense to him. Not that there had been even five minutes to consider them. He and Raffin and Nicole had spent most of the night being questioned by police. A long, sleepless night. And then, this morning, he had been summoned to Paris and a rendezvous with the French Minister of Justice, otherwise known as the *Garde des Sceaux*, literally the Keeper of the Seals, one of the most powerful and prestigious posts in government. Political master of both the police and the French justice system. Enzo had assumed that the Minister wanted to congratulate him on the success of his investigation.

Raffin had a more cynical take on it. "They're going to warn you off."

"If I was going to be warned off, surely I would have been summoned to her office at the Ministry? Not invited to a private dinner at her apartment."

Raffin shook his head. "If she called you to her office, that would make it official. And you would run from the building screaming 'Cover up!' Dinner in her apartment means it's all off the record. She'll appeal to your sense of duty, request that you desist, rather than order it."

"But why? What has the government got to hide?"

"Its embarrassment. Ten years ago the top advisor to the Prime Minister disappeared. It was a mystery. No one could explain it. The papers were full of it. For a while. And then it just went away. And it remained a mystery. Everyone could live with that. But you've just proved that he was murdered. Not only murdered, but dismembered, and bits of his body strewn about the country. And now people are going to want to know why. It's already caused an uproar in the press, and when my piece appears in *Libération* tomorrow on the discovery in Toulouse, the government is going to have a very red face. The leader columns are going to be asking why, with all the resources at their disposal, in ten years the government and the police were unable to solve the mystery of Gaillard's disappearance, when a biology professor from Toulouse could do it in under a week." Raffin grinned. "I tell you, Enzo, your name'll be mud at the Élysée Palace."

"Well, at least it's mud in classy places," Enzo said.

Raffin turned his car into the Avenue Georges Mandel. A treelined walkway between the two carriageways was named after the opera singer Maria Callas. Raffin pulled up outside the apartment block at number thirty-three, opposite the late diva's former apartment. Enzo got out and stood uncomfortably on the pavement, unaccustomed to the formality of a suit and collar and tie. The air was soft and warm after the heat of the day. Kids on roller blades drifted past. A young couple stood embracing and kissing unashamedly in the middle of the street. A man with a young girl perched on the back of his bike cycled by at a leisurely rate. The child turned her head to stare at Enzo with naked curiosity.

Raffin leaned across to the open passenger door. "Don't let her bully you, Enzo. Let me know how you get on."

Enzo watched Raffin's car head back towards the Trocadéro, and he turned to look up at the apartments behind him. Five floors clad in pale stone hacked from the catacombs of Paris. An inner courtyard reverberated to the sound of voices from the open windows of a first-floor apartment. Enzo could see figures in dinner jackets and evening dress milling around a large *salle* with champagne flutes in their hands. But that wasn't his destination. He pressed a buzzer, and after some moments a woman's voice responded.

"Enzo Macleod for Madame Marie Aucoin," Enzo said, and an electronic mechanism released the lock on the door. He crossed a mosaic floor, passing between marble pillars to a red-carpeted staircase, and climbed two floors to the apartment of the Minister of Justice.

She opened the door herself. He had seen her on television many times and had always thought her a handsome woman. But she was even more attractive in the flesh. She was just forty-five years old, young to have been appointed to such a powerful position. Long, black hair fell to her shoulders, a loosely parted fringe above a lean, youthful face. Her full lips parted in a wide smile. Dark blue eyes radiated unusual warmth. She was smaller than Enzo had imagined, a sheer black evening dress clinging to a slim figure, the slash of her V-neck revealing the ivory white skin of her neck, and just the hint of a cleavage between small breasts.

"Monsieur Macleod, I'm so pleased you could come."

Enzo wondered if he'd had any choice in the matter. "It's my pleasure, Madame Le Ministre."

She smiled at his clumsiness in addressing her and presented him with her hand. He took it awkwardly. "Please," she said. "Come in."

Light spilled into the hall from leaded windows. Exotic, hand-carved wooden figurines stood on a

154

marble-topped dresser. A huge antique armoire reached almost to the corniced ceiling.

"Lyonnaise," Marie Aucoin said. "Louis Quatorze." She smiled. "You know, there is a depository in the thirteenth *arrondissement* of priceless antique furniture from which government ministers can choose to furnish their offices. Sadly we must furnish our homes at our own expense. Which is a pity, since they don't really pay us very much."

She led him through double doors into a classical French dining room with moulded ceilings, marble fireplace, and gilded mirror. But there France ended, and China began. The furniture was oriental. A long, black-lacquered table with eight chairs. Matching mahogany buffets with bamboo panelled doors, inlaid with mother-of-pearl, and dressed with carefully arranged Ming and Qing Dynasty vases and ornaments. Ceramic dragons flanked the *cheminée*. Vividly coloured Chinese rugs were strewn about the parquet floor, and original Chinese scroll paintings hung from cream-painted walls. Bridges and Buddhas and pinkfaced children. Even the Venetian blinds were mahogany-slatted in the Chinese style. A red lantern diffused soft light above the table. The strings of a classical Chinese orchestra scraped and wailed gently somewhere in the background.

"I thought Chinatown was on the Left Bank," Enzo said.

She smiled. "I went to school in China. My father was ambassador in Singapore and then Peking. I speak Putonghua and Cantonese." She led him through to an

155

adjoining sitting room, and two men and a silver-haired lady of around sixty rose from armchairs. The younger of the men stepped forward with his hand outstretched. He was tall, with thinning brown hair, a little younger than Enzo.

"Christian Aucoin," he said.

"My husband," the Minister of Justice added unnecessarily. And she turned to her guests. "Juge Jean-Pierre Lelong and his wife Jacqueline."

Enzo shook hands with each of them. *"Enchanté."*

A young man in a white jacket was hovering by the door. Marie Aucoin signalled to him. "A drink for Monsieur Macleod. What will it be, whisky? That's what the Scots drink, isn't it?"

"That'll be fine."

"Any particular *marque?*"

"Glenlivet, if you have it." Enzo thought that she almost certainly would not.

But she was unperturbed. "Of course." She nodded to the waiter and ushered Enzo to a seat. "Juge Lelong is one of the foremost *juges d'instruction* in Paris. You know what a *juge d'instruction* is, don't you?"

"A judge who instructs the police in the investigation of a crime, I believe."

"You're familiar with our legal system, then?"

"I have lived here for twenty years, Minister."

"Of course you have. Left your wife and family in Scotland to set up a *concubinage* in Cahors with a young lady who died giving birth to your daughter. Sophie, isn't it?"

156

The fact that she felt no need for subtlety in conveying that she had done her homework on him left Enzo feeling a little uneasy. "Yes."

"Tell me." She perched on the edge of her seat and leaned confidentially towards him. "What makes a man abandon his family and a successful career to come and live in a foreign country and teach biology at a second-rate university?"

Enzo looked at the Minister of Justice and decided that he did not like her very much. She was superior and patronising. He said solemnly, "It was the sex, Minister."

He enjoyed the moment of shocked silence which invaded the room like a fifth presence, before Marie Aucoin burst out laughing and clapped her hands in childlike delight. The others took her lead, smiling politely, but were clearly unamused by Enzo's vulgarity. "Bravo, Monsieur Macleod, bravo. I think you and I are going to get on very well together."

Enzo was pretty sure they weren't. His drink arrived, and a perfunctory toast was made to good health. They drank and made desultory conversation. Christian Aucoin told him that he was the Director of the Banque Agricoles, which explained how they could afford a Louis Quatorze armoire and an apartment in the Avenue Georges Mandel. Enzo knew from newspaper articles that the Aucoins had no children, and he noticed that they never once made eye contact. Their body language spoke of a relationship fractured beyond repair, but glued together for the sake of appearances. Juge Lelong kept his own counsel,

157

watching Enzo cautiously from beneath furrowed brows while his wife prattled nervously about making preparations for the August evacuation to the summer house in Brittany. The judge dragged his eyes momentarily away from Enzo to his wife and said, ominously, "You may very well be on your own this year, Jacqui."

Finally, they adjourned to the table, where bamboo mats and chopsticks awaited them. Jasmine tea was served in delicate china cups, and a succession of Chinese dishes was brought out from the kitchen by two waiters. The food was excellent, and Enzo didn't need a second invitation to eat.

The *Garde des Sceaux* was well-practised in the art of conversation, asking questions, making observations. She elicited from Enzo his passion for music, and disclosed to him her love of potholing. "I'm quite often in your part of the world," she said. "I once abseiled into the Gouffre de Padirac." The wine flowed freely, and Enzo began to relax a little. Which was when she caught him off guard. "I understand your Scottish daughter is working in Paris at the moment."

He looked up from his plate and felt the colour rising on his cheeks. "Yes."

"Translation and interpretation. It's a job with a future in an expanding Europe. An internship, isn't it?"

"I believe so."

The Minister leaned her elbows on the table. "I could get her a better position in one of the ministries."

"I'm not sure she'd be very happy about that."

Marie Aucoin seemed taken aback. "Why ever not?"

"She's not very well disposed towards her father. I suspect she'd reject out of hand an opportunity connected with me in any way."

The Minister shrugged. "Foolish girl, then." And she changed the subject abruptly. "So what do you think of the new parliament sitting in Edinburgh?"

"I think anything that brings decision-making closer to the people is a good thing."

"Do you really? Some political observers believe that 'the people' are not particularly well-qualified, or informed, to make decisions about anything."

"Oh, I forgot," Enzo said. "You French think that the state should be run by an intellectual élite. From what I understand, it wouldn't be unusual at any given time for the President, the Prime Minister and half the Cabinet to be graduates of ENA. *Énarques*. Isn't that what you call yourselves? And, of course, you send out unelected provincial governors to administer the populace. That is what Préfets do, isn't it?"

She was unfazed. "Interesting view, Monsieur Macleod. But by the same calculation, at any given time at least half of those of us in government are not *énarques*. But, at least all of us are there on merit."

By now, the meal had run its course, and Enzo had had enough. Emboldened by wine, his patience frayed by fatigue, he crumpled his napkin and dropped it on the table. "Minister," he said. "Why am I here?"

Marie Aucoin's eye flickered almost imperceptibly in her husband's direction and he immediately stood up. "Jacqueline," the banker said. "I found those prints I promised you. Why don't you come through to the study and tell me which of them you'd like? We can join the others for coffee and *digestifs* in the *séjour* later."

"Of course." Madame Lelong rose from the table with a fixed smile.

"Excuse us," Christian Aucoin said.

When they had gone, Enzo found himself facing Marie Aucoin and Juge Lelong across the table, and he suddenly felt very much on his own.

"We have the DNA results back from the arms you found in Toulouse," the Minister said. "Confirming that they are, indeed, part of the remains of Jacques Gaillard."

"I never doubted it."

"We're still waiting for the pathologist's report."

"Which probably won't tell you much," Enzo said. "Except that those chips and grooves on the bones of the forearms were probably made when he raised his arms to protect himself from the blades of his attackers."

"Plural?" said the judge. "What makes you think there were more than one?"

"There was a lot of damage to the radius and the ulna on both arms. Either the attack was very frenzied, or there was more than one attacker."

Marie Aucoin looked thoughtful. "Why do you think the killer — or killers — left clues leading to the next body part?"

"It's strange, isn't it?" said the judge, before Enzo could answer. He was clearly intrigued. "It's almost as if finding one body part will lead inexorably to the others."

160

"If you can decode the clues," Enzo said. "But it's clear that the pieces we have recovered so far were never meant to be found."

"Which somewhat undermines your theory, Jean-Pierre," the Minister said. She glanced at the judge and then folded her hands on the table in front of her, fixing Enzo with dark blue eyes. But there was very little warmth in them now. "Monsieur Macleod, I want to thank you on behalf of both the government and the police for the work you have done in bringing Jacques Gaillard's murder to light. You have performed a very valuable service, and I will be making our gratitude public at a press conference tomorrow." She paused.

"But?"

"Now that the circumstances of his killing have been brought to our attention, I have appointed a special investigation team to look into it. The team will be led by Juge Lelong." Enzo glanced at the judge, who was watching him impassively. "Which means that your help will no longer be required."

"In fact," said Juge Lelong, "were you to involve yourself in further investigations, it might be regarded as interference in official police business."

"Although, of course, given your familiarity with the background of the case, any further insights that you might have would be gratefully received," Marie Aucoin added quickly, and she smiled sweetly across the table. A long silence hung in the soft light of the red lantern. "Well?"

"Well what?"

The judge stressed each individual word. "Do you have any further insights?"

"No." Enzo realised that Raffin's words of warning had, indeed, been prophetic.

"Good." Marie Aucoin sat back smiling, business accomplished. She lifted a little bell from the table and tinkled it. "Time for coffee, I think."

CHAPTER
ELEVEN

Enzo sat in the back of the taxi and pulled off his tie. He stuffed it in a pocket and opened the top two buttons of his shirt. He took a deep breath. It was late. Nearly midnight. The air was still hot, heavy with humidity and pollution, and night had settled on the city like a warm, damp blanket. Streetlights drifted past, streaking darkness, like disembodied beings from another world. Enzo's own world felt very small, confined to the space he occupied in his taxi. A world filled with confusion, anger, frustration. He was damned if he was going to give up his investigation just to save the further blushes of the government and the police. They had failed to make any progress in ten years. What guarantee was there that they would make any now? Perhaps they were hoping that Gaillard would simply go away again. And, yet, he knew how difficult it would be for him to proceed if the authorities were against him. Interfering with official police business. Juge Lelong's words rattled around in his head. The warning could not have been clearer.

They crossed the river at the Pont de la Concorde. The Boulevard St. Germain was deserted at its eastern end. Enzo stared out bleakly at the empty pavements,

163

shuttered shops, and darkened apartments. As they passed the junction with the Boulevard Raspail, he could see the lights of the sixth *arrondissement* ahead of them. The cafés would still be full, and only now would late-night diners be debouching from bars and brasseries. He could almost hear the narrow streets around his studio echoing with their laughter, and he was not sure that he could face it. On an impulse he told the driver to take him to the Île St. Louis instead, and he got out in the Rue des Deux Ponts.

The street was quiet as he watched the taxi recede into the night. The café on the corner where he had sat watching for Kirsty just a few days earlier was closed. They were sweeping out in the restaurant where he had eaten lunch. He stood on the pavement and wondered what he was doing here. He walked to a point opposite the entrance to her apartment. The buildings on this side had been recently renovated. There was a For Sale sign outside the first floor apartment above him. He craned his head up towards the attic studios opposite and wondered if Kirsty's place looked down into the street. There were lights on in a few windows. Was one of them hers? Did she ever think about him, except in anger? His own father had died when he was a young man, so he knew what it was to be fatherless.

Why had he come here, drawn back like a moth to the flame? Guilt? The realisation that, in truth, he had given Kirsty every reason to hate him? He knew, after all, that his own pain was self-inflicted. He sighed. This was stupid. He thrust his hands in his pockets and turned towards the Rue St. Louis en l'Île. It would take less than fifteen minutes to walk back to his studio. A taxi passed on the other side of the street and pulled up outside the door to Kirsty's apartment. A young couple stepped out and the taxi remained idling at the kerb. The girl had long, chestnut hair drawn back in a loose knot, and he heard her laugh, a familiar sound to him, even after all these years. He drew back into a doorway and watched as the young man cupped her face in his hands, talking to her earnestly for some moments, before drawing her face to his and kissing her. They embraced, then, and kissed once more. A long, lingering kiss. Enzo watched, with an ache in his chest and a knot in his stomach. When they broke apart, the young man said something and they both laughed. She was happy, and Enzo would have given anything to be able to share in that happiness. Her young man climbed back into his taxi, and she stood waving as it headed off towards the Pont de la Tournelle. She glanced back along the street, and Enzo pulled further into the shadows. For a moment he thought she had seen him, but then she turned and punched in her entry code and was swallowed up by the building.

He stood in the dark for ten, maybe fifteen, minutes. After all the misery with which he had tainted her life, she was still capable of laughter, and happiness. He had no right to make her unhappy again. He was just being selfish, in search of forgiveness to exorcise the guilt which had haunted him all these years. It was the same selfishness which had prompted him to leave in the first place. To steal away the father she had loved. *Nor all*

*thy piety nor wit shall lure it back to cancel half a line,
nor all your tears wash out a word of it.*

He made a decision, standing in the doorway, her
laughter still echoing distantly in his memory, that he
would never bother her again. She didn't want him. It
was her choice to make. And he had no right to try to
change her mind. He had had his chance once and
failed her. The least he could do now was let her get on
with her life, free of him, free of the past. A past that he,
too, must put behind him, and move on.

He stepped out of the shadows and crossed the
street, turning left into the Rue St. Louis en l'Île. The
lights of shop windows fell out across the street.
Patches of shadow where apartment buildings and
doorways stood in darkness were like missing teeth. It
was oddly quiet here in the heart of the city, the calm at
the centre of a storm. The traffic was a distant rumble.
There was no one else in the street. At the far end, the
Brasserie St. Louis was shut, tables and chairs stacked
up on the pavement under its awning. He heard his
own footsteps echoing back from the apartment blocks
rising on either side, each step laden with resignation.

But the echo seemed odd, unsynchronised, and he
realised that they were not his footsteps. There was
someone else in the street. He stopped, turning to look
behind him, but he could see no one. The dislocated
echo had stopped, too. A trick of acoustics, perhaps. He
continued towards the end of the street and heard the
sound of following footsteps again, some way back. He
swivelled and caught a fleeting movement in the
shadows of a gateway leading to a courtyard. Again the

166

echoing footsteps had ceased abruptly. Was there someone lurking there? His mouth felt dry, and he became aware for the first time that his pulse rate had increased. He realised he was afraid, and was not sure quite why. Except that someone seemed to be following him, and didn't want to be seen.

He picked up pace towards the Brasserie St. Louis. And there it was again. An echo that wasn't quite an echo. He glanced over his shoulder and this time saw a man following in his wake, about twenty metres back. He was making no attempt to conceal himself. His pace had picked up to match Enzo's. As he neared the end of the street, Enzo started to run. Scaffolding forced him off the pavement. He thought he could hear the other man running behind him. He stole another glance over his shoulder, but the scaffolding obscured his view. He turned left at La Chaumière en l'Île, emerging from the darkness of the narrow Rue St. Louis into the brightly lit expanse of the Pont St. Louis leading over to the Île de la Cité and the floodlit towers of Notre Dame.

If he had hoped to find people here, he was disappointed. The bridge was deserted, and he could still hear footsteps in the street he had just left.

He was halfway across the bridge when he saw the second man. A thickset figure in a dark suit standing on the far side, silhouetted against the lights of the cathedral behind him. Something about the way he stood, legs slightly apart, hands at his sides, gave Enzo the immediate impression that this man was there to bar his way. He stopped running, and stood staring

167

breathlessly at the man, uncertain of what to do. Behind him, footsteps emerged from the Rue St. Louis and came to an abrupt halt. Enzo looked back. His pursuer stood at the other end of the bridge, and Enzo could hear him breathing hard in the night air. He was trapped. There was no way off the bridge. Enzo looked around in a panic, willing a taxi to appear, or a group of revellers to spill out from a bar somewhere. But there was no one. No traffic. No redemption. No escape. The man behind him began moving forward. In the distance Enzo could see the lights of traffic drifting past on the Quai de l'Hôtel de Ville. But they might as well have been a million miles away.

The sharp blast of a horn startled him. He turned to see the lights of a *péniche* approaching on the river below. In fact, there were two barges, end to end, being shunted down river by a small tug. They sat dangerously low in the water, weighed down by their cargo of sand. Enzo could see the figure of the helmsman in the window of the wheelhouse. The first of the barges was already passing under the bridge immediately beneath him. The sand looked soft and inviting. A drop of four or five metres. He turned and clutched the rail. It would be a desperate thing to do. If he jumped and misjudged it he could break his legs and God knows what else on the crossbars, or even end up in the water.

Almost as if they realised what was in his mind, the two men started moving towards him. Enzo no longer had any choice. He hoisted himself on to the rail, balancing precariously for a moment. He heard one of the men shouting, and he jumped. Even as he fell through the air, it occurred to him how absurd this was. What on earth was he doing?

He hit the sand with more force than he had been expecting. His legs folded under him, and he landed on his back. The sand was not as giving as he had hoped, and all the air was knocked from his lungs. He found himself looking up at the underside of the bridge passing overhead, unable to breathe, unable to move. If either of these men had a gun, he would be an easy target when he emerged on the far side.

He lay helplessly, face up, as the star-studded sky emerged once more, and he saw the two men peering down at him from the parapet. One of them seemed to be laughing, the other serious and unsmiling. What if the danger had only been imagined, and the two men on the Pont St. Louis were simply on their way home after a night out. Here he was, leaping off the bridge like a madman. Enzo tried to imagine how he would have reacted, had he encountered a man who had suddenly, and for no apparent reason, thrown himself off a bridge on to a passing barge.

With something between a cough and a retch, his lungs were suddenly released from their paralysis, and they filled painfully and rapidly with air. His first few breaths were difficult. He seemed to have to fight to empty and then refill them. He inclined his head to see the two men still standing on the bridge watching as the barge took its course around the north side of the Île de la Cité. He saw the flare of a match as one of them lit a cigarette. He let his head fall back, and lay

169

for several minutes waiting for his breathing and his heartbeat to stabilise.

Apparently the helmsman had not noticed him drop from the bridge. Enzo could still see him in the wheelhouse. He was smoking a cigarette and occasionally lifting a mug of coffee to his lips. They passed under four bridges and were clearing the tip of the Île de la Cité, emerging again into the full flow of the Seine. Enzo scrambled unsteadily to his feet and began shouting and waving his arms. If he didn't get off this thing now he could end up in Rouen.

He saw the helmsman's expression of incredulity in the light of the wheelhouse, and the man's mouth began working. Enzo could only imagine the stream of imprecations which issued from it. He couldn't hear him above the thrum of the tug's motor. A group of young people passing across the pedestrian Pont des Arts looked down in astonishment. Enzo heard the motor slip into reverse. And as it roared and revved, the *péniche* slowed, turning in towards the quay at the Port des Saint-Pères. Enzo clambered up out of the hold and on to the nearside skirting. As the barge drew alongside the quay, he took his life in his hands and leaped across the narrowing gap, slipping on the cobbles and landing on his hands and knees. He felt his trousers tear at the right knee, and when he staggered to his feet saw blood smearing white flesh revealed by the tear. The palms of his hands were grazed and stinging.

The helmsman was out of his wheelhouse shouting at Enzo, who could hear him now. He reflected briefly on how colourful and expressive the French language

170

could be. The crowd on the bridge had doubled in size and a dozen people or more gathered along the rail watching with interest. Enzo wondered why there couldn't have been more people around when he needed them. Across the river, he could see the long, south-facing elevation of the Louvre, huddled in muted lighting down the length of the quay. Above him, the floodlit dome of the Institute de France was stark against the night sky. He realised he was only minutes away from his studio.

Still the helmsman was shouting. What on earth could Enzo tell him? How could he explain? He decided not to even try, and he turned and ran, fleeing from the scene of the crime like a schoolboy playing truant, up the ramp to the Quai Malaquais, slithering in his haste, shedding sand in his wake.

The Rue Mazarine skirted the Institute de France, and he ran up it without stopping until he reached the Café Le Balto on the corner of the Rue Guénégaud. There, he stood gasping for several minutes, leaning against the wall beside the door to his apartment block, until he was composed enough to tap in the entry code and step into the safety of the hall.

He knew immediately that there was something wrong. The light did not come on. The light always came on. It was on a timer which kept it burning long enough to reach each landing and hit another switch to take you up to the next. It saved electricity. But without it, the stairwell was pitch dark. Enzo stood, holding his breath, listening intently. His own heartbeat seemed deafening. But above it, he heard the unmistakable creak of the wooden staircase, like a footstep in dry snow. And then silence. There was somebody on the first floor landing. Somebody waiting in the dark. Somebody waiting for him.

He made his way across the lobby in the darkness, arms extended, until he felt the stair rail cool and smooth in his hand, and one by one he began climbing the stairs as quietly as he could. The silence in the building was pervasive and unnerving.

Enzo stopped at the mezzanine level and listened. Now he could hear the slow, regular sound of someone breathing, and realised that if he could hear them, they could hear him. On the halflanding he stopped and listened again. A dim light shone through a window from the street outside, but it only seemed to plunge the shadows on the landing above into deeper darkness. This time he heard nothing. As hard as he strained to hear, it seemed that the breathing had stopped. Was it possible for someone to hold their breath that long? It was time to take the initiative. Another half-dozen stairs and he would be at his door.

He sprinted up, two at a time, with a rush of adrenaline, and was blinded by a light that shone suddenly and directly into his eyes. He yelled and swung out blind, with a clenched fist, punching the wall and gasping in pain.

He heard a startled exclamation and a woman's voice. "For God's sake, Enzo, what are you doing?"

As he hopped around the landing, waving his injured hand, and dredging up infantile swear words from his childhood, it occurred to him that it was a voice he knew. He shielded his eyes from the light and saw Charlotte's frightened face peering at him out of the dark. "Could you please stop shining that thing in my face?" And when she diverted it to the floor, he saw that it was the kind of small penlight you might carry on a key ring. "How did you get in?"

"I remembered the code from the night you brought me up for coffee. The lights weren't working, but I had this little flashlight, so I decided to sit on the stairs and wait till you got back."

Enzo was opening and closing his hand, flexing bruised joints.

Charlotte added, "But I didn't expect you to try to assault me."

"I didn't know it was you." Enzo realised he wasn't making a very good impression.

"So do you normally try to punch people you meet on the stairs?"

"I thought someone was waiting to jump me."

"Why on earth would you think that?"

"Because it wouldn't be the first time someone had tried it tonight." Enzo unlocked the door to the studio and reached in to switch on a light.

Charlotte laughed. "Wha-at?"

"I was being followed. On the Île St. Louis. At least, I think I was."

"What were you doing on the Île St. Louis? I thought you were having dinner with the *Garde des Sceaux*."

"It's a long story."

She followed him into the studio and watched as he poured himself a large whisky. "What on earth have you been up to?" She looked at the state of his suit. "You're covered in sand. And your trousers are ripped."

"I jumped off the Pont St. Louis into a passing barge." He avoided her eye.

"I think I'd better have one of those, too." She nodded towards the whisky bottle. "And maybe you should tell me what happened."

As Enzo related the story to Charlotte, his fears seemed absurd, and his response to them verging on the ludicrous. She was hardly able to drink her whisky for laughing.

"It's not funny," he said. "I really thought these guys were after me."

"But why?"

He shrugged. "I don't know. Maybe I'm just getting paranoid. This whole Jacques Gaillard thing is getting out of hand. His killers must know I'm getting close to them." He looked up, struck by a sudden thought. "How did you know I was having dinner with the *Garde des Sceaux?*"

"Roger told me."

"Oh, did he? You two seem to do a lot of talking for a couple who've just broken up."

"It wasn't an acrimonious split," Charlotte said, and then immediately qualified herself. "Well, not really." But it wasn't something she was going to discuss further. "So what did Marie Aucoin have to say for herself?"

"She's set up a special team to investigate Gaillard's killing. And it was made clear to me that I was to have nothing further to do with it."

"So what are you going to do?"

"I'm going to have everything further to do with it."

Charlotte smiled. "Of course you are." She took his whisky glass from him. "Why don't you take off your trousers and sit up on the breakfast bar, and I'll dress that wound for you."

"Best offer I've had all night." Enzo kicked off his shoes, undid his belt and stepped out of his trousers. He hoisted himself up on to the breakfast bar, his legs dangling, and for the second time that night felt like a big kid. He remembered his mother sitting him up next to the kitchen sink to clean the gravel out of skinned knees when he was a little boy in Scotland.

Charlotte found a sponge in an unopened pack under the sink, and some disinfectant. She boiled a kettle and mixed up a solution of water and disinfectant to clean out the gash on his knee. It stung, and he yelled out, flinching from the sponge. "Don't be a baby," she said. "You don't want to get an infection in that." She discovered a roll of bandage in a drawer and taped it over the wound. "I think you'll live."

Enzo wanted to keep her close. "Tell me, in your considered opinion as a forensic psychologist, why would Jacques Gaillard's killers leave clues with each of his body parts?"

"Clues to what?"

"To the location of the next body part."

She shrugged. "Without knowing more about the case I can only offer an uninformed guess."

"Which is?"

"He, she, they . . . want to be caught."

"But that's crazy. Why?"

"Well, if they don't get caught, no one will ever know how clever they were. After all, they got away with murder. It's not uncommon for a killer to want to be caught so he can claim the credit."

"But they went to great lengths to hide the body parts so that they would never be found."

Charlotte sighed. "Then your guess is as good as mine."

Beyond the initial jagged pain when she dabbed his knee with the sponge, he had enjoyed the cool, soft touch of her fingers on his skin. And after she had finished, she left a hand draped over his thigh, her belly still pressed against his other leg as they talked. He could smell her perfume, and felt the warmth of her through her dress. She looked up at him, and her face was very close. Her eyes were like big, dark saucers, and they fixed him with a twinkle that was half serious, half amused. He felt blood rushing to his loins, and on an impulse leaned forward to kiss her. To his surprise and delight, she made no attempt to move away. Her lips were soft and moist, and there was a sweetness on her tongue. He cupped the back of her head in his hand, feeling the soft, silky texture of her curls, the smooth curve of her skull as it swooped down to her neck. He felt her hand on his chest, fingers moving up to his face.

And then it was over, and they broke apart and looked at each other for a long time without a word passing between them. Finally Enzo said, in almost a whisper, "Stay over."

But she shook her head. "I have an early client. Another time."

"There might not be another time. I have to go to Toulouse tomorrow."

"Why?"

"The President of my university has requested an audience. I think he's going to sack me." He tried a smile, but it was a poor attempt at masking his disappointment.

CHAPTER
TWELVE

I

The Université Paul Sabatier was smudged across a great, sprawling campus on the southern outskirts of Toulouse. Sabatier had been the Dean of the Faculty of Science at Toulouse University in the early part of the twentieth century, and winner of the Nobel Prize for Chemistry in 1912. Enzo had often thought how the great man would have been horrified to see the crumbling collection of faculty buildings thrown up in his name thirty years after his death. The science-based university consisted of disparate, ugly concrete blocks separated by vast car parks and scrubby patches of sun-scorched grass which turned to mud in winter.

From the dilapidated administration building, an avenue of trees flanked a long rectangle of green, stagnant water leading to a series of lawns providing a perspective to the distant, classical Lycée Bellevue on the other side of the Route de Narbonne.

Enzo parked in front of the administration block and climbed broken steps, past graffitied pillars, to the main entrance hall. The office of the Président was one floor up on the mezzanine level. His secretary ushered Enzo into his office and told him that the Président would be with him shortly. Huge glass windows gave out on to the view towards the Lycée Bellevue whose beautiful view the university was spoiling. Students attending summer courses ambled across the concourse below, unhurried in the striking heat of the southern sun. The office was airless and hot. There was no air conditioning, and Enzo took a handkerchief from his satchel to mop his forehead. He sat down in front of the Président's vast desk and let his eyes wander across the shambles of paperwork which littered it. The Président's glasses lay, half open, on top of a pile of exam papers. Designer tortoiseshell frames, lenses divided in two for distance and close work. On an impulse, Enzo reached over to pick them up. They were handsome spectacles, and he wondered if they might suit him. He put them on and stood up to try to catch his reflection in the window. As he did, he heard the door opening behind him, and he snatched the glasses from his face. He turned, slipping his hands behind his back to hide them.

"Macleod," the Président said, and he held out his hand.

Enzo swapped the Président's glasses from one hand to the other, and firmly shook the one being proffered. When he returned his right hand to its place behind his back, it was only to discover that somehow the index finger of his left had become jammed in the bridge between the two lenses. He pulled discreetly, but it wouldn't budge.

The Président dropped into his chair and regarded Enzo thoughtfully. "You're a damned nuisance, Macleod."

"Yes, Monsieur le Président."

"Well, sit down." He waved a hand at the chair opposite.

But Enzo knew he could not very well sit down with his hands behind his back. He yanked again at the glasses. "I'd rather stand." He felt awkward and foolish.

"As you wish." The Président began searching about his desk, lifting and laying papers, a frown forming itself in deep lines between his eyes. "I spent an unpleasant fifteen minutes on the phone with the Chief of Police yesterday. I suppose you can imagine the topic of conversation?"

"I suppose I can."

The Président flicked him a fleeting glance, suspecting sarcasm, then returned to his search. "He was adamant that the place for a Professor of Biology is in the classroom. And I have to tell you, I agreed with him."

"Yes, Monsieur le Président."

Finally, the frustrations of his fruitless search boiled over. "Where the hell are my glasses! I'm sure I left them on the desk. Damned things cost an arm and a leg." He looked up at Enzo. "You didn't see them, did you?"

"No, Monsieur le Président." Enzo wedged the glasses in his right hand and pulled hard with his left. There was a loud crack as the frame broke in two across the bridge.

The Président looked up. Enzo moved his head around as if his neck was troubling him. "Good God, man, I'd get that seen to," the Président said. He

180

opened a drawer and pulled out that morning's edition of *Libération*, and Enzo slipped the broken halves of the glasses into his pocket. "And then this appears in the paper this morning." He held it up. But Enzo didn't need to look. He had read Raffin's account of the find in Toulouse during his flight down from Paris. "I know your background is in forensic science, Macleod, but that is not the capacity in which you are employed by this university. Your antics are attracting unwelcome publicity. We require state as well as private funding, and we cannot afford to offend our political masters. There could be financial implications. You understand?"

"Yes, Monsieur le Président." Enzo was wondering what to do with the broken pieces of the Président's glasses, which were burning a hole now in his pocket.

"I've always thought you were a maverick, Macleod. You're too chummy with the students. I hear that you've been known to go drinking with them, and that they even invite you to parties. Is that true?"

"Yes, Monsieur le Président."

The Président shook his head. He was feeling about in his pockets. "Doesn't do. Doesn't do at all. Not good for discipline."

"Is there a problem with my student pass rates?"

"No." The Président gave a little defensive shrug of each shoulder. "But that's not the point."

"What is the point, Monsieur le Président?"

"The point is, Macleod, that I want you to lay off this amateur detective nonsense."

"I'm on holiday, Monsieur le Président."

181

The Président stood up. "Yes, you are, Macleod. And I can arrange for it to be permanent if that's how you'd prefer it."

"No, Monsieur le Président."

"Good, then we understand one another." He stretched out a hand to indicate that the interview was at an end.

Enzo shook it. "Yes, Monsieur le Président."

And as he walked through the outer office he heard the Président shout to his secretary, "Amélie! Have you seen my glasses?"

"No, Monsieur le Président." Amélie hurried through to help him look for them.

Enzo took the pieces from his pocket and dropped them in the wastepaper bin. He didn't feel so bad now about breaking them.

II

It was early afternoon by the time he stepped off the Toulouse train in Cahors. He was depressed and disheartened. Warned off the Gaillard case twice. Once by the government, once by his employer. And he had spent most of the previous night dwelling on what might have been with Charlotte. He had known from their first meeting at Raffin's apartment that she was special. She was affecting him in a way no woman had since Pascale. Dry mouth, palpitations, loss of self-confidence. It was uncomfortably like being a teenager again. He hardly knew her, and yet he knew

182

that what he felt was more than just attraction. And last night, when they kissed, he had wanted simply to possess her. Entirely. It had been hard for him to accept her rejection, and he had lain awake most of the night thinking about it. There was no knowing when he would next be in Paris. And so he had no idea when he might see her again. The only redeeming thought in which he found comfort was that last night it was she who had come to see him.

He let himself go with the flow of disembarking passengers, out through the station foyer and into the afternoon sunshine.

It was a fifteen minute walk back to his apartment, where the final straw awaited him. He saw it as soon as he opened the door. Bertrand's metal detector. He could not believe it was still there. "Sophie!" he bellowed. But there was no response. The apartment was empty. He had no idea where Nicole might be. He picked up the metal detector and stormed off down the stairs in search of his car.

Bertrand's gym was on the west side of the river, across the Pont Neuf, at the far end of the Quai de la Verrerie. The gym had been converted to its present purpose from a disused *miroiterie*. Tall windows along the front of the building flooded the interior with light. It was divided in two. There was a *salle des appareils*, filled with heavy weightlifting and fitness training equipment. A room beyond it with a sprung wooden floor was used for aerobics and dancing. One of its walls was lined entirely with mirrors so that overweight housewives could watch their flesh heaving as they tried to exercise it away.

Enzo had never visited the gym. He knew that it had an older clientele during the day, and that in the evening it was a popular haunt for the town's teenagers. There were nearly twenty cars parked outside, and Enzo had trouble getting parked himself. He took the metal detector and pushed open the door. A number of middle-aged men and women looked up from miscellaneous pieces of equipment, and nodded and mumbled *bonjour*. A television set mounted on the wall was belting out MTV music videos. There was a sour smell of body odour and feet. Through windows along the back wall, he could see thirty or more women, ages ranging from twenty-five to sixty-five, dance-stepping in time to an endlessly repetitive beat. Bertrand was leading them, calling out each change in step. He wore a muscle tee shirt, and close-fit shorts that cut off just above his calf. Enzo had only ever seen him in jeans and loose-fitting tee shirts, and was almost shocked by his beautifully sculpted physique. God only knew how many hours of muscle-burning weight training it took to build a body like that.

Now that he was here, the metal detector in his hands, Enzo was not quite sure what to do with it. He could hardly burst into the aerobics class waving it at Bertrand. He decided to wait until the class was finished. He sat down on an exercise bench and waited through another ten minutes of mind numbing dance beat before the women began streaming out towards

184

the changing rooms, a babble of breathless, excited voices.

He stood up and saw Bertrand laughing and joking with a group of them. Hard as it was to see past the facial piercing and the gelled, blond-tipped spikes, with reluctance Enzo supposed that Bertrand was a good-looking young man. The women couldn't keep their hands off him, all anxious to kiss him goodbye. And he seemed to be enjoying it, flirting with them, encouraging them. His smile faded when he saw Enzo and the metal detector. He detached himself from the ladies and came across to shake his hand, the diamond stud in his nose glinting in the sunlight that slanted in through the front windows. Enzo grudgingly took the proffered hand. "You left something at the apartment." He thrust the metal detector into Bertrand's chest. He was taller than Bertrand, but the boy's physical presence was almost intimidating. A confrontation between the young buck and the grizzled old stag.

"I can't leave it lying around here. It would be dangerous."

"I can vouch for that. And I don't want it in my home."

"Fair enough." Bertrand turned and headed out of the door with it. Enzo followed him across the car park to a battered white Citroën van. Bertrand opened the back doors and threw the metal detector inside. He closed the doors and turned to face his girlfriend's father. "You don't like me much, do you, Monsieur Macleod?"

"So you're quick as well as fit."

Bertrand looked at him with hurt in his soft brown eyes. "I don't know why."

"Because I don't want Sophie throwing her life away on a waster like you. I saw you in there with those women. Like some kind of . . ." Enzo searched for the right word, ". . . gigolo. Disgusting."

"Monsieur Macleod," Bertrand said patiently, "these women pay good money to come to my fitness classes. It does no harm to be nice to them. It's good for business. And as far as women are concerned, there's only one in my life. And that's Sophie."

"She's not a woman, she's just a girl."

"No, she's a woman, Monsieur Macleod." Bertrand's patience was wearing thin. "She's not your little girl any more. So maybe it's time you started letting her grow up."

Enzo exploded. "Don't you tell me how to bring up my daughter! I've done it for twenty years without any help from anyone. If it wasn't for you she'd still be at university. She's thrown away her future. And for what? Some muscle-bound dickhead who spends his days prancing about a gym with a bunch of middle-aged women. What possible future could she have with you?"

All the colour had drained now from Bertrand's face. He stared back at Enzo with eyes that blazed anger and humiliation. He pointed at the gymnasium. "You see that gym? That's mine. I created that. It was a derelict old factory until I raised the money to convert it. My father died when I was fourteen, and my mother couldn't afford to put me through college, so I did it myself. I took two jobs, working nights and weekends."

Enzo was already regretting his outburst. "Look . . ." he said, determined that things should take a more conciliatory turn. But Bertrand wasn't finished.

"I've got a diploma on the wall in there. Top of my year. Do you know how hard it was to get that? Ten gruelling months at CREPS in Toulouse, studying anatomy, physiology, accounting, diet, muscle development. Do you know how many people apply for entry each year?"

Enzo shook his head. "No."

"Hundreds. And do you know how many they take? Twenty. The physical test's tough. Twenty tractions, twenty push-ups, forty dips, twenty squat-lifts, and as many laps of the stadium as you can run in twenty minutes. Then there's the written exam. General knowledge. An oral address to a panel on motivation and ambition, and then a gruelling question and answer session where they can ask you any question they damn well like for half an hour. It would be easier getting into one of the *Grandes Écoles*."

He paused for a moment, but only to draw breath. "So don't call me a waster, Monsieur Macleod. I may be many things, but I'm not that. I do what I'm good at, and I'm good at what I do. I've worked damned hard to achieve what I have. And as far as Sophie's concerned, I did everything I could to persuade her to stay on at university. But she's the one who wanted to drop out. She told me there was no point in even trying to compete with her genius of a father."

187

Enzo was stunned to silence, and felt the colour rising on his face.

"Thanks for bringing the metal detector." Bertrand turned and went back into his gym.

CHAPTER
THIRTEEN

I

Enzo retreated to the apartment like the wounded stag that he was. The young buck had given him quite a mauling. There was still no one there when he got back. He picked his way into the *séjour* which seemed, if anything, even more cluttered. There were empty cola cans lying around, and pizza crusts in carryout boxes. The air was stale, and the heat stifling. He opened the French windows, only to be hit by a wall of even hotter air. Which was when he noticed that his whiteboard had been cleared of its first set of clues, and a new set of images fixed around its edges. A crude drawing of two skeletal arms; a bottle of Dom Perignon champagne; a photograph of a crucifix with the date 1st April written beside it; a picture of a dog tag with *Utopique* handwritten across it; a diagram of a dog's skeleton with one of its front legs circled in red; a photograph of a lapel pin, complete with two men on a single horse and the inscription, *sigilum militum xpisti*. And someone had already begun trying to decipher them. There were words written up and circled, with arrows criss-crossing the board.

"Oh, you're back." Enzo turned to find Nicole standing in the doorway grinning at him. He hadn't heard her come in. Her long hair tumbled over her shoulders and down her back, and her breasts seemed more prominent than usual in a tight-fitting tee shirt. Its V-neck exposed a substantial amount of cleavage. Enzo tried not to let his eyes be drawn by it. "I didn't know when you'd be, so I started without you," she said.

"So I see." She brushed past him and sat herself at the computer, hitting the spacebar to wake it up. "Where did you get the images?"

"On the internet."

Enzo looked at the board and frowned. "Why the skeleton of a dog?"

"Ah." Nicole beamed with pleasure. "Remember the bone that was in the trunk? The one that didn't seem to go with the arms? It's a shinbone from a dog's foreleg."

Enzo was astonished. "How do you know that?"

"A boy I was at school with is studying zoology at Limoges. It was his professor who was called in by the Toulouse police to try to identify the bone." She grinned again, pleased with herself. "Word gets around."

But Enzo was distracted from her self-congratulation by an odd, acrid smell that he noticed wafting into the room for the first time. He screwed up his face. "What the hell's that?"

"What's what?"

"That smell."

"Ah . . ." Nicole said. "That'll be the ducklings."

"Ducklings?"

"I put them in the bath. I didn't know where else they should go"

Enzo looked at her in disbelief. He turned and stalked out into the hall and threw open the bathroom door. The stink hit him like a blow from a baseball bat. Half a dozen tiny ducklings had settled themselves in the bottom of the bath, which was covered with a mixture of grain and shit. "Dear God! Is this some kind of a joke?"

Nicole had followed him out, and stretched on tiptoe to look at them over his shoulder. "They're a gift from my father. By way of an apology for the other night." She sniffed several times. "You get used to the smell."

Enzo looked at her over his shoulder. "I can't keep ducks in my apartment. They can't stay here."

Nicole shrugged. "You must know someone with a garden. My papa says he'll slaughter them for you when they're big enough." She turned away into the hall, irritated by the interruption to her flow of explanation. "Do you want to know how far I've got with these clues or not?"

Enzo raised his eyes to the heavens and closed the door on the problem. He'd worry about the ducklings later.

He followed her back into the *séjour*.

Nicole settled herself in front of the computer again and said, "You'll see I've written *dog* up there, and circled it and drawn arrows to it from the dog's skeleton and the dog tag."

Enzo looked at the board, still distracted by the smell, and nodded. "You'd better tell me why."

191

"Well, it was the guy from the *police scientifique* who said it — about the disk with Utopique engraved on it. A name tag for a dog, he said it looked like. And it did. Just the sort of thing you would attach to your dog's collar. And if it is a name tag, then it's reasonable to assume that Utopique is the name of a dog. We know that the extraneous bone was a dog's shinbone, so it just seemed kind of obvious that both these clues were pointing towards a dog."

"Called Utopique."

"Exactly."

"It's possible," Enzo conceded. He couldn't argue with the logic. "Go on."

Nicole beamed with pleasure. "Okay. The champagne. Moët et Chandon, Dom Perignon 1990. You have to figure that they didn't choose a 1990 vintage by accident. I've no idea why, but the date's got to be important."

"Agreed," Enzo said. "Which is probably why it was in a box, wrapped and protected by the wood wool, so the label would be kept safe from the damp."

Nicole nodded and moved on. "You'll see I've written *Poisson d'avril* below the date 1st April, beside the crucifix."

"April Fool's Day, we called it in Scotland," Enzo said.

Nicole chided him. "Don't you remember when Sophie was little, kids sticking paper fish on each other's backs?"

Enzo shook his head. "No."

192

"Well, it probably happened at school. It's what you do on April 1st in France. You try and stick a paper fish on other kids' backs without them knowing. Which is why we call it *Poisson d'avril*."

"I didn't know that," Enzo confessed. He smiled. "Maybe it's a red herring."

Nicole frowned. "What do you mean?"

"A red herring. Something that misdirects you from the truth. Isn't there a French equivalent?"

Nicole looked at him as if he were mad. "I don't think so, Monsieur Macleod." She shook her head. "Anyway, I searched the internet for things that might have happened on 1st April. And guess what? Another Napoléonic connection. Napoléon Bonaparte married Marie Louise of Austria on April 1st, 1810."

Enzo looked at the board where Nicole had written and circled *Napoléon* and drawn an arrow to it from the crucifix. He chewed his lip thoughtfully. "But what's the connection with the crucifix? It seems to me that the date and the crucifix are inseparable, and that whatever they point to should have a relevance to both." He took a cloth and wiped off the circle and the arrow. "Let's just keep that in mind, and maybe we'll come back to it."

"Oh, okay." Nicole was momentarily crestfallen. And then she brightened up. "But here's the real breakthrough. The lapel pin. *Sigilum militum xpisti*. Do you know what that means?"

"The seal of the army of Christ," Enzo said without hesitation.

It was as if he had stuck a pin in her. She was instantly deflated. "How do you know that?"

"I studied Latin at school."

"I suppose you also know what it is, then?"

"I haven't a clue."

She brightened up again. "Two men on a single horse bearing shields, encircled by the words *sigilum militum xpisti*, is the chosen seal of the Knights Templar." Her fingers spidered across the keyboard and she read from the screen. "The seal was introduced to the Order in 1168 by its Grand Master in France, Bertrand de Blanchfort."

Enzo breathed a small jet of air through clenched teeth. Bertrand! It seemed there was no escaping him.

Nicole continued, "It is said that fifty years earlier, when the founding Christian knights took a vow of poverty, chastity, and obedience at Jerusalem, they could only afford one horse between two of them. And the depiction of two knights astride a single mount also recalls the passage in the book of Matthew, where Christ says, 'Wherever two or more of you are gathered in My name, there am I, in the midst of you.' "

"Well that seems pretty conclusive," Enzo said. "Well found." And he picked up a marker pen and wrote up *Knights Templar*, and circled it and drew an arrow to it from the lapel pin. "I wonder if we can connect April 1st in some way with the Knights Templar. Maybe it's an important date in the history of the Order."

"That's a thought." Nicole called up Google and began a search. But after nearly fifteen minutes, she had found nothing that linked the date with the Order.

194

She grinned to cover her disappointment. "Another 'red herring.' "

"What about trying to link the date with the crucifix?" Enzo felt that he was clutching at straws now. But anything was worth a try.

Nicole tapped in *crucifix* and *April 1st*, and initiated a search. After a moment she let out a tiny yelp of excitement. Enzo crossed the room to take a look. There were three hundred and seventy-eight results. But halfway down the first page of ten was a link headed, THE FIRST MIRACLE OF FATIMA — 1385, and below it an extract from the page it would take them to — *He died in his cell clutching a crucifix on April 1st, 1431*. Nicole clicked on the link and brought up a lengthy document detailing the canonisation of the Blessed Nuno, whom it described as the last great mediaeval knight. But their initial interest was short lived as they read through a dull account of the man's life and death. A Portuguese knight, widowed in 1422, he had given away all his worldly wealth and joined a Carmelite monastery in Lisbon. There did not appear to be any connection with the Knights Templar, or with France.

Enzo blew his frustration through pursed lips. "April 1st, April 1st, April 1st." He repeated it over and over under his breath as he made his way across the room to the open windows. He stood holding the rail and looking out over the treetops in the square. "What other significance might April 1st have in the French calendar?" No sooner had the words left his mouth than he checked himself. "Calendar," he said. "What Saint's day falls on April 1st?"

Nicole made a quick internet search. "Saint Hugues." She looked towards him. "Does that mean anything to you?"

Enzo turned back into the room. "No." He sighed. "Try a search of Saint Hugues and see what we come up with."

As Nicole tapped at the keyboard she said, "You know, whoever put these clues together ten years ago wouldn't have had the help of the internet."

It wasn't something Enzo had considered before. "No, of course they wouldn't. The internet was still in its infancy in those days."

"And most of the stuff we're digging up wouldn't even have been on it then."

"You're right." Enzo realised that Gaillard's killers could never, in their wildest dreams, have imagined that ten years on, the information which, then, would have taken days, weeks, even months to find, could be accessed in seconds on the internet.

"Oh, my God," Nicole said suddenly. "This is the only problem with the net." She was gazing forlornly at the screen. "Information overload. There are six thousand, four hundred and forty links to pages containing mentions of Saint Hugues. There seem to be lots of Saint Hugues too. Saint Hugues de Cluny . . . de Grenoble . . . de Chartreuse . . . Do you want me to go on?"

Enzo shook his head. "I need a drink."

Nicole looked at her watch. "It's too early, Monsieur Macleod."

"Nicole, it's never too early." Enzo picked his way through to the dining room and opened a fresh bottle of whisky from the drinks cabinet. "Do you want something?"

"A diet Coke. There are bottles in the fridge."

He poured himself a large measure and took her a bottle of diet Coke. After removing a pizza carryout box from his recliner, he settled himself in the chair. "I see you've been eating well."

"I'm not much of a cook, Monsieur Macleod. My dad really wanted a boy, so I know more about ploughing and shearing and milking than I do about cooking."

Enzo took a long sip from his glass and closed his eyes as the whisky burned down inside him. Immediately, he sat upright again. "We're missing something here. None of these clues stands alone. I mean, they always connect in some way with one or more of the others." He took another slug of whisky and pinched the bridge of his nose between thumb and forefinger, closing his eyes again to try to concentrate. "April 1st already has a religious connotation because it's engraved on the back of a crucifix. So maybe we're not looking for Saint Hugues. Just Hugues."

"So?"

"So why don't we try combining Hugues with one of the other clues?"

"What, like with the Knights Templar?"

"That, or ... Dom Perignon. Or even just champagne."

Nicole shrugged and typed in *Hugues* and *champagne* and hit the return key. Enzo watched her face closely as her eyes flickered back and forth across the screen. Suddenly they lit up, and she threw her arms in the air. "Monsieur Macleod, you're a genius!"

And the word genius was like a finger poking at an open wound. *She told me there was no point in even trying to compete with her genius of a father*, Bertrand had told him.

"There are links all over the place to an Hugues de Champagne. And you're not going to believe this — to the Knights Templar as well."

Enzo stood up. "How? What's the connection?"

"Wait a minute ..." Her fingers danced across the keyboard, and he went to stand behind her so that he could see what she was pulling up on screen. It was a page headed HUGUES DE CHAMPAGNE 1074–1125. Enzo leaned over to read it. Several paragraphs detailed his parentage, his childhood, his marriage, and then his first trip to Palestine in the year 1104. His first marriage in 1093 to Constance, the daughter of King Philip the First of France, was annulled in his absence, and when he returned three years later he was remarried to a young girl called Elisabeth de Varais. Evidently it didn't take quite as long for the shine to wear off the second union, for seven years later he took off again for Palestine, this time in the company of his vassal, Hugues de Payens, along with Geoffrey de St. Omer, Hugues d'Hautvillers, and five others. There, in Jerusalem, in 1118, they established the Order of the Knights of the Temple, and Champagne's vassal Hugues de Payens became its first Grand Master.

"What a lot of Hugues there were in those days," Nicole said.

"Yes, yes, yes!" Enzo whispered into the afternoon heat. And he nearly danced across the room to the whiteboard. "Hugues de Champagne." He wrote it up on the board and circled it. Then he drew extravagant arrows to the name from the crucifix, the lapel pin, the champagne bottle, and the Knights Templar. He stood breathing heavily, gazing at it, and took another gulp of whisky.

Nicole was regarding it with something less than conviction. "And?" she asked, finally.

"And what?"

"Just and."

He looked at the board again, and his enthusiasm began to wane. "Okay, so I don't see any tie-up with the dog."

"And what about the date on the champagne bottle? And why specifically Moët et Chandon and Dom Perignon?"

Enzo sat on a pile of books and emptied his glass with less enthusiasm than he had filled it. "I don't know. Maybe there's something on the label. Maybe we need to get a bottle of that vintage to see." He sighed. What a roller coaster ride this was. "What does it say about the 1990 on the net?"

Nicole had anticipated the question and was already pulling up search results. "It's nearly all wine-sellers," she said. "Oh, wait a minute, here's a magazine piece . . ." She tapped some more, then read, "Dom Perignon was launched in 1921 by Moët et Chandon as their top of the line champagne. It is a single vineyard wine, made only from grapes grown in that one vineyard, and only made in certain years when the harvest is exceptional. It is renowned for its colour and flavour and the longevity of its finish." She looked up. "Between 1978 and 1993, the 1990 vintage gets the third highest points rating. Hmmm. Wouldn't mind a glass of that. I like champagne."

They heard the door from the landing open and then Sophie's exclamation, "Oh, my God, what's that smell?" There was the sound of another door opening, and then a shriek even more shrill than the first. Sophie appeared in the doorway, her eyes full of astonishment and repugnance. "Papa, there are ducks in the bath!"

"I know," Enzo said wearily.

"Well, what are they doing there?"

"Shitting and eating," he said. But it was not a conversation he wanted to pursue. "I'm going out for some air." He crossed the room, stopping briefly in the doorway to give Sophie a peck on the cheek.

"But what are they for?" she called after him.

"Roasting," he shouted back.

He was halfway down the stairs when she called again. "Where's Bertrand's metal detector?"

"Ask Bertrand!"

II

It was a relief to escape the apartment, and the head-banging process of trying to decipher the clues. Enzo felt as if he was beginning to understand the thought processes of Gaillard's killers, to get inside their heads. And it was not a pleasant place to be.

The town was crammed with tourists and with farmers who had come in from the country for the morning market in the Cathedral square. The market was over now, the square once more fulfilling its regular function of car park. But people had stayed on to eat in the restaurants and shop in La Halle, and to idle the day away in pavement cafés, drinking coffee and watching the world go by. This week, the town was filled to bursting point for the annual blues festival. Enzo pushed through the crowds and into La Halle, and made his way to the wine merchant's stand.

Michel was a ruddy-faced man with a fuzz of wiry, steel-coloured hair. He smoked Voltigeur cigars, and his silver moustache was tinted nicotine yellow. But he knew his wines. He shook Enzo's hand warmly.

"Don't tell me you've finished that Gaillac already?"

Enzo laughed. "My God, Michel, if I'd drunk it that fast I'd have drowned in it. I've still got two cases left." Enzo preferred the softer, rounder tones of the Gaillac wines to the sharp tannins of the Cahors vintages. "It's champagne I'm looking for today."

Michel's eyebrows shot up. "Champagne?" He issued some staccato nasal farts that Enzo supposed indicated mirth. "Something to celebrate?"

"Just life."

"What would you like? I can offer you a toasty little Veuve Clicquot. Yellow Label. Not too expensive."

"I'm looking for a Moët et Chandon, Dom Perignon 1990."

Michel's jaw fell. *"Merde alors!* You're kidding!"

"You don't have any?"

Michel laughed. "I certainly do not." He held up a finger. "But wait." He turned to his computer, flickering behind the counter, and tapped away at the keyboard, staring intently at the screen. "Here we are. Dom Perignon. 1990." He made a moue with his lips and blew a jet of air through them. "A rare wine these days, my friend. Robert Parker described the 1990 vintage as 'brilliant.' " He grinned at Enzo. "It's a sad state of affairs when it takes an American to tell us how good or bad our wines are." He tapped some more. "Ah-ha! Got you!" He looked up triumphantly. "I can get you a bottle."

"Today?"

Michel gave a very gallic shrug of the shoulders and pouted pensively. "About two hours?"

"Ideal."

"Come and get it before we close up."

"Thanks, Michel." Enzo turned away.

"Don't you want to know how much it is?"

Enzo stopped in the arched gateway leading to the street. "I suppose I should. How much is it?"

"Well, normally, it would be a hundred and fifty."

Enzo nearly choked. "Euros?"

Michel nodded and smiled. "But, well, given the special circumstances . . ." He thought for a minute, and Enzo reflected warmly on just how much he loved it here. People knew you. People did you favours. "I'm going to have to charge a hundred and ninety."

After two hours and several beers at Le Forum, Enzo returned to the apartment clutching his bottle of Moët et Chandon. He was in mellower mood, in spite of his wallet being nearly two hundred euros lighter. All the windows were wide open, and Sophie was on her hands and knees in the bathroom scrubbing the bath with disinfectant. There was no sign of either Nicole or the ducklings. The smell had all but gone.

"Where's Nicole?"

"Gone." Sophie kept her head down, still scrubbing.

"Gone where?"

"Home."

"Why?"

"Because I told her the ducks couldn't stay here and that she would have to take them back to her father."

Enzo flapped his arms in exasperation. "Sophie, they were a gift. I don't want to offend him."

Sophie looked up and shook her head. "There are times I think I'll never understand you, Papa. We're talking about a man who broke into our apartment and beat you up. And you're worried about offending him?"

Enzo shrugged. "That was a misunderstanding."

Sophie spotted the bottle of champagne. "What's the occasion?"

"There isn't one."

She followed him through to the *séjour*, peeling off her rubber gloves. "Well, you don't just go buying champagne for no reason."

"I got it for the label."

"What?"

He placed the bottle on the table and searched through the drawers of his writing bureau until he found what he was looking for. A large magnifying glass. "This is the make and year of champagne they found in the trunk in Toulouse." He started examining the label through the magnifying glass. "I can't figure out why they chose this particular *marque* or vintage. There has to be something on the label."

It was a classically shaped sloping-shouldered bottle in dark green glass. There was a gold stamp on the black foil around the cage and cork. It said, simply, Cuvée Dom Perignon. The label was in the shape of a three-pointed shield, greenish ochre in colour. Across the top of the label was the legend *Moët et Chandon à Épernay — Fondée en 1745*. Beneath it, *Champagne — Cuvée Dom Perignon — Vintage 1990*. Beneath that was a five-pointed star, and the alcoholic content, *12.5% VOL*. At the very foot of the label, Enzo's glass magnified *75cl* and *Brut*. He hissed his exasperation.

"Well? What revelations on the label?"

Enzo flicked a look of annoyance over the top of his magnifying glass, and then peered through it again. "Wait a minute. There's something written around the edge of it." He read out, *"Elaboré par Moët & Chandon à Épernay, France — Muselet EPARNIX"*

"Illuminating."

Enzo turned the bottle around to look at the label on the back. There was nothing but the Cuvée Dom Perignon logo, a couple of recycling symbols, and a bar code. He banged the bottle down on the table. *"Putain!"* A complete waste of money.

"Papa!" Sophie was mock shocked. "That's terrible language."

Enzo picked up his satchel and his jacket. "I'm going to get drunk."

III

He hadn't really meant to get drunk. It had been more an expression of his disgust than a statement of intent. But after a pizza at the Lampara, he had fallen into bad company at the Forum, and his words had taken on more prescience than he intended. It was one in the morning by the time he made his way unsteadily back to the apartment. His meal and a night's drinking had cost a fraction of what he'd wasted on the bottle of Moët et Chandon. But that was of little comfort.

The apartment was in darkness when he opened the door into the hall, confident that tonight he would not trip over Bertrand's metal detector. He did, however, manage to stumble over a pile of books in the *séjour* and almost went sprawling. He banged into the table and knocked over his bottle of Dom Perignon. It rolled away across the tabletop with a strangely hollow ring. He grabbed the bottle and, although the glass was heavy, it was not as heavy as it should have been. He carried it across the room and switched on the light. The foil wrapping had been torn off, the wire cage unwound and the cork removed. The bottle was empty. Enzo stared at it in disbelief. He looked across the room and saw the discarded cage and cork on the table, and two empty glasses. Anger fizzed up inside him. "Sophie!" His voice resounded through the silence of the apartment. He stood breathing hard, listening for a response. But there was none. Perhaps she was still out. "Sophie!" He stamped through the hall and threw open her bedroom door. Moonlight spilled through the window across the bed, and two frightened faces peered back at him from beneath the sheets. A night's drinking at Le Forum left him momentarily confused, and briefly he thought he was seeing double. Until a diamond nose-stud twinkled in the moonlight. "Bertrand!" The boy was in bed with his daughter. In his own house. He couldn't believe it. "Jesus Christ!" he spluttered.

"Papa, I can explain."

"No, you can't." He pointed a finger at Bertrand. "You. Get out!"

"Yes, sir." Bertrand slipped, stark naked, from the bed, hunched modestly to conceal his embarrassment. He struggled to pull on his shorts and tee shirt, hopping from one foot to the other.

"You drank my champagne!" Enzo wasn't sure which made him angrier — finding Bertrand in bed with Sophie, or knowing that they had drunk his Moët et Chandon.

Sophie was sitting up, clutching the sheet to her neck. "You said you only bought it for the label."

"Jesus Christ!"

"You did!"

"Have you any idea how much that bottle cost?"

Bertrand was trying to undo the buckles on his sandals. "Probably about a hundred and fifty euros."

Enzo swung blazing eyes in the unfortunate young man's direction. "And you still drank it?"

"Papa, it was my fault. I thought you were only interested in the label. And it didn't go to waste, honestly."

"Oh, didn't it?"

"No, we really did have something to celebrate." She glanced at Bertrand, who prepared himself for an explosion. "Bertrand asked me to marry him."

A black cloud descended on Enzo, and he felt a strange stillness. "Over my dead body." He turned a steady gaze in Bertrand's direction. "I thought I told you to get out."

Bertrand shook his head in despair. There was no point in arguing. "Yeah, okay, I'm going." A sullen calm had overtaken him.

"Papa-a-a," Sophie wailed.

Bertrand brushed past her father and into the hall, sandals dangling from his hand. He muttered something as he went.

Enzo turned on him. "What was that?"

Bertrand swivelled to face him. "Why would anyone in their right mind pay a hundred and fifty euros just for a label?"

"A hundred and ninety," Enzo corrected him.

"Then you were robbed."

Enzo glared at him, inflamed by the knowledge that he was probably right. "It's an important clue in trying to solve a man's murder."

"This Jacques Gaillard thing?"

"Yes. Only, I can't figure out what it is."

"What's to figure about a bottle of champagne?"

"The vintage. It has to have been chosen for a reason."

"1990?"

"Yes."

Bertrand thought for a moment. "When, exactly, was Gaillard murdered?"

"In 1996."

The young man shrugged. "Well, there's your connection." Enzo frowned. "What do you mean?"

"The 1990 Dom Perignon wasn't released until 1996."

"How do you know that?"

"Before I went to CREPS, I trained as a wine waiter for a year."

"And that makes you an expert?"

"No. But I do know a bit about wine."

Enzo's frown deepened. "Next you'll be telling me the significance of Dom Perignon."

"In relation to the murder of Jacques Gaillard, no." Bertrand was standing his ground defiantly. "But I do know that he was born Pierre something, sometime in the mid-seventeenth century, and that he became a Benedictine monk before he was twenty. He was less

208

than thirty when he was appointed cellar master at the Abbey of Hautvillers. I know that some people have credited him with inventing champagne, but actually sparkling wine was being produced a century earlier by monks in the south of France. I also know he was supposed to have been blind, allegedly heightening his sense of taste. But that's another myth. The truth is, he was just a damned good winemaker. He introduced blending to the Champagne region, and was the first person to successfully contain local sparkling wine in reinforced glass bottles with Spanish corks."

Enzo looked at him in amazement. Sophie shuffled into the hall from the bedroom, the sheet wrapped around her. "I didn't know you knew all that stuff," she said.

"I can show you his tomb, if you want."

Enzo scowled. "How do you mean?"

"On the internet. There's a site where you can make a three hundred and sixty degrees tour of the church where he's buried."

Enzo had forgotten his anger. Through a fugg of drink and fatigue, a strange clarity was starting to emerge. "Okay, show me."

The three of them trundled through to the *séjour*, and Bertrand seated himself at the computer. "I can't remember the URL, but I'll find it." He made a quick search. "Here we are." He clicked on a link and up came a site about Dom Perignon, with another link that took them to a pop-up photograph of his tomb — an engraved black slab set in a stone-flagged floor. Beneath it were arrows pointing up and down, right and left. By pointing the mouse at the arrows it was possible to make the image move. Bertrand panned up from the tomb to an altar behind a black-painted rail, and three stained-glass windows beyond that. It was possible to pan all the way up to the roof. By pointing at the left arrow, he swung them along a wood-panelled wall down the side of the church to rows of benches leading to the back. A massive, old-fashioned chandelier hung from the beams overhead. Bertrand kept the cursor over the left arrow and they went through three hundred and sixty degrees, returning to the altar where they'd begun.

Enzo had never seen anything like it. Sunlight fell in through the stained glass and lay across the floor in geometric patterns. There was a sense of being there, of being able to look in any direction, to focus on anything you wanted. Enzo shook his head in awe. "That's extraordinary. How do they do that?"

"Six pictures taken with a very wide-angled lens, then somehow they get stitched together to give you the panorama," Bertrand said.

Sophie slipped her arm through her father's, and snuggled up close to him. "Am I forgiven, Papa?"

But Enzo was distracted. "No," he growled. And to Bertrand, "What church is this?"

"It's the abbey at Hautvillers, just outside Épernay in the Champagne region."

"Hautvillers." When Bertrand had spoken of the abbey a few minutes earlier, it had lodged somewhere in the back of Enzo's consciousness, ringing tiny alarm bells that he wasn't hearing until now — the second mention of it.

"It's the home of Moët et Chandon," Bertrand added.

But Enzo was remembering something else. "Here, let me in." He moved Bertrand out of the chair and sat himself in front of the computer. He pulled down the History menu and began searching back through all the sites Nicole had visited earlier, stopping only when he found the link that took him back to the page on Hugues de Champagne. All the time he kept hearing Nicole's voice. What a lot of Hugues there were in those days. He ran his eye down the page. "*Putain con!*"

"Papa, what's wrong?"

"Nothing." Enzo was grinning stupidly. "Nothing at all." He jumped up and clambered over piles of books to the whiteboard, and then he turned, marker pen in hand, for all the world as if he were lecturing a class at Paul Sabatier. "Hugues de Champagne went back to Palestine in the year 1114 in the company of eight other knights. One of them was his vassal, Hugues de Payens, who went on to become the first Grand Master of the Knights Templar. Another was Geoffrey de St. Omer. But here's the thing . . ." Sophie and Bertrand had no idea what he was talking about. "There was another Hugues. Hugues d'Hautvillers." His face was shining. "Don't you see?" But they didn't. He turned to the board and wrote up Hautvillers and drew a circle around it, and then arrows to it from almost everywhere else. "Everything leads to *Hautvillers*. The

211

champagne, Dom Perignon, the crucifix and St. Hugues, the lapel pin, and the Knights Templar. Everything." He frowned. "Except for the dog. But I'll work that out when I get there."

"Where?" Sophie asked. "When you get where?"

"Hautvillers," Enzo said triumphantly. "First thing in the morning."

CHAPTER
FOURTEEN

I

White dust rose from the wheels of a tractor like smoke. Everything was white. The dust, the soil. Even the sky was bleached white by the afternoon sun. The chalk gave the grapes their distinctive dry flavour, and turned the rivers and lakes a strange, milky green.

The rolling hills that folded one over the other looked as if they had been combed. Enzo had never seen such fastidiously pruned vines. There was something almost manic in their neatness, endless unwavering lines of green and white stretching away into a hazy distance.

Neither had he seen so many castles, as he drove through the tiny stone villages nestling in the folds and valleys of the Aube.

Épernay was surrounded by twenty thousand hectares of vineyards. It was a classic eighteenth-century French provincial town in the heart of champagne country, just a few miles south of the cathedral city of Reims. It was home to many of the most famous brands of champagne, household names in wealthy homes around the world. But, in Épernay, everyone drank champagne, from the street cleaner to the lord of the manor. It had been said that drinking

213

champagne in Épernay was like listening to Mozart in Salzburg.

Enzo had booked two rooms in the Hôtel de la Cloche in the Place Pierre Mendès-France. The last two rooms available. They had told him he was lucky to have got one room anywhere in town, never mind two. Raffin had called him on his mobile earlier in the afternoon to confirm that he would be arriving at seven forty-five that night on the train from Paris. Enzo arrived shortly after five, and passed the time with a glass of wine on the *terrasse* looking out over a square dominated by the municipal theatre and a host of restaurants serving it. Trees grew in a small park in the centre of the square, and fountains played in the early evening sunlight. The station stood at the end of a short boulevard on the far side of the *Place*. Enzo resisted the temptation to make the ten-minute drive out to the tiny village of Hautvillers. He had promised Raffin that they would go together in the morning. But the waiting was almost more than he could bear. One glass of wine became three, and he watched with impatience the slow progress of his watch towards eight.

At seven-thirty, he crossed the square and walked down to the station. Le Nivolet restaurant was doing brisk business. The station concourse was filled with people waiting for the Paris train. Enzo went out on to the platform, slipping between two Asian nuns in champagne white, to stand gazing out towards the distant vine-covered hills. There did not seem to be a single square metre that was not given over to the growing of grapes. He saw the tall figure of Raffin, a

214

head higher than most of the other passengers streaming on to the platform from the train. The collar of his neatly pressed white shirt was open at the neck and turned up, and his jacket was, as usual, slung carelessly across his shoulder. He carried a handmade leather overnight bag. No matter how hot it was Raffin always looked cool and unruffled, as if he had just stepped from the dressing room immediately after a shower. At his shoulder Enzo saw a flash of dark curls, and his stomach flipped over. Charlotte slipped out from Raffin's wake and smiled when she saw Enzo waiting, eyes flashing darkly, full of fun and mischief. She wore pale pink tennis shoes and white cotton calf-length trousers. A man-sized denim shirt hung loosely from her shoulders. She had a canvas bag slung over one of them. She and Raffin made a handsome couple.

Raffin shook his hand warmly. "You've been busy."

"I have," Enzo acknowledged with a grin.

"Hi," Charlotte said, and she reached up to kiss him on both cheeks.

He breathed in the familiar scent of her perfume and felt the first hint of desire stir in his loins. "What are *you* doing here?"

"There was no keeping her away," Raffin said. "When I told her where I was going she cancelled all her appointments for today and tomorrow."

She smiled up at Enzo. "I'm hooked. I want to know how the story ends."

Enzo laughed. "So do I. But there may be a problem."

"What's that?"

"There are no hotel rooms left in town, and I've only booked two."

Raffin said, "She can always share with me."

And Enzo felt a sudden, unpleasant jolt of jealousy. They had been an item until recently. It was not an unreasonable suggestion. But he was relieved when Charlotte said, with a slight tone, "I doubt if there'll be any need for that, Roger. There's almost always a bed available somewhere, if you ask nicely."

They ate on the *terrasse* at La Cloche, clouds of swallows dipping and diving across the square in the dying light, their chattering chorus taking over from the roar of traffic as the roads emptied and the restaurants filled. Charlotte pulled up a chair and joined them as the *entrées* were being served. She looked pleased with herself. "They gave me a single room up in the attic. It's kept for staff who have to stay over. I told you there's always a bed somewhere."

Raffin seemed disappointed. He turned to Enzo. "So tell us why we're here."

Over the meal, Enzo took them step by step through his deconstruction of the clues found with Gaillard's arms. "Everything leads to Hautvillers."

"Except for the dog clues," Charlotte corrected him.

"I have to figure that's something that's going to become apparent. Like the scallop shell in the garden in Toulouse. I had no idea what we were looking for until we got there."

They drank pink champagne with their meal and sat on the *terrasse* until almost midnight drinking

Armagnac. At a quarter to, Charlotte stood up suddenly and announced that she was going to bed. Enzo and Raffin stayed on for one more drink. Raffin seemed pensive, almost distant. Finally, he turned to Enzo and asked, "Is there something going on between you and Charlotte?"

Enzo was surprised by his directness and by the hint of jealousy that was apparent in his tone. He had thought the relationship was over. "I wish. She's a very attractive woman."

"She is," Raffin agreed. "But she's been on her own too long. Do you know what I mean? She's not easy to live with." And Enzo had the impression that without actually warning him off, Raffin was doing his best to put him off.

"I've been on my own for twenty years." Enzo grinned. "I'd probably be impossible to live with."

They climbed the stairs together and shook hands outside Raffin's door, and Enzo carried on along the hall to his own room. Light from the floodlit Église Saint Pierre-Saint Paul, on the other side of the street, fell unevenly across the room, following the ruffled contours of the bed. As he closed the door, he became aware of her perfume hanging in the still, warm air, and as his eyes adjusted to the light, he saw her dark curls fanned out across the pillow. His mouth was so dry he could hardly speak. He said, in a whisper, "I thought you had a room in the attic."

"I lied." He could hear her grin.

"How did you get into my room?"

"I told them I was with you and they gave me the key to bring my bag up. I left the door on the latch when I took the key back."

So she had been planning this from early evening. "That's pretty devious of you."

She sighed. "Are you coming to bed or not?"

He released his hair to tumble over his shoulders, and undressed in the light of the church. Butterflies hatched out and flew around inside him, before he slipped under the sheet and felt the warmth of her skin next to his. He turned his head and looked into her eyes, and her smile made him almost giddy. He could not remember wanting anyone so much in a very long time. She moved towards him and kissed him gently, and he felt her breath soft on his face and the sweet taste of champagne on her lips. This was nectar. He let himself go, drawn into all the folds and softnesses of her mouth and her body, his hardness pressing into her belly as she climbed on top of him and slid slowly down his chest and stomach with her lips and her tongue, until finally she found and swallowed him whole. He drew a sharp intake of breath and held on to each side of the headboard, hips lifting as she worked him into a state of complete helplessness. She was relentless and unforgiving, taking complete control and leaving him with none. Until years of frustration exploded inside, and she sucked him dry, leaving him limp and spent and regretting his selfishness.

"What about . . . ?"

"Shhhhh." She put a finger over his lips, and slid up to pepper his chest with kisses. "It's my gift to you."

But he didn't want it to be just about him. He wanted it to be about her, too. About them. He slipped out from beneath her and turned her over so that she was face up. She seemed so slight and fragile in his hands. He found her neck with his mouth and felt her shiver as he kissed her and dropped down to the rise of her full breasts. He heard her moan as he grazed her nipples with his lips and moved down again, across the soft swell of her belly. A fine fuzz of hair led down to a soft triangle of dark, damp growth, and he breathed in the musky smell of her sex. She gasped aloud as he found her with his tongue and worked it as relentlessly as she had hers with him. She arched and arched against him, until finally she shuddered and called out, and he felt both of her hands clutching his hair and holding him there between her legs.

Her pleasure had aroused him again and, before she had time to recover, he moved up to find her mouth with his and force her legs apart with his knees. Her fingers dug into his back, and then found his hair and pulled on it hard as he slipped inside her. Again she arched herself to meet his thrusting, frantic and fighting and pushing until they both arrived at a shuddering climax and collapsed, exhausted, and perspiring, and wrapped around each other in a tangle of sheets and pillow.

They lay for a long time, breathing hard, exchanging tiny kisses. There was nothing they could say that wouldn't be an anticlimax. And as he slipped away into a languid, dreamy sleep, Enzo briefly and belatedly wondered if Raffin might have heard them through the wall.

II

Hautvillers nestled in a cleft of the hillside, surrounded by trees and looking out across endless miles of vineyards. They passed the Moët et Chandon factory at the foot of the hill as they turned off the main road and drove through the early morning sunshine up towards the village.

Charlotte had been gone when Enzo wakened, leaving only her scent and the impression in the pillow where her head had lain. He found evidence in the bathroom that she had taken a shower before she left. He could not believe that he had slept through it. When he got downstairs, he found Raffin and Charlotte having breakfast. She greeted him with a subdued *bonjour* and a perfunctory kiss on each cheek. There was not the slightest hint of acknowledgement in her eyes of what had passed between them the previous night. Raffin offered him a cursory handshake, and was reserved all through the coffee and croissants. The three of them drove out to Hautvillers in silence.

The village was already filling with tourists, who were arriving by the coachload. Enzo found a parking place just off the Place de la République, and he and Raffin waited while Charlotte went into the tourist office. She emerged with a map and a handful of leaflets. Raffin

220

took the map and led them along the Rue Henri Martin in the direction of the abbey. As they walked, Charlotte flicked through her leaflets. "You know, this place is pretty old. The village was founded in the year 658. It's supposed to be the birthplace of champagne. It says here that the *méthode champenoise* was invented at the abbey of Hautvillers more than three hundred years ago by the Benedictine monk Dom Perignon."

"Actually," Enzo said, "they'd been making sparkling wine in the south of France for a hundred years before that."

Raffin glanced at him curiously. "How do you know that?"

Enzo raised his shoulders casually. "I have a friend who knows these things," he said, and felt a twinge of shame. The thought that he had been premature in his judgment of Bertrand had haunted him through all the long drive north.

"My God . . ." Charlotte still had her nose buried in the leaflets. "Did you know that all the major champagne houses have their *caves* down in Épernay? Well, actually, down below Épernay. According to this, over the last three hundred years, they've dug a hundred and twenty kilometres of tunnels out of the chalk under the town, and there's more than two hundred million bottles of champagne stored down there." She looked up, her eyes shining. "Two hundred million bottles!"

"That's a lot of bubbles," Enzo said.

Everywhere they looked there were makers and sellers of champagne. Gobillard, Tribaut, Locret-Lachaud, Lopez-Martin, Raoul Collet, Bliard-Moriset. At the Square Beaulieu, they turned into the Rue de l'Église, and climbed the hill, past the walled garden of the priest's house, to a mosaic path of polished and unpolished granite leading to the back of the nave. The side door of the abbey stood ajar beneath the steeply pitched roof of a stone porch. They had arrived at this holiest of shrines to the God of champagne before the tourists, and as they entered the dark cool of the church, they felt subsumed by its silence, compelled to take soft, careful steps, and to communicate by eye contact and the merest of whispers.

For Enzo, there was a powerful sense of *déja vu*. Sunlight fell through the three tall windows behind the altar just as it had on the website. The polished black slab inscribed to the memory of Dom Perignon lay side by side with the the tomb of Dom Jean Royer, the last *abbé régulier* of the monastery, who died in 1527, nearly two hundred years before Dom Perignon. Enzo ran his eyes along the wood panelling which lined each side of the front half of the nave. He supposed it might be possible to somehow hide a body, or parts of a body, behind it. But it would not have been an easy matter to remove and replace pieces of the panelling without leaving obvious traces.

"Look at this," Raffin whispered, and all three of them gathered around a carved and gilded casket which stood on a marble-topped table to one side of the altar. It held the remains of St. Nivard, the archbishop of

222

Reims who founded the abbey in the year 650. The bones of the archbishop were clearly visible through two oval portholes, tied together with ancient ribbon. His skull stared back at them from the shadows. "You don't think . . . ?"

Enzo shook his head. "There was still flesh on Gaillard's bones when they hid them. They would have been rather obvious behind glass. And I think someone might have noticed the smell."

Raffin wrinkled his nose in distaste and turned away. He looked along the length of the nave to the organ pipes rising to the ceiling at the far end. "Not easy to hide body bits anywhere in here," he said.

Enzo found himself in reluctant agreement. He was not sure what he had expected to find. He had been hoping that something obvious would suggest itself, just as the shell fountain had done in Toulouse. But the naked whitewashed walls, the stark wood panelling, the statues of saints, the paintings of biblical scenes, and the cold, stone floor did nothing to excite the imagination. He walked to the back of the church and inspected a marble memorial to the dead of two wars. Enzo gazed at the names of dead men and wondered if they had any relevance. But somehow he felt that the trail had just gone cold. He glanced back along the length of the church to the stone altar, with its pillars and cross and praying angels, and had no confidence that there was anything of relevance here.

Quite unexpectedly, the church was filled with the sudden, eerie sound of soprano voices echoing back from ancient stone walls. A stereo system on a timer, hidden speakers. The effect was almost chilling, and Enzo felt all the hair stand up on the back of his neck. He also felt depression descend on him like a cloud. He had raised his expectations to a level which made it hard, now, to accept failure. But he had no idea what he was looking for, or where to turn when he couldn't find it.

Charlotte was sitting among the pews, still going through her leaflets. She looked up and turned to see where Enzo was. Her voice rose boldly above those of the soprano choir. "One of the clues was a bottle of 1990 Dom Perignon, right?" Enzo nodded. "Well, suppose they didn't actually hide the body here, in Hautvillers, but in the *caves* of Moët et Chandon? Down below Épernay, where the 1990 vintage is stored."

Raffin turned towards Enzo. "That's possible, isn't it?"

Enzo was less certain. The clues had led to Hautvillers, not Épernay. But he had no alternative suggestion. He shrugged. "I suppose."

III

Brick tunnels with arched roofs led off into a fog of humid air clouding around electric lights. "The temperature in the *caves* remains constant all year round," the girl was saying. "Between ten and twelve degrees. Humidity is a constant seventy-five to eighty percent."

Enzo felt the chill seeping deep into his bones after the heat of the morning sun. Thousands upon thousands of dark green bottles, laid on their sides between rows of wooden slats, lined the walls as far as he could see. A-framed racks called *pupitres* held yet more bottles, at angles that kept them neck down.

"The bottles in the *pupitres* are turned just a little every day by expert *remueurs*," the guide said. "This is to encourage the remaining sediment to gather in the necks, which are then rapidly frozen. The sediment is trapped in the ice and, when the bottles are reopened, natural pressure expels the ice and the sediment with it, which is when the winemaker completes the process. A small quantity of *liqueur d'expédition*, composed of sugar and some wines from the company's reserves, is added before the bottles are finally corked and wired."

The official tour of the *caves* of Moët et Chandon had seemed like the easiest way to check out Charlotte's suggestion, and so they had joined a tour group of more than twenty, and followed a guide through the tunnels immediately below the company's headquarters in the Avenue de Champagne.

Enzo was learning things he had not known about champagne. That it was a blend of three grapes: Chardonnay, Pinot Noir and Pinot Meunier. That two of those grapes were red, and must be pressed very gently in order not to transfer colour from the skin to the juice. That the vines of Champagne were the most northerly in France, and were constantly pruned to ensure that the sun got to the grapes. That the chalk soil, which so characterised the bleached, white landscape, retained the warmth of the sun, as well as the rain, which it released gradually to regulate the growth of the vines.

They had stopped, now, in front of a deep recess set into the tunnel wall. Racks of champagne bottles disappeared into the shimmering darkness beyond. The girl continued with her mechanical commentary. "Notice the plaque, with its six digit code which identifies what year and brand of champagne is stored here. These are secret codes, known only to the cellar master. They are constantly changing as the champagnes move through the processes of *fermentation, remuage, dégorgement, dosage,* et cetera."

Enzo interrupted her. "So if you knew what these codes were, you would be able to identify where a champagne from any given year was stored?"

The guide seemed irritated by the interruption to her well-practised flow. "In theory. But as I just told you, the codes change as the wines move."

"Which they do all the time?" Charlotte asked.

"Space in the *caves* is at a premium," the girl said. "Bottles are moved on, and eventually out, displaced by each new harvest."

Raffin said, "So the Dom Perignon 1990, for example, wouldn't be stored in the same place as it was ten years ago?"

"Absolutely not. In fact, I'm not sure how many bottles of that particular vintage we have left. But even if I knew the cellar master's codes from ten years ago, I wouldn't know where to find the 1990 today."

They emerged, blinking, into the sunlight, the bubbles from the three free glasses of champagne they had received at the end of the tour still fizzing on their tongues. Charlotte spread her palms apologetically. "Sorry. It seemed like a good idea at the time." Body parts hidden behind or amongst bottles of the Dom Perignon 1990 would have been discovered years ago.

Fourteen grand villas, each one home to one of the prestigious *Maisons de Champagne*, marched up the hill to the top of the Avenue. Across the street, the *Hôtel de Ville* stood in its own park behind a high stone wall. They crossed the road and wandered into the park, uncertain of what to do next. None of them had voiced it, but it was clear that each of them was convinced their trip was turning out to be little more than a wild goose chase. Enzo gazed despondently across a small, blue lake surrounded by willows. He felt personally responsible for their failure. And yet, there was no doubt in his mind that the clues had led him irrevocably to Dom Perignon and Hautvillers. Raffin was idly skimming stones across the surface of the lake, and Charlotte had wandered up uneven steps to a pavilion whose roof was supported on a circle of pillars.

"We've got to go back," Enzo said.

Raffin turned to look at him. "Back where?"

"Hautvillers. We must have missed something."

"What?"

"Well, if I knew that, we wouldn't have missed it." Enzo was annoyed with himself for getting irritated.

But Raffin just shrugged. "If you like." He glanced at his watch. "But I'll have to be getting back to Paris soon."

Enzo looked up and saw Charlotte watching them from between the pillars. She inclined her head and offered him the palest of smiles. "Let's go."

They drove in silence once more over the huge expanse of rusting railway junctions on the outskirts of town, abandoned rolling stock mutilated by vandals and left to rot. The waters of the Marne, on the far side, were a soupy chemical green. In a matter of minutes they were out among the vines, hills rising around them, Hautvillers cradled amid the trees and basking in sunshine. It was hard, now, to get parked, and by the time they got back to the abbey it was filled with tourists wandering the aisles, cameras flashing in the gloom.

"I'm going to have a wander around the graveyard," Charlotte said, and she headed off through a small gate in the cemetrey wall.

Enzo and Raffin walked again through the abbey looking at the same things they had looked at two hours before. Nothing had changed. Nothing new struck them. Enzo pulled down a folding seat below the wood panelling and sat down, gazing despondently along the length of the nave. Raffin stopped in front of him and lowered his voice. "I don't like being lied to."

Enzo looked at him, startled. "What are you talking about?"

"You and Charlotte."

"For God's sake, man!" Enzo's raised voice turned heads in their direction. He lowered it again. "I thought it was over between you and Charlotte."

Raffin's jaw set. "It is."

"So what's the problem?"

"I asked you last night if there was anything going on between you —"

"And I told you there wasn't. Which was true. Then." Enzo looked away self-consciously. "Things change."

"Yes, so I heard."

Enzo wondered if he meant that Charlotte had told him. Or that he had heard them, after all, making love the night before. "Do you have a problem with that?"

Raffin looked at him hard for a very long time, and then let his eyes drift away towards the altar. "No," he said finally.

The church door creaked as it opened again and light flooded across the flags. Charlotte's voice cut through the hush. "Enzo . . ." They turned to see her framed in the doorway, and she waved an urgent hand towards them. "There's something you should see."

They left the church and followed her quick footsteps into the graveyard, and she took them along a narrow path between rows of tombs, to a vault like a miniature temple. It was weathered and streaked with black, and a sad bunch of wilting flowers was placed at its door. The earliest inscriptions had been eroded by time and were almost unreadable. But the most recent was sharp and clear. Dated October 1999, it was dedicated to the beloved memory of Hugues d'Hautvillers and his wife, Simone, who died together on October 26 that year in a car accident on the road between Épernay and Reims.

Enzo stared at it in disbelief. Hugues d'Hautvillers. So perhaps the clues had been leading, not to the place, but to the person.

"It's a very old family vault," Charlotte said. She knelt down to touch the dying flowers. "But there's still someone around who cares."

There was a bell push set in the wall beside the gate to the priest's house. A sign read: *Sonnez et entrez*. Enzo did as bid, and they heard a bell sounding some way off beyond the wall. He pushed one half of the white gate and it opened on to an overgrown path between two lawns, leading to a small house almost adjoining the front end of the nave. The door opened before they reached it, and the priest looked at them with mild irritation. "Can I help you?"

"I wonder what can you tell us about the d'Hautvillers family vault in the graveyard?" Enzo said.

The priest seemed surprised. Apparently it was not a question he was asked very often. "There's nothing to tell. It's the family vault of the d'Hautvillers. They've lived at Château Hautvillers for centuries."

"Hugues d'Hautvillers died in a car crash in 1999, is that right?"

"Yes."

"Did he have any heirs?"

"His son still lives at the *château*."

"What's *his* name?" Raffin asked.

230

"The eldest son of the family has been called Hugues since the days of the Knights Templar, and probably before."

"So there's an Hugues d'Hautvillers living at the château now?" Enzo said.

The priest was running out of patience. "I think that's what I just said."

"How do we get there?" Charlotte asked.

IV

Château Hautvillers was less than three kilometres away in the next valley, rebuilt in the seventeenth century from the remains of a mediaeval fortress. An odd hybrid of French country manor and fortified *château*, it stood foresquare at the end of a long drive flanked by lime trees, and was surrounded by a deep, wide moat. Well-kept parkland rose up behind it to the treeline, and a fountain sparkled and frothed in the centre of a cobbled courtyard in front of the house. Horses snorted and snuffled and stamped in stables along the west wing of the courtyard. A group of working farm buildings huddled along the east bank of the moat. As Enzo turned his car into the drive, they saw the blue-flashing lights of several police vehicles on the far side of the stone bridge. A white ambulance stood in the courtyard, backed up to the main entrance. Its rear doors were open. A group of people stood at the nearside of the bridge watching the proceedings in silence. Staff from the *château*, and farm workers, and

231

a couple of *gendarmes*. They all turned at the sound of the arriving vehicle.

Enzo swung his car off the drive just before the bridge and parked under the trees. One of the group detached himself and approached as they stepped out on to the grass. He was a man in his late sixties or early seventies, with silver hair short-cropped around a polished bald pate. He had the demeanour of a *maître d'hôtel*, and wore a dark suit with polished black shoes. "Can I help you?"

"What's going on?" Charlotte said.

"There's been a suicide, madame."

"Oh, my God. Who?"

"I'm afraid it was young Hugues d'Hautvillers."

"Suicide?" Enzo could hardly believe it.

"Yes, Monsieur. He hanged himself in the *grande salle*. Did you know him?"

Raffin said quickly, "We came from Paris to see him."

"Oh, I see. Were you friends? At ENA together, perhaps?"

"That's right."

Enzo marvelled at the way Raffin could lie so easily.

"Then, I'm terribly sorry to be the bearer of such bad news." The old man turned and glanced across the moat towards the *château*. "They're just removing the body. Perhaps if you'd care to wait fifteen minutes or so, I can speak to you, then."

"Of course," Raffin said.

"Why don't you take a walk in the grounds?" The old man nodded towards the gardens, evidently anxious not to swell the ranks of the *voyeurs*. He returned to the group, and Enzo, Raffin and Charlotte followed the moat to its south-west corner where a gate opened on to wooded parkland. A brown hen and a clutch of chicks went clucking away across the lawns ahead of them.

Raffin turned to Enzo. "Interesting that the man whose name is evoked by the items found in Toulouse should turn up dead just three days later."

"Do you think he had something to do with Jacques Gaillard's murder?" Charlotte asked.

Raffin raised an eyebrow. "Who knows? But if he had, then perhaps he knew that exposure was inevitable, and killed himself to avoid the consequences. What do you think, Macleod?"

But Enzo felt less than happy with the thought that his actions had caused a man to kill himself, even if he was a murderer. "I don't know." He half-hoped that Hugues d'Hautvillers had nothing to do with any of it, and that his death was just a strange, sad coincidence. He looked back along the moat towards the bridge with its stone balustrade and four arches rising out of the dark water, and saw that the ambulance was leaving. As it crossed the bridge the onlookers moved aside to let it past. Enzo was overtaken by an odd sense of despair. It seemed as if his investigation would end here, with the death of a man whose body was being taken away even as he watched. Literally, a dead end.

He stuck his hands in his pockets and walked off along the edge of the moat. The three metre drop was guarded by a low, mossy wall. Pointed turrets were built out into the water at each corner of the castle. There were arrow slits in the thick stone walls, from where defenders had once drawn bows to repel attackers. Away to his left, ancient trees grew among well-tended lawns, leading to woods beyond. A gardener with a wheelbarrow was tending flowers in a rockery, apparently unaffected by the activity at the château. A group of deckchairs sat around a wooden table, flapping gently in the hot breeze. Enzo reached the north-west corner of the moat, where the ground rose away steeply, and sat on the edge of a retaining wall. Unlike the patterned brick façade at the front of the château, the back of it was rendered in grey concrete, damp creeping up from still water, seeping into its very foundations.

As he looked back along the moat, Enzo saw Charlotte approaching. Raffin had remained by the gate, leaning on the wrought iron, watching the proceedings in the courtyard. Enzo looked up as Charlotte stopped in front of him, and had to shade his eyes from the midday sun. "Did *you* tell him about us?"

She said, "There is no *us*. I told you, I'm not ready for another relationship yet. We had sex, that's all."

Enzo was wounded by her words. It had felt like more than just sex to him. He took the shading hand from his forehead and leaned forward on his knees, staring at the grass. "Why's he so pissed off? It *is* over between you, isn't it?"

"Oh, yes." She hesitated. "But it wasn't his idea. He's having trouble letting go, that's all." She sighed, and sat on the wall beside him, and scuffed idly with her tennis

234

shoes at a slab of stone set in the grass. "I'm sorry, Enzo. It's just a little difficult right now." And she took his hand briefly in hers and gave it the smallest of squeezes.

They sat in silence then, and with the toe of her shoe she traced the outline of letters carved into the stone slab. He watched her, unseeing, distracted by all the emotional contradictions she had brought into his life. Until, quite unexpectedly, the letters she was following with her toe seemed to jump into sudden, clear focus, and he realised what those tiny movements had just spelled out. He grabbed her arm, fingers digging deep into the soft flesh above her elbow. She turned, alarmed, to see him staring fixedly at the ground in front of her. "What is it?"

"*Utopique.*" Even as he whispered the name he felt goose-bumps raise themselves across his back and shoulders.

"What are you talking about?"

He nodded towards the slab and moved her foot aside with his. He read, "*This stone was set in the ground in the year 1978, in loving memory of our faithful family retriever, Utopique, who died in the act of rescuing his beloved eight-year-old master, Hugues, on the occasion of his falling into the moat. Utopique jumped after him into the water, keeping him safe from drowning until he could be rescued. Sadly, Utopique was drowned before he, too, could be saved. We will be forever grateful for his sacrifice.*"

Enzo stared at the words he had just read aloud. Words that swam now in front of his eyes. Utopique

235

had been Hugues d'Hautvillers' dog! Finally, the dog tag and the shinbone made sense. "It's got to be under this stone." He stood up.

"What has?"

"The next piece of Jacques Gaillard. Probably another trunk. And probably more clues." He looked at Charlotte, eyes shining with renewed anticipation, and saw that she had turned pale.

"Right here? Beneath our feet?"

"It has to be." Enzo looked around wondering what he should do, and saw Raffin coming towards them. Beyond him, he saw the gardener wheeling his barrow down the hill. Enzo shouted and waved, and the gardener stopped and turned to look. Raffin glanced behind him at the gardener, and then again at Enzo.

"What's going on?"

Enzo said, "Read the stone slab." And he shouted again to the gardener and waved him over.

"Jesus!" Raffin looked up from the slab. "You think it's under here?"

"What do *you* think?"

"I think there's a damned good chance of it."

The gardener left his barrow and wandered across. He was a man in his sixties, weathered and worn by a life spent outdoors. He was wearing blue dungarees over a grubby white vest, his flat cap pushed back from a forehead beaded with sweat. He looked at them suspiciously, each in turn, then fixed Enzo with cloudy blue eyes. "Can I help you, monsieur?"

"We think there might be something buried under this stone." Even as the words left his mouth Enzo thought how ridiculous they sounded.

The gardener looked at the slab and shook his head slowly. "Nothing under it but earth, monsieur."

"How do you know?"

"Because I laid it there myself. Monsieur Hugues senior had it engraved and asked me to set it in the ground."

"But after that," Raffin said. "Someone could have lifted it and buried something underneath."

The gardener looked at them as if they were insane. "Why would anyone want to do that, monsieur?"

"It would be possible, though?" Enzo said.

The old man shrugged. "Of course. But I would have known about it."

"How?"

"Because I've spent my life here, monsieur. Every single day of it. I've kept these gardens for nearly forty years, just like my father before me. I know every blade of grass. You couldn't lift that slab and lay it down again without me knowing it."

Enzo didn't want to believe him. This had to be the place. "Do you remember young Hugues falling into the moat?"

"It was me that pulled him out."

"And Utopique?"

"Dead by the time I got to him."

"I suppose the dog is buried under the stone?" Raffin said.

"No, monsieur. The stone was just to commemorate the occasion and mark the spot. Utopique was buried in the same place the family have buried their dogs for centuries." He pointed towards the treeline. "Up there in the woods, with a view down to the *château*. There's dozens of them buried up there, each with its own headstone. A kind of dog cemetrey, you might say."

Enzo thought about the dog's shinbone found in Toulouse, and he and Raffin exchanged glances. An unspoken communion on a single, shared thought. "Can you show us?"

The old gardener sighed. "I suppose I could."

As they walked up the hill Charlotte said to him, "You know what's happened down at the *château?*"

"I do."

"Are you not concerned to see what's going on?"

"There's nothing about the family that concerns me, mademoiselle. I've never had any time for the aristocracy."

"They pay your wages," Raffin said.

"And I look after their estate. It doesn't mean I have to like them. I saved that young boy's life, but it pleased them better to credit the dog. And now he's killed himself. Good riddance, I say."

When they reached the treeline, the cut grass gave way to long, tangling undergrowth. Young saplings grew in all the open spaces, trying to reclaim the land taken from nature by man. The gardener led them through the trees to a clearing bounded by the remains of a dry stone wall and a tumbled-down gate. Ancient headstones poked up at odd angles through long, dry grass. There was a sad air of neglect about this hidden burial place.

"You don't look after the cemetrey, then?" Raffin said.

"I never come here. It's none of my concern."

"So somebody could have buried something up here and you wouldn't know."

"The only thing that gets buried up here are dead dogs, monsieur."

They found Utopique's grave at the far side of the plot. The headstone was marked simply, *Utopique 1971–78*. It seemed as undisturbed as all the other graves, but then it would after ten years. Raffin turned to the gardener. "We'll need a couple of shovels."

The old man looked at him distrustfully. "What for?"

Raffin opened his wallet and took out two fifty euro notes. He folded them and held them out to the gardener. "You never come up here. You don't need to know."

It took him ten minutes to return with two stout spades. A small enough request in return for a hundred euros. But he was determined to stay and watch, nonetheless. He might have no loyalty to the family, but his curiosity was aroused.

Enzo threw his jacket and satchel to one side and began digging like a man possessed. Raffin laid his jacket carefully on the remains of the wall, and neatly folded back the sleeves of his shirt. He set his feet carefully on the ground to try to avoid getting dirt on his shoes, and joined in. Within minutes both men were perspiring freely and, for all his precautions, Raffin's shoes were quickly covered with dry, chalky dust. His shirt, wet with sweat, was sticking to his back.

About a foot down they began uncovering bones. Not a skeleton, but individual bones, as if perhaps they had been dug up once before and tossed back in when the hole was refilled. They gathered them in a small pile on one side.

Charlotte leaned against the wall and watched them in silence, her dark eyes deeply brooding. Whatever was in her mind, she kept her own counsel, chewing anxiously on her lower lip as the hole got deeper.

Through the trees they could see blue lights flashing down at the *château*. Although the body had been removed nearly half an hour earlier, the *gendarmes* were still there. Taking statements, perhaps, awaiting officers from the *police scientifique* to confirm that it was, after all, just a suicide.

Enzo struck something solid. Metal on metal. Both men stopped digging, and Enzo told Raffin to step back. The journalist moved away from the open grave, his neatly coiffured hair falling across a face smeared now with dirt. The gardener stepped forward to take a closer look as Enzo began working more carefully to scrape the earth away from around the lid of a battered, military-green tin trunk. It was just like the others. When, finally, he had removed all the dirt from around the latches, he stepped out of the hole to take a pair of latex gloves from his satchel. He snapped them on and crouched over the trunk again. Carefully, he released the catches and opened the lid. Rusted hinges protested loudly. A fusty, damp smell rose to greet him, and he

240

recoiled with disgust. "Jesus . . ." The others crowded around to look. The skeletal remains of two legs were folded back at the knee and tied loosely together with plastic twine. The bones were yellow and stained, but undamaged, every tiny metatarsal in the feet preserved intact.

Enzo heard Charlotte gasp. And the gardener said, "What the hell is that?"

"It's a man's legs," Enzo said. But they were not alone in the trunk. As before, there were another five items. Without looking up he said to Raffin, "Get my digital camera out of my bag, Roger." The journalist retrieved the camera and handed it to Enzo. Enzo said, "We have to be very careful. Don't want anyone accusing us of contaminating the evidence."

One by one he lifted the items out to place, singly, on the lid of the trunk and photograph them. There was a brooch, in the shape of a salamander, studded with precious and semi-precious stones. A large gold pendant made in the image of a lion's head. A lapel pin flag with three vertical stripes of colour — green at the hoist side, yellow and red — a small, green, five-pointed star centred in the yellow band. A replica of a trophy, like a sports cup, with a lid and two large ear-shaped handles. It was engraved with the date 1996. The final item was what appeared to be a referee's whistle, attached to a neck cord. There were three faint numbers, divided by an oblique, scratched into the metal plating: 19/3.

Enzo replaced each item in the trunk where it had lain and looked up at the faces around him. "We're going to have to tell the *gendarmes.*"

241

V

The old retainer who had first greeted them on their arrival walked with them now from the house across the uneven cobbles of the courtyard. He seemed older than just three hours ago. As if one death hadn't been enough! He had served the family for more than forty years, he told them. He had known three generations of d'Hautvillers. And now they were gone. He had outlived them all, and it would fall to Hugues' first cousin to carry on the line.

"He was a very bright young man," he said of Hugues. "Too bright, really. They say the star that burns twice as bright burns half as long. But his light burned out when his parents died. He was an only child, you see. And his only *raison d'être* seemed to be gaining the approval of his parents. He did everything to please them. It broke his heart when they sent him to military *lycée* in La Flèche, the Prytanée National Militaire de la Flèche. He was a gifted child, and it was a gift that required nurture. I think he understood that to achieve his full potential he had to go to La Flèche. But it was probably reason enough that it pleased his parents. All the same, it distressed him to be away from them."

They crossed the bridge and turned west, past a couple of *gendarmes* and several unmarked police vehicles, and followed the moat along to the gate.

"Of course, you know that he had a brilliant career ahead of him in the Conseil d'État."

242

Enzo felt guilty that they had kept up the pretence of knowing the young Hugues.

"But when news reached him of the death of his parents in that dreadful car crash, he simply bought himself out and came back here to mourn. Seven years of solitude." The old man shook his head. "He was not interested in company, or in travelling. Occasional trips to Paris to deal with legal and financial affairs. But he spent most of his time locked away in the library reading. Endlessly reading. Or walking the estate. He would be gone for hours on cold winter days, striding over the hills. Didn't even keep a dog. Wouldn't have one after . . . well, you know. Said no dog could ever serve him so well as Utopique."

When they reached the gate, Enzo could see crime scene tape fluttering in the breeze up along the treeline, and a scribble of blue and pink where a group of *gendarmes* stood waiting. That was when they heard the first distant drone of the helicopter, thrumming rotors beating warm air as it dropped altitude over the vineyards at the end of its short flight from Paris.

The old man gazed up into the clear sky, searching for a first sight of it. When, finally, he saw it, he seemed disappointed and turned away. Enzo walked with him, and Raffin and Charlotte followed. He drifted along the edge of the moat, staring gloomily into its stillness. "You've no idea why he did it?" Enzo asked.

"Why he killed himself?" The old man shook his head. "None. If he'd been going to do something like that, I'd have thought it would have been after his parents died." He lifted his arms, then let them fall again to his sides, as if signalling the futility of ever trying to understand what moved men to do what they did.

"Had he been depressed recently?" Charlotte asked.

"He was a very melancholy young man. He was only thirty-six. But, of course, you know that. Hardly old enough to be carrying the weight of the world on his shoulders. But he always seemed to." The old family retainer stopped to remember, and Enzo reflected that he must have known Hugues from cradle to coffin. "Not depressed, as such," the old man said suddenly. He searched for the right word. "Agitated. Yes, I'd say he was agitated these last days. Spent more time in bed than usual. Wasn't eating properly. Drinking far too much. But, then, that had become something of a habit."

The distant beat of the helicopter had become a roar, and they turned to look as it swooped down, slowing abruptly and then settling itself gently on the grass. Its nearside door swung open and Juge Lelong climbed out, aided by a uniformed officer of the *Police Nationale*. A third, plainclothes officer, followed. The judge spotted Enzo. He ducked and hurried out from beneath the rotors, before straightening up and running a hand back through ruffled hair. His suit was creased from the flight, and he tried to tug a little style back into its skewed lines. He strode purposefully towards Enzo and the others, his minions trotting in his wake like well-trained dogs. Behind him, the helicopter pilot cut its motors and the blades slowed with a descending whine. Enzo knew that the judge was not going to be pleased with him.

Juge Lelong stopped in front of Enzo and lit a cigar, blowing smoke into the hot afternoon air. "You're a persistent man."

"So I've been told."

"You were *told*," said the judge, "to keep your sticky little fingers out of the honey pot. But you just couldn't resist, could you?"

"As far as I'm aware, we don't live in a police state. Yet."

The judge delivered a long look of withering contempt. "You're an amateur, Macleod. And I think the *Garde des Sceaux* made it perfectly clear that you were to leave matters to the professionals."

"If we were to wait for the professionals to get a result, we'd all be picking up our pensions," Raffin said.

Juge Lelong swung his head slowly to encompass Raffin within his glare. "And who are you?"

"Roger Raffin." Raffin smiled affably and held out his hand.

If Lelong saw it, he chose to ignore it. "Ah, *yes*. The journalist." He spat out the word *journalist* as if it had a bitter taste.

"That's right. I'm following Enzo Macleod's investigation. He's just uncovered what are certainly more of Jacques Gaillard's remains. And when the story appears in *Libération* tomorrow, I think it's you people who are going to look like the amateurs." He pulled a small notebook from his pocket and drew a pen from its spine. "Any comment?"

Juge Lelong's comment was contained within the look he drew the journalist. And if his look had been words, they would have been unprintable.

CHAPTER
FIFTEEN

I

The Rue des Tanneries, in the thirteenth *arrondissement*, was in the heart of what had once been the poorest *quartier* of Paris. The tanneries, which crowded the narrow streets and filled the air with noxious odours, washed their leather in the river Bièvre, polluting the water that powered the mills along its banks. And when Jean Gobelin opened his tapestry factory in the fifteenth century, his new techniques with scarlet dyes turned the river blood-red. It was here, in the offices and warehouse of a former coal merchant, that Charlotte had chosen to establish her home and consulting rooms.

"I'm told," she said, "that in the old days, on a moonlit midsummer's night, the streets looked as if they were covered in snow. Everything was layered with a fine, white dust from the treatment of the leather. I guess people must have breathed that stuff in every day. No wonder life expectancy was low."

Enzo looked from the open kitchen window down into the street below. Most of the buildings were commercial, occupied by offices and wholesale suppliers. The ground-floor windows of Charlotte's place were barred, the door grilled and padlocked. A heavy, retracting metal door guarded the entrance to the ground-floor storage area of the old warehouse.

Enzo turned to watch her preparing food on the worktop. It was a bright, modern kitchen with a large, blue-painted table at the window. "What on earth made you set up base here?"

She smiled. "So I wouldn't bump into any of my clients in the street when I go out shopping." She returned to the chopping of vegetables. "I've made a few changes to the place. Why don't you take a look around?"

They had come in through a waiting room downstairs, and climbed up a narrow staircase to the first-floor living area. Another three steps led up from the kitchen to a huge, sprawling *séjour* beyond a sliding Japanese screen door. Venetian blinds diffused the light from windows which ran along the front wall from floor to ceiling. A superstructure of metal cross-supports held up a steeply pitched roof. Brick walls were painted white. A bank of computer screens and monitors flickered on a long table pushed up against the windows. Beyond them, two low settees defined a living space subdivided by shelves lined with files and books.

Raffin sat at one of the computers, searching the internet for background information on Hugues d'Hautvillers. They had driven back to Paris in the early evening, and Raffin had directed Enzo to his parking place in an underground car park in the basement of an apartment building in the Rue St. Jacques, near the Luxembourg Gardens. His own car was in for repair. They had taken the métro, then, to Glacière — one stop from Corvisart, and two from Place d'Italie, names that seemed to be haunting Enzo — and walked to the Rue des Tanneries.

Enzo went down another three steps leading to a metal gallery overlooking the old warehouse storage area. Large interior windows opening into a bedroom immediately opposite made Enzo feel like a voyeur. He could see pale lilac sheets thrown back from a large bed, discarded clothes draped over a chair. He assumed it was Charlotte's bedroom.

Late evening sunshine streamed in through a pitched glass roof above a second gallery and, when Enzo looked down into the well of the space below, he saw that it had been transformed into an indoor garden, filled with potted plants and gravelled walkways. The constant tumbling of a small fountain filled the whole space with its gentle cadence. Upholstered garden furniture sat around a low, teak table at the centre of the garden. It was an extraordinary oasis in the heart of the city.

"It's where I interview my clients." Charlotte's voice startled him, and he turned to find her at his side. She leaned on the rail. "Good *feng shui*. It relaxes them. It relaxes me. It's almost a therapy in itself." She pointed out video cameras mounted on metal struts that criss-crossed the space overhead. "I quite often record my sessions so that I can replay them later." She nodded towards monitors next to where Raffin was still working at the computer. "It means I never have to take notes." She paused. "Where are you staying tonight? At the studio?"

"Probably."

She lowered her voice a little. "I have a spare room here." And Enzo thought that no matter how much he was attracted to Charlotte, he hated this subterfuge.

"You'd better come and have a look at this," Raffin called over his shoulder, almost as if he had heard her, and they went back up to the *séjour*. Enzo drew a chair in beside him. "Most of the stuff about d'Hautvillers is pretty well buried. Unlike Utopique. But I'm beginning to get a picture of him." He rubbed his hands enthusiastically, and started pulling up sites he had already visited. "We knew from the old servant at the *château* that he went to the Prytanée National Militaire de la Flèche. Apparently this was to prepare him for the competitive exam you have to sit to gain entry to the École Polytechnique." He glanced at Enzo, and must have realised that an explanation was required for the dumb foreigner. "That's the *grande école* that trains the top engineers required for public administration. Seems he came out top of his year at the *lycée* and won the *Concours Général* for maths."

He pulled up another site. "Of course, he had no difficulty getting into the Polytechnique. He went on to become one of the top students of his year, and was selected on graduation for the Corps des Mines, which is pretty much the *crème de la crème* of the engineering *cadre*."

He ran his finger down the screen until he found what he was looking for. "But he turned that down to follow in the footsteps of a pretty famous predecessor, Valéry Giscard d'Estaing. Apparently if you're smart

250

enough to be offered a place in the Corps des Mines, you're smart enough to gain direct access to ENA. Which is what he did." He turned eyes filled with light towards Enzo and Charlotte.

"Now, here's the thing. Each period of study at ENA is called a *promotion*. Each *promotion* is given a name by its students, who choose it during a two-week bonding holiday in the Vosges. In d'Hautviller's case, his *promotion* was named after Victor Schoelcher, who was a nineteenth-century campaigner against slavery and colonial injustice. The Schoelcher Promotion ran from 1994 to 1996 — the same period that Gaillard was teaching at ENA." He beamed triumphantly. "So Hugues d'Hautvillers must have been one of his pupils."

Enzo drew a long, steady breath. A direct connection between Hugues d'Hautvillers and Gaillard. Did that mean that d'Hautvillers was one of his killers? Enzo was reluctant to make that leap. But it was, at least, a starting point in the search for a motive.

"Wait a minute." Charlotte sat down on the edge of the table and looked at Enzo. "The name of Hugues d'Hautvillers came out of the process of decoding the clues you found in Toulouse, didn't it?"

"That's right."

"So wasn't there a name associated with the first set of clues? The ones found at Place d'Italie?"

"Philippe Roques," Enzo said. "But that was just a clue to lead us to the Hospital St. Jacques."

"Are you sure about that? The Hugues d'Hautvillers that you originally unearthed was one of the founders of the Knights Templar, wasn't he? Not the Hugues d'Hautvillers who went to ENA."

The implications of what she was saying started to dawn on Enzo.

"She's right," Raffin said. "Maybe the clues don't just lead us to the next body part, but also to one of the killers." He typed *Philippe Roques* into his search engine and hit the return key. "Let's see what comes up."

There were nearly five hundred links to sites with references to the name of Philippe Roques.

"*Merde!*" Raffin began scrolling through them. There was a financial expert, a professor of film studies in New York, an expert on downloading music from the internet. There was the Philippe Roques they already knew about, recipient of the *Ordre de la Libération*, and a Philippe Roques who was head of the Inspection Générale de l'Administration at the Ministry of the Interior. Raffin's cursor hovered momentarily over the last name, and he tilted his head slightly, staring off into the middle distance. Then he clicked on the name, and up came a biography. Raffin scanned it quickly, and then slapped the palm of his hand down on the table. "I knew it!" And he read, "Philippe Roques, fifty-two, rose through the ranks of the IGA before taking advantage, in 1994, of one of several internal promotion opportunities offered each year by the École National d'Administration." He turned shining eyes on his ex-lover. "Spot on, Charlotte. Roques was at ENA at the same time as d'Hautvillers. Part of the Schoelcher Promotion. Another one of Gaillard's pupils."

★ ★ ★

They ate in silence in the kitchen, each nurturing his or her own private thoughts. Charlotte had prepared a smoked salmon salad, and they washed it down with a cool, crisp Chablis. A beige, short-haired cat with a huge head and enormous green eyes watched them enviously from the window sill. It looked like an alien, or something recovered by archaeologists from a Pharaoh's tomb. Charlotte called it Zeke, and when she let it, it would leap on to her shoulders and drape itself around her neck. It was Charlotte who finally broke the silence. "So how many killers do you think there are?"

"Probably as many as there are body parts," Enzo said.

"And how many body parts?"

"Well, we've already found the head, the arms, and the legs. You have to figure there's not a whole lot more of him left."

Talk of body parts was not putting Raffin off his salad. "This is very good." He pushed a final forkful of smoked salmon and Roquefort into his mouth. Then he mopped up the remaining dressing with his bread, cleansed his palate with the last of his Chablis, and wiped his lips with his napkin. "I've got to make a few phone calls." He pointed up the stairs towards the workstation. "Is it okay?"

"Sure," Charlotte said.

Enzo was still lost in thought. "I don't understand it. Why? I mean, who did they leave these clues for? And why are they giving themselves away, one by one? What kind of game were they playing?"

"Well, maybe that's exactly what it was," Charlotte said. "Some kind of a game. But maybe they thought they would be the only ones ever to play it."

Enzo looked at her. "You've studied the psychology of crime. What is it that makes people kill?"

Charlotte shook her head. "Like this? I have no idea. There are various theories about what makes people commit crime. There are the so-called social causes — environment, peer pressure. There are situational causes. A set of stressful circumstances perhaps. People crack under stress. Then there are those who commit crime impulsively, usually sexual crimes. Or compulsively, as part of a character disorder or fantasy obsession." She sipped at her wine. "They are all fairly predictable. My favourite, though, is Fredric Wertham's theory of catathymic behaviour."

"What's that?"

"Wertham describes catathymia as the urge to carry an idea through to a violent act. The person imbues the violence with symbolic meaning, and his thinking acquires a delusional quality, which is often marked by rigidity and incoherence. Some situation then arises, creating extreme emotional tension, and leads to the crisis of violence. When it's over, the person returns to a superficial normality, and the tension appears to have been expunged."

"Do you think that catathymia could have played some part in Gaillard's murder?"

Charlotte smiled. "Well, we all get stressed when we're sitting exams. But we don't usually kill our teachers. And it would be hard to imagine a group of people all becoming catathymic at the same time."

Raffin appeared in the doorway at the top of the steps and waved a piece of paper at them. "I've got an address for Philippe Roques. Why don't we go and ask him?"

II

It was nearly ten-thirty by the time their taxi dropped them outside Roques' apartment. The last light of the day was almost washed from the sky, and even through the light pollution of the city it was possible to see the first faint stars putting in their nightly appearance. The apartment was on the third floor of an upmarket block on the Boulevard Suchet, on the edge of the Bois de Boulogne, not far from the Hippodrome. Charlotte had decided not to come with them.

At a tall gate, Raffin rang the bell for the *concierge* and, after a few minutes, an elderly lady peered at them suspiciously through the wrought iron.

"Sorry to trouble you, madame," Raffin said, turning on the charm. He held up his Press pass. "My name's Raffin. I'm with the Press corps at Matignon. We're here for a briefing with Monsieur Roques. He *is* expecting me, but I'm afraid I've mislaid my entry code."

She raised a sceptical eyebrow and it was clear that she did not believe him. But, still, she sighed and opened the gate. "Always the same," she said. "Young men, old men . . ." She glanced at Enzo. "All with their stories. You people must think I came up the Seine in a bubble."

Enzo and Raffin exchanged puzzled glances. What on earth was she talking about?

"Follow me," she said, and they did as they were told. She took them through a brightly lit passageway to a wide, paved courtyard ringed by extravagant gardens. Her apartment was on the ground floor adjoining a marble lobby with an lift and a carpeted staircase. "Wait here. I'll call him." She went into her apartment and left the door open.

"What are we going to tell her when Roques says he doesn't know us?" Enzo whispered.

But Raffin was unfazed. "I'll think of something."

They waited a long time before the *concierge* returned, scepticism replaced by consternation. "I don't understand it. I saw him coming in. And I know he hasn't gone out."

"There's no reply?" Raffin asked. She shook her head. "Then he must have slipped out when you weren't looking."

"No." She waggled a finger emphatically. "If he had gone out again, I'd have seen him." She nodded towards a barred window giving on to a small sitting room. A television screen flickered blue in the dark. "I always hear the lift. Besides, young Luc hasn't been out all day." She was clearly at a loss for what to do, and more than a little apprehensive. "Will you come up with me?"

"Of course, madame."

256

The three of them took the lift to the third floor and stepped out on to a thick-piled carpet. The walls of the landing were painted a rich cream above polished mahogany panelling. There were doors to two apartments set into opposite angles of the hallway. Roques' nameplate was on the left-hand door.

The *concierge* went to ring the doorbell and stopped suddenly, recoiling as if from an electric shock. "It's open," she said. And Enzo moved forward to see that the door stood very slightly ajar, as if someone had left in too much of a hurry to close it properly. He pushed it wide. The apartment beyond lay in darkness.

"Hello?" he called into the void; it seemed to swallow up his voice, and gave nothing back in return. "Hello!" he called again, only louder. Still nothing. But now he caught a scent that seemed vaguely familiar. A perfume, or an aftershave. For some reason it spooked him, and he began to feel decidedly uneasy.

"There must be a light," Raffin said, and Enzo leaned in to feel for a light switch on the wall. He found it and flicked it down. Nothing happened.

"The *disjoncteur* must have blown," the *concierge* said. "I'll go and get my flashlight. Wait here." And she seemed relieved to have found an excuse to leave.

They stood on the landing listening to the whine of the lift as it descended to the ground floor. And then an unnerving silence. Enzo and Raffin exchanged uneasy glances. Finally, Enzo said, "I'm going in."

Raffin nodded bravely. "I'm right behind you."

The hall was long and narrow, and went beyond the reach of the light from the landing. There were doors

257

off to left and right. Enzo stepped forward cautiously, pushing open a door on his right-hand side. A glimmer of light sloped in through a window and lay across the cool tiles of a bathroom floor. Further on, a door to the left opened into a bedroom. There was more light here, from the street lamps in the boulevard. The bed was unmade, and there were clothes strewn across the floor. A stale smell of socks and bodies. Enzo could hear the murmur of distant traffic.

Raffin followed behind him like a ghost as he moved down the hall to the next door. On the right this time. Another bedroom. Less light. The bed was made, pillows leaning decoratively against the headboard. There was an odd, unlived-in feel about the room. A guest bedroom, perhaps.

At the end of the corridor, the hall divided into passageways leading off at right angles, and they found themselves facing tall double doors to what Enzo assumed must be the *séjour*. One of the doors was off the latch, and a faint crack of light drew an angled line across the floor of the hall and up the wall opposite. As Enzo gently pushed it open, the crack widened. Through it, he could see windows overlooking the street whose lamps were the source of the light. Otherwise, the room seemed mired in deep shadow. The scent which Enzo had first noticed on the landing was stronger here. And, oddly, even more familiar.

Behind them they heard the drone and clatter of the lift as the *concierge* returned with her flashlight. Emboldened, Enzo opened the door wide. Now the scent of perfume gave way to something else. Again, strangely familiar. But unpleasant, like singed flesh and hot metal. The warm air was thick with it. Enzo scanned the room, eyes adjusting to the dark, and stepped in as he heard the *concierge* at the far end of the hall.

But suddenly the floor beneath his feet turned soft, and he felt his ankle turn, and he tipped forward losing all spacial awareness as the window flew up through his line of vision towards the ceiling, canted at a peculiar angle, and he hit the floor with a force that took his breath away. Almost at the same moment, the world flooded with a light that burned and dazzled, and he found himself looking into half a face. A single, staring eye. A mouth that gaped in a grotesque smile, revealing bloodied teeth and jawbone, and disappearing into deep, black red. Enzo opened his own mouth to scream, but all he could hear was the screaming of the *concierge*.

He spun on to his back, feeling the blood sticky on his hands and soaking into his shirt, and as he heaved himself on to one elbow, he saw a young man sitting in a chair, arms hanging at his sides. His head was tipped backwards at an impossible angle, and most of the back of it was splashed across the wall behind him. Bits of brain and bone and hair. A gun lay on the floor beside the chair, immediately below one hanging hand.

The *concierge* was still screaming, standing in the doorway, both hands clutching at her face. Raffin stood a little way in front of her, and his face was as white as Champagne chalk.

III

Enzo heard the high-pitched whine of a flash recharging after each photograph, and then the splat sound it made with the next shot. There was a low murmur of voices, and footsteps moving around. Something fell to the floor, and a voice raised itself above the others with a curse.

Raffin was pacing by the window, speaking rapidly into his mobile. He had made several calls in the space of a few minutes, but Enzo was paying him very little attention. He was still in shock. The blood had dried, turning rust-brown and crusting on his hands. Like Lady Macbeth, all he wanted to do was wash them. His shirt was stiff where the blood had dried on it and, despite the warmth of the Paris night, Enzo found himself shivering. He wanted out of these clothes, he wanted to stand under a hot shower and wash away the blood and the memory at the same time.

Both men in the next room were dead. That much was certain. And one of them was Roques.

Enzo and Raffin had been made to wait in the guest bedroom when the first officers of the *Brigade Criminelle* arrived. No one had talked to them. No one had asked them anything. But they had heard the shrill, near-hysterical voice of the *concierge* in another room describing everything that had happened from the moment they had shown up at the gate.

The door opened, and the plainclothes officer who had arrived at Château Hautvillers in the helicopter with Juge Lelong stood looking at them thoughtfully.

"Who gave you permission to make phone calls?" he said sharply to Raffin.

Raffin hung up and slipped the phone into his pocket. "I don't need your permission."

"Wrong." The officer closed the door behind him. "From now on you don't breathe without my permission."

Raffin stood his ground. "I don't think you have the right to withhold my air. Are we under arrest?"

"That could be arranged. For the moment you're helping us with our enquiries into two suspicious deaths."

"Murders," Raffin corrected him.

"That might be one interpretation."

"And what's the other?" Enzo asked.

"A lover's tiff. Luc Vidal had been living here with Roques for nearly nine months. They had a furious row. Vidal shot Roques in the face and then in a fit of remorse sat down, put the gun in his mouth, and blew the back of his head off."

"Obviously, that's what you're supposed to think," Raffin said.

"I don't think anything." The detective slipped his hands into his pockets and leaned against the wall. "I'll wait for the autopsy reports, and the results from the *police scientifique* before I come to any conclusions. Meanwhile, I would like you to tell me what you were doing here." He waited for a response, and when none was forthcoming, he said, "Monsieur Roques was a well-known homosexual. Apparently he and his boyfriend had frequent gentlemen callers."

Enzo had no appetite for playing games. "I think you know perfectly well why we were here. The names of Philippe Roques and Hugues d'Hautvillers both arose from the clues found with Jacques Gaillard's body parts."

"Only, we seem to have figured that out ahead of you," Raffin said. "As usual."

"Okay." The detective pushed himself off the wall and held out a hand towards Raffin. "I'll take your mobile now."

"What for?"

"I think Juge Lelong made it perfectly clear to both of you this afternoon that he would take a dim view of any further interference in this case. I'm pretty sure we can bring charges of obstruction, and withholding evidence in a criminal investigation." He opened the door and shouted down the hall. A uniformed officer appeared. The detective said to him. "Take these gentlemen down to the Quai des Orfevres." And he turned to Enzo and Raffin. "Accommodation for the night courtesy of the *République*." He held out his hand towards Raffin again. "Your phone, please, monsieur."

IV

The police cells at *La Crime* were on the second top floor at No. 36 Quai des Orfevres, immediately below the cells kept by the Brigade des Stup — the drug squad. They were blind cells, without windows. One entire wall was made of reinforced Plexiglas. From the darkness of an observation room on the other side, a prisoner could be kept under constant surveillance.

Enzo and Raffin were put in separate cells. In the police van Raffin had told Enzo, "They can only keep us *en garde à vue* for twenty-four hours." Then he had hesitated. "Unless, of course, Juge Lelong decides to sign an extension." He looked apologetically at Enzo. "In which case they could hold us for forty-eight."

Almost two of those hours had already passed. Crawling by in a glare of fluorescent light. Even if he had felt like it, Enzo knew that sleep would have been impossible. Once or twice, shadows had moved around beyond the Plexiglas, but he had been unable to see who had come to take a look at him. He sat on the edge of a hard bunk bed, leaning forward, elbows on his knees. They had taken his belt and his shoes, but left him his bloodied shirt. He had pulled it off and thrown it across the cell, to where it still lay on the floor, and they had let him rinse the blood from his hands and arms. Bare-chested, and in his socks, he felt very vulnerable.

He was still suffering from the shock of finding Roques with half his face missing. Two deaths in a single day. Two names that he had unearthed from the clues left by Gaillard's killers, and both men were dead. He felt responsible. He felt sick. His reflection in the Plexiglas looked haunted, like a vision of his own ghost staring back at him from the shadows.

The cell door opened and he thought for a moment that he was hallucinating. A woman in full evening

263

dress stood framed in the doorway. Cream silk, cut straight across the chest to off-the-shoulder sleeves. The contrast with the black hair that tumbled over her shoulders and the black opal which hung on a fine chain around her neck was startling. She looked stunning. Red-painted full lips pursed in a thoughtful pout, a frown gathering between her eyes. "You know, I was having a good time tonight, until you spoiled things." She let her eyes wander over the silvered black hair that curled across his naked chest. "They pulled me out of the party just after midnight."

"Sorry about that." Enzo had difficulty keeping the sarcasm out of his voice.

She turned and nodded to a uniformed officer lurking in the shadows, and stepped into the cell. The door closed behind her.

Enzo stood up. "Is it usual for prisoners to receive personal visits from the *Garde des Sceaux?*"

"An old French custom. From the days when the *guillotine* was still in use."

"I hope you're not going to cut my head off."

"I feel like knocking it off," she said with feeling. "Good God, Macleod, you're a stubborn Scottish bastard."

"It's a national character trait. We don't like being told what to do. The English have been trying for centuries."

She canted her head to one side and looked at him with something like laughter in her eyes. "What *are* we going to do with you?"

"Well, you could tell them to let me go, for a start."

"Actually, that's just what I was planning."

"Oh, really?"

"But I would like something in return."

"I've never been one to turn a lady down."

A smile flickered across her face, then faded. "I'm sure your experiences today with suicides and murders cannot have been very pleasant for you. More than enough, I would have thought, to convince you of the folly of your ways. But if not, I'd like your word that this business will stop. Right here. Right now."

"Or?"

"Or . . ." She looked at her watch. "You can spend another forty-five hours or so kicking your heels in here." The good humour slipped from her face like a mask. "And believe me, Monsieur Macleod, there are many other ways in which I can make your life more than difficult. When I tell someone to do something I expect it to be done. I have set up an official inquiry into the Gaillard case, and I would like it to proceed without further interference from you. The daily revelations in Raffin's left-wing rag are both a hindrance to the police investigation and an embarrassment to me. And I want them to stop. Is that clear?"

The cell door opened, and Marie Aucoin swung towards it in a sudden fury. Her voice was tense with anger. "I thought I told you I wasn't to be interrupted!"

Raffin stood in the doorway, his jacket draped over his shoulders, smoking a cigarette. He smiled and said languidly, "Sorry. Must have missed that." And to Enzo, "Come on, Macleod, time to go home."

"What are you talking about?" The Minister's face had coloured with anger and humiliation.

"The lawyers my 'left-wing rag' sent down seem to have convinced Juge Lelong that he has no grounds whatsoever for detaining us. And that the consequences of ignoring their advice on the legality of our detention would be both grave, and very public." He slipped the jacket from his shoulders and tossed it to Enzo. "For God's sake cover yourself up, man. You'll be arrested for indecent exposure."

Enzo slipped into Raffin's jacket and nodded to the *Garde des Sceaux*. "You and the good judge should make sure you're singing from the same hymn sheet next time. *Bonne soirée*, madame."

CHAPTER
SIXTEEN

I

At the foot of the stairs, Enzo and Raffin stepped out into an inner courtyard. Lights from windows lay in geometric patterns across its cobbles. A police car stood idling, its diesel purr reverberating around the cloistered inner sanctum of the *Brigade Criminelle*, just one part of this sprawling complex on the Île de la Cité which made up the Palais de Justice. They followed their shadows down a long passageway, footsteps echoing back from scarred walls. Ahead of them, one half of the huge wooden gates stood open. And beyond it they could see across the Seine to the lights of the Left Bank. They passed through it into the Parisian night with an enormous sense of relief. A black, uniformed policewoman watched them without curiosity.

The street was jammed with police vehicles, marked and unmarked. Enzo glanced up towards the second top floor and wondered where exactly it was he'd spent the last few hours.

"Hey!" They turned at the sound of Charlotte's voice, and she came running along the riverside pavement to meet them, soft curls streaming out behind her. She stopped and looked at them breathlessly. "I couldn't get parked any closer. My car's on the other side of the river."

"Was it you who phoned *Libé?*" Raffin asked.

She nodded. "After you called I kept phoning the desk at *La Crime* asking what had happened to you. Eventually I think the duty officer got fed up with me and told me you were being held for questioning. The only thing I could think of was to phone the paper."

"Good girl." Raffin embraced her and kissed her on the cheek. She responded and hugged him back. Enzo watched awkwardly, and was annoyed by the tiny worm of jealousy he felt stirring inside. They broke apart and Raffin said, "I've got to go to the office and update my story. Two dead now. Three if you include Gaillard."

"Four, if you include the boyfriend," Enzo said.

"Was Roques really murdered?" Charlotte asked.

"He was murdered all right," Raffin told her. "If not by his lover, then by someone else." He looked at Enzo. "Makes you wonder about Hugues. Either someone is prepared to kill again and again to cover up the original murder. Or fate has conspired to take three lives by pure coincidence."

"I don't believe in fate or coincidence," Enzo said.

"No, neither do I." Raffin tugged at Enzo's lapels to straighten his ill-fitting jacket, and he looked at it ruefully. "I'll get the jacket another time." And he kissed Charlotte on the cheek again. "Catch you later." He went running off towards the Pont St. Michel,

268

waving and shouting at a taxi which had appeared from the Boulevard du Palais.

Charlotte and Enzo stood looking at each other. "You're a little underdressed," she said.

But Enzo couldn't even bring himself to smile. "Jesus, Charlotte, this is getting scary." And he took her in his arms, and held her for a very long time. She moulded herself into all his contours and held him just as tightly, and he felt a huge rush of fatigue and relief and affection.

"Come on," she said finally, dark eyes looking intensely into his. "Let's get you home."

As they walked along the quay, past the Préfecture de Police, and towards the floodlit Notre Dame, she slipped her hand into his, and he squeezed it, grateful for the comfort. They crossed the Pont St. Michel and turned down past the oldest tree in Paris, a grizzled acacia which stood at the centre of a garden brooding darkly behind spiked railings. Charlotte's car was parked beyond the Église St. Julien-le-Pauvre. A down-and-out slept opposite the church in the doorway of a tea shop.

At her car, Charlotte turned and reached up to hold Enzo's face in both her hands. She gazed at him for a moment, a fleeting infusion of mixed emotions, then reached up on tiptoe to kiss him softly on the lips. He was caught off-guard by her sudden tenderness. "I'm sorry," she said.

"What for?"

She shook her head, smiling sadly. "Just . . . everything."

Hot water beat down on his head and shoulders, streaming over his chest, and hanging in droplets from a million hairs. He wanted to stand there forever, just letting it wash over him, taking with it the taint of a dead man's blood, the awful image of his gaping, lifeless face. The shower door opened and Charlotte stood naked before him, a slight, quizzical smile on her lips. She stepped up to share his water, and her dark curls unfurled into long, black ribbons over her shoulders. She stared at him through the steam. "I love your eyes," she said. And she touched his face and pushed his wet hair back behind his ears. Then she dropped both hands to find and hold the softness of his penis, and he immediately felt the blood rushing to it. Her breasts pressed against his belly and, as his passion flowered, she slid her hands behind him to hold his buttocks and pull him towards her. She turned her head to one side and pushed her face into his chest.

They stood like that for a long time, under the running water, before stepping out to towel each other dry, skin glowing pink, wet hair hanging in damp ropes. She peppered him with kisses, and ran her fingers gently through the wiry hair on his chest, then took his hand and led him back through to the bedroom. Beyond the walls of glass which looked down on the garden courtyard below, the dark seemed very intense. Enzo felt strangely exposed. Anyone out there on the gallery opposite could see right in, just as he had the previous evening. Now he was lying among the lilac

270

sheets that he had seen earlier, Charlotte on top of him, something frantic in the ferocity with which she bit his lip and pushed her tongue in his mouth. She reached down to find his erection and guide him inside her and thrust her hips at him with an energy he found hard to match.

He came quickly, almost overcome by fatigue and a strange melancholy, and she immediately lay down beside him to curl into his hip. "I'm sorry," he whispered. His turn to apologise.

"Why?" She seemed surprised. "You were lovely." She reached over and turned out the light, and they lay in the dark for ten or fifteen minutes without stirring. Moonlight spilling across the rooftops washed down through the angled glass roof of the warehouse, into the garden below, and through the tall windows of the bedroom. Enzo lay with his eyes open, and they adjusted to the light, so that he could follow every shape and contour. His brain refused to stop. He caught the slightest movement in his peripheral vision and turned his head to find himself looking into two luminous, saucer-like green eyes. Zeke sat on the bedside cabinet staring at him, and Enzo wondered if the cat had watched them making love. Wondered if it was jealous.

His thoughts were broken by Charlotte's voice, small and hoarse in the dark. "You know, I bought this place ten years ago from an old couple who'd lived here in the war. They were just newly married when the city was occupied by the Nazis. They ran a coal merchant's business, and the Germans forced them to supply them with coal. They told me that the street was known as Little Italy, because of the number of Italian soldiers billeted here. They had been made to provide food and lodgings for two of them." She reached across his chest to twirl the long strands of his hair idly in her fingers. "Then after the allies landed, and the Libération of Paris was close, Parisians all over the city rose up against the occupiers. The couple who owned the coal merchant's shot and killed their two Italian lodgers. They told me this because, when I was buying the property, I asked them why the cellar below the warehouse had been bricked up and cemented over. And they said that's where they had buried the Italians. They were in their seventies by then, and they said I was the first person they had ever told."

"And did you believe them?"

She laughed a little. "I don't know. But I'd like to. I've come to think of the bodies in the cellar as my Italians. Buried for eternity. And that I'll always have their ghosts for company on cold winter nights."

Enzo thought about the sense he'd had earlier of vulnerability, of exposure to anyone who might have been watching from out there in the dark. And he thought about the ghosts of the two Italian soldiers who had never, after all, made it back to the olive groves in the southern sun. "I hope you're not thinking of adding a third Italian to the collection," he said.

He heard the rustling of sheets, and then her lips, soft and cool, on his cheek. "I'd like to think that maybe my real-life Italian would stay voluntarily."

272

He closed his eyes and felt himself drift off into confusion. She had a powerful effect on him. There was no doubting that. And yet the signals she gave him were mixed and conflicting. She didn't want a relationship, she said. And yet she was happy to make love to him. Her relationship with Raffin was over, but she didn't want to make him jealous. And now she wanted her *real-life Italian* to *stay voluntarily*. What did she mean? *I love your eyes*, she had told him. Had she changed her mind about not wanting a relationship? He was nearly fifty years old, and he still had no greater understanding of women than when he was fifteen.

He began drifting backwards in space, falling softly through the dark, as tiredness overwhelmed him and sleep started wrapping him in its embrace. And then her voice drew him back to the surface, coming, it seemed, from a very long way off.

"Do you really think Jacques Gaillard was killed by a group of his own students at ENA?"

He broke the surface of consciousness with his heart pounding. "Yes," he said, with a sudden, frightening clarity. "I do."

"So what are you going to do now?"

"There's another set of clues to decipher."

"Will you stay in Paris?" Her voice was barely a whisper.

He hesitated. "No. I have to go back to Cahors." Her disappointment was almost palpable, even in the dark. "But first I'm going to go to ENA to see if I can't get a photograph of the Schoelcher Promotion, and a list of the names of all the students."

"Then you'll have a long way to go."

"What do you mean?" Enzo raised himself up on one elbow and made out the pale shape of her face looking up at him from the bed. "I checked. ENA's based here in the Rue de l'Université, about ten minutes' walk from the studio in St. Germain."

"Not any more, it's not. They quit that building earlier this year, and moved everything, lock, stock and barrel, to Strasbourg."

III

The building at No.2 Rue de l'Observatoire stood cheek by jowl with the huge Lycée Montaigne opposite the south end of the Luxembourg Gardens. Even from the outside, it was apparent that its architecture was influenced by a history of North African colonialism. Arabic arched windows and doors, intricate mosaic and ceramic decoration. It had taken Enzo most of the day to discover that this place even existed.

Madame Francine Henry was close to retirement. Which, Enzo reflected, was probably why ENA had left her behind when the school moved to Strasbourg. She had worked as a publicity officer for the École National d'Administration for nearly thirty years, she told him. And now she was based here, in this oddly arabesque building, originally built to train administrators from the French colonies in Africa and Indochina. It had been taken over by ENA in recent years to house its international school, and

274

was the only part of the institution to remain in Paris.

She led him through an inner courtyard which more resembled a Moroccan *riad* than a Parisian school. Windows rose in peaked arches through three tiers on all sides. A square of lawn was gently shaded by two tall silver birches. A patterned frieze of moulded green ceramic separated the first and second floors.

"It's beautifully tranquil, isn't it?" she said. "Hard to believe that Paris is just out there." She turned and pointed up into a corner of the main building. "You can't see it because of the lower roof on this side. But there's a painted panel just below the gable which bears the name *Schoelcher*. Quite a coincidence, really."

"Yes," Enzo agreed.

"I suppose they must have chosen to dedicate the building in his name because of his fight against colonial injustice."

"That would make sense."

"You know, you're very fortunate," Madame Henry told him. "Almost all of the archival material went to Strasbourg with the school. But I suppose when they realised they were going to be tight for space, it made a kind of poetic sense to store the archives from the Schoelcher Promotion here."

"It's very good of you to help"

"It's the least we can do." Madame Henry composed a solemn expression. "I remember him, you know. The young Hugues d'Hautvillers. He was a character. A stunning intellect. It must be a terrible blow for the family."

Madame Henry was an attractive woman for her age. Gently old-fashioned. But her soft, brown eyes were filled with a warmth and sympathy which only increased Enzo's sense of guilt at his deception. "Yes, it is," he said. "They'll be very pleased to receive any mementos you might have of his time here."

He followed her through a wide arch, and she pushed open glass doors into a lobby at the far end of a long, narrow corridor lined with paintings. Down steps, then, into a gloomy stairwell. Madame Henry indicated the door at the foot of the stairs. "It opens on to the street. It used to be the private entrance for overseas students when they lived here in rooms on the upper floors." She opened a door to their left. Enzo could see a staircase descending into darkness. She flicked a light switch, and they went down into the cellars.

It was a rabbit warren of brick walls supporting the building above. They were lined with shelves, piled with papers and box files and books, and Madame Henry pointed up to a row of levers high along the facing wall. Ceramic panels beneath them were labelled *Séjour, Salle à Manger, Cuisine*. "The original mechanisms," she said, "for opening up the heating vents around the building."

He followed her along a dimly lit passage.

"So much history, just shut away in the dark. Sometimes I wonder what purpose there is in keeping it all. And then someone like you comes along, and you realise why." She stopped, and started searching through files along the upper shelves, which were labelled alphabetically. "Fascinating thing, history. You

276

wouldn't know it now, but this place was built on the site of a former monastery, established by the monks of the Order of Chartreux in 1257. They dug the stone to build it out of the ground underneath, and created a network of tunnels and *salles* down there in the process. Somewhere right below where we're standing now. They used them for the brewing of beer and the distillation of liqueur. I'm sure you've heard of Green Chartreuse."

"Yes," Enzo said.

"Well, this is where they used to make it. Right beneath your feet." She moved along the shelf. "Ah. Here we are." And she drew a box file out from among the others. "Schoelcher." She took the file to a table and opened it up, and began riffling through wads of documentation. Finally, a gasp of satisfaction. "Ah-ha." She pulled out a photograph. "I knew there would be one somewhere." Enzo peered at it in the poor light. It was a black and white group photograph, like any school photograph. Something more than a hundred pupils and professors, arranged in five ascending rows in front of a long building, all smiling for the camera. It was captioned, *Promotion Victor Schoelcher 1994–1996*.

Straight away, he spotted Gaillard sitting near the middle of the front row, hands folded in his lap, legs crossed, looking faintly bored. Neither Hugues nor Roques were immediately apparent. "I can have a copy of this made upstairs," Madame Henry said. Then from deep in the box she pulled out a VHS video tape marked *1994–96*. She waggled it triumphantly. "Each *promotion* makes its own video record of the year. A

277

pretty amateur hotchpotch. But I'm sure Hugues will be on it somewhere. If you want to wait about twenty minutes, I can have a copy made of that, too."

"It's very kind of you," Enzo said. "You wouldn't have a list of all the students from the Schoelcher Promotion, would you? It may be that the family will want to contact some of them."

"Yes, there'll be a list in the *annuaire*. I can photocopy that for you in the blink of an eye."

Enzo sat in the still of the courtyard, sunlight sloping in across the rooftops. Through glass doors leading to the entrance lobby, he could see delegates coming and going from a conference in the amphitheatre. He had been staring for some time at the copy of the photograph that Madame Henry had made for him. By now he had identified both Hugues d'Hautvillers and Philippe Roques among the rows of faces. He looked at all the others, and wondered how many more of them had been responsible for the murder of their *maître*. Most of them seemed so young, such innocence in all their open, smiling faces. He turned to the photocopied list of names and ran his eye down them. And there they were. D'HAUTVILLERS Hugues, and ROQUES Philippe, and one hundred and twelve other names. In his hand he held the faces and the names of Gaillard's killers. He had identified two of them. Both were dead. He had no way of knowing if he would ever unmask the others. And if he did, how long they would live.

Madame Henry bustled into the courtyard and he stood up. "There." She handed him a large manila envelope containing the video tape. "All done."

Enzo slipped the photograph and the list of names in beside it. "Thank you very much, madame."

"Oh, it was the least I could do." She smiled sympathetically. "Please pass on my condolences to the family."

IV

It was less than five minutes' walk from the Rue de l'Observatoire to the underground parking in the Rue St. Jacques. Enzo's overnight bag was still in his car, along with a change of clothes. He had felt uncomfortable all day wearing a forgotten shirt and slacks left at Charlotte's place by Raffin. It was a constant reminder of a history Enzo cared not to know about. There had been nearly half a wardrobe of Raffin's things in her bedroom. Enzo didn't like to think of Charlotte expending the same sexual energy and passion on Raffin that she had on him. But he knew they'd had a long relationship.

The car park was on three levels in the basement of an apartment building between the Rue des Feuillantines and the Rue des Ursulines. Raffin's lockup was two down. Raffin had been unable to give Enzo a key for the lift, but told him he could get access by walking down the ramp. Enzo left the late afternoon sunshine behind him as he slowly descended the steeply curving concrete. The first level was deserted. Night-lights cast a faint gloom among the shadows of the cars. Ten lockups along either side of a central lane. Each with its own up-and-over door, each parking space separated from the other by a metal grille. Raffin had left the door of his lockup open so that Enzo could pick up his car any time he liked.

He carried on down the next ramp, and noticed that the overhead lamps were not working. A feeble, flickering yellow light followed him down from above, but as he approached the second level he seemed to be descending into absolute darkness. By the time he reached the foot of the ramp, he could not see his hands in front of his face. He knew that somewhere there was a light switch. But he had no idea where. This was infuriating. It was his intention to drive back to Cahors tonight, a good six hours by car. He was anxious to get on the road as soon as possible.

At the far end of the aisle he could see now the faint glow of an exit light above the door leading to the lift. Raffin's lockup, he knew, was right next to it. With his hands held out in front of him, he walked forwards, very gingerly, until his fingers touched cold metal. The door of a lockup. It rattled beneath his touch, and he moved cautiously along, from one door to the next. He was beginning to be able to see by the light of the exit sign, and for the first time vague shapes were taking form. His hands disappeared into space. Raffin's lockup. The door was somewhere up above his head. He searched for his car keys and felt the notched rubber on the remote controller. He pressed it, and heard the doors of his car unlock. His sidelights flashed twice. And in that moment, a piece of darkness detached itself from the shadows, warm and heavy, and enveloped him completely. Enzo toppled backwards. He heard the crack of his head as it hit the concrete, and some inner explosion of light filled it. The darkness was on top of him, forcing the breath from his lungs, and Enzo realised it had hands. Hands made soft by woollen gloves. One of them was around his neck.

Enzo panicked, bucking and kicking, but the darkness was stubbornly strong, pinning him to the floor. And then he saw the merest flash of light reflected from the exit sign as a blade rose above him, and he realised that his attacker was about to plunge a knife into his chest.

"I'm sorry," he heard a breathless voice whisper in the dark.

"What!" Enzo gasped in disbelief. He grabbed his attacker's wrist before it could begin its deadly descent. But he immediately felt the strength in the man's arm, and knew that it was stronger than his. He would not be able to resist its power. With his other hand, he clutched at the face above him, and felt hot breath through a woollen mask. Desperate fingers found the eyeholes, and he clawed at them with all his strength. The man's scream reverberated around the car park, and immediately the pressure of the knife arm was released. Enzo heard the blade go clattering away across the concrete in the dark, and both of his attacker's hands flew to his face to prise Enzo's fingers away. Which gave Enzo the chance to ball his fist and throw it hard in the direction of the man's head. It made contact with a sharp crack, and he only barely heard the man's cry above his own. Bone on bone was a painful experience.

Sudden light flooded their conflict. Hard, yellow light, that fell from a gaping crack in the wall. Enzo turned his head and saw a young couple framed in the exit door, the stairway illuminated behind them. The girl screamed. Enzo looked up to see his attacker's black, masked head turn towards her, and he grabbed the mask with both hands and tore it away. For a confusing moment, it seemed as if there was another mask beneath it. And then Enzo realised that his attacker was black. He saw frightened rabbit eyes turn briefly towards him in the dark, and then the man was up and running in the direction of the ramp. Soft footsteps slapping concrete, all shape and form quickly consumed by shadow.

The young couple seemed frozen by fear as Enzo staggered to his feet, shocked and groggy, and still reeling from the dawning realisation of just how close he had come to being murdered. These young people could easily have opened the door to find his body lying bleeding on the car park floor. He swallowed hard to stop himself from being sick and stooped to pick up his manila envelope.

"Are you all right?" the young man asked tentatively.

"I'm fine," Enzo said. As fine, he thought, as anyone could be who had just fought off an attempted murder. And he remembered his attacker's whispered apology.

I'm sorry. Sorry! It filled Enzo as much with anger as confusion.

Enzo winced as Charlotte dabbed the back of his head with cotton wool soaked in antiseptic. She shook her head. "Enzo, this is getting to be a habit."

"It's not funny, Charlotte. That guy really was trying to kill me." A lump the size of an egg had come up on the back of his head. Blood had coagulated and stuck to his hair. "Ow!" He jerked away from her hand. "I hope you take better care of your patients' minds."

She grabbed his ponytail. "Hold still. Why are men such babies over a little pain?" And she dabbed him with more antiseptic. "You can't go back to Cahors now."

"Why not?"

"Because if they knew where you'd parked your car, do you not think they'll know where you live?"

"Well, if they do, then they'll probably know where you live, too." Enzo had driven like a maniac through the fifth *arrondissement* into the thirteenth and abandoned his car half on the pavement outside Charlotte's warehouse.

Charlotte paused, and acknowledged the thought with a grave nod of her head. "So they might come looking for you here."

"Jesus, Charlotte, I'm not cut out for this sort of thing. My strengths are cerebral, not physical. Maybe I should go to the police."

"And tell them what? That someone's trying to murder you for pursuing an investigation they've twice asked you to stop?"

"Hmmm." Enzo paused to think about it. "You might have a point."

Charlotte handed him a clean wad of gauze. "Here, press that against the back of your head until the bleeding stops." She tidied away the bits and pieces of her first aid kit from the kitchen worktop. "Give me fifteen minutes to change and pack a bag."

"Where are we going?"

"My parents have a holiday home in the Corrèze. It's an old farmhouse. A little primitive. Very remote. We used to go there for our holidays every year when I was a kid. I still use it when I want to escape from everything. My little hidey-hole away from the world. I think we'll be pretty safe there." She looked at her watch. "It's after six already. We'll be lucky if we get there by midnight."

CHAPTER
SEVENTEEN

I

Although the sky was clear the night was dark. There was no moon, and the *autoroute* was virtually deserted. They had stopped at services just past Limoges for something to eat, and now Enzo was feeling the onset of fatigue. He needed to occupy his brain in order to resist the temptation to shut his eyes, and he had forced himself to recall, one by one, the items found with the legs in the trunk at Château Hautvillers. The salamander brooch, the lion's head pendant, the lapel pin flag, the sporting trophy, the referee's whistle with the numbers scratched into the plating.

"Is there anything that occurs to you about any of them?" he asked Charlotte.

"Well, the lion's head is an interesting pointer. The lion is pretty much symbolic of Africa. So I'd say there was a good chance that the flag on the lapel pin is probably the national flag of some African country."

"A lot of countries in Africa."

"Given that most of these clues relate to France, it's probably a former French colony."

"Good thought." Enzo watched the broken white lines coming at him in a never-ending stream. "And the salamander?"

"The salamander was the emblem of the French king, François Premier. I don't know if that's relevant or not. There were dates engraved on the back of the brooch, weren't there?"

"1927 to 1960."

"Hmmm." Charlotte sounded doubtful. "François Premier was early sixteenth century. The dates don't really connect, do they?"

"Only about three hundred years out." Enzo saw headlights in his rear mirror approaching at speed. He had never developed the French penchant for fast driving and had been sitting at a steady one hundred and ten kilometres per hour. The vehicle coming up behind was going considerably faster.

"What about the sports trophy and the referee's whistle?" Charlotte asked.

"What about them?"

"I don't know, I'm looking for a sporting connection. It's hard to see one with François Premier and an African flag. The trophy had a date on it, too, didn't it?

Enzo nodded and glanced at the approaching car. It was taking its time pulling out to overtake. "1996 again. The year Gaillard disappeared."

"And you think that's the only point of it?"

"It's the same date that the 1990 Dom Perignon vintage was released, and there didn't seem to be any other point to that." The lights behind were dazzling now. Headlamps on full beam. "Jesus Christ!"

"What is it?"

"You'd think this idiot was trying to blind me!"

286

Charlotte glanced back into the full glare of the lights. "My God, he's far too close!"

Enzo felt a sudden jolt of fear, as if he had touched the naked copper of a live wire. "And he's going far too fast!"

The bang as it hit their rear bumper seemed inordinately loud, and both their heads jerked back against the headrests before they pitched forward again, straining against the seat belts. Enzo struggled to keep control of the steering as his car began serpentining across the white line. He stood on the brakes, but the vehicle at their back was propelling them forward. There was a sickening screaming of tyres. Smoke billowed up in the headlamps, and the car was filled with the smell of burning rubber. Enzo immediately took his foot off the brake pedal and accelerated hard. They pulled away from the following vehicle and the car stopped swerving.

Charlotte had turned in her seat and was staring out through the back windscreen. "It's a truck." Enzo could hear the fear in her voice.

"What the hell is he trying to do?"

She faced front again. "You cut up a truck coming out of the parking at that last stop."

"I did not," Enzo protested. "He was on my right. The road was unmarked. I had right of way."

"Well, he didn't think so, did he? He honked loud enough."

Enzo looked at the lights in the mirror and screwed up his eyes. They were getting closer again. "Do you think it's him?"

"I don't know. It seems a pretty extreme reaction if it is."

As the truck bore down on them once more, Enzo moved into the outside lane. The truck followed. He swerved back to the inside, and his tyres shrieked in protest. The truck stayed out as if it was going to overtake. The cab drew level with the back of Enzo's car, and just as Enzo was about to hit the brakes again, it nudged his rear wing. That was all it took to send the car into an uncontrollable spin. The world seemed to be revolving hopelessly around them. Smoke and light and burning rubber. And more smoke, and more light. Enzo pulled the steering wheel one way, then the other. And miraculously they stopped spinning. But they were sliding side-on, now, and a large green drum with a white arrow was flying towards them at speed. Criss-crossed white lines passed beneath them before they hit the drum and spun off again on to a steeply curving exit ramp, coming to a sudden and unexpected stop halfway up it, facing back the way they had come. The truck flew past on the *autoroute*, and as its lights and the roar of its engine receded, a dreadful silence settled on them, like dust after an explosion.

Enzo clutched the wheel to stop his hands from shaking. He glanced across at Charlotte. Her face was an almost luminous white. Her hands were pressed against the dashboard, arms at full stretch. "He was trying to kill us," she whispered. And her voice seemed to thunder inside Enzo's head.

All he could do was nod in acknowledgement. It felt as if he had left his voice somewhere back there on the *autoroute*. Twice in one day he had been within seconds of death. The first time, there was no doubt that someone had premeditatedly tried to murder him. Whether this time he was a victim of road rage, or another deliberate attempt at murder, he had no way of knowing.

The road was still empty, the countryside around them lost in blackness. There were no lights visible anywhere, except for Enzo's headlamps pointing back down the ramp. The engine had stalled. He collected himself to try to restart it. It was not until the third attempt that he managed to coax it back to life.

"We're not going back on the *autoroute*, are we?" There was something like panic in Charlotte's voice.

Enzo finally found his. "No. There's a map in the glove box." With legs like jelly, he manipulated the pedals to put the car in reverse and take them through a three-point turn so that they were facing the correct way. Then he pulled gently away and followed the road to a junction where a road sign reflected brightly in their headlights. TULLE 27km.

Charlotte turned on the courtesy light and squinted at the map. "This must take us to the N120. If we get to Tulle, I know the way from there. We should be at the house in just over an hour."

It was after midnight, and Enzo's car strained up a narrow road through a tunnel of trees and lush, green foliage. On the main road from Tulle they had passed through village after village swaddled in darkness. Houses shuttered, street lamps extinguished. It was hard to believe that anyone inhabited these grim stone dwellings huddled along the roadside. Everywhere seemed abandoned to the night. The only life they had seen since leaving Tulle were occasional sets of furtive eyes caught in the headlamps, unseen creatures skulking at the roadside.

Now the road rose steeply through the wood-cladded hillside, twisting and turning, headlights picking out creepers dangling from overhanging oaks. An owl swooped through their lights, intent on some invisible prey, and shrieked with alarm before veering off sharply and disappearing into the forest.

Suddenly they emerged from the claustrophobia of the trees, on to an open ridge. The moon had risen, and cast its colourless light across the valley below. They could see distant twinkling pockets of streetlights, a church floodlit on the far horizon, the river Cère a thin, meandering band of silver far below. The land rose and fell dramatically all around them, smeared black with trees, and punctuated by shimmering silver-green pasture. The road curled up, then, through a tiny stone village with a huge, crumbling church, and began its descent on the other side. A white ironwork cross at the side of the road reflected the lights of the car, and Charlotte told Enzo to turn left into a tiny metalled road which took them down a steep incline. They passed a holiday home, all closed up behind high hedges, and carried on to the treeline and beyond. The road reached an unexpected dead end, and Charlotte told him to take another left, down a rough, cobbled path. Enzo nursed his car gently down the track, wondering where on earth Charlotte was taking them.

"You can stop here," she said suddenly.

Enzo jerked to a halt and looked around. They were surrounded by trees, and tangling briar amongst thick undergrowth. "Here?" He was incredulous. "Where on earth are we?"

"You'll see." She reached into the back to retrieve her overnight bag and her laptop, and she got out of the car.

Enzo cut the engine and the lights and followed her out into the night. It took several moments for his eyes to adjust to the sudden darkness, and for the world to take shape again in the moonlight that filtered down through the trees. She plunged off into what seemed like thickly wooded hillside, and he scrambled along behind her, afraid of losing her in the dark. But in just a few short steps, they emerged again into bright moonshine, a clearing cut into the slope, and Enzo could see, about four metres below them, the dark shape of an old house nestling in a natural fold of rock. Primitive steps had been cut into the hill and reinforced by old railway sleepers. Charlotte followed them down to a covered patio at the front of the house, and snapped on her penlight to track down the lock on the door. She fumbled with a set of huge old keys, and in a moment pushed the heavy front door inwards into the house.

"Wait here a minute," she said, and disappeared inside. Enzo turned to take in the moonlit view that dropped away almost sheer below the house. The air was shimmering in the night heat. He could still see occasional snatches of the silvered Cère through the trees. And then it was all wiped out, the *terrasse* washed with sudden light as Charlotte switched on the electrics somewhere inside the house.

He turned to see her through the doorway standing at the far side of an old farmhouse kitchen with tiled floors and pointed stone walls. She was pale, and tired, and still shocked by their brush with death, but he remembered again, in that moment, how beautiful he'd thought her that first time he'd seen her. Then she had been defiant and self-confident. Now she seemed vulnerable, defeated. He walked into the kitchen, and immediately felt the chill contained within its thick stone walls. A stark contrast with the warm air outside. He put his bag on the table and took her in his arms, and held her tightly. One way or another, he knew, she was going to have a huge impact on his life. And he didn't want to let her go. Ever.

"What are we going to do?" she whispered.

"The only thing we can do."

"What's that?"

"Find them before they find us."

II

There was a renewed urgency now about the need to make sense of the clues found at Hautvillers. In the barn adjoining the house, Charlotte dug out the white cardboard wrapping from a dishwasher installed the

292

previous summer, and Enzo opened it out and taped it to a wall in the kitchen. A makeshift whiteboard. In the huge open fireplace, the flames of a log fire licked up blackened stone, dry oak crackling in the grate, taking the chill off air undisturbed since the house was closed up for the winter at Christmas. The comforting smell of woodsmoke filled the kitchen.

Charlotte heated soup on the stove while Enzo set up her laptop at one end of the kitchen table, connected it to a printer she kept at the house, and downloaded the photographs he had taken at the dog cemetrey above Château Hautvillers. One by one he printed them out and stuck them up around the edges of his whiteboard. Beneath the salamander and the sports trophy he marked up the dates that were engraved on them. He wrote *19/3* below the referee's whistle.

Then he sat down at the long wooden table and tried to clear his mind. At first he closed his eyes, and then he opened them again and let them wander around the kitchen. It was a large room. For living in, as well as cooking and eating. It was the centre of the house. Great blackened beams supported the floorboards of an attic room above. Pots and pans and keys and rusted chains hung from ancient nails hammered into them long ago. Behind a curtain next to the fireplace, an old staircase led up to the attic. Crooked wooden doors opposite led to a bathroom and a double bedroom. The original stone *souillarde*, set in an arched alcove, was still used as a sink. There were bookcases and an old walnut buffet, an antique grandfather clock whose

293

pendulum hung still and silent. Every surface was covered with dust, and framed family photographs.

Enzo got up to take a look. Most of them were old. Cheap prints, garish colours. There were several taken on the patio outside. A middle-aged couple with a skinny young girl posing coyly between them. Long, curling black hair. A summer dress, a dark tan. Charlotte aged ten, or twelve. Enzo let his eyes linger on her for a moment, and he smiled fondly. There were several black and white photographs, faded and discoloured with age. Memories of another era, another generation. A young couple on a beach, in strangely dated swim wear, grinning gauchely at the camera. He had a moustache curling around either cheek and wore heavy-rimmed, round glasses. Her hair was a nest of flyaway curls. They both had bad teeth.

"My grandparents," Charlotte said, glancing across from the stove.

Enzo picked up one of the photographs taken on the patio. "Your parents?"

"Yes. I think I was about eleven when that was taken."

"Are they still alive?"

She nodded. "They live in Angoulême."

Enzo looked at them. Oddly unremarkable people. He was losing his hair. She was overweight. Enzo could not see Charlotte in either of them. He said, "Hard to tell which of them you take after."

"Neither," Charlotte said. Enzo looked across, but she was focused on her soup. "I was adopted."

"That explains it, then."

"But I couldn't have loved them more if they'd been my real parents," she said unnecessarily, as if in response to some unspoken criticism. "They'd have done anything for me." She was lost for a moment in some other world. "And still would." She started ladling soup out into deep bowls. "I used to love coming here when I was a kid. Playing in the woods, making up my own games. I'm glad I didn't have any brothers or sisters. I liked being on my own." She hesitated. "Still do."

Enzo wondered if that was her way of telling him not to get too close. Yet more mixed messages?

"They were devastated when I tried to track down my blood parents."

"Why did you do that?"

"I'd just gone to university. I was starting to try to figure out who I was. Or, at least, who the adult me was. It's funny. There's always this thing inside you that needs to know where you came from. No matter how happy, or how settled you are." She shook her head and took the bowls to the table. "Hardly ever works out well."

"How did it work out for you?"

"It didn't. All I managed to do was hurt my parents. Stupid, thoughtless, selfish . . ." Enzo saw, with a slight shock, that she had tears in her eyes, and she turned quickly to get cutlery and wipe them discreetly away.

He didn't want to embarrass her and focused his attention, then, on the contents of the bookcase. The top shelf was lined with children's editions of famous books. Reading for the young Charlotte. *La Petite*

Dorrit, Le Tour du Monde en 80 Jours, Les Misérables (Tome II). Enzo picked out a book he remembered buying for Sophie when she was young. *Le Père Tranquille*. He opened it up and read the handwritten inscription on the title page. It was a gift for Madeleine on the occasion of her seventh birthday, from Mama and Papa. "Who's Madeleine?"

She sat at the table and put a spoon beside each bowl. "Come and get your soup."

He slipped the book back on the shelf and went to sit opposite her. The soup was a thick vegetable and lentil mix. Comfort food in an uncertain world. He took several mouthfuls, and Charlotte opened a bottle of red wine and poured them each a glass. Enzo took a sip. "So who is she?"

"Who?"

"Madeleine."

Charlotte shrugged. "No one special."

Enzo was intrigued by her evasion. "Why won't you tell me?"

She sighed. "She's me. All right? I'm Madeleine. Charlotte's my middle name. There were two other Madeleines in my class at school, so they called me Charlotte to avoid confusion. The only people who still call me Madeleine are my parents, and . . ." She stopped. "Well, just my parents."

"It's a nice name," Enzo said. "Maybe I'll call you Madeleine."

"No!" she said sharply. Then, more softly, "I don't want to be Madeleine. If you want to call me anything,

296

call me Charly." She pronounced it *Sharlee*. "It's what my friends call me."

"Is that what Roger calls you?"

Charlotte laughed. "Oh, no. Not Roger. That was far too common for him. He always called me Charlotte."

Enzo liked the way she spoke of him in the past tense.

Charlotte cleared away the empty soup bowls and went in search of a cable to connect her laptop to the telephone line. Once connected she pulled the Google search page up on screen, and refilled both their wine glasses. She watched as Enzo wrote *Africa* in the centre of his makeshift whiteboard, circled it and drew an arrow to it from the lion's head. Neither of them felt tired. There was still adrenaline flowing through their veins from the incident on the *autoroute*, and the soup and wine had infused flagging spirits with new energy.

Enzo stared at the board for a long time. The previous clues had taken him to an uncomfortable place, inside the heads of Gaillard's killers. He needed to get back there now. To think the way they thought, to follow the same processes. Make the same connections. He heard Charlotte tapping at the keyboard behind him, and he let his gaze drift to the lapel pin. "We need to figure out what flag that is," he said. "There must be something on the net that would make it easier for us to identify it."

"I'll have a look."

Enzo's eyes wandered back to the lion's head. "What about Ethiopia? Haile Selassie was known as the Lion of Judah, and he was the last emperor of Ethiopia."

"Wasn't a French colony," Charlotte said. "Wait a minute. Here's what you wanted." She tapped some more, then read, *"Ivan Sarajcic's flag finder*. This is amazing. You can select from a choice of flag types, colours, and what he calls *devices* — objects that appear on the flag."

Enzo came to stand behind her and look at the screen.

"Flag type. Three stripes vertical." She selected a black and white flag with three vertical stripes. The image was highlighted in white. "Colours are green, yellow, and red." And she selected them from a choice of eleven colours. Again, they were highlighted in white. She moved the cursor to a pull-down menu listing devices that might appear on the flag and scrolled down the choices until she came to *star*. She selected it and moved to a choice of colours, picking green. Then she clicked on a button which read *Find the Flag*. Within seconds, a large scale image of the flag appeared. "*Senegal*," Charlotte read from the caption. "It's the Senegalese flag."

"Was Senegal a French colony?"

"Yes, it was." Charlotte entered *Senegal* into the search engine and came up with a World Factbook site. She read, "Senegal. West African state bordering the North Atlantic Ocean between Guinea-Bissau and Mauritania. Gained its independence from France in 1960."

"1960," Enzo said. "That's the second of the two dates engraved on the salamander."

"What about the other date?"

"1927."

"Maybe it's significant in Senegalese history." Charlotte typed *Senegal* and *1927* into the search engine and then groaned. "Two hundred and six thousand results. We could be here for a month wading through these."

But Enzo was still excited. He went back to the board and wrote up *Senegal*, circled it and drew arrows to it from the flag and from *Africa*. "Let's leave the dates for the moment," he said. "What about the salamander itself? You said it was the emblem of François Premier. Let's see what we can find out about him."

Charlotte's fingers rattled quickly across the keyboard. "There's a mountain of stuff about François." She scanned yards of text as she scrolled down the screen. "A champion of the Renaissance. His motto was, *I am nourished and I die in fire*, which seems to be why he chose the salamander as his emblem. It's supposed to be so cold, it will extinguish all fire on contact. Even his hat was fastened with a jewelled salamander." She looked up. "Just like the one in the trunk."

Enzo shook his head. "It's not doing anything for me."

"Wait a minute." Charlotte typed some more. "Apparently François Premier was also known as François d'Angoulême."

Enzo raised an eyebrow. "Your home town."

"It seems that's where his family came from. The Valois Angoulême. His son and grandson were the last of the line." She looked up. "Maybe Angoulême is a clue. Maybe that's where we should be looking for the rest of the body."

Enzo looked doubtful. "I'm not seeing any connections here. Except . . . Gaillard's family came from Angoulême." He thought briefly. "I'll write it up for the moment." And he turned and wrote *François Premier (Angoulême)* in a circle and drew an arrow to it from the salamander. He faced Charlotte again. "What other symbolic meaning might a salamander have?"

Charlotte initiated another search and came up with an article on salamanders and symbolism. "Fire," she said simply. "There was a fifteenth-century Swiss physician who dubbed the salamander as the symbol of fire. And a famous Australian explorer who wrote of the aborigines, *The natives were about burning, burning, ever burning; one would think they were of the fabled salamander race and lived on fire instead of water.*" She scrolled down more of the article and shook her head. "Fire. That's it. Apparently salamander is derived from an Arab-Persian word meaning, *lives in fire.*"

Enzo wrote the word *fire?* beside the photograph of the salamander brooch, but did not circle it. There were still no connections. For a moment he closed his eyes, and from nowhere a wave of fatigue washed over him. He staggered, and put his hand on the table to steady himself.

300

"Are you okay?" Charlotte stood up, concerned.

"I'm fine." He stepped back and looked at the board again, but it was burning too brightly on his retinas, and he had to screw up his eyes to focus on it. He knew now that he would make no further progress tonight.

"It's nearly four o'clock," she said. "The sun'll be up in less than an hour."

He nodded, succumbing to the inevitable. "We'd better go to bed, then."

She put the computer to sleep and took away his empty wine glass. Then she took his hand and led him through to the bedroom at the back of the house. The double bed, with its heavy, carved wooden head and foot boards, took up nearly the whole room. An enormous *armoire* occupied the remainder. Lurid green and pink floral wallpaper covered the walls and the door. A single, naked light bulb cast its cold light around the room. The air was chill in here, and smelled of damp cellars. "I should have had it airing," Charlotte said. "It's my parents' room. My room's in the attic. It would be warmer and drier. But there's only a single bed up there." She opened the windows and threw the shutters wide, then slotted a fly screen into the window frame.

The bed was cold and damp, and they huddled their naked bodies together for warmth. She fitted perfectly into his foetal curl, and he wrapped an arm around her, cupping one of her breasts, feeling a nipple pressing into his palm, aroused by the cold. But there was no thought of sex. Just comfort. And within minutes of Charlotte turning out the light they were both asleep.

III

It wasn't the daylight that wakened him. It had been light for hours. Sunshine streaming through the open window lay hot across the bed. The room smelled of the forest, and the hum of insects filled the air from outside. It must have been the church bell that pricked his consciousness. He heard it ringing distantly in the hilltop village. He had no idea how many times it had rung. Seven, eight, nine times? He lay with his eyes closed, luxuriating in the warmth, listening to see if it would ring again. Sometimes they would ring the hour for a second time after an interval of two or three minutes. Just in case the workers in the fields had miscounted the first time. The bell began again, and this time he counted it all the way up to twelve. It was midday. They had slept for almost eight hours.

He rolled his head to one side and saw that Charlotte was still asleep. Her hair lay tangled beneath her head, smeared across the pillow. Her mouth was slightly open, soft lips almost pouting, blowing out tiny puffs of air. He was seized by an incredible tenderness. He wanted to run his fingers lightly over her lips, and then kiss them softly, so that she would wake to the taste of him. He wanted to make love to her. Not frantically as they had before, but gently, taking their time, losing themselves in a long, slow oblivion.

But he did not want to wake her, so he slid carefully from the bed, lifting his clothes from the floor where last night he had simply let them fall, and tiptoed out to the kitchen. There, he pulled on his cargos and tee shirt and slipped into his running shoes, dragging his hair out of his face to gather it loosely in a band at the nape of his neck. In the bathroom he slunged his face with water and went back out to the kitchen to make coffee. He opened the window and shutters on either side of the main door to let in light and air, and went out on to the patio. In daylight, he saw that the *terrasse* was shaded by a vine trained across a rusted metal frame. No doubt the family would eat out here on summer evenings, looking out upon their own private view of paradise. He saw, now, tiny villages of honeyed stone nestling in the river valley, or sitting proudly on hilltops, church spires poking out from amongst the trees that marched up every hillside. Ravines and gorges cut through greenery, marking the outer limits of valleys where once huge, fast-flowing rivers carved their way relentlessly through the rock.

It was a wonderful, solitary place. Somewhere to reflect. To be at peace. To be yourself. Enzo saw two magpies chasing each other across a meadow full of summer flowers immediately below the house. He heard the coffee-maker gurgling and spitting inside, and he went in to pour himself a coffee. He found a mug, and a jar of sugar cubes, and made it sweet. He took a long sip, and almost immediately felt the caffeine kick. There was still no sound from Charlotte.

It was curiosity that led him to the staircase behind the curtain. He drew it back, and climbed carefully up into the dark, his coffee still in his hand. At the top of the stairs a low door opened into a tiny bedroom built into the slope of the roof. Sunlight sneaked through the cracks around the edges of a small dormer window. Enzo opened it and unlatched the shutter. Light poured in and filled the intimate space around him. The view across the valley was spectacular. He could imagine the young Charlotte waking to it every summer's morning, filled with excitement, and an eagerness to be out exploring the world around her, probing the outer limits of her imagination.

He turned back into the room, stooping to avoid the angle of the ceiling. Her bed was pushed against the far wall. He pictured her lying in it, the child in the photographs. Sleeping, dreaming, free to fantasise, before adulthood reined her in to face an altogether less attractive world. More photographs lined themselves up along a wooden dresser, around a bowl and pitcher, carefully arranged on lace doilies. Family groups posed in the garden with the view behind them. A pergola hanging with flowers. He recognised Charlotte's parents, and an older couple. Perhaps the grandparents he had seen, much younger, in the photograph taken on the beach. Her grandfather still had the same curling moustaches. Only now they were pure white. Charlotte looked radiant, touched by a happiness that sparkled in her dark eyes and glowed in her smile. She was sitting on the knee of an older man. Not as old as her grandfather, but with the same extravagant moustaches, and a head of wild, untamed hair.

Enzo felt as if someone had just punched him in the gut. He felt dizzy and sick, his mind clouded by pain and confusion. His mug of coffee fell to the floor and smashed, and he picked up the photograph with a shaking hand. His mouth was dry and he couldn't even swallow. There was absolutely no doubt. The man on whose knee the young Charlotte was sitting was Jacques Gaillard.

CHAPTER
EIGHTEEN

I

As he got to the foot of the stairs, Charlotte was padding naked from the bedroom wiping the sleep from her eyes. "What happened?" she asked dreamily. "I thought I heard the sound of something breaking." And then she saw his face. Chalk white and etched with hurt and anger. "What's wrong?" The alarm in her voice was clear.

He threw the photograph on to the table, and the glass cracked in the frame. She looked shocked, her eyes full of incomprehension. He said, "I think there's something you forgot to tell me."

She walked to the table and glanced at the photograph behind the broken glass, and he saw realisation break over her like a wave, leaving her drenched with weary resignation. But her first instinct was to cover her nakedness, to dress up her sudden vulnerability. "It was none of your business," she said, almost under her breath, and she turned back to the bedroom.

Enzo went after her. "Well, I think it's my business now." She pulled on a towelling dressing gown and held it tight around her, then stood her ground defiantly. "Are you going to tell me?" he asked.

"He was my uncle."

Enzo felt his anger simmering and bubbling inside him. He fought to keep it from boiling over. "You lied to me."

"I didn't lie to you. I didn't tell you, that's all."

"You lied by omission. It's the same thing."

"Oh, crap!" She pushed brusquely past him and out into the kitchen again. He followed her. She said, "I just met you a week ago. I didn't know you. And I certainly didn't owe you. The truth or anything else."

"Does Raffin know?"

"Of course he does. That's how I met him. When he was researching the book."

A tiny explosion of air escaped from the back of Enzo's throat. "Oh, right. Of course. It all becomes clear. You got involved with Raffin because you thought you might learn something about what happened to your uncle. But when he failed to come up with anything you didn't already know, you dumped him. Just as I appeared on the scene promising to take a fresh look."

"It wasn't like that." She folded her arms across her chest and faced him off.

"Well, tell me how it was, then."

She glared at him, angry and defiant and defensive. "I never thought for a minute that Roger was going to turn up anything new about my Uncle Jacques. I fell for him, that's all. I thought he was charming and funny, and we had great sex."

Enzo almost flinched. This was more than he wanted to know.

"I dumped him because I got to know him. After that first flush of infatuation, I discovered that the more I knew him the less I liked him. It happens all the time. You meet someone. You think they're great. Then you find out they're not as great as you thought they were, and you move on."

"To me."

She shook her head. "It was you who asked me up for coffee, remember?"

"No. You asked yourself. And you're the one who kept turning up at *my* door. Not that I wasn't happy to see you. But it was you who came to Épernay. It was you who got the key to *my* room, you who got into *my* bed."

She was only able to meet his angry gaze for a moment before she turned away. "You were the first person in ten years who seemed like he might actually find out what happened to my Uncle Jacques. And I wanted to be around when you did." She swung back to face him, vindication burning in her eyes. "I loved that man. A lot of people didn't. I don't know why. Because to me he was the kindest, sweetest, gentlest person. And someone just took him away from me. Wiped him off the face of the earth, without reason, without trace."

"So you used me."

"Yes."

Enzo felt the bottom falling out of his world.

"Not that I didn't find you attractive."

"Oh, please!"

"But, yes, I thought there was a good chance you might turn up something new." She drew a deep breath. "And then I got to know you. And the more I got to know you the more I got to like you. Just the opposite of how it was with Roger."

"You don't know me at all." This was hurting more than he had thought it would.

"I know enough to know that you make me feel like I've never felt before about any man."

But Enzo didn't want to hear it. This could only get worse. He started lowering the portcullis. "You know what I think?" He answered his own question. "I think you use people. I think you used Raffin, and I think you're using me. And when this is all over I'll be nothing more to you than a piece of history."

She looked at him with her big, dark eyes, like some wounded animal. Full of hurt and incomprehension. She shook her head slowly. "You're wrong, Enzo."

And suddenly the fire of their argument was extinguished, as if a salamander had come between them and put out the flames. Enzo felt spent. He walked past her and out into the early afternoon sunshine. The heat was building, and he felt the sun burning his skin. He thrust his hands in his pockets and walked off through the long grass choking the garden, until he found a stone bench placed so that it gave on to an undisturbed panorama of the valley below. He felt the stone hot through his trousers as he sat down, and he closed his eyes. The air was filled with the sound of a million humming insects, and then the church bell chimed one. It was extraordinary, he thought, how a single hour could change your life.

309

And in that moment of introspection, as anger subsided, the first doubts crept in to undermine his self-righteous certainty. Had he, after all, judged her too hastily, too harshly? He opened his eyes to the full glare of the sun and knew that whatever the truth, it was too late now to unsay the things that had been said.

II

He had no idea how long he sat there staring out over the Cère valley with its hills and gorges and tangling forests. It seemed like forever, but the church bell had not yet struck two. Ten minutes earlier he had heard the distant chatter of Charlotte's printer, and now he caught a movement out of the corner of his eye, and turned to see her wading through the grass towards him. She was wearing jeans and a large, shapeless tee shirt with a faded Bart Simpson head on it. A sheaf of papers was fluttering in her trailing hand. She stopped a metre short of him, and he looked up to see that she had been crying. Her eyes were bloodshot and watery, and sadness was smudged in the shadows beneath them. But she looked at him without emotion.

"Get over it." She held out a sheet of paper.

"What's this?"

"I got to thinking about the clues again," she said. "It seemed a little more constructive than sitting about feeling sorry for myself."

Enzo ignored the barb. "And?"

310

"And, I got to thinking about those dates. 1927 to 1960. They seemed kind of like the dates you see in brackets after the name of someone who's dead. A life span."

"A short life. Just thirty-three."

"He was."

"Who?"

She pushed the sheet of paper at him. "See for yourself. I just put the dates into the search engine and that's what came up."

Enzo glanced at the printout, squinting at it in the bright sunlight. DAVID DIOP — POET (1927–1960). It was an entry on a page of the library section of the University of Florida website. Diop had been born in Bordeaux, the son of a Senegalese father, and his work had reflected a deep hatred of colonialism in Africa. Killed in a plane crash in 1960, most of his poetry had been destroyed with him, leaving for posterity only the twenty-two poems published before his death.

He looked up at Charlotte. "So? He had a Senegalese father."

"So I looked at that list of Schoelcher students you got from ENA." She held it out to him. "I've marked the name with a highlighter."

He looked at the green, highlighted name on the list. François Diop. And through the mist of blood and anger and pain which had clouded his last hour, an extraordinary clarity emerged. The dates engraved on the salamander. François Premier. Africa. Senegal. All leading incontrovertibly to the name of another of Jacques Gaillard's students. François Diop. He turned shining eyes on Charlotte, and for the moment everything that had passed between them was forgotten. "What do we know about him?"

She shrugged. "I haven't looked yet."

He wrote *François Diop* up on the board, circled it, and drew arrows to it from everything else, except the cup and the whistle. "Okay, so we know who, but not where." He crossed to the kitchen table and picked up the group photo of the Schoelcher Promotion. There were four black faces amongst them. One of them was François Diop, and François Diop had tried to murder him. Of that he was certain. But he had not got a clear enough sight of the face to be able to recognise him. Certainly not from a tiny image in a ten-year-old photograph. "Have you found anything yet?"

Charlotte was still typing and working the mouse. "There are quite a number of François Diops. Apparently Diop is one of the commonest names in Senegal." She was scrolling down a list of more than one hundred and thirty links. "Wait a minute, I'll try to narrow the search by linking the name to ENA." She searched again, and this time only a handful of links appeared. Mostly articles or official documents relating to a high-ranking *fonctionnaire* in the French diplomatic service. She pulled up an article headed: DIOP TIPPED AS NEXT DIRECTOR OF PEACEKEEPING OPERATIONS. She quickly scanned the text. "This is him." And Enzo rounded the table to stand beside her and lean over the laptop to peer at the screen. He smelled the traces of perfume in her hair, felt the heat of her body next to his, and suffered a huge rush of regret. He forced himself to focus on the text of the article.

Diop was based at the Quai d'Orsay, in the Ministry of Foreign Affairs. During the previous nine years he had been appointed to a string of diplomatic postings in Washington, Tokyo, and Moscow. He had embarked on that golden path after graduating from the Schoelcher Promotion at ENA as one of the top students of his year. His ethnic background had stood him in good stead and, according to this particular journalist, he was now being groomed by friends in the Foreign Minister's office for a top position at the UN.

There was a photograph of Diop grinning lopsidedly at the camera. He was a good-looking young man. The caption claimed he was just thirty-five years old, a child prodigy who was more than fulfilling everything which had been predicted for him.

The article went on to delve into his "extraordinary" background as an underprivileged black kid, the son of Senegalese immigrants, who grew up in one of the most notorious *banlieues* in Paris. His exceptional intelligence was noticed early by his teachers, as was his wonderful natural ability as a footballer. It was rare to be blessed with one outstanding talent. But such brilliance, in both academic and sporting disciplines, was unheard of, certainly in a black Parisian ghetto kid. As a teenager he had been pursued by several top French football clubs: Paris St. Germain, Metz, Marseilles. But he had been persuaded by his French teacher to take the academic route. While his star might

313

have shone brightly for a few short years as a top sportsman, his teacher had told him, it would have dimmed as surely and quickly as his body was destined to decline. But his mind would grow and expand for decades to come. It was good advice.

Diop gained easy access to the élite Université de Paris Dauphine, renowned for turning out the future captains of French commerce and industry. There he quickly developed into a brilliant all-round mind, so that by the time he graduated he was able, with just one year's preparation at Sciences-Po, to sail through the *Grand Oral* and the stringent entry exams for the École National d'Administration at his first attempt. He was, then, still only twenty-three.

Even today, however, he had not completely given up his football. As a student he had been the star player in ENA's official student football team — a mix of current and former pupils who played in a Monday night league. Since his return to Paris, he was still turning out every Monday as a former pupil, and was still their star player.

Enzo put his hand over Charlotte's to scroll back up to Diop's photograph. He stared at him hard for nearly half a minute. It was difficult to believe that this smiling young man had tried to kill him. That ten years earlier he had been part of a ruthless and savage group of students who had murdered their teacher. All of them endowed with rare intelligence, each of them on the threshold of brilliant careers. Why on earth had they done it?

He had left his hand resting on Charlotte's, and he became suddenly self-conscious. He quickly removed it. "So there's our sporting connection," he said. He glanced up at the whiteboard. "The cup and the whistle must lead us, somehow, to the next body part." It felt awkward now to talk about body parts with the victim's niece. Like speaking carelessly about a dead person to a recently bereaved relative.

"I suppose the cup could be some kind of football trophy," Charlotte said. "The division one championship, or the *Coupe de France*."

"Or any cup won by one of those teams who was interested in Diop as a teenager." Enzo pulled a sheet of paper towards him and scribbled the names down. "Paris St. Germain. Metz. Marseilles."

Charlotte stood up. "Football's for boys. I'll leave you to it." And she crossed to the fireplace and pulled the curtain aside, to disappear into the darkness of the attic staircase.

Enzo stood for a moment, wondering whether he should go after her. But decided against it, and sat down instead in front of the laptop. It only took him a few minutes to track down a UEFA website bristling with football statistics from around Europe. He scrolled back to the year 1996. The *Championnat de France* and the *Coupe de France* had both been won that year by Auxerre, the League Cup by FC Metz. The UEFA Cup had been won by Bayern Munich, and the Champions' League by Juventus. Paris St. Germain, more affectionately known as PSG, had won the European Cup Winners' Cup, and Germany had won the European Football Championship at the end of a three-week competition in England. So two of the clubs who had pursued Diop as a schoolboy, PSG and Metz, had won trophies in 1996.

He heard Charlotte coming back down the narrow wooden staircase. She pulled open the curtain at the foot of the stairs, and emerged carrying a small television set which she placed on the far end of the kitchen table. It was an old set, with a built-in video player. She began searching in a drawer of the *buffet* for a mains extension.

"What are we watching?" he asked.

"If the television still works I thought it might be useful to take a look at this." She lifted Enzo's manila envelope from the table and took out the video record of the Schoelcher Promotion that Madame Henry had given him in Paris. Enzo had forgotten all about it. He had no idea what Charlotte thought they might learn from it. Perhaps she just wanted to take a closer look at her uncle's killers.

He left her to set up the TV, and returned his attention to the computer. He typed *PSG* into the search window and hit the return key. The official website of Paris St. Germain came up at the top of the page. He clicked on the link. A menu down the left-hand side of the home page offered him a range of options from *Matches* to *Ticket Sales*. He selected *Club* and, from a submenu, *Histoire*. The page which downloaded offered a brief history of the club from its creation in 1970 to the present day. Enzo scanned the text, but nothing jumped out at him.

From a range of options along the top of the page he selected the period 1990–2000. A detailed history took him through that decade. The events of the 1995–96 season focused on the winning of the European Cup Winners' Cup — their first European trophy. He also read through an account of the following season. But again there was nothing to connect the club to any of the other clues. Or to François Diop. Enzo breathed his frustration into the rafters.

Charlotte had found a cable and was plugging in the TV set. She switched it on, and white noise issued from tiny speakers. She turned it to mute and said, "I was thinking about those numbers on the referee's whistle."

Enzo glanced up at the board, where he had written *19/3* beneath the photograph of the whistle. He had not yet given them any consideration. "What about them?"

"What do they look like to you?" She pushed the cassette into the slot beneath the screen, and like a mouth it opened up to swallow it whole.

Enzo looked at the numbers, vaguely shaking his head. He took a stab in the dark. "I don't know . . . a date?"

"Exactly."

He sat up. Why had he not thought of that? "Nineteen, three. March 19th." He looked at Charlotte. "Does that mean anything to you?" But even as he asked, he knew the answer. "19th of March, 1962. The date of the ceasefire in the Algerian War. There are streets and squares all over France named *19 Mars 1962*."

"That's the problem. There are too many of them, unless you can tie one to a specific location."

Enzo looked at her, surprised. "You'd already thought this through?"

"Of course."

"So when were you thinking of sharing it with me?"

"I just did." She stabbed the play button on the set. "Do you want to watch this or not?"

He left the computer and moved around the table as a piano began playing some soft classical music. The group photograph that Enzo knew so well came up on screen, with the caption: PROMOTION VICTOR SCHOELCHER 1994–96. Then, VIE D'UNE PROMOTION, followed by close-up shots of the faces in the photograph. They were all there. Gaillard, Hugues d'Hautvillers, Philippe Roques, François Diop. Enzo stared at it grimly. How many others had they not yet identified?

With a bad sound cut, the picture jumped to a shot of hanging French flags, and the caption, LE CONCOURS. This was an extract from some French television news item. A voiceover full of gravitas listed the names of famous *énarques*. Jacques Chirac, Alain Juppé, Lionel Jospin, Valéry Giscard d'Estaing. The leaders of a generation. And, thought Enzo, a roll-call of crooks. The camera lingered on the *façade* of ENA's former Paris HQ in Rue de l'Université. These presidents and prime ministers, the voice-over intoned gravely, had all passed through these hallowed gates. And today, it went on, there were more than four thousand *énarques* running both the French government and the private sector.

The camera wandered, then, into the torture chamber where ENA's panel of experts conducted the *Grand Oral*. Five smug interrogators sat behind a long, oval table smiling sadistically in anticipation of the inquisition to come. An elaborate timer stood on the table to count off the minutes.

The short film then segued through various sequences, amateur footage, and excerpts lifted from professional news reports. Students sitting in the ENA library discussing their course, shots of skiers at Puy St. Vincent during their bonding break. A lecture room full of students listening in rapt silence to their lecturer.

Enzo heard Charlotte's sharp intake of breath, and realised that the lecturer was Jacques Gaillard. He was brusque and business-like, addressing his students with the absolute confidence of a man free of self-doubt. Even in this fuzzy clip, with its bad ambient sound, his charisma was electrifying. He commanded total attention, complete respect. As the camera panned around the students, Enzo saw the languid figure of Philippe Roques, leaning one elbow on the arm of his chair, listening intently to his teacher. Enzo hit the pause button, and the picture froze on Roques' face. "Philippe Roques," he said. And he turned to see silent tears running down Charlotte's cheeks.

"Bastard!" she whispered.

Enzo let the tape run on. More shots of students, borrowed this time from BBC World. A caption, LA VIE À STRASBOURG. Students walked around the ancient streets of this centre of European power. In the language labs, yet more students conducted debates in foreign languages. German, Italian, English. They all seemed fluent. One student had enough confidence and wit to correct his chairman in English. "First, I would like to point out," he said, "that I am not *Mister* Mbala, I am *Chief* Mbala."

And then there was Hugues d'Hautvillers, smiling, cocky, cracking jokes in German, aware of the camera on him and playing to the gallery. Enzo wondered what on earth had led him from precocious childhood to murder and suicide — if that's what it had been.

The film cut to LES SPORTS. A mini-marathon. Students rowing and doing press-ups. And then a football match. A black player scoring a spectacular goal. François Diop. Fit. Strong. No wonder he had been able to overpower Enzo so easily. Enzo felt a huge surge of resentment and anger. These people had been given every advantage nature and society could offer. Intelligence, talent, privilege. And yet they had chosen to exercise their advantage by indulging in murder. Both then and now. Only now, it seemed, they were disposing of one another.

The end caption came up. BONNE CHANCE, TOUS NOS VOEUX, A BIENTÔT, EN FORMATION PERMANENTE. The film was dated March 1996.

"They graduated in March," Charlotte said quietly. "So they had five long months to plan and carry out the murder of my uncle. No rush of blood to the head,

320

no *crime passionel*. Just cold, calm, premeditated murder."

She switched off the recorder, and it spat the tape back out at them, as if the cassette had left the same bad taste in its mouth as in theirs. They sat in silence, staring at the blank screen. Then Charlotte said, out of nowhere, "What about the Saint's day? That came up in one of the previous sets of clues, didn't it?"

Enzo did not immediately understand. "April 1st," he said. "But I don't see . . ."

"March 19th," Charlotte said patiently.

Enzo glanced at the board again and shook his head doubtfully. "We've already got a name."

She shrugged. "It wouldn't do any harm to know."

Enzo returned to the computer and tapped the date into Google. "Saint Joseph," he said. "It's Saint Joseph's Day."

In the moments of silence that followed, neither of them could think of any relevant observation. Then Charlotte said, "I'll pack the TV away." And Enzo returned to his search of football clubs. He typed *FC METZ* into the search window, and when he punched the return key a link to the official website of FC Metz appeared at the top of the page. He clicked on it and was immediately subjected to a passage of loud rock music accompanying flashing animated images of a footballer intercut with the club's official shield.

"What in God's name's that?" Charlotte asked.

But Enzo had frozen, his eyes locked on the screen, his heart pulsing in his throat. The animated sequence

321

finished on a final image of the club shield, and then cut to the home page. "Jesus . . ."

"What is it?" Charlotte came around to look.

"The official emblem of Metz football club. It's a salamander." He pushed back his chair and crossed quickly to the whiteboard. He wrote up *Metz FC* and circled it. "That's it. That's the place."

"Metz?"

"Yes."

"More body parts? More clues?"

"It must be." Enzo turned back to the board and started slashing arrows across it. "All the arrows that pointed to Diop carry on to Metz. Then we have another arrow from the salamander. Metz won the league cup in 1996, so another arrow from the football trophy. And then a final arrow from the referee's whistle. Another football connection."

But Charlotte was not convinced. "What about March 19th?"

"I don't know. Maybe the football stadium's in *Rue du 19 Mars 1962*. We'll find out when we get there."

Charlotte began studiously winding up the mains extension cable. "*You* might. *I* won't."

Enzo felt an unpleasant stillness settle on him. "You're not coming with me?"

"No. I have to get back to Paris."

"Don't you want to know who killed your uncle?"

She turned on him, anger flashing in her eyes. "What do you care? All you're interested in is winning your bet."

322

If she had plunged a knife into his heart, she could hardly have hurt him more. But maybe it was no more than he deserved. He watched her in silence as she packed away the cables. "How will you get back to Paris?"

She shrugged, "You can drop me at the railway station in Tulle." And she lifted the television to take it back up to her room.

CHAPTER NINETEEN

I

The car stood where they had left it, abandoned on the track. But there was no traffic here. Not even the local farmer came down this way. The back of the car was buckled and scorched where the truck had rammed them, and scraped all down one side where they had struck the dividing drum a glancing blow at the off ramp.

On his fourth failed attempt to start the car, the engine made a sound like tearing metal and abruptly seized. Now it would not even turn over. Charlotte got out and walked around to the front of the car. "There's oil all over the path."

Enzo released the hood and went to have a look. A small river of oil had run down among the stones, dividing and subdividing, before soaking into the earth. He lifted the hood and the pungent stench of warm lubricating oil wafted up into their faces. It glistened on every surface of the engine and its mountings. "Shit!" Enzo dropped the hood and thought about it. They were miles from anywhere. And even if they could persuade a *garagiste* to come out, the car was unlikely to be on the road again anytime soon. He felt in the leg pocket of his cargos for his mobile. Its tiny screen told him there was a strong signal here. He thought for a moment, then became aware of Charlotte looking at him.

She said, "Who are you calling?"

"My daughter."

Sophie answered quickly. "Hi, Papa. Where are you?"

"Sophie, I've been in a road accident."

"Oh, *mon dieu*! Papa, are you all right?"

"I'm fine. But I need you to do me a favour." He took a deep breath and swallowed his pride. "Actually, it's Bertrand I need to do me the favour."

"Bertrand?"

"He's got transport, hasn't he?"

"He's got a van, yes."

"I need him to come up to the Corrèze and pick me up. And then take me to Metz." He paused. "Oh, and ask him to bring a couple of spades."

II

They went back to the house, and Charlotte made coffee. Then she climbed the hill and lay in the grass, propped on one elbow, sipping her hot drink and staring gloomily out across the valley. Enzo returned to his stone bench, and they waited, neither of them speaking to the other, through three long hours, as the sun sank lower in the sky.

By eight, Enzo was about to call Sophie again when they heard an engine straining on the road above.

325

Charlotte locked up again, and they followed the railway sleepers up through the trees to Enzo's car. When they got there, Bertrand's white van was pulled in behind it, engine idling, and he and Sophie were out looking at the damage.

Sophie hurled herself at her father, wrapping her arms around his neck and nearly knocking him over. "Oh, Papa, I've been worried about you all the way here." She held his face in her hands to look at him. "Are you sure you're all right?"

"I'm fine, pet, really." And he pulled her to him and hugged her tightly.

"That's some mess you've made of your car, Monsieur Macleod," Bertrand observed dryly. "What happened? Did you back into a tree?"

Enzo glared at him. "No, Bertrand. A truck tried to run me off the road."

"It not only tried, it succeeded," Charlotte said.

Sophie spun around to look at her. "Hi." She waited expectantly for a moment. "I'm Sophie."

"I'm Charlotte." Charlotte held out her hand and Sophie shook it with unabashed curiosity.

"So you and dad are . . . friends, then?"

"Yes," Enzo said quickly. "And this is Bertrand."

"So I gathered." Charlotte and Bertrand shook hands, and she touched a fingertip to her nose. "Love the stud. Is it a real diamond?" Enzo felt as if she was only saying it to annoy him. But, then, they had never discussed Bertrand, and she had no idea what he thought of facial piercing.

326

Bertrand nodded enthusiastically. "Yeah. Eighteen carat." Then, "Do you live here?" He sounded incredulous. "It took us forever to find this place."

"It's a holiday home. I live in Paris."

"Are you coming with us to Metz?" Sophie asked eagerly. She was evidently anxious to learn more about her Papa's "friend."

"I'm afraid not." Charlotte was awkward. "Your father said you would drop me off at Tulle. I'm getting the train back to Paris from there."

"Oh." Sophie was disappointed. "Sure."

"Do you have any idea how long we're going to be away?" Bertrand asked Enzo. "I've had to pay someone to look after the gym."

"I'll pay you back," Enzo said abruptly. "Can we go? It's getting late."

But before anyone could move, the back door of Bertrand's van swung open and a sleepy-looking Nicole jumped out. She stretched, thrusting juddering bosoms toward the treetops and blinking in the late evening sun. "Why did no one wake me?"

Sophie and Bertrand exchanged looks.

Then Nicole's gaze fell upon Enzo and she rushed to give him a crushing hug. "Oh, Monsieur Macleod, are you all right? I've been so worried about you."

Enzo prised himself free of her, and glanced self-consciously towards Charlotte. "What are you doing here, Nicole?"

Sophie pulled a face. "She's been hanging around the apartment for days waiting for you. As soon as she knew you'd phoned, there was no dissuading her from coming with us."

III

The sun had dipped behind the hills, but there was still light in the sky when they dropped Charlotte at the station in Tulle.

Enzo had squatted on the floor in the back of the van, Nicole prattling in his ear, while Charlotte sat up front in the passenger seat, with Sophie squeezed in between her and Bertrand. The teenager had chatted animatedly to Charlotte, eliciting more information in half an hour than her father had managed in over a week.

They all got out of the van in the station car park. Sophie kissed Charlotte on both cheeks. "You've got to come and see us in Cahors," she said. "You'd love it there, and Papa's a great cook."

"Charlotte's a very busy woman," Enzo said.

Charlotte avoided his eye. "That's right." She shook Bertrand's hand. "Thanks for the lift, Bertrand."

"*De rien.*" He gazed at her admiringly.

She turned to Enzo. "You'll let me know how you get on?"

"Of course."

And she turned and walked into the station. Sophie looked at her father. "You didn't kiss her goodbye."

"No, I didn't."

Sophie cocked an eyebrow. "Lover's tiff?"

"Don't even go there," Enzo growled.

"She's a beautiful looking woman," Bertrand said.

Sophie tipped her head at him. "And don't you go there, either." And then she grinned.

"Can we go, please?" Enzo opened the passenger door and held it open for Sophie.

She flounced past him and jumped in. "You're in a right mood tonight, aren't you?"

They got on to the A89 *autoroute* for Clermont-Ferrand just outside Tulle, Enzo, Sophie and Bertrand all squeezed into the front, Nicole in the back, the roar of the engine and the smell of diesel filling the cab. It was Bertrand, finally, who broke the silence. "You said you were run off the road by a truck."

"That's right?"

"On purpose?"

"Yes."

Nicole leaned forward from the back and peered at him in the gathering darkness. "Why?"

Enzo took a deep breath. "I suppose you all have the right to know." He hesitated. "This murder I've been trying to solve —"

"Jacques Gaillard?" Sophie said.

Enzo nodded. "I've found three of his killers so far. Two of them are dead, and the third one has tried to kill me at least once."

The youngsters were shocked to silence. Then Sophie said in a very small voice, "Why are we going to Metz?"

"To find another body part, and the clues that'll lead us to the fourth killer."

By midnight, Enzo could not keep his eyes open. His head was rolling about on his chest. At Vierzon, Bertrand left the *autoroute* and took a D-road cross-country towards Troyes. Metz was an industrial town in north-west France, not far from the German border. It would be several more hours before they got there.

Bertrand said, "Why don't you lie down and sleep, Monsieur Macleod? There's a mattress rolled up in the back there. Nicole was using it earlier." He flicked his head towards the back of the van.

"It's very comfortable," Nicole said. "And I could do with some company back here."

Sophie stifled a smile. "On you go, Papa. We'll wake you up when we get there."

Bertrand pulled in at the side of the road, and Enzo got out into the warm night air. There was nothing else on the road. He went around the back and climbed into the dark interior. The courtesy light below the rear-view mirror barely reached beyond the driver's seat, but what little light it cast illuminated Nicole's beam of pleasure. "Over there behind the seats," she said, pointing. "I tied it up again."

Enzo fumbled about until he found the mattress, rolled up and tied with string. As he untied it, the mattress flopped open across the floor of the van, and something struck him a glancing blow on the side of the head

"Ow!" he yelled. "What the hell . . ."

Bertrand retrieved a flashlight from the glove compartment and shone it into the back. Caught in its

330

beam, Enzo saw the familiar shape of Bertrand's metal detector.

"Bloody thing!" It was as if it were following him. And he heard a muffled snigger coming from the front. He kicked it to one side and lay down on the mattress as Bertrand extinguished the flashlight and forced his gearbox through shot synchromesh into first gear. They moved off with a jerk.

"Night, Papa," he heard Sophie saying, then after a moment felt the warmth of Nicole's body as she plumped herself down next to him.

"You don't mind, do you?" she said in the dark. "There's plenty of room for both of us."

He had no recollection of whether or not he responded. The rhythm of the engine, the thrum of tyres on tarmac, very quickly dragged him down into a dark, dreamy sleep where he was chased by salamanders and confronted by creatures with bloodied faces. He had no idea how much later it was that he awoke with a sudden, startling thought in his head. It was still dark, and the ever-present roar of the diesel seemed never-ceasing. Like jet engines on a transcontinental flight, it had become part of the very fabric of his existence. Nicole was fast asleep. He scrambled on to his knees and pulled at Bertrand's shoulder from behind. Bertrand half-turned his head and Sophie looked back in surprise and alarm.

"Are you all right, Papa?"

"Why have you got a mattress in the back of your van?"

Bertrand turned away and fixed his eyes on the road. He said nothing. Enzo was sure he could see colour rising on his neck.

Sophie laughed. "Don't be silly, Papa. What do you think it's for?"

This was not a thought that Enzo wanted to entertain. "For heaven's sake, Bertrand, she's my *daughter*," was all he could think to say. And immediately it occurred to him that his concern was more for himself than for his daughter, his fear of losing her.

Bertrand kept his eyes front. "I'm sure Sophie's mum was someone's daughter, too. And I'm sure you loved her just as much as I love Sophie."

Sophie reached out to touch Bertrand's cheek. Enzo could almost feel her pleasure in Bertrand's words.

"There's no room at my mum's," Bertrand said to Enzo. "And I know you don't approve of me. So . . ." He left the sentence hanging, with all its implications. Where else were they to go? Enzo was depressed by the thought that somehow he was to blame. Forcing them to make love on some seedy mattress in the back of a van. He felt even more uncomfortable on it now, and he retired silently into the back of the van like an animal with a self-inflicted wound.

He lay on his back, then, leaving a discreet distance between Nicole and himself, and thought of Pascale. How she had turned his life upside down, touched him with a forbidden happiness, and then left him with only the memory of it. He remembered Bertrand angrily saying to him of Sophie, *She's not your little girl any more. So maybe it's time you started letting her grow up.* Sophie was just three years younger now than her mother had been when Enzo first met her. But all Enzo could think of was the little girl he had raised, all her moments of tears and triumph. Her tearful first day at school, the first wobbling moments on a bicycle. *Don't let go, Papa, don't let go!* The hours spent in the open-air pool on the Île de Cabessut teaching her to swim. The joy of passing her *baccalaureate*. Moments replayed, some of them too close to those he had lived through once before with Kirsty as a child. Only, he had lost Kirsty through his own selfishness, and had no idea what he would do if he lost Sophie, too. Bertrand would never know how hard it was for him to let go.

He closed his eyes and succumbed to dreams of Charlotte, with her beautiful black eyes, and the soft touch of her fingertips on his face. Even in sleep there was no escape from the melancholy reminders of his life's failures. And somewhere, in the last shreds of consciousness, he found regret again that he had not handled his confrontation with her differently.

IV

Sunlight poured in the back window and splashed across the mattress, hot through the glass, burning his clothes and his skin. Enzo stirred and rolled over, turning face-first into the large, round sensor pad of Bertrand's metal detector. He awoke, startled and disorientated.

"Morning, Papa."

He turned to see Sophie smiling back at him from the passenger seat. "Where are we?"

"Metz. We got here in the middle of the night. It seemed a shame to wake you. And, anyway, there was nothing you could do while it was still dark. So we just snatched a few hours' sleep here in the front."

The driver's door opened, and Bertrand's face appeared. "Is he awake yet?"

"Yes, he is," Enzo said.

Bertrand grinned at him. "Morning, Monsieur Macleod."

Enzo looked around. "Where's Nicole?"

Sophie couldn't resist a smile. "Still in seventh heaven after spending the night with you. If only her father could have seen you."

Enzo glared at her and Bertrand said, "She went for a wander round the stadium."

Enzo opened the back doors and climbed stiffly out into the morning sunshine, blinking in its glare. He slipped on his jacket and saw that they were parked beside a small river running along behind the stadium. He also noticed, with some disappointment, that they were not in the Rue du 19 Mars 1962. This was the more prosaically named Rue du Stade. Trees grew alongside the river, opposite a row of terraced houses and a sports shop. He turned to see the main stand stretching away towards the distant motorway. Stade Symphorien. The home of FC Metz since 1987. He saw the club shield on the side of the north stand, the double-cross of Lorraine on one side, a salamander on the other.

And then Nicole appeared from behind the east stand. As she approached them Enzo saw that she was frowning. "Why are we here, Monsieur Macleod?"

Enzo sighed. Facts were easier to explain than instinct. "Because Metz won the League Cup in 1996. A replica trophy was one of the clues we found at Hautvillers. And because the club's emblem is a salamander. That was another of them."

"Do you have photographs?"

"Yes."

"Let's have a look at them, then," Sophie said, and they all crowded around Enzo at the open back door as he took the prints out of his bag and laid them along the floor of the van.

Bertrand craned his neck to see. "Is that the trophy?" He stabbed a finger at the picture of the cup.

"Yes."

"Then that's not the League Cup. Not even the old one. The League Cup's a unique design. Unmistakeable."

"So what is it, then?" Nicole asked.

Bertrand lifted the photograph. "This is the *Coupe de France*."

"What's the difference?" Sophie said.

"The difference is that, in 1996, the *Coupe de France* was won by Auxerre. Not Metz."

"And," said Nicole, as if to rub salt in the wound, "the Metz emblem is not a salamander." She looked up at the graphic on the stand. "Very similar, Monsieur Macleod, but it's actually a graoully. A sort of dragon."

CHAPTER
TWENTY

I

The mediaeval city of Auxerre stood on a hill on the banks of the river Yonne, one hundred and seventy kilometres south-east of Paris, in the heart of the Bourgogne. It was early afternoon by the time they reached it, and ominous, dark clouds had already begun rolling in from the west. The air was humid, hot, filled with the promise of summer rain. As they crossed the Pont Paul Bert, daylight darkness settled like a shroud on the towers and buttresses of St. Étienne Cathedral, which dominated the skyline on the west bank. Cruise boats lined up along the quays opposite, rising and falling as if in slow motion on the gentle slate grey swell of the river.

The stade Abbé-Deschamps stood along the banks of the Yonne at the south end of town, surrounded by playing fields and running tracks. Bertrand turned left off the main road into the car park in front of the main stand, and Enzo got out of the van stretching and flexing limbs that had stiffened up during the three-and-a-half hour drive.

Kids were playing football on the far side of a fence, aspiring future stars, shouting and chasing, attracted to the ball like metal filings to a magnet. Enzo left Sophie and Bertrand and Nicole in the van and walked along the length of the stand, past the boutique and the ticket office and the administration block. He had a sickening sense of *déjà vu*. One football stadium was much like another. Metz had been a wild goose chase. Auxerre might well be the same. He had no idea what he was looking for.

Behind the Leclerc stand, which backed on to the river, youngsters were chasing one another up and down the concrete steps, their catcalls and laughter echoing between rows of grey plastic seats. In the dark beneath the overhang, he saw two young lovers backed up against a wall, oblivious to the kids playing on the staircases and landings above them, driven by adolescent hormones to fulfil some desperate fantasy amongst the broken bottles and discarded beer cans. Beyond the trees, two teams of rowers cut through choppy waters, the blades of their oars rising and falling in perfect unison, throwing cool spray into warm air.

Even as he found his way between the stands to the very edge of the pitch, secure behind its moat and fences, he knew that there would be nothing for him here. Cut grass and advertising hoardings, rows of empty seats rising into the stands.

When he got back to the van Nicole looked at him expectantly. "Well?"

He shook his head. "I'm wasting my time here. And yours. We should go back to Cahors."

"It's a long drive," Bertrand said.

Enzo looked at him. The young man was exhausted. He had driven through the night to Metz, and then again all morning to Auxerre. It would be six or seven hours back to Cahors. "Why don't we stay overnight?" Enzo said. "I'll pay for a hotel. We can head back in the morning." After all, what was there to hurry back for?

The Hôtel l'Aquarius was at the end of the Avenue Gambetta, east of the river, in the new part of town. The rooms were small, windows looking out over a shambles of red-tiled rooftops and seedy backyards. Nicole went off with Sophie and Bertrand to explore the old city, and Enzo lay down on his bed staring at the cracks in the ceiling. He thought again about all the clues which had brought him here. There were too many anomalies. The referee's whistle with the numbers 19/3 scratched into the plating. They didn't seem to fit with anything else. The salamander which had sent him on a fool's errand to Metz. How certain he had been that he would find the answers he was looking for at Metz football club. A certainty so easily punctured by Bertrand's revelation about the *Coupe de France* and Auxerre. As well as Nicole's graoully. Perhaps Enzo had misread the clues completely. Perhaps there was no football connection at all. When conviction is fractured, doubt creeps in through all the cracks.

The silence in Enzo's room pressed in around him. He wondered what awaited him in Cahors. Was he still in danger? He wished he had never heard of Raffin and his seven most celebrated unsolved murders. It was one thing to make an argument in the abstract during the course of a dinner, to deliver bold statements and accept wagers, it was quite another to come face to face with reality. Real life. Real death. Murder. Personal tragedy. He thought of Charlotte, and of how things had been between them, and he remembered an old Chinese proverb. *It is not an easy thing to mend a broken mirror.*

He reached for the remote control and turned on the television. The melodramatic orchestral overtures of some dubbed American soap filled the room. But anything was better than the silence which accompanied regret. He closed his eyes and let the sounds of it wash over him without listening.

He was not certain how long he had been asleep, but something in the voice that wakened him penetrated deep into his subconscious to bring him bubbling back to the surface. The national television news was playing on France 3, and he realised with something of a shock that it was after seven. His thoughts were quickly focused on the commentary of the reporter. He squinted at the picture to see helicopter footage of long traffic tailbacks on the *périphérique* ring road around Paris. His heart was pounding, but he wasn't quite sure why. *It took firemen more than half an hour to cut through the wreckage to recover the body,* the voiceover told him. *An investigation has already begun into what caused the vehicle to swerve across three lanes of traffic and into the containing wall before bursting into flames.* A still photograph filled the screen, and Enzo sat abruptly upright. It was the same

339

photograph he had seen on the internet yesterday. A stock shot, apparently in use by all the media. Diop's unmistakable lopsided smile. *François Diop was being tipped for high office at the United Nations before today's tragedy. He is survived by a wife and two young children.*

Enzo sat with the blood pulsing at his temples. Diop was dead. The man who had tried to kill him just two days ago. The man whose footballing past had led Enzo to this provincial hotel room in the ancient city of Auxerre. Dead because of Enzo. He was sure of that.

An urgent knocking at the door startled him. Sophie's voice called from the hall. "Papa? Papa, are you there?" He slid off the bed, and as he stood the blood rushed to his head. He steadied himself against the door jamb and unlocked the door. Sophie and Bertrand and Nicole stood in the darkness. Sophie seemed shocked by his appearance. "Papa, are you feeling all right?"

"I'm fine, Sophie. What's all the noise about?"

She grinned then, her eyes gleaming with anticipation. "You'll never guess what we found up in the old town."

"You're right, I'll never guess."

"A restaurant," Nicole said before Sophie could respond.

Enzo sighed. "Is that a hint that you're hungry?"

Nicole shook her head triumphantly, but Sophie beat her to the punchline. "It's called The Salamander."

II

La Salamandre restaurant was at number 84 Rue de Paris, next door to a wine merchant's, and opposite a shop supplying flowers for funerals. The three youngsters led Enzo up through the narrow streets of the *cité médiéval*. A cat sat in an open window, above an old bicycle, and watched them go by. Geraniums poured in carefully pruned cascades from hanging pots on almost every corner. Tourists filled the cafés in Place Charles Surugue, soaking up the burgundy wines and the centuries-old ambience of the ancient, beamed buildings that leaned and tilted at odd angles all around them. Enzo watched the town slide by, like a man seeing the world through a fisheye lens. There was nothing here out of the ordinary, and yet none of it seemed quite real. He felt oddly detached, as if fate had taken away his powers of decision-making, and given over his life to the vagaries of chance and serendipity. The same clues which had led Enzo to Diop were leading him now to a restaurant in a quiet back street in this *capitale départementale* of the Yonne. A chance find by these young people he had unwittingly involved in this foolish venture.

Painted salamanders climbed the pale green frames around the door of the restaurant. *Poissons — Fruits de Mer*, it said in both windows. They stood outside on the pavement, looking at a menu offering oysters, large roasted king prawns, half lobster roasted in its shell with pan-fried chanterelle mushrooms.

"What do you want to do?" Nicole asked.

Enzo could almost hear her salivating. "I suppose we'd better go in and eat."

It was still early, and they were seated at a table near the window. The waiter was a young man in his early twenties. Bertrand, at Enzo's bidding, ordered a 1999 Pouilly Fuissé to wash down their seafood. Sophie asked for a bottle of Badoit, Nicole a diet Coke, and Enzo asked the waiter if he knew of any connection between the restaurant and Auxerre football club.

The young man gave him an odd look. "Why on earth would there be?"

Enzo shrugged, a little embarrassed. It must have seemed like a very peculiar question. "I don't know. I just wondered, that's all."

The waiter looked puzzled. "Not that I know of. I could ask the owner if you like. Monsieur Colas. He's also the chef. He opened this place more than twenty years ago."

"No, that's all right." Enzo knew now that this was a waste of time. No more than a bizarre coincidence. And then a thought occurred to him. "Are you a supporter?"

"Of Auxerre? Sure. My father started taking me when I was just five years old."

"You know that the salamander was the emblem of François Premier?"

The waiter looked at him as if he were a sandwich short of a picnic. This was all getting a little surreal. "Was it?" It was clear that he didn't.

Enzo was disappointed. "So you wouldn't know of any connection between Auxerre football club and François Premier."

"I could tell you more about the English Premiership than François Premier. And apart from where they finished in the league last season, the only unusual thing I know about Auxerre football club is their patron saint. Saint Joseph. And I only know that because it's the name of the school I went to."

Enzo was beginning to feel like one of the Three Princes of Serendip. "There's a school in Auxerre called Saint Joseph's?"

"Sure. Saint Jo's. It's a *lycée* and *collége* and commercial school all rolled into one. Just up the hill there in the Quartier Saint Simeon." He paused. "Is there anything else I can get you?"

Enzo shook is head. "No. Thank you."

Nicole looked at him. "Is that significant?"

"One of the items we found along with the clues that led us here was a referee's whistle with numbers scratched into the plating. A nineteen and a three, separated by an oblique."

"Nineteen, three," Bertrand said. "March 19th."

Enzo was taken aback. It had taken Charlotte to point that out to him. "It's Saint Joseph's day," he said.

Bertrand thought for a moment. "So you think the clues only led to Auxerre football club, in order to take you on to the school, via the club's patron saint?"

Enzo shrugged his eyebrows. "It's possible."

"But what could there be at the school?" Sophie asked.

"Playing fields, perhaps." Enzo shook his head. "There has to be some reason for the inclusion of a referee's whistle." The waiter brought an ice bucket to

343

their table, Pouilly Fuissé chilling in iced water. "We'd better go and see." He caught Nicole's look of alarm and added, "after we've eaten."

III

Saint Jo's Collège and Lycée was at the top of the Boulevard de la Marne on the northern edge of town. It was flanked on its west side by suburban villas and bungalows. At the foot of the hill there was a development of residential apartments, and a franchise for Mitsubishi Motors. The school itself stood, in the gathering gloom, behind white walls and blue fencing, in several acres of forested parkland. The sky was a pewtery blue-black, low clouds scraping the surrounding hills. Street lamps fought to make any impression in the growing twilight. Bertrand drew his van up to electronic gates that were closed and padlocked. There were no lights beyond them, and no sign of life. Immediately opposite, the offices of the Crédit Agricole bank were shuttered and dark. The only light was a moth-infested pool of yellow at a roadside cash dispenser.

There was little or no traffic on the boulevard as Enzo stepped out of the van to feel the first spots of rain, warm and heavy on his face. Somewhere beyond the far hills, the sky flashed and crackled, and several seconds later they heard the distant rumble of thunder. The air was filled with the smell of ozone. A sudden *courant d'air* moved among the trees beyond the fence like a sigh. The first turbulent breath of the coming storm.

Enzo scaled the gate with the minimum of effort and dropped down on the other side.

"Papa, you can't just go breaking into the place," Sophie hissed at him from the van.

"I'm not breaking anything. I'm just having a look."

"I'm coming with you," Bertrand said suddenly. And before any of the others could object, he was out of the van, and vaulting easily over the gate. He grinned at the scowling Enzo. "Safety in numbers." He snapped on his flashlight. "And it helps to be able to see."

Nicole climbed out of the back. "Be careful, Monsieur Macleod."

"And for goodness' sake be quick!" Sophie called after them as they moved off into the grounds and were consumed by the dark.

They followed the beam of Bertrand's flashlight along a metalled drive, an empty car park brooding silently away to the right. To their left, a roadway ran off through trees to a cluster of single and two-storey flat-roofed buildings. Up ahead, floodlights mounted on the roof of the school gymnasium were trained on an area of playing fields behind a high wire fence. In the distance, Enzo could just make out a patchwork of baseball and volleyball courts. Immediately to their right was the football pitch. A dusty, chalky, burned-up stretch of what might once have been grass. Bertrand swung his beam across the pitch to pick out the white of the goal posts. The nets had been removed. Big fat raindrops were leaving craters in the dust.

"We're going to get wet," Bertrand said.

Enzo nodded absently. He was staring off thoughtfully across the football pitch in the final glimmer of the day's light. "You know a bit about football, don't you?"

"I used to play for an amateur side."

"Where does the referee usually stand when he blows for kick-off?"

He heard the young man expel air through his teeth. "Well, I don't think there's any set place." Bertrand thought for a moment. "I guess he usually stands somewhere around the centre circle."

"That's a big area to dig up."

"What, you mean you think that what you're looking for is buried somewhere in the centre circle?"

"I don't know. I really don't. I'm clutching at straws here. If we're in the right place — and I've got to believe that we are, since all the clues have led us here — then there has to be a reason for the referee's whistle." Enzo sighed, frustrated, trying to articulate his reasoning. "The clues have always been symbolic or representative of something else, Bertrand. So maybe it's not the whistle itself that's important, so much as the person who blows it."

He began walking out across the pitch towards the centre circle. The lines delineating the field of play were faded almost to the point of obscurity. The rain would very soon obliterate any remaining traces. Bertrand followed him to the centre circle, his flashlight trained on the halfway line that led them there.

"My God," Enzo said surveying a diametre of something close to twenty metres. "It's huge. We couldn't possibly dig up an area this size."

"We don't have to," Bertrand said. "Wait here." And he took off, running back towards the gate before Enzo had the chance to ask him what he was talking about. He stood, then, a solitary figure, in the centre of the football pitch, where generations of breathless kids had chased elusive aspirations in the shape of a leather ball, and when genius had eluded them, gone on to become doctors, lawyers, waiters. For a moment, he felt surrounded by the ghosts of failed ambition, until lightning tore open the sky and he saw that he was completely alone.

All daylight had bled, now, from the evening. The darkness was absolute. Thunder cracked so loudly overhead that it felt like a physical blow. Enzo ducked involuntarily, and as lightning flashed again beneath dangerously low clouds, he saw the lean, fit figure of Bertrand loping back across the pitch, his flashlight in one hand, his metal detector dangling from the other. Bertrand was grinning when he reached him. "I knew this would come in useful for something."

Enzo looked at him for a long moment. Words escaped him. Then finally he said, "Well, I hope the damned thing works!"

Bertrand began a first circuit of the centre circle, the metal detector hovering just centimetres above the parched ground as he swept it methodically from side to side. And then the rain began in earnest, almost tropical in its intensity. Within seconds both men were soaked to the skin. Enzo held the flashlight and followed Bertrand's progress. The hard-baked earth was slow to soak up the rain, and it began lying in ever widening puddles on the surface of the playing field. The metal detector emitted a steady, high-pitched whine, only just audible above the drumming of the rain.

"Papa . . ." Enzo turned as Sophie and Nicole ran into the circle of light, a shared raincoat held over their heads and shoulders.

"You can't stay out in this," Nicole said.

"It's crazy, Papa."

"You should have stayed in the van," was all he said.

And suddenly the wail of the metal detector rose half an octave. In that moment lightning filled the sky, infusing every single drop of rain with its light so that the world was lost in a brief, blinding mist. But even above the crash of thunder that followed, Enzo could still hear the shriek of the metal detector.

"There's something here," Bertrand bellowed above the noise of the rain. "Right below here!" He had completed about two thirds of his circuit and stood at ten o'clock on the circle. Gelled spikes had dissolved into streaks of black hair striping vertically on his forehead. Water dripped from his eyebrow piercings and nose and lip studs, and he was grinning like an idiot. "We'd better start digging."

"We can't dig in this rain," Enzo shouted back. "The hole will just fill with water."

"I've got an old two-man tent in the back of the van. If we put up the outer skin we can cover the hole."

"Did you bring the shovels?"

"Of course."

"You're mad!" Sophie shouted at them.

But Enzo just turned to the two girls and said, "Go and get the tent and the spades."

Within ten minutes they had erected the arched cross frames of a small igloo tent, stretching its plastic outer skin tightly across it and pegging it into increasingly soft earth. Bertrand began digging first, until he had made enough of a hole to allow Enzo in beside him, and the two men dug furiously by the light of the flashlight, expelling shovel after shovel of mud through the open flap on to the pitch beyond. The rain hammered an unrelenting tattoo on the taut plastic. Sophie and Nicole stood outside, beneath their raincoat, watching the silhouettes of the two men in the tent rise and fall like some distorted shadow theatre playing out on its curving walls.

They were almost a metre down before Enzo's spade hit metal. It jarred up through his arms and shoulders, but the dull clang of metal on metal was sweet music to accompany the drumming of the rain. In spite of the tent, water was seeping back into the hole. Enzo knew they would have to get the chest out completely, to be sure of keeping its contents dry and free from contamination. It took another fifteen minutes to prise it from the mud suction of its ten-year resting place and lift it carefully up on to the rim of the crater they had made. The flashlight's batteries were failing fast, and they both stood panting, and staring at the trunk in the fading yellow light. It was the same military green as all

349

the others. Enzo glanced at Bertrand, and saw that his face was sweat-streaked and covered in mud. They were like clay men, standing ankle deep in liquid earth, breathing hard and filled with anticipation and trepidation.

The girls crouched down at the opening and peered in. "Is that it?" Sophie said.

Enzo nodded. "Take a pair of latex gloves from my bag and give me something to dry my hands with."

Nicole held out a handkerchief for him to wipe the mud from his hands and face, and Sophie handed him a pair of surgeon's gloves from his bag. He tore them out of their plastic wrapping and snapped them on. Very carefully he unclasped the lid of the trunk and lifted it open. It was stiff, complaining loudly as he forced it back against the will of rusted hinges. Bertrand shone his flashlight inside.

"Jesus!" Enzo heard him whisper.

The skeletal remains of Jacques Gaillard's torso almost filled the interior. Bleached white bones. Shoulders, ribs, pelvis, spine. Enzo had to reach carefully through a ribcage chipped and scarred by the blades which had killed Gaillard, to remove one, by one, what he knew now to be the final set of clues. A short meat cleaver. A baking tray with twelve moulds in the shape of seashells. A bunch of chopsticks tied together with a piece of string. Even before he counted them, Enzo had guessed how many there might be. Thirteen. Unlucky for some. There was a green glass model of the leaning tower of Pisa, and a key ring replica of the Eiffel Tower. Enzo looked at it closely and saw that it was made in China. Just one more confirmation. The final item was a small rock hammer with a rubberised handle grip.

He laid them out side by side on the inside of the lid. The only thing he had not yet worked out was the name of the last surviving killer.

"Give me my camera," he said to Sophie, just as Bertrand's flashlight delivered its final flicker and plunged them into blackness.

Almost at the same instant, they were dazzled by a blinding white light, and the sound of revving motors soared above the storm. As Sophie and Nicole spun around to see what was happening, Enzo saw lightning flash through the tent flap, and the silhouettes of half a dozen vehicles behind a phalanx of lights were thrown into momentary sharp relief as they came hurtling towards them across the football pitch. Then blackness swallowed the sky, and their eyes were filled again only with the light. The vehicles pulled up abruptly, engines still revving, and a dozen or more figures streamed out into the rain-filled glare, automatic rifles clutched across their chests. A voice crackled through a megaphone.

"Step out into the light. Keep your hands above your heads."

Enzo and Bertrand pulled themselves from the hole and crawled out of the tent into the rain and the light. The girls had abandoned their shared raincoat and stood with their hands high above their heads. The rain streamed down Sophie's frightened face. Before either man could get to his feet, boots came splashing through the wet, and strong hands forced all four of them face first into the mud. Enzo felt the cold bite of handcuffs around his wrists as they snapped shut.

IV

Sophie was furious. She paced restlessly around the cell. "It's ridiculous. A complete over-reaction. We were digging a hole in a football field, for God's sake. And they send men with guns?" She waved her arms in the air. "And look at me. Look!"

They all looked. The mud was drying on her now, cracking and flaking. It was stuck in her hair like glue, smeared across her face, and caked on her tee shirt and jeans. But she was just a mirror image of the rest of them.

"It's assault!" she railed. "I bet I'm covered in bruises. I'm going to sue them!" She hammered on the steel door with her fists. "I demand to see a doctor! It's my right to see a doctor!"

She was answered by a resounding silence. Digging a hole in a football field, it seemed, had been enough to deprive them of their rights.

They had been denied their right to a telephone call. They had no means of exercising their right to a thirty-minute private interview with an *avocat*, since no one knew they were there. And now, Sophie claimed, she was being denied her right to be examined by a doctor. Enzo supposed they had been granted their right to silence, since nobody had asked them anything.

They had been bundled into a police van and driven, under armed guard, to the Hôtel de Police in the Boulevard Vaulabelle, less than a kilometre from the stade Abbé-Deschamps. Through a barred window at the back of the van, Enzo had seen the painted dragons and white lions of the Golden Pagoda Chinese restaurant before they turned into the Rue de Preuilly and through a sliding blue gate into a walled yard. There they had been hustled out through the rain and along a dark corridor before being pushed unceremoniously into this holding cell, its stout steel door slamming resoundingly behind them.

Since then, Enzo supposed, more than two hours must have passed. He had no idea what time it was, since they had taken his watch, along with everything else. Sophie's fury was intermittent, punctuated by long periods of sullen silence during which indignation simmered and gathered momentum before exploding again in another outburst.

Bertrand had not said a word, sitting silently on the floor, his back to the wall, legs pulled up to his chest. They had made him remove his nose and lip studs, and the shards of metal from his eyebrow. Strangely, Enzo thought, he seemed almost naked without them. Nicole, too, had been unusually quiet, tearstains dried now on her cheeks. Their clothes were still damp beneath the drying mud, and in the chill of their cell, it was all Enzo could do to stop his teeth from chattering. Sophie threw herself down on the single bunk bed and lapsed into another period of brooding silence.

It was Bertrand who broke it. He raised his head suddenly and said to Enzo, "You knew what they meant, didn't you?"

"What?" Enzo dragged himself back from a gathering of dark thoughts.

"The things we found in the trunk. You weren't surprised by anything."

Enzo shrugged. "They complete the circle, that's all. They lead us back to the place we started — with the skull under the Place d'Italie."

"I don't understand."

"The first body part, the skull, and the first five clues were found by accident in a collapsed tunnel beneath the thirteenth *arrondissement* in Paris," Enzo explained patiently. "Each set of clues led us to the next body part. The ones we found tonight lead us back to the skull."

"How?"

"The Eiffel Tower . . . What does it symbolise?"

"Paris," Nicole said, emerging suddenly from her cocoon of depression.

Enzo nodded. "That's the first clue to the location. The key ring was made in China. That's the second. The leaning tower of Pisa. Well, that's Italy, isn't it? So now we have Paris, Place d'Italie, and a Chinese connection. We already know that the skull was found beneath the Avenue de Choisy, just off Place d'Italie, right in the heart of Chinatown."

"I'll bet there were thirteen chopsticks," Nicole said.

Enzo managed a pale smile. "You're right. Thirteen chopsticks, representing the thirteenth *arrondissement* and Chinatown."

354

"So the rock hammer must symbolise the quarriers." Nicole's interest was fully engaged now.

Enzo nodded again. "Who dug out the catacombs that run right under the Avenue de Choisy. Had we got that far, I'm sure we would have found some sign down there that would have led us to the trunk. As it was, fate beat us to it."

"What about the cleaver and the baking tray?" Bertrand asked.

Enzo shook his head. "I don't know. Each set of clues provided us with a location, and the name of one of the murderers. Presumably the cleaver and the baking tray will lead us to the name of the final killer. But I haven't really given it any thought yet."

"You don't have to. It's easy."

Enzo, Bertrand and Nicole all turned towards Sophie, who had hoisted herself up on one elbow on the bunk bed. She looked back at them, wide-eyed.

"Well, it's obvious, isn't it?"

"Is it?" asked Bertrand.

"Of course. I mean, who uses a meat cleaver like that?"

"A Chinese chef," Nicole said. "And I suppose that would also be another Chinese clue."

Sophie shook her head in irritation. "Who else uses a meat cleaver?"

"A butcher." This from Bertrand.

"Exactly." Sophie looked at her father triumphantly. "Butcher in English, *boucher* in French. It doesn't matter which, it's a surname in both languages."

Enzo looked doubtful. "You can't jump to quick conclusions with these clues, Sophie. We'd need something else to confirm it."

"What about the baking tray?" Bertrand said.

"Well, that doesn't need any confirmation." Sophie was piqued by her father's lack of enthusiasm.

Enzo and Bertrand looked at her expectantly, and Nicole said, "Of course, being men, they wouldn't know."

Sophie hesitated then, and Enzo saw that her eyes were beginning to fill up. "Every young girl makes them with her mum," she said. "Except me, of course. I made them at school." She quickly brushed away a tear with the back of her hand and made a brave attempt at a smile.

Enzo looked at her and felt his own emotions well up inside. However hard he might have tried, and for all the love he had given her over all these years, there were still things she had missed out on. Things that only a mother and daughter can share. And now he had let her down, exposed her to danger. It had been his duty as a parent to protect her, and he had failed in that, too. "What's that?" he asked, and he heard the crack in his voice.

"Madeleine cakes," Nicole said. "As every little French girl would tell you, that's what the seashell moulds in the baking tray are for. Making Madeleine cakes."

"Madeleine Boucher." Bertrand tried the name out for size. "I suppose it's possible."

356

Sophie looked to her father for his approval. But it was as if he had set eyes on the face of the Gorgon and turned to stone.

If Enzo had believed it possible for his heart to stop, then he would have said it had done so. And for the first time in his life he understood how it might feel if his blood were to turn to ice. He remembered the handwritten inscription in the book so very clearly. *For Madeleine, aged seven. Happy Birthday, darling.* And he remembered how evasive she had been. *Why won't you tell me?* he had asked her. And finally she had sighed and told him, *She's me. All right? I'm Madeleine.* He remembered, too, how strongly she had reacted against his suggestion that he call her that. *No! I don't want to be Madeleine!*

"Papa?" Sophie had risen from the bed and crossed to touch his face with her fingertips, leaving a little trail of mud flakes in her wake. "Papa, what's wrong?"

"*Mad à minuit*," Enzo said. "Madeleine at midnight. That's who he was meeting in St. Étienne du Mont."

Bertrand was watching him closely. "Do you know her?"

Enzo pulled himself back from the brink of an abyss he dared not peer over. "Maybe."

Sophie frowned. "Do *we*?"

"You met her last night. Charlotte's her middle name. Her given name is Madeleine."

CHAPTER
TWENTY-ONE

"Papa, I don't believe it!"

Enzo did not want to. It was almost impossible for him to think of those dark, smiling eyes as the eyes of a killer. He remembered the tenderness of her touch, the softness of her lips, the sweet taste of her on his. He closed his eyes and drew a deep breath.

"I mean, how many Madeleines must there be in France?" Sophie persisted. "Thousands, tens of thousands. And, anyway, Boucher isn't her second name, is it?"

Enzo shook his head. "It's Roux."

"There you are, then."

"We don't know that Boucher is the right name. But, in any case, she was adopted, Sophie. She told me herself that she tracked down her birth parents when she went to university. It's quite possible that her mother, or her father, was called Boucher. Or something else that we haven't figured out yet."

Sophie threw a defiant hand in his direction. "Well, there's another thing. When she went to university, you said. That was the Sorbonne, right? She told me that last night." Enzo tipped his head in reluctant acknowledgement. "And you told us that all the other

358

killers were students of Jacques Gaillard's at ENA. Well, Charlotte wasn't at ENA, was she?"

"We don't know that," Enzo insisted. "We only know what she's told us." He was playing devil's advocate to his own feelings. "But we do know that she was Gaillard's niece. And most murders are committed by people known to the victim. Usually a member of their own family. God knows what kind of motive she might have had for hating him. For wanting him dead. Maybe he abused her as a child."

"Oh, for Heaven's sake, Papa!"

"Sophie, she tried to conceal from me that he was her uncle, that her real name was Madeleine. Why?" And then he answered his own question. "She must have known that in the end I was going to get to these clues in Auxerre." The voice of his rational self was fighting to be heard above the emotional one in his head. A voice that screamed down everything he was saying. It wasn't true. It couldn't be true. She was the gentlest, loveliest creature he had met in the twenty years since Pascale's death. She had issues, yes, and dark places in her head that she guarded closely. But there was a spiritual centre to her that was as still and beautiful as her smile.

He tried to picture again all the faces in the photograph of the Schoelcher Promotion, all the students who had flitted across the screen in the video record of the class of '96. Had she really been somewhere there amongst them? Ten years younger — hair a different cut perhaps, a different colour? If Charlotte really was Madeleine, then she must have been supremely confident that he would not recognise her. It had been her idea to watch the video. Maybe she had just been playing with him. For wasn't this, after all, really just a game? An extreme IQ test where the cracking of clues was rewarded with the pieces of a murdered man?

But why? It's what he kept coming back to. What was the point of it all? He knew now that there had been four killers. But three of them were dead, and so there was only one person left alive who could answer that question. And her name was Madeleine.

The four of them spent the next hour in reflective silence until Bertrand said, "Don't we have the right to make a phone call?"

"Yes," Sophie said immediately. "And they can only hold us for twenty-four hours without charging us. But there's some stupid clause that says if they think it would be against the interests of the investigation, they can withhold the right to the call. Which means we don't have the right to one at all. It's ridiculous!"

Enzo never ceased to be amazed by how much kids knew about their rights. Things that had never crossed his mind as a young man. Perhaps it was a sign of the times, that young people had higher expectations of conflict with the authorities.

The cold in the cell was getting into his bones now and, like Bertrand, he pulled his legs up to his chest and wrapped his arms around them for warmth. He felt the bulge of something hard in the knee pocket of his cargos. "Jesus Christ!" he said suddenly, startling the others.

"Papa, what is it?"

"I've still got my phone. They never took my *mobile*." They had removed rings and watches and piercings, and made them empty their pockets. But Enzo had forgotten about the leg pockets of his cargos and, in their hurry to lock them up, so had the police. Perhaps they had been obscured by mud.

He squeezed fingers into the pocket and pulled out his mobile. He pressed the on button. The screen lit up and the phone beeped loudly. They all froze, listening for any indication that someone out there might have heard it. But there was nothing, except the same interminable silence. Enzo looked at the indicator and saw that the battery was low. But there was a strong signal. He hesitated. Who would he call?

Then, to his horror, it started ringing. He was so startled by the electronic rendition of *Scotland the Brave* that echoed thunderously around the cell that he almost dropped it.

"For goodness' sake, Papa, answer it!"

He fumbled for the answer button and pressed the phone to his ear. "Jesus Christ, Magpie, where the bloody hell are you?" It was Simon. In spite of years in London, his Scottish brogue was always particularly strong when he was stressed. Enzo started telling him that he was in a police cell in Auxerre, when the voice cut over him, and he realised it was a recording on his messaging service. "Call me when you pick this up. It's important." And the line went dead. There was something in Simon's voice that sent a strange chill of premonition through Enzo. He hung up on the soporific voice telling him that he had no more messages.

"Who was it?" Sophie asked.

"A message from Uncle Simon."

"Well, call him back, quick. He's a lawyer, isn't he?"

"In England, not France."

"Well, he must know someone in France who can help."

Enzo pulled up the recall option and and listened as the phone began ringing at the other end. It was answered almost immediately. "Magpie, where in God's name have you been? I've been trying to get you all bloody day."

"Simon, just shut up and listen." Enzo knew he had to make this quick and concise. "I'm in a police cell in Auxerre. Nicole, Sophie, Bertrand and I have been arrested. We need help. Legal representation. Someone to get us out of this mess."

"Jesus, Magpie, what have you been up to?"

"It's a long story. I'm going to give you a name and a number in Paris." He flicked through the *répertoire* in his phone's memory and rhymed off the number. "His name's Roger Raffin. He's a journalist. His paper's lawyers got us out of trouble before. Tell him I know the names of all of Gaillard's killers." There was a long silence at the other end of the line. "Simon, are you still there?"

"Give me his address," Simon said. "I'll go and drag him out of bed personally."

Irritation creased Enzo's face. "Simon, there's no time for you to fly to Paris."

362

"I'm *in* Paris."

And something in his voice brought earlier forebodings flooding back. "What are you doing there?"

"Enzo, that's why I was trying to get you." Enzo heard him draw a deep breath. "Just don't panic, okay?"

"Why would I panic?" But he was starting to already.

"Magpie, Kirsty phones her mum once a day, every day. She has done ever since she arrived in Paris."

Just the mention of Kirsty's name made Enzo tense. "What's happened to her?"

"Just listen!" Simon's voice was insistent. "She hasn't phoned home in three days. Her mum's tried to get her several times on her mobile, but it's always switched off, and she hasn't responded to any messages. Linda phoned me in a panic yesterday, and I got the first flight over. According to the *concierge*, Kirsty hasn't been home in three days. She hasn't been at work either. Magpie, she's just vanished. Into thin air. And no one seems to know where the hell she is."

The single fluorescent strip in the ceiling burned out everything around it. The world turned a blinding white. Enzo closed his eyes tight to shut it out. A line had been crossed, and there was no going back. His life, he knew, was about to change again. Forever.

"Magpie?"

"Just get me out of here, Simon. As fast as you can?" His voice was barely a whisper.

He hung up and the phone slipped from his grasp and clattered to the floor. He stared at it blindly.

"Papa?" Sophie was kneeling beside him. She picked up the phone and looked at him. He could hear the fear in her voice. "Papa, what's happened?"

He looked at her, and saw her mother in her, as he always did. "They've got her." His voice was strained and quiet. There was no doubt in his mind. No question of innocent coincidence.

"Who's got who?"

"Gaillard's killers." Then he corrected himself. "Killer." He looked into Sophie's eyes. "Madeleine. Whoever she is, she's got your sister."

CHAPTER
TWENTY-TWO

I

They had no idea what time it was, or how long they had been sitting in the interminable fluorescent glare of this square, featureless police cell. Without windows they did not know whether dawn had broken, or if it was still dark outside. But they had not slept. Tired eyes scratched and burned with every blink, heads aching, necks stiff, faces shadowed and drawn.

The first indication that things were about to change came with the sound of raised voices from the corridor. Then the door flew open, and Simon stood there grinning, his beard bristling, and he looked greyer than Enzo remembered. In spite of the smile, he too had dark penumbrae beneath his eyes.

Sophie hurled herself across the cell and threw her arms around him. "Don't do that," he said, mock embarrassed. "You're dad'll think I'm only after your body."

"Thank God you're here," she said, and she gave him a big hug.

Simon put his arm around her and shook hands with Enzo and Bertrand and Nicole. "You guys okay?"

Enzo nodded.

"No, we're not!" Sophie protested. "We weren't allowed a phone call, we weren't allowed to talk to a lawyer."

"You called me, didn't you?"

Sophie's laugh of contempt sounded more like a bark. "Only because they forgot to take my Papa's *portable* off him. I was refused access to a doctor after all their manhandling."

Simon raised an eyebrow. "Were you? One more to add to the list, then. These guys are in deep shit. Roger figures they were trying to keep you under wraps and out of the way for forty-eight hours so they could make some kind of announcement to the press."

Enzo nodded, realising now why they had been locked up like this. "To claim the credit for finding Gaillard's remains and revealing his killers."

"Before we could run the story in *Libé*." Raffin appeared next to Simon. He looked flushed and weary, and he shook all their hands gravely. "Your detention order was signed by Juge Lelong. Again." He nodded back along the corridor. "He's here, you know. He might try to argue that you damaged public property, or that you were interfering with a police investigation. But it's not going to wash. Not now."

Simon grinned. "He's fucked," he said. "And you guys are free to go."

Enzo put a hand on his arm. "Any word of Kirsty?"

Simon's grin faded and he shook his head. "Nothing."

Raffin said, "We've got a car waiting for you outside. We can be in Paris in a couple of hours."

366

★ ★ ★

At the charge bar, they had all their possessions restored. Bertrand was told that his van was in the yard behind the police station. "Take Sophie and Nicole straight back to Cahors," Enzo told him. "And don't let either of them out of your sight."

"No!" Sophie stood her ground defiantly. "We're going to Paris, too."

"All of us," Nicole said.

For almost the first time, Sophie and Nicole were in accord. "We'll follow you." Sophie thrust her chin out and dared her father to challenge her. But he knew better than that. She was, after all, her father's daughter. And in many ways he was happier to keep her close. The thought of anything happening to Sophie, too, was almost more than he could bear. He sighed and nodded, and they were led through to the foyer. It was daylight outside, but the rain from the night before had not stopped, and it streaked the windows all along the front of the Hôtel de Police. Through them, Enzo could see the blurred shape of a rain-stained church tower across the street. Traffic sat in long, patient queues, windscreen wipers beating countless paths back and forth through the endless summer downpour.

The *accueil* was filled with uniformed officers and men in dark suits. There was some heated debate in progress. As they followed Raffin out through the front door, Enzo caught sight of the pale face of Juge Lelong among the men in suits. Their eyes met for just a moment, and Enzo saw defeat in the set of the other man's face. Long gone the arrogance which had so characterised their first meeting. He had made a mess of this, and the *Garde des Sceaux* would be furious. Only scandal and humiliation awaited them both now. But Enzo had other things on his mind.

"What time is it?" he asked Simon.

"Just gone ten."

They had lost nearly twelve hours, and it would be after midday before they got to Paris. God only knew what might have become of Kirsty in that time.

II

The seventeenth century wooden staircase was protected by the Beaux Arts, the *concierge* told them.

It had taken ten minutes, and a studious examination of Enzo's *Carte de Séjour* to convince her that he was Kirsty's father. Finally, reluctantly, she had given him the key. She would not come up with them, she said. She was no longer able for the climb.

The staircase ended abruptly on the third floor, and a narrow corridor led to a spiral stairway which took them up another three flights. By the time they reached the top landing, Enzo was breathless. Sophie, too, was breathing hard. But she was impressed. "She must be fit, my half-sister. You wouldn't go out casually for a coffee, though, would you?"

Enzo waited with Sophie and Bertrand until Raffin, and finally Simon and Nicole, completed the climb. Simon was panting and red-faced. "Jesus," he said. "She certainly knows how to discourage visitors."

Rain battered against a narrow window in the stairwell. It opened on to a fire escape. Six floors of flimsy steel ladder. It was a long way down. Enzo slipped the key in the lock and opened the door. Immediately he smelled her perfume, the same scent she had been wearing the day he left her shopping bags at the foot of the stairs. Its almost tangible presence seemed only to underline her absence, and it caused a sickening lurch in his stomach. He feared the worst.

The studio apartment was tiny, built into the slope of the roof. There were two windows on the east side, and one facing west over a wet Paris roofscape of tall chimneys and television aerials, towards the twin towers of Notre Dame. It was a stunning view, almost unreal, like a set from a fifties Hollywood movie. The sun, Enzo realised, would go down behind the cathedral. His daughter must have had one of the most privileged sunset views in Paris.

Kirsty's personality filled the room, even though she had not been there for days. Her clothes were draped over a chair. A bed settee, pushed up beneath one of the east-facing windows, was folded down, unmade since the last time she had slept in it. The shape of her head was still pressed into the pillow. With a jolt he recognised the soft toys lined up along the top of the settee. A threadbare panda with one of its eyes missing, a large cartoon pussy cat with its head tipped to one side, an old-fashioned dolly in a faded blue ruffled dress. One of its red shoes had been lost. These were things he had bought her when she was barely old enough to walk. Much-loved toys which had gone with her everywhere. Overnights at her grandparents, weekends at the home of her best friend, midge-infested camping holidays in the Highlands. Panda, pussy and dolly always went, too. Even here, to Paris, apparently. Even after all these years.

But wherever she was now, for once she had left them behind.

Sophie followed his gaze. "Pretty crappy toys." Enzo heard the jealousy in her voice.

"No one touch anything," he said. And with difficulty added, "We might be looking at a crime scene."

He cast his eyes quickly around the room. The walls were painted a pale yellow. There were some cheap pictures on the gable, bought from street artists in Montmartre. Clichéd views of the old square. A huge movie poster of *Gone With The Wind*, the lurid flames of Atlanta glowing red behind Clark Gable, the prostrate figure of Vivien Leigh draped in his arms. There were shelves of books and CDs. A laptop computer open on a small table below the west-facing window. A stout wooden beam followed the slope of the roof, creating a semi-partition between the living area and a minuscule kitchen flooded with light from the window on the east side. A small, cluttered dining table was pushed in below the beam.

Enzo saw, lying on a kitchen worktop, a hand-written card with a thumb tack pushed through its centre. *Kirsty, elle est chez elle*. A note, left perhaps for friends downstairs, so that they knew whether or not she was at home before embarking on a long, fruitless climb to the sixth floor. Today her father had made the climb because he knew that she was not at home, and he wondered why the note was here. Surely she would keep it with her when she was out, so that she could pin it up at the foot of the stairs when she returned?

"Monsieur Macleod . . ." He turned, and Nicole nodded towards the dining table. "Look."

He looked, and at first saw nothing unusual. An untidy pile of books, an open box of sponge cakes, a medal of some kind. "What?"

"The cakes," she said insistently.

And he realised with a shock that drew the skin tight all across his scalp, that it was a box of Madeleine cakes. A message. He knew it instantly. This casual arrangement on the kitchen table was a carefully constructed note, just for him, the box of Madeleine cakes a signature.

Raffin stepped forward to look at the table. "What is it?" He saw only what anyone else would have seen. Innocent clutter in a young woman's apartment. Had the police made a search of the place they would certainly have missed it, probably disturbed it, destroying it in the process.

Enzo was having trouble controlling his breathing. "I'd say it was probably a ransom note."

Simon frowned. "What are you talking about?"

"Madeleine. She's telling me she's got Kirsty." He carefully lifted the box of cakes and laid it to one side. He had run out of latex gloves, but he did not believe that the woman called Madeleine would have been foolish enough to leave finger-prints. He pulled up a chair and sat down to examine the remaining items on the table. The others crowded around. "I've already been inside her head. She knows that I know how she thinks. But, in any case, she won't have made this too difficult."

There were three books. An unabridged version of Victor Hugo's *Les Misérables*. A book called *Les Artistes Font le Mur*, which appeared to be a largely photographic record of a fresco sixty metres long created by a group of school children. And the prosaically titled *Computers, an Illustrated History*. The only other thing on the table was a metal cross with four flared arms of equal length, attached to a piece of ribbon. It was black, with the letter W in the centre, the date 1914 on the lower arm, and a faded silver trim around its edges. It was about four centimetres across.

"What is it?" Bertrand asked.

"An *Eiserne Kreuz*," Enzo said. "A German Iron Cross, a medal given out during the First World War."

"So what's the message?" Simon said.

Enzo raised his hand in irritation. "I don't know. I'm going to have to work it out." Somehow the urgency of it was making his mind go blank. It was Nicole who kick-started his thought processes.

"Victor Hugo's hero in *Les Misérables* was called Jean Valjean," she said. "But he had another persona, didn't he?"

"Monsieur Madeleine," Bertrand said suddenly, as it came back to him from some long-ago reading.

372

Enzo's mind was racing. "Yes." But there was something else significant, something just beyond his reach. Then all at once he grasped it. "There's a long sequence in the book where Valjean rescues a man by taking him through the sewers of Paris."

Simon pulled a face. "You mean you think she's taken Kirsty down into the sewers?"

"No, not the sewers. Below that. The catacombs. After all, that's where the first body part was found. It would kind of be like coming full circle."

He picked up the book about the children's fresco and flipped through its colourful pages of naively painted tropical fish and underwater seascapes. He could not, for the life of him, see the relevance of it. A mural painted on a wall sixty metres long. And a book about the history of the computer. He picked up the Iron Cross and held it between thumb and fore-finger. If she was making this easy for him, why was he finding it so hard? And, in his mind, he answered his own question. Because he was looking for difficult answers.

He dropped the cross and picked up the computer book. *Computers, an Illustrated History.* Why couldn't he see it? And then suddenly he did. "Goddamn!" he said, angry with himself for trying to make it so complicated. He stood up, pushing past the others, and crossed the studio to Kirsty's laptop on the desk below the west-facing window. He checked the cables. It was connected to the mains, and to the telephone line via an ADSL modem, which meant she had a high-speed connection to the internet.

"What is it, Papa?" Sophie asked.

"It's in here," he said, and he switched on the computer. It would take a minute or so to boot up.

"What is?" Raffin stood behind him as Enzo pulled a chair up to Kirsty's desk and sat down in front of her laptop.

"When you're on-line," Enzo said, "you leave a trail of the sites you've visited. They get stored under History, in the browser."

"Of course," Nicole said. "*Computers, an Illustrated History.*"

They watched and waited in silence while the computer took what seemed like a lifetime to load its desktop screen. And when, finally, it did, Enzo stared in shocked disbelief at the picture Kirsty had chosen for its background. It was an old photograph, taken more than twenty years ago, in the back garden of their red sandstone terraced home on the south side of Glasgow. Kirsty was maybe five years old. She had been almost blond at that age, a head full of big, soft curls. She was wearing a pale lemon sleeveless dress and a wide-brimmed straw hat with a blue ribbon which she had pushed back on her head. Her eyes were sparkling, and an impossibly wide grin revealed one missing front tooth. Crouched beside her, an arm around her waist pulling her towards him, a young Enzo smiled self-consciously at the camera. His hair was shorter then, darker, his white streak more pronounced. Kirsty had one arm dangled around his neck. Father and daughter as Kirsty remembered them. As she wanted to remember them. The father she had loved. The father who had loved her. A moment shared. And not all the years which had passed since could take that away from her. Enzo bit his lip and fought to hold back his tears. How could he have been so careless with his daughter's love?

"I thought she hated you." It was Sophie's voice that broke the spell, and again he heard an edge of jealousy in it.

"I thought she did," he heard himself say, almost in a whisper.

"You don't put a picture of someone you hate up on your computer screen," Sophie said. "Not when you have to look at it every day."

"She never hated you," Simon said. "Just . . . just never forgave you."

Enzo took a deep breath and dragged his eyes away from the photograph. There was no time to be distracted.

"Here, let me in." Nicole nudged Enzo aside and her fingers rattled across the keyboard. He blinked away his tears and watched as she opened up the browser, then clicked on the History tab on the left-hand side of the screen. The History drawer slid open. It was empty, except for a single link:

http://14e.kta.free.fr/visite/AssasObservatoire/index.html.

Nicole clicked on it. Immediately, they were connected to a page under the heading, LE QUARTIER ASSAS — OBSERVATOIRE. Down the left side of the screen were twenty or thirty links to streets and boulevards and other *quartiers* in the fourteenth *arrondissement*. In the top right corner was

375

a tiny map labelled VILLE DE PARIS. An area of it was patched in blue. Most of the rest of the screen was filled with an enlarged plan of the blue area. It was a shaky, confusing, hand-drawn map, with streets represented by single, often broken lines, and names squeezed into spaces that were sometimes too small for them. It was, Enzo thought, how you might represent a rabbit warren. It certainly looked liked one.

"What is it?" Bertrand asked.

It was Raffin who replied. "It's a map of the Grand Réseau Souterrain. The catacombs. Or, at least, a part of them." He leaned forward to peer at the screen, and then he traced a line with his finger. "There's the Rue d'Assas."

And Enzo realised he was looking at a map of the tunnels immediately below ENA's international building in the Avenue de l'Observatoire, where only two days ago he had been given the photograph and video tape of the Schoelcher Promotion. He remembered the helpful Madame Henry telling him how monks had established the Order of Chartreux there in 1257, digging the stone to build it out of the ground below, creating a network of tunnels and chambers in the process. *Somewhere right below where we're standing now*, she'd said. And there it was, immediately south of the Luxembourg Gardens. Above a mess of squiggles and loops and dead-ends, the author of the map had written *Fontaine des Chartreux*, and drawn an arrow pointing down into the muddle.

376

"What's that?" Enzo guided Nicole's mouse hand slightly to the left so that the arrow was pointing at two words.

They all squinted at them. They were far from clear. "It looks like *Abris Allemand*," Nicole said.

Enzo frowned. "German shelters? What does that mean?"

"Aren't we looking for something with a German connection?" Bertrand said. "The Iron Cross."

"Yes . . ." Still Enzo could make no sense of it. Nicole moved the mouse fractionally to her left and the arrow turned into a tiny hand, which meant there was an invisible link there on the map. She clicked on it, and a new page wiped across the screen. It was headlined, LE BUNKER, and beneath it was a detailed map of something called the BUNKER ALLEMAND DU LYCÉE MONTAIGNE.

"It's the plan of an old German bunker," Raffin said. "Right below the Lycée Montaigne. They must have built it during the occupation. It looks like some kind of communications and command centre."

It was huge, a labyrinth of rooms and corridors, each carefully delineated and notated. Arrows indicated old entrances which had long since been bricked up. There were warnings about obstacles and pitfalls.

"There!" Bertrand stabbed a triumphant finger at the map. Enzo peered at where he was pointing. Three tiny, blurred words. *Salle avec fresques*.

Suddenly they had made sense both of the Iron Cross and the book about the children's fresco. Deep in the bowels of the city, in the triangle between the

Avenue de l'Observatoire and the Rue d'Assas, there was an old German wartime bunker with a room full of frescoes.

Nicole scrolled down the page, then, to discover a series of photographic images of the tunnels and rooms in the bunker, walls covered with graffiti. And beneath them was a link directly to the *Salle des Fresques*. She clicked on it, to download thirteen different images of graffiti art plastered over the walls of a single room in the bunker. An Aztec warrior facing down a dragon. An astronaut on the moon with an American flag. A skeleton in dinner jacket and bow-tie holding up a notice about AIDS.

"That's where I've to meet her," Enzo said.

Simon scratched his beard. "How do you know that?"

"Because that's where the clues have led us. That's her message. Go to the Salle des Fresques."

Raffin looked at the screen thoughtfully. "When?"

"What do you mean?"

"When have you to meet her? You might know the where, but not the when."

"Yes, we do." Everyone turned in surprise to see Sophie standing at the table. She was holding the box of Madeleine cakes. She folded back the lid and held it out, as if offering them one. "It's written on the inside of the lid."

There was a series of numbers scrawled on the white card. *19070230*. And they were followed by two words. *Toute seule*.

Enzo got up and crossed the room to take the box from her. He looked at the numbers, and knew at once what they were. The 19th of the 7th at 02.30 hours. He checked his watch. Today was July 18th. Madeleine was making a rendezvous to meet him alone in the Salle des Fresques in a long-abandoned German bunker twenty metres below the streets of Paris, at two-thirty tomorrow morning.

III

The rain beat a constant rhythm on the taut canvas of the maroon awning overhead, filtered daylight casting red shadows on all of their faces. Enzo sat hunched over their table watching tourists in brightly coloured plastic raincoats hurry by. They sat in silence, waiting for Raffin, who was still inside speaking on the telephone. Simon had ordered a whisky and told Enzo that he should have one, too. But Enzo wanted to keep his head clear. As clear as it could be after a night without sleep, and only twelve hours to prepare for a meeting with the woman who had kidnapped his daughter. A woman who had killed at least four times. As it was, his head was aching. There was a loud tinnitis ringing in his ears, and his eyes were burning. Sophie sat silently sipping a *tisane*, and Nicole was leafing through a pile of papers and photographs she had taken from Enzo's satchel. Bertrand stared gloomily across the bridge opposite, towards the Île de la Cité.

It was the same bridge from which, just over a week earlier, Enzo had thrown himself into a passing barge. He sat now watching the rain mist as it thrashed down on the swollen waters of the Seine, and he found it hard to believe he had done something so stupid. He had been someone else then, in another lifetime. So much had happened since that evening in Cahors when he had accepted the Préfet's wager. But he could never have foreseen that it would lead to this.

He turned and looked through the window, beyond the reflections of Notre Dame, into the brasserie. Waiters in black waistcoats and long white aprons were clearing debris from tables. He could see Raffin speaking animatedly on a telephone by the bar, a poster on the wall behind him of an Alsatian Frenchman feasting on German sausage courtesy of *Produits Shmid*. Raffin hung up and walked briskly to the door, emerging from the restaurant on to the *terrasse*. For once he seemed less than stylish. His raincoat hung damply from his shoulders, and his wet hair had fallen forward across his forehead. He swept it out of his eyes and lit a cigarette.

"He's coming to the apartment at midnight."

"Do you trust him?" Enzo asked.

Raffin pulled up a seat. "When he took me down to do that piece for *Libé* I could not have been more completely in his hands. Frankly, Macleod, I doubt if there's anyone who knows the catacombs better. He has his own maps and charts, meticulously accumulated during years of personal exploration. It's his life's work."

"And he makes a living from it?" Bertrand asked. "I mean, taking people down there illegally?"

"A very good living from all accounts."

"I don't want him to take me down," Enzo said. "All I need him to do is get me in, and provide me with enough information to get me where I need to be."

"Papa, you *can't* go down there on your own." Sophie's eyes were red from tears already spilled as a result of her father's stubbornness.

"She's right, Magpie," Simon said. "I mean, think about it. Why does this Madeleine woman want you to go down there in the first place. So she can can hand Kirsty back and tell you to be a good boy? I don't think so. I think she's using Kirsty as bait to lure you down there so that she can kill you to stop you from revealing her identity."

"We already *know* who she is," Nicole said. Enzo flashed quick eyes at her, and she held up the list of Schoelcher students that she had dug out from amongst his papers. "And Sophie was right about the butcher's cleaver." She handed the list to Enzo. "Marie-Madeleine Boucher. Right after Marie Bonnet and before Hervé Boullanger."

Enzo ran his eye down the list, and there it was in black and white. MARIE-MADELEINE BOUCHER.

Raffin said, "And it's not Charlotte, Enzo." He had been shocked on the drive from Auxerre to learn of Enzo's fears. "I'd stake my life on it."

"You don't have to," Sophie said. "My Papa does."

"Marie, Madeleine, Charlotte, whoever the hell she might be," Simon said, "even if you knew for sure, she doesn't know that." He took a long, deep breath, and Enzo heard the tremor in it. "And I hate to say this, Enzo, but it's possible that Kirsty's already —"

"Don't!" Enzo cut him off. "Don't even think it!" He took a moment to compose himself. "I *have* to go alone. Because that's what Marie-Madeleine Boucher wants me to do. I can't just do nothing. And I can't go to the police. I have to believe that Kirsty's okay, so I'm not going to do anything to put her in more danger than she's already in. I'll keep the appointment, and I'll take my chances. Because there's nothing else I can do."

CHAPTER
TWENTY-THREE

I

Nicole had spent several hours during the afternoon trying to track down Marie-Madeleine Boucher on the internet. But there were nearly a thousand references to the name, in both France and Canada, and not one of them linked directly to ENA. It could take days to find out who she really was.

Enzo had passed the remains of the day in something close to a trance. Now, in the glare of a desk lamp, the maps spread across Raffin's desk burned themselves on to his retinas. It was pitch-black outside, and still the rain fell. A dense, slow-moving storm cloud had been dumping its precipitation on the city for nearly twenty-four hours. The television news was reporting that the Seine had burst its banks in several places. There had been flash floods all across Paris. But it was a warm, summer rain, the air sticky and breathless, and several times Enzo had found himself wiping a fine film of cold sweat from his forehead. A black cloud of swallows was swooping and diving around inside his stomach. He glanced at his watch. It was nearly a quarter past midnight.

The smoke from Samu's constant roll-ups hung still and blue in the lamplight. Raffin said that the tunnel rat was reputed to have got his nickname because in another life he had been a medic with the SAMU, the Service d'Aide Médicale Urgente. But he did not know if that was true. Samu's real identity was a secret he guarded closely.

He was a tall, thin, nervous man in his middle forties. He grew greying hair to collar length and gelled it back from his face. He had the pallor of a man who spent his life below ground, his complexion grey and pasty and scarred by adolescent acne. The thumb, index and middle fingers of his right hand were nicotine orange. His jeans and tee shirt hung loosely from a skeletal frame, and he seemed incapable of staying still for two minutes. His very presence was unsettling. He circled the desk slowly like an animal stalking prey.

"You really don't want to go down there on your own," he said to Enzo. It was the obligatory health warning, like the caution on a cigarette pack that smoking will kill you. "If you get lost you're fucked. You could be wandering those tunnels forever. And then again, you might encounter some of the undesirables. Most of the folks who do the catacombs are all right. It's a bit of fun, a bit of excitement. Something different. You find a room down there, you light some candles, you smoke some dope, you play some music. The graffiti artists are okay, too. Dedicated boys and girls. Like pigs in shit with all those virgin walls. But there's some bad dudes, too. Drug dealers, junkies. Guys who'd slit your throat for ten *centimes* and not think twice about it. And that's not to mention the tunnel cops. They'll lock you up and fine you a fucking fortune." He pulled on the last of his current roll-up and drew his lips back in a grin. Smoke seeped through brown-stained teeth. "So you really *don't* want to go down there on your own."

Enzo really didn't. "All the same, I *am* going." Madeleine had already made the decision for him. Samu had no idea why he wanted to go down into the catacombs, and Enzo wasn't about to enlighten him.

Samu glanced at Raffin. He knew there was more to this than he was being told. But he just shrugged. "Your funeral." He turned and leaned over the desk, sifting through the various maps. "I'm only going to give you three plans. No point in confusing you." He smoothed the first of them out on top of the others. It was headed, GRANDE AVENUE DU LUXEMBOURG (NORD). He clamped his roll-up between wet lips and screwed his eyes up against the smoke as he searched in his pockets for a red marker pen. When he found it, he leaned over the map again, spilling ash and brushing it aside with the back of his hand. "This is your master map. I'm going to mark out your route on it. You don't deviate from this, my friend, or you're fucked, okay? It's a labyrinth down there, a maze. Once you're lost, you're lost. Lots of the tunnels are *murés*, they've been bricked up by the authorities. We've knocked cat holes in some of them." He looked appraisingly at Enzo. "But you're a big guy. You could have trouble squeezing through. Most of them were made for skinny guys like me."

He took his marker pen and traced a thick red line along a route running north to south. "This is the Grande Avenue du Luxembourg. Most people get access to it through a couple of hidden entrances in the Luxembourg Gardens. The authorities deny they're there. But they exist all right. Trouble is . . ." he glanced at Enzo again, ". . . I doubt if you're up to climbing the railings. But I know another way in. We'll come to that." He returned to the Grande Avenue du Luxembourg. "You keep following this straight down. It's pretty easy going. You don't take any of these turnoffs until you get to here." He stopped his pen tip at a junction which branched off to the west. "If you miss this one you'll know soon enough, because the tunnel comes to a dead end where they've built a multilevel underground car park."

Enzo wondered fleetingly if it was the one where Diop had tried to murder him.

"You're around ten metres down at this level. The deepest you'll go is fifteen." His pen followed the turnoff. "Keep going west. You can't go wrong. Ignore any branches, just stick to my line. Until you get to here . . ." At which point he pulled over a second map. This one was headed RÉSEAU DES CHARTREUX. "This shows the area in more detail. You can see the German bunker marked out here at the top left, and down below it are the tunnels quarried by the Chartreux monks. Right down at the bottom here is the Fontaine des Chartreux. It's a big, hollowed out chamber with a stone sink to collect water that runs down the walls. They call it the Fontaine des Chartreux because the water is green, just like the liqueur made by the monks. If you find yourself there, you'll know you're in the wrong place. It's a dead end. You used to be able to get in from the tunnels under the Rue d'Assas, but it's all been bricked up. If you do get lost, you can always try and get into the Rue d'Assas through some of the *chatières* at the south-west corner of the German bunker. It'll be a tight squeeze, but you might make it. If you get into the Rue d'Assas you'll see there are two tunnels, one either side of the street. They're linked by these transversals, kind of shallow tunnels that cross under the road at right-angles. You might need to use one or more of them to find an exit up to the street above. It's a general principle. Most of the main overground avenues and boulevards have two tunnels running beneath them linked by transversals."

Samu stood up to roll another cigarette, and Enzo could only see his hands in the light of the desk lamp as they manipulated the paper and tobacco shreds. His voice came disembodied from the darkness outside the circle of light. "Anyway, the main thing is not to get lost. And you won't, if you follow the red line."

From his brief visit to the catacombs beneath the Place d'Italie, Enzo had a good sense of what to expect. Low, arching tunnels, cold, damp, fetid air, darkness, claustrophobia. He would be completely and utterly alone, venturing voluntarily into a trap set for him by the woman who had stolen his daughter. It was madness. Madeleine had every possible advantage. And he had absolutely no idea what he was going to do when he got there. He felt a creeping cloak of hopelessness start to wrap itself around him. But there was nothing else for it. He had to follow this through.

"Okay, this is where you'll come in off the Luxembourg map." Samu had lit his roll-up and was tracing his red line into the Chartreux map from the top right-hand corner. "Down to what looks like a roundabout here. You're more or less below the Rue Auguste Comte at this point. It was walled up in eighty-eight, and we knocked a *chatière* in it in ninety-two. A lot of people have squeezed through that hole, so you might just make it." He switched maps again, to a detailed plan of the bunker, and circled the roundabout at the top right. "Okay? You see where we are?"

Enzo nodded.

"Right, now you're in the bunker. It's a mess. A real bugger's muddle." He drew a careful red line that zigzagged south and then west through what seemed like an impossible maze. Then he made a small circle and stood up triumphantly. "And that's it. The Salle des Fresques." Enzo could barely see his grin through the smoke. "It's quite something. A bit like a bad trip."

Enzo thought that this whole undertaking was one big, bad trip. "How long will it take me?"

Samu shrugged. "Thirty to forty minutes. Depends how fast or how slow you are. Could be quicker, could be longer." He unfolded three clear plastic ziplock bags. "I'm going to put the maps in these to protect them from the wet. After all this rain you might find there's a bit of water down there." He began slipping the maps into their bags. "Guard them with your life, my friend, because it may well depend upon them."

II

The marble woman reclining on the left slope of the triangular headed doorway opposite held her sword upright in the rain, impervious to the wet, unblinking in the glare of the floodlights that washed the building. There was something stoic about her. She wore a Mona Lisa smile of quiet confidence. Enzo sat in the dark by the window of Raffin's study and regarded her jealously. He wished he could find an inner calm to mirror her stony self-confidence. But in truth, he was afraid. More afraid than he had ever been in his life. Afraid for Kirsty, for what might already have become of her. Afraid that he lacked both the courage and the resources to be able to change her destiny. Or his. The rain made tracks down the glass, like tears, and in the light from the street, their shadows streaked his face.

A shaft of pale electric yellow fell across the floor as the door opened from the *séjour*. Enzo heard the television, and the low murmur of voices coming from the other room. Raffin closed the door behind him and shut them out. He stood for a moment before crossing to the window. He had a parcel of soft cloth in his hand, which he held out and unwrapped to reveal the shiny, blue-black barrel of a gun with a polished wooden handgrip. "It's loaded. I want you to take it."

Enzo shook his head. "No."

"Why not?"

"Because I could never use it."

"Enzo —"

"No, Roger!"

Roger stood for a long time in the dark, the gun still in his hand, before finally he wrapped it up again. Enzo heard his shallow breathing. "You've got about ten minutes."

As he opened the door, Enzo called after him. "Roger . . ." The journalist stopped and looked back. "Thanks."

Raffin and Simon passed in the light of the open door and Raffin closed it behind him, leaving Simon standing in the dark.

Without taking his eyes from the lady with the sword, Enzo said, "We're closed. Didn't you see the sign?"

"Magpie, I don't want you to do this." He started across the room.

"We've already covered that ground."

"I don't want to lose the two people I love most in this world."

Enzo turned to look at his friend. Even in the faint reflecting light from the street he could see how pale he was.

"You know that Linda and I always kept in touch. I saw a lot of Kirsty over the years. Whenever there was a problem, her mum would always call me." He looked down at his hands. "I guess, you know, because I never had any kids of my own . . . she became kind of like a daughter to me." He looked up and said quickly, "Not

390

that I could ever take your place. She wouldn't have had that. She always loved you, Magpie. That's why she never found it possible to forgive you. It's hard for a kid to take rejection."

"I didn't —!"

"I know." Simon held up quick hands to pre-empt his protest. "I've told her a thousand times. But you can't rewrite the history she has in her head. However wrong she's got it, it's so ingrained it's written in stone."

"That was her mother."

Simon nodded. "Linda didn't help. You hurt her, Magpie. Kirsty was the only way she could get back at you." He sighed deeply. "It's an old story." He looked past Enzo towards the statue across the street. "I want to call the police."

"No."

"Enzo —"

"No!" Enzo faced up to his friend, two old stags prepared to lock horns to defend their territory. "It would be like signing her death warrant."

"Like you're not signing your own?"

"I'd rather die than know that I was responsible for her death."

"Jesus, Magpie," Simon's voice whispered at him in the dark. And their foreheads came together in gentle acceptance that the fight was over, even before it had begun. Simon wrapped his arms around the boy he'd met on their first day at school together, and hugged him so hard Enzo could barely breathe. His beard scratched Enzo's cheek. "Jesus," he whispered again.

III

Enzo slipped on his waterproof leggings, and pulled the light-weight plastic cagoule over his head. He folded his maps in two and zipped them into an inside pocket. He felt better now that the waiting was over. All the hours he had spent treading water felt like wasted time. Samu adjusted the webbing inside Enzo's hard hat and got him to check the fit. Then he double-checked the lamp set above the peak. It shone bright and strong, powered by a brand-new battery. He handed Enzo a small, waterproof flashlight as backup. "Keep it safe," he said. "The last thing you want to be down there is in the dark."

The others stood around Raffin's *séjour* watching in silence. Their tension was tangible. It was time to go, and no one wanted to acknowledge it. Enzo looked at his watch. It was nearly one-fifteen. "Be back in a few hours." He followed Samu out into the hall and on to the landing.

They were crossing the courtyard when Sophie came running after him. "I'll catch you up," Enzo told Samu, then turned to his daughter. "Go back inside, pet, you'll get soaked."

"I don't care!" Sophie stood defiantly in the rain, looking up into her father's face with her mother's eyes. "If anything happens to you I'll never forgive her." And Enzo couldn't tell if she was crying, or if it was just the rain.

"Kirsty?"

"She's got no right to take you away from me."

Enzo shook his head gently. "Sophie, none of this is Kirsty's fault. The only person to blame is me."

Her lower lip quivered. "I love you, Papa."

She fell into his arms and he held her, the rain crashing all around them, rising off the cobbles in the courtyard in a mist like smoke. "I love you, too, Sophie." He cupped her face in his hands. "I want you to promise me something."

"No, I'm not promising anything. You're the one that's got to promise — that you're going to come back. Okay?" He closed his eyes. "Papa!"

He opened his eyes again. "I promise."

She held his gaze for a long, sceptical moment. "I hate her."

"No you don't."

"I do."

"Sophie, there's too much of me in her. You can't love me and hate her."

Her face turned sulky. "I'll hate you both if you don't come back."

"I promised you I would, didn't I?"

Her eyes narrowed. "You'd better."

Samu was revving the motor of his car in the street outside, blowers working overtime to stop the windscreen from misting. His wipers were thrashing back and forth at double speed. Enzo slipped in beside him, dripping wet. "Okay, let's go." And as the car pulled away, heading through the rain towards the floodlit edifice of the Sénat at the top of the street, neither of them noticed the dark figure of a woman flitting through the downpour beneath the sheltering cover of a black umbrella to punch in the entry code to Raffin's apartment building.

IV

The sound of Raffin's bell ringing shattered the tense silence in the apartment. Had Enzo and Samu forgotten something? Sophie was towelling her hair dry. She cast a quick glance towards Raffin. "I'll get it," she said quickly. And she padded through to the hall and opened the door. Charlotte stood on the landing, her raincoat and umbrella dripping on the floorboards. Her hair was lank and damp, her curls had lost their lustre. She was ghostly pale. She seemed surprised to find Sophie there. Sophie looked at her suspiciously. She had found it hard to believe that Charlotte could be Madeleine, but she knew that her father had been tortured by doubts. Raffin appeared behind her. "Charlotte —"

"Is Enzo here?"

Sophie said, "Someone's kidnapped his daughter." She paused. "His other daughter. He's gone down into the catacombs to try to get her back."

Charlotte closed her eyes and shook her head. "I should have phoned."

"You'd better come in," Raffin said.

She left her umbrella leaning against the outside wall and followed him through to the *séjour*. Sophie came in behind them.

"I know who the last killer is," Charlotte said.

394

"So do we," Sophie told her. "Madeleine Boucher." And she watched for Charlotte's reaction.

"You found the last set of clues then?"

"In Auxerre," Sophie said. "How do *you* know who she is?"

"Because I went back five months through my uncle's diaries. They never meant anything before. But now that I knew I was looking for references to students at ENA, there they were. Right under our noses the whole time. His little coterie of favourites. His little geniuses, he called them. Roques, and d'Hautvillers, and Diop. And Madeleine Boucher." She looked around the blank faces. "You don't know who she is, do you? Who she really is?" She turned to Raffin. "Roger, if she has his daughter, and Enzo's gone to meet her, then she'll kill them both."

CHAPTER
TWENTY-FOUR

The Rue Rotrou was just two streets away from Raffin's apartment. Samu parked on a carpet of light laid down in the road by the large, overlit window of an art gallery on the east side of the street. The two men abandoned the car and splashed across the pavement to the shelter of an adjoining doorway. Samu rapped sharply on the glazed door with the back of his hand, and his signet ring almost cracked the glass. Through the condensation, they saw a silhouette loom against the light, and the door opened to reveal a much smaller man than his shadow would have had them believe. He wore a suit, his tie loosened at the neck and the top button of his shirt undone. He was bald, with a sallow complexion, and darting, frightened eyes.

"Come in, quick." He glanced into the street and closed the door behind them. "It's one thing when we're open for business, Samu. But it looks pretty damned strange to have all my lights on at this time of the morning."

"Turn the fucking things off, then." Samu took a white envelope from an inside pocket and handed it to him. "You'll get the rest when Monsieur Macleod gets back."

The gallery owner glanced nervously at Enzo. "How long will you be?"

"As long as it takes," Samu said. "Come on, take us down. And turn out the lights when you come back up."

The cream-painted walls of the gallery were hung with movie poster originals by Alain Lynch. There was an exhibition of Ellen Shire abstracts, and several of Gilbert Raffin's stylised Paris-scapes. Enzo wondered briefly if the artist was related in some way to Roger.

"This way." The little man led them down a steep, narrow staircase to the basement of his shop. It was dry and cool down here. Dozens of paintings were stacked against the walls and draped with cloth. He took out a bunch of keys and unlocked a door beneath the staircase. It opened into blackness. He reached into it to find a light switch, and a single yellow bulb brought sudden hard light to a narrow passage with brick walls and an earthen floor. There was a smell of damp and the sound of small creatures scuttling into the shadows. Old cobwebs hung in folds, draped from the ceiling like fine-spun gossamer curtains. "You know your way from here."

"I do," Samu said, and he stepped into the passageway, stooping to avoid a rusting steel beam. Enzo followed and shivered. It felt cold here in the dark and damp. The basement door slammed shut behind them, and he heard the key turning in the lock. Samu said, "Mostly these cellars are used to access the sewer system, but if you know where to look you can get right down into the catacombs. Come on." And he set off briskly along the passage. They hurried past locked doors leading to the basements of shops and apartment blocks. And as the light faded behind them, they switched on their helmet lamps, sharp beams cutting through damp air, swinging left and right with the turn of their heads.

Samu seemed to know his way by heart, taking right turns, or left, without hesitation. To Enzo, one turn looked like any other. Brick walls and steps and narrow openings. Rusting steel doors. Samu delivered a breathless commentary as they moved through the dark. "We just crossed under the Rue de Médicis. If we turned right we'd come up against the wall of the car park beneath the Sénat." He opened a door and they went down a short flight of steps into a huge tunnel that arched above their heads and roared with the sound of rushing water. Drips fell like rain from the brickwork overhead. The beam of Enzo's lamp flashed across the black streaked surface of what looked like an underground river in spate. A narrow walkway with a rusted iron rail ran along the side of it. It was slippery like ice underfoot. "Jesus!" he heard Samu's voice rise above the roar of the water. "I've never seen it like this before!"

"Where the hell are we?" Enzo shouted back.

"We're in the sewers! But don't worry, the shit's all in the pipes. This is just rainwater draining down from the streets." They slithered along the walkway for twenty or thirty metres. "We're under the Jardins du Luxembourg now."

"Maybe it would have been easier climbing the fence," Enzo shouted.

Samu grinned and turned off into a feeder tunnel. The water was calf deep, and the power of it was almost strong enough to take Enzo's feet from under him. They waded against the flow of it to a flight of steps leading up to a metal door set into the wall. Samu heaved it open and they climbed into a dry, circular, concrete chamber. Metal rungs set into the wall ascended into blackness. Even with his head tipped back and the beam of his lamp pointed straight up, Enzo could not see where they went. The darkness above them seemed to snuff out the light. When Samu slammed the door shut, the roar of water in the sewers became a distant rumble. He produced from somewhere beneath his waterproofs an iron crossbar with metal lugs at one end, and knelt on the floor. Enzo tilted his head to direct the beam of his lamp downwards, and saw that there was a circular IDC metal plaque set into the concrete. Samu slipped the lugged end of his crossbar into a slot beneath the letters and turned it like a key to lock it in place, and then he braced himself to pull the lid aside. He strained and grunted as the cast iron slipped out of its circular groove and dragged across the concrete. The darkness it uncovered was profound.

Samu stood up, breathing hard and grinning triumphantly. "*Et voilà*. You're in." Enzo could see the first rungs gleaming dully in the light of their helmets. "It'll take you straight down into a little antechamber right off the main drag. There's a short stretch of tunnel. It'll take you west about fifteen metres. When you get to the end you turn left. That's south. You'll be right below the Grande Avenue du Luxembourg, and then you're following the map." He fumbled in his pocket and pulled out what looked like a wristwatch with a velcro strap fastening. He held it out. "Put that on your right wrist." Enzo took it and realised that it was a compass. "You'll find that you get pretty disorientated down there. That should keep you straight." He went into an inside pocket and brought out a tarnished silver cigarette case. He opened it to retrieve a pre-rolled cigarette and lit it, his lighter bringing fleeting colour to a bloodless face. "What are you going down there for, man?"

But Enzo just shook his head. "You don't want to know."

Samu shrugged. He looked at his watch. "It's just after one-thirty. How long are you going to be?"

"I don't know. Two, maybe three hours."

"I'll be back here at three-thirty. I'll wait till five. If you haven't shown by then, you're on your own."

Enzo nodded.

"*Bon courage.*" Samu extended a hand. It was cold and limp when Enzo shook it.

Enzo crouched on all fours and dropped a leg into the hole to find the first rung. He tested his weight on it before lowering himself carefully to reach the next. It was a tight squeeze. By the time he was a dozen rungs down, the hole had swallowed him entirely. The sound of metal dragging across concrete forced him to crane his head back and look up. He saw the light of Samu's helmet extinguished as the iron plaque slid back into place above him. For a moment, he panicked, crushed by darkness and claustrophobia. He wanted to shout, like a child at bedtime whose parents have turned out the light. He was breathing too rapidly and knew that he was in danger of hyperventilating. He fought to control it, holding down the acid in his stomach until the first flush of panic passed. He had to get to the bottom as fast as possible.

With arms and legs trembling, he climbed down as quickly as he could, and found himself standing in a small space crudely hacked out of the rock and shored up with brick. A narrow tunnel stretched ahead of him. It looked as if it had been bored out of the rock by a giant drill. Bent almost double, and bracing himself with hands and feet against its curving walls, he made slow forward progress until he reached a barrier crudely constructed from rough-cut blocks of masonry. Some of them had been knocked out. He peered through the hole to see that he would have to climb backwards through it to get down into the wide, square tunnel which crossed at right-angles beyond. He heard his cagoule tear as he eased himself through the gap, its hood catching on a jagged edge of rock. He cursed and yanked himself free, jumping, almost falling backwards into the tunnel. He steadied himself against the brick, legs quivering from the effort, and found himself looking at a street sign painted on a smooth stone slab set into the opposite wall. G.DE AVENUE DU LUXEMBOURG CÔTÉ DU COUCHANT. It was covered in graffiti, red and blue and silver arrows, the letter A inside a circle. Already he seemed to have lost his bearings.

Turn left, Samu had said. South. Enzo double-checked with his compass. Of course, now he was facing the other way, and had to turn right. He steadied himself for a moment, then began south along the tunnel. The roof and floor seemed smooth, hacked out of solid bedrock. The walls were made from roughly-cut stone bricks. It was narrow, little more than his own width again, and he had to stoop to avoid scraping his helmet on the roof. His breath condensed in white clouds in the lamplight as he pushed on as quickly as he dared. He passed several junctions branching off to east and west. In places the walls had collapsed, and he had to clamber over fallen masonry. Occasionally the tunnel widened, and crude brick columns had been constructed to support the roof. In other places the walls bulged, narrowing to the point where he could barely squeeze himself through.

He stopped frequently to consult his map. He had crossed four junctions, and was certain that the next turn to his right was the one that Samu had marked in red. He must have passed beyond the Luxembourg Gardens by now, and be heading south beneath the Avenue de l'Observatoire. In spite of the cold, he was sweating profusely. His helmet felt hot and uncomfortable and chafed above his ears. His back ached from the constant stoop.

He arrived at the fifth junction. The wall on the east side was partially collapsed, and he had to scramble across the rubble to get into the tunnel heading west.

He was certain that this was his turnoff. Almost. But that single, tiny, nagging grain of doubt was enough to completely undermine his confidence. What if it wasn't? If he got lost, then Kirsty would be lost, too. He forced himself to try to think calmly. He had to trust his judgment, and Samu's map. And, in any case, Samu had said that if he missed his turn he would come up against the new multistorey car park and know that he had made a mistake.

He wondered if, perhaps, he should carry on to that dead end, just to be sure, and then make his way back to the turnoff. But there wasn't time. He looked at his watch. He had no idea how long any of this was going to take.

So he headed off west, checking constantly with his compass. The tunnel should start curving to the south-west. But if the compass was to be believed, he seemed to be heading north-west. It was impossible to tell if the tunnel was curving or not. He could not see far enough ahead to make that judgment, and he had to keep his eyes down to avoid tripping over debris or falling into holes.

After several minutes, to his great relief, the tunnel seemed to arc south, just as it did on the map. He passed another opening veering off to his right, turning north this time. He looked at the map. There it was, leading off into a parallel network. He did not want to go that way. According to the plan there should not be any turnoffs on his left. If he hugged the left wall all the way, it should lead him to what Samu had called the roundabout beneath the Rue Auguste Comte.

He had gone, perhaps, twenty or thirty metres when he heard the first blood-curdling howl. It was almost feral, and it stopped him in his tracks. He could hear the faint thump, thump, thump of distant music. Another shriek. And then laughter. Several voices, whooping and hollering. The music was getting louder, finding form in the dark. He could distinguish now the monotonous rhythm of a repetitive rap track. The thumping of a bass drum, the vibration of a bass guitar. More shrieking. It was getting closer, coming towards him from the direction of the bunker.

Enzo stood rooted to the spot. He had no idea what to do. There was nowhere to go. Maybe they were just kids out for a good time. Maybe they would say *hey man*, and shake his hand, and go on their way. Now he could see the light of their flashlights beyond a curve in the tunnel. And if he could see theirs, then they could see his.

Suddenly the music went dead, and the lights went out. The silence was absolute. And terrifying. Much worse than the music and the shrieking. He heard the faintest rustling, and then dark shapes moved into the farthest reaches of the beam from his helmet. He saw its light reflected in their eyes as they inched around the curve of the tunnel towards him. Five, six sets of them. They stopped, and there was a short, tense period of assessment, and then they all switched on flashlights and Enzo was momentarily dazzled. Another standoff, before a repetition of the howl which had first alerted Enzo to their presence. Like a bugler trumpeting the command to attack. It sparked off a chorus of shrieks, and their lights came flying towards him like frenzied fireflies. There was clearly going to be no *hey man*, and shaking of hands. Enzo turned and ran as fast as he could, back the way he had come. But they were younger, faster. It would only be a matter of time before they caught him.

He saw the rubble gathered around the north turn he had passed moments earlier, and he slithered over it into the turnoff. He fumbled for the switch on his helmet and turned off the light. A wall of blackness smothered him before his eyes adjusted to the reflected lights of the youths streaming in his wake. They were just out of sight beyond the turnoff. Enzo scrambled forward, tripping and stumbling, and almost fell into another turnoff on his left. He groped his way around a support column and felt where the wall had collapsed to create a shallow recess. He climbed over the rock-fall and rolled into it. He felt around for a sharp piece of rock that would fit into his hand, and pressed himself against the stone, trying to stop his breath from grating in his throat.

The light grew stronger and he could see out into the tunnel now. It was narrower than the others, and its walls were in a poor state of repair. The pursuing voices had gone quiet, but Enzo could hear them breathing and whispering. The beams of several flashlights shone down his tunnel, beyond his hiding place, criss-crossing, searching out every crevice and rock-fall. There was a brief, whispered discussion, and then the flashlights carried on along the top passage, until gradually their light faded completely and silence returned to the catacombs.

Enzo did not stir for nearly two minutes, until he was certain that they were not coming back. Then, cautiously, he eased himself out into the tunnel. He felt for the switch on his helmet and turned on the light. The face caught full in its beam was that of a young man with a completely shaven head. He had a deep scar through his left eyebrow, and black smeared like war paint across either cheek. He opened his mouth to yell as he raised a baseball bat above his head. Enzo smashed him full in the face with the rock he still held in his hand. He both heard and felt the breaking of bone, and saw blood spurting in the lamplight. His attacker folded at the knees and pitched forward face-first. Enzo had no idea how much damage he had done, but he was not going to wait to find out. He picked up the baseball bat where it had tumbled among the fallen stones and scrambled out into the main tunnel, turning right, and right again, hoping that he was accurately retracing the steps he had taken just minutes before. He ran as fast as he could, semi-crouched, shoulders glancing off the tunnel walls as he propelled himself forward into the darkness.

Even as he ran panic was setting in. What if he had turned the wrong way? Supposing he was heading north instead of south? Or east. He might be anywhere. He was sure he had passed this stretch of collapsed wall before. The tunnel narrowed here and took a jagged turn. It all seemed horribly familiar. He stopped running, and leaned against the wall to catch his breath, searching in his pocket for his maps. And then his heart nearly stopped. He could only find two. The bunker, and the Réseau des Chartreux. His Luxembourg map was gone. He remembered it had been in his hand when he first encountered the rappers. What had he done with it? He tried to think. In his panic he must have dropped it somewhere. "Fuck!" he shouted at the top of his voice, but his cry of despair was choked off by the weight of the city above him. He dropped his face into his hands and screwed his eyes closed and wanted to weep.

But there was no point in feeling sorry for himself. Again, he forced himself to focus. Still breathing stertorously, he checked his compass. He was, it seemed, still heading south-west. He must be going the right way. With his eyes shut he tried to visualise the map. The tunnel took a loop at the bottom end, and curved around to Samu's roundabout. If he could only get to the roundabout, then he would be on to the Chartreux map, and back on track. He was not going to help himself by panicking. He forced all the air out of his lungs and drew a long, deep breath. With the wall to his left, all he had to do was keep going. He set off again, this time at a less frantic pace.

Time and space and direction had no place here in the catacombs. Enzo had lost track of them all. It seemed that the only thing he could do was focus on the tunnel ahead and keep going. And going. Interminably onwards, despair creeping back with every negative thought. And then the tunnel began visibly curving away to his right. This had to be the bottom end of the loop. He stopped to check the Chartreux map. It showed a tunnel branching off to the right. But there was no sign of it. He pushed on. Still no tunnel. Panic was returning. And then there it was. A crooked support column, a section of collapsed ceiling, a tunnel leading directly north.

Immediately ahead, the tunnel opened out without warning into a crude chamber, where ceiling and floor folded one into the other, and several misshapen columns supported the roof. Another tunnel fed into the space from the north, and a cemented brick wall blocked the way out. Near the foot of it someone had taken a sledgehammer to break a way through. A *chatière*. It was a small, ragged-edged hole, and Enzo looked at it doubtfully, wondering if he would be able to force his big frame through it. He stripped off his cagoule and got down on his knees. He got an arm through, and then his head, and he twisted to get his shoulders in. Even as he managed finally to drag himself through to the other side, he realised that it would not have been possible for Madeleine to force Kirsty all this way through the catacombs against her will. Either she had been tricked into going voluntarily, or Madeleine knew another way in.

He reached back to retrieve his cagoule and the baseball bat, and he sat on the floor with his back to the wall, examining his two remaining maps. At the bottom left of the bunker map, on the Rue d'Assas, almost immediately adjacent to the Salle des Fresques, there was a notched circle with an arrow drawn to it. *Plaque IDC en face de la librairie d'Assas*, it said. Samu had

408

told him all the exits into the Rue d'Assas had been walled up. But maybe Madeleine had made her own *chatière*.

Enzo looked around and realised for the first time where he was. This was the north end of the German bunker. Concrete floors, pointed walls. Corridors rather than tunnels. Doorways, some with old metal doors, buckled and torn, still hanging from rusted hinges. The walls were covered in graffiti. Arrows pointed to *Hinterhof, S. Michel, N. Dame-Bonaparte*. Black letters painted on a white background warned, *Rauchen Verboten*. A more recently constructed red-brick wall barred that way forward. Enzo got to his feet and checked his map and his compass and then turned due south. Even after all these years, the German passion for order was still apparent in the ruins of this wartime bunker. Out of the haphazard chaos of the catacombs, they had created a grid-system of corridors and passageways, rows of doorways leading off to rooms and offices. It made Samu's map easy to follow.

The graffiti artists had been everywhere. Enzo saw several ghostlike white figures painted on brick. A skull and crossbones beneath which someone had scrawled RAMBO 21 DEC 1991. A mock street sign read, *Passage of the Invisibles*. An explosion was painted in red and white on another wall, a skull at its centre. *NP NB* was stencilled into it, and below it the legend, *CONTAMINATION*. Side by side in one corridor, he passed a row of what had once been chemical toilets. The remains of a wooden seat still straddled the pit in one of them. A primitive tribal figure with red facial war markings leered at him from a freshly bricked-up wall.

Everywhere he turned, strange images were caught in the light. He saw old junction boxes fixed high on the walls, cables still spewing from the busted interiors from which they had been ripped more than half a century before. More recently someone had tried to make navigation easier by painting colour-coded arrows on the walls where corridors divided and led off in different directions. But Enzo had no way of making sense of them.

He passed through a doorway and into one of the original tunnels hacked out of the rock by the ancient *carriers*. It ran east to west, effectively dividing the bunker in two. At the end of it, the map showed a corridor leading further west and through another doorway into the Salle des Fresques. Another thirty metres and he would be there. He turned off his light and stood in the pitch-black listening to the silence. It was as dense as the darkness, and just as impenetrable. His own breathing was deafening. He waited for his eyes to adjust to any other light source, and somewhere very faintly in the far distance he picked up the merest glimmer. Very carefully, fingertips picking their way along the wall, he drifted as quietly as he could through the darkness of the tunnel towards it. Slowly the light grew stronger, until he reached the end of the passage and moved back into the regimented world of German planning. He passed three rooms on his right, before turning into a short corridor. A doorway on the left opened into the Salle des Fresques. The light was strongest here, although still feeble. A soft, flickering light that danced gently around the opening. Enzo advanced one cautious step at a time. There was still no sound, except for the ringing in his ears and the rapid beat of his heart pulsing in his throat.

He moved into the doorway, and the Salle des Fresques opened out in front of him, beyond a heavy, rusted iron door which stood ajar. It was a long space, brick walls giving form to a chamber hewn roughly from solid bedrock. He recognised some of the paintings from the internet. The Aztec Indian, Armstrong on the moon, the skeleton with its warning on AIDS. There were others. Marlene Dietrich, Spiderman, a penis with wings, a green man from outer space, a couple of big-booted thugs with mohican haircuts and an axe. But otherwise the *salle* was empty. The light came from a single candle which stood burning in the middle of the floor, set solid in a pool of its own melted wax. Next to it, the glass of what looked like a wine bottle glowed green in the flickering flame. The shadow of the bottle fell across the floor to flit around the walls with the frescoes.

Enzo did not know whether to be alarmed or relieved. He stepped into the room and switched on his helmet lamp. He was quite alone. He crossed to the candle and crouched beside it to examine the bottle. It was a bottle of Chartreuse. And he saw then that the glass was clear. It was the liquid that was green. Green Chartreuse. The liqueur made by the Chartreux monks. He swore, and spat his frustration at the floor. Right to the end Madeleine was playing with him, leaving him clues to decipher. And this one was, perhaps, the easiest of them all.

He took out his maps. The Réseau des Chartreux was immediately south and east of the bunker. At its southernmost tip was the Fontaine des Chartreux. Samu had told him that it got its name from the green water that ran down the walls to collect in a stone sink made centuries before by the monks. There was an exit marked from the German bunker into the *réseau* at its south-east corner. And from there it looked a fairly straightforward route to the *fontaine*. He checked the time. It was twenty past two.

As he stood up, he heard the same blood-curdling howl which had greeted him on the turnoff from the Grande Avenue du Luxembourg. It was followed by a series of whoops and hollers. He wheeled around and ran back along to the near end of the tunnel which transected the bunker. This time he turned south, and then east, following a long, straight corridor past door after door giving on to deserted concrete rooms. It was hard to believe that all this had once been inhabited by German intelligence officers and administration staff, a command and communications centre controlling the occupation of the city. At the far end he turned south again, still running, passing more ghostly figures white painted on the walls, until he reached an arched stone doorway. An iron gate blocked his way. Beyond it was the *réseau*. Rusted hinges screamed their protest as he pulled the gate wide enough to let him slip through. On the other side he stopped again to look at the map. He

412

was fifteen metres below ground here. The route he wanted to follow was marked on the plan as the Chemin du Bunker. It dog-legged south towards the *fontaine* at the bottom end. He stood listening. The screams and catcalls had faded. He hurried through the chamber beyond the gate and loped out into the network of tunnels that ran beneath the former Chartreux monastery.

He was now in one of the tunnels dug out by the monks themselves, and he had to stoop low to avoid cracking his helmet on the roof. These must have been small men. In some places the tunnel narrowed to the point where he had to turn sideways to squeeze through. In others it seemed unusually wide, with a shelf sloping away to the ceiling along the left-hand wall. Some of the walls appeared to have been constructed from cement and pebbles, repairs perhaps where some of the original walls had tumbled down and left the structure unsafe.

At the bottom end of the Chemin du Bunker, there were passageways leading off left and right and his tunnel narrowed to another iron gate set into a squared doorway. Enzo stopped to listen. All he could hear now was the drip, drip, drip of water. He turned off his lamp, and after a moment saw the faint flickering glow of distant candlelight beyond the gate. Moving more cautiously now, he slipped past it and into a large, cavernous chamber whose curving roof was supported on crooked pillars. The light was coming from a narrow opening in the far wall. Enzo approached slowly, until he could see that there was a flight of stone steps leading down through the rock to a lower level. And there, at the foot of the steps, was the basin the monks had chiselled out of limestone to collect the water that dripped from the ceiling and ran down the walls. A candle burned in an alcove immediately above it, and the water itself gleamed a luminescent green by its light. Drips, like raindrops from the ceiling, broke its surface in ever increasing hypnotic rings. There were stone shelves set into the wall on either side of the basin and, on the left-hand wall, a figure sat cross-legged in the gloom staring down into the water as if in a trance. A slight figure, a woman, dark hair falling across her face. She appeared to be wearing a ski-suit and climbing boots. There was a small rucksack strapped to her back.

As Enzo moved into the doorway she heard him and turned to look up the stairs. It was Marie Aucoin. The *Garde des Sceaux*. She was wearing no make-up and looked older than on the two previous occasions they had met. Her face was a sickly white, all humour leeched from her eyes. She swung her legs around to dangle from the shelf and placed her hands palm-down on the edge of it.

"Surprised?"

He stared at her for a long time, anger slow-burning inside him. "Yes," he said finally.

"Good." She managed a wan smile. "Then perhaps I'm not too late."

CHAPTER
TWENTY-FIVE

I

"I was married to Christian when I was still working at the Société Générale," she said. "But finance was his forte, not mine. Still, it was useful to have a wealthy husband to support me through two-and-a-half years as a student at ENA." She gazed back up the stairs at Enzo. She was a woman who liked the sound of her own voice. "It was starting to become fashionable at that time to accept students from the *real world*. It went against the stereotype of the cloistered academic, even though I already had my degree from Sciences-Po. But I preferred to be enrolled under my maiden name. Didn't want to be thought of as a kept woman. So I was Marie-Madeleine Boucher, then." She smiled. "But when I ran for Députée in Val de Marne, the name seemed a little too religious for a secular politician. And so I was happy to become Marie Aucoin and take my seat in the National Assembly."

"Where's Kirsty?"

The *Garde des Sceaux* seemed disappointed by his lack of interest in her story. She sighed. "All in good time."

"Whose good time?"

"Mine, of course."

"What do you want?"

Something hardened in her cold, blue eyes. And there was an edge to her voice. "To fulfil my destiny. I am forty-five years old, Monsieur. I am a woman, and I am the *Garde des Sceaux*. Do you have any idea how impossibly difficult it is to be all those things at the same time?" She allowed herself a small smile of self-satisfaction. "And that's just the beginning. Already they're whispering in the corridors of Matignon about the possibility of my appointment as Prime Minister. But the Élysée Palace is my real destiny. To be the first woman elected to the office of President. An office from which I can change the future of my country. To which I can restore the vision of Napoléon and the genius of de Gaulle. I can lead France back to greatness."

"I admire your modesty."

"Modesty is for fools!" She jumped down from her shelf. "Why don't you come down and join me?" It wasn't so much a request as an instruction. She moved away from the foot of the stairs to the far side of the small chamber the monks had built to accommodate the *fontaine*. She took off her rucksack and laid it on the shelf beside her and folded her arms.

Enzo hesitated. He knew that once he had descended into the chamber he would be trapped there. "Where's Kirsty?" he demanded again.

"She's nearby."

"If you've harmed her —"

"She's alive and well. And it is not my intention to do anything to change that."

Still he hesitated.

"Unless you force me to."

He had no choice then. Slowly, reluctantly, he climbed down the six steps into the pit and turned to stand facing her across the green basin. They were only two metres apart, and he saw now that her eyes were quite dead. Almost opaque. She saw the world through cataracts of self-deception. She looked at the baseball bat dangling from his right hand and smiled.

"Really, Monsieur, did you think you were going to beat me to death?"

"It's dangerous down here."

"Not if you know your way around. I've been exploring the catacombs since I was a student. I love it. It's like life, really. You need to know what lies beneath, to understand what's on the surface."

"Why did you kill him?"

The sudden directness of his question seemed to ruffle her surface calm, and for a moment he caught a glimpse of the darkness that lay beneath.

"He humiliated us." Her mouth curled in anger. "Picked us out as the brightest and best and then told us how much smarter he was than we would ever be. A process of daily, ritual humiliation. He had this compulsive need to demonstrate his superiority. Always at our expense. In private he would tell us that we were the future of France, in public he made fools of us in front of our fellow students. He wanted to mould us in his image, but made it clear we would always be inferior copies. He wanted us to worship at the altar of his brilliance, an acknowledgement from the intellectual cream of our *promotion* that we were mere cerebral midgets in the shadow of his towering intellect." She almost laughed. "And what had he become, this great brain? A reviewer of films."

"So you killed him?"

"Have you any idea of what it is like to be mocked and ridiculed, Monsieur Macleod? To be *fêted* and flattered in one breath, and then denigrated in the next?" She paused. "Yes, we killed him. He needed to know, in the end, that we were smarter than he was. That the future was ours, not his. It was a demonstration of *our* superior intelligence."

Enzo began to see how twisted minds worked. They had all been child prodigies. Little geniuses. Groomed for greatness. The cream which had risen to the top of the Schoelcher Promotion. The elite of the elite. "I've always thought that violence was the first and last resort of the inferior intellect," he said.

"You sound just like him."

"Is that why you want to kill me, too? Because I found out you weren't as smart as you thought you were? Because, in the end, you couldn't get away with murder after all?"

She shook her head. "Oh, but we did. No one even knew he was dead. It was the perfect murder, Monsieur Macleod." She smiled. "The thing about intelligence is that in itself, it has no real value. It must be practised and applied. If you have a vision, you need the courage to see it through. My co-conspirators turned out to lack the courage of their convictions, that's all."

"So you killed them, too."

She shrugged. "Hugues saved me the trouble. Philippe was weak, and his weakness was a danger to me."

"And Diop?"

"An old favour repaid, by someone who knows better than to ever open his mouth."

"Juge Lelong?"

"Good God, no. Lelong's a pedant. A zealot. As straight as the day is long. He really believed you were raising a middle finger to his precious enquiry."

"So it wasn't the good judge that you delegated to try to dispose of me?"

A frown of genuine consternation crinkled her eyes. "You? What *are* you talking about?"

"The two men on the bridge. The truck on the *autoroute*."

Now her consternation gave way to amusement. "I think you've been letting your imagination run away with itself, Monsieur Macleod."

Enzo experienced a fleeting embarrassment. Had he really just been a victim of his own paranoia? He moved on. "What I don't understand is why you left clues with the body parts in the first place."

"There is a great deal you don't understand, Monsieur Macleod. I'm not sure it's even worth your while trying."

"Indulge me." He needed to keep her talking. He needed every moment he could claw back from her to think of a way out of this.

She sighed, bored now, it seemed. "Each of us took responsibility for burying one piece of the Maître. And each of us revealed that location to only one other. The clues were then designed to lead from one trunk to the next, revealing the identity of one of us each time. That way, none of us could betray the others, without the circle of clues leading eventually back to him."

"Or her."

She inclined her head in acknowledgement. "Or her. Of course, we couldn't make the trail too easy. If one of the trunks was discovered by accident, we didn't want some knuckle-headed policeman putting it all together. We had to make the clues hard enough that it would take someone of equal intellect to solve the puzzle."

"Someone like me."

She laughed, then. And her mirth seemed genuine. "No, Monsieur. You were never in our league. You had the internet at your disposal. In 1996, we had no idea what the internet might become, or how it might unravel all our carefully considered clues. It took us five months to assemble them and put our plan together."

"And one bloody night to carry it out."

"You should have seen his face, Monsieur. That moment of realisation. When he knew, for all his arrogance, that those he had humiliated were capable of far more than he ever suspected."

"So, really, you just killed him to show how clever you were. An intellectual game of murder which no one would ever know you had won."

"Until now." She held his gaze for a moment, enjoying the opportunity to echo his words.

"So what are you going to do?"

She turned and removed a small gun from her rucksack and levelled it at him. "I'm going to kill you, and then it'll just be our little secret. A fitting reward for your obstinate persistence, don't you think?"

Fear flooded his being like a poison gas. "What about Kirsty?"

"Oh, I won't have to kill her. Nature will do that for me. A very trusting girl."

"Where is she?" Enzo looked around for some way out.

"Chained to a wall in one of the transversals below the Rue d'Assas. Water's pouring in from the sewers. A fortuitous summer storm. It was more than half full when I left her. I doubt if her misery will last for too much longer."

The full horror of the circumstance she had so calmly described created a still centre to Enzo's fear. "Kirsty!" he bellowed at the top of his voice and, when its echo faded, silence was the only response.

"Too late already, perhaps."

And, then, very faintly, they heard a voice calling out of the darkness. It seemed a long way off. A tiny voice full of terror and despair. And disbelief. "Daddy?"

He felt as though someone had plunged a knife into his heart. He could not remember when she had last called him that.

"Daddy, help!" It was a scream filled with both fear and hope.

But he was powerless to help her. Marie Aucoin had let her gun drop for a moment, but now she raised it again. Enzo's breathing became rapid and shallow, and he turned his eyes to heaven as if appealing for help from a higher power. And like the answer to a prayer, he heard a voice from above. "There's no point in killing anyone, Madeleine."

Both he and the *Garde des Sceaux* turned to see Charlotte standing on the top step. She had a gun pointing at the other woman, trembling slightly in an unsteady hand. Enzo recognised the polished wooden handgrip. It was Raffin's revolver. Just behind her he saw the gleam of Bertrand's nose stud, and the shadow of someone else.

Marie Aucoin's self-confidence seemed shaken. She turned blazing eyes on Enzo. "I told you to come alone!"

"It doesn't matter now," Charlotte said. "The whole world knows who you are. Marie-Madeleine Boucher. The police are on their way."

"And who the hell are you?"

"You murdered my father."

Marie Aucoin frowned in confusion. "Gaillard had no children."

Charlotte glanced at Enzo. "I'm sorry, Enzo. Another deception. I didn't know myself until I tracked down my birth parents. I'd always called him uncle and thought he was an old friend of my adopted parents. It seems I was one of his early indiscretions. My mother wanted nothing to do with him, and I was to be aborted. But he couldn't bear to destroy any part of himself. And so he bought her off, and persuaded the son and daughter-in-law of an old family retainer, a childless couple in Angoulême, to adopt me. I think I

422

was the only thing he ever loved apart from himself. A man of strange contradictions. Flawed in ways that maybe only a daughter could love." She saw Enzo flinch from the thought, and looked back at Marie Aucoin. Her hand had stopped shaking. "But you, you're a much more interesting case. Would you like my professional diagnosis?"

"What are you talking about?"

"Narcissistic Personality Disorder. It's quite rare. At first I thought you were displaying the classic symptoms of catathymia. You remember we discussed that, Enzo? But I was wrong." Charlotte paused, and refocused her attention on the *Garde des Sceaux.* "No doubt someone of your academic background will have read Dostoevsky." Marie Aucoin remained unresponsive. "And so no doubt you'll remember how in *Crime and Punishment* the murderer, Raskolnikov, wrote an essay on *extraordinary* people, and how such people are above the law. People like you, Madeleine. People who value themselves above all others. People who have no empathy. People who become so preoccupied by grandiose fantasies that they will commit any crime to achieve their goals. People who believe that they are above the laws that lesser beings like us must follow." She shook her head. "How ironic that we should have made you the guardian of the very laws you feel so at liberty to ignore." Anger filled her dark eyes. "Narcissism is the beating heart of psychopathy. I shouldn't hate you, I should pity you."

Marie Aucoin let her gun fall to her side. She seemed smaller now, diminished by her defeat. But no more so

423

than in her own eyes. "You came to kill me, didn't you?"

Charlotte nodded. "Yes."

Marie Aucoin took a deep breath and pulled herself up to her full height.

Enzo watched with horror as Charlotte's finger tightened on the trigger. "Don't!" he said. She was trembling once more. The gun shook increasingly as she tried to hold her aim. And then suddenly her eyes cleared. She lowered Raffin's gun. She had found her pity.

And that, Enzo realised, was probably the hardest pill of all for Marie Aucoin to swallow. She would probably never know, as they did, that she was not the extraordinary person she believed herself to be. She would never see herself through their eyes as the pathetic, deluded individual she really was.

"That's the trouble with you people." Her defiance was brittle. "You have no courage. To realise your vision you need the courage to carry it through." She raised her gun, bit down hard on the barrel and pulled the trigger.

Green turned to red.

"Daddy!" Kirsty's scream echoed through the dark chambers of the catacombs.

"Jesus . . ." Enzo stepped over the prone figure of the *Garde des Sceaux* where she had fallen at the foot of the steps and leapt up the stairs. "Kirsty's going to drown."

"Where is she?" Enzo saw now that Samu was the shadow beyond Bertrand. His face was blanched, shocked.

"Somewhere beneath the Rue d'Assas. In one of the transversals. It's flooding."

"We'll have to go back to the bunker, then," Charlotte said. She put a hand on his arm and squeezed it. "That's how Samu brought us in. Bertrand made a *chatière* with a sledgehammer."

"No time," Enzo said. "Marie Aucoin must have had her own way of getting in. So there must be a way out to the Rue d'Assas from here."

"It used to be bricked up at the far side there," Samu said, and they followed him through the dark cavern, Bertrand hefting his sledgehammer on his shoulder. A tunnel led off from the north-west corner. Two metres along it they reached a dead end. It was sealed off. Red brick covered in graffiti, a cartoon image of a white pig with a curling tail, the names of countless visitors sprayed in red and black and green. There was a pile of loose rubble gathered against the foot of the wall. Enzo dropped to his knees and started pulling the stone away with desperate fingers.

"There's a hole behind this."

They all joined in, and very quickly uncovered a hole hacked in the brick. It was wide enough for only a very slight person to crawl through.

"Get out of the way," Bertrand said quietly. And when they had moved aside he swung his sledgehammer at the brick, sending sparks and splinters flying through the air. He let the heavy head of it fall to the floor before heaving it back above his shoulder and swinging it down again through an arc at the wall. Enzo saw the impact of it shudder through the young man's

425

body. There was sweat trickling down from his scalp. It took five swings before, finally, brick and mortar cracked, and the wall collapsed around the initial hole. Cold, damp air rushed through the opening.

They could hear Kirsty screaming now, desperate pleas for help. Enzo clambered over the shattered brickwork and into the east tunnel of the Rue d'Assas. "Which way?" he shouted.

"Turn right." Samu's voice was right behind him.

Water fell like rain from the cold stone above their heads, making it slippery underfoot. The light of their flashlights barely penetrated the fog of humidity that filled the tunnel, and they very nearly ran into a second wall blocking their progress. It, too, had been holed, but this time the gap was big enough even for Enzo to get through.

Kirsty's voice was closer now, but it had lost its fire, shredded and chopped by sobs and tears.

"Kirsty, hold on!" Enzo shouted.

"Da-ad-y!" she screamed back, and he felt tears of shock and fear fill his eyes, burning them like acid.

"There, on your left," Samu called, and Enzo saw a narrow opening on the west side of the tunnel, just ahead of them. The ground sloped away steeply into the turn, and down into the transversal. Somewhere along the way, Enzo had lost his helmet. He shone the flashlight Samu had given him down into the tunnel and saw that it was full of water.

"Oh, my god!" He started wading into it, almost surprised at how warm it seemed, and very quickly he was up to his chest. He raised the flashlight above his head and kept going. The water was almost up to his neck before finally the ceiling levelled off, and he found himself looking along the gap between the water and the roof. It was maybe fifteen centimetres. He shone his flashlight along the surface and saw Kirsty's head tipped back so that her mouth and nose were above the water level, only just still able to draw breath. She turned her head towards the light, and he saw the terror in her eyes.

"Daddy!"

"Hold on, baby, I'm coming." Enzo plunged under the water, kicking hard to propel himself forward. It was cloudy. The light of his flashlight barely penetrated it, and he could hardly see his hand in front of his face. He bumped into Kirsty before he saw her, and immediately surfaced to gasp for air. The water level was rising fast. There was hardly any gap left at all now. He ducked under again and grabbed his daughter's arms, following them to find metal cuffs at the wrists attached to a chain. The chain was half a metre in length and looped through an iron ring set into the stone. The loop was padlocked. He took the chain in both hands, braced his feet against the wall, and pulled with all his might. There was not even the hint of movement. The chances were the ring had been sunk in the stone years ago and was rusted solid into it.

His lungs were bursting now, and he surfaced again for air. This time he smacked his head against the roof. There was no longer any gap. There was no more air. He saw his own blood colour the water red. And he turned to see Kirsty looking at him through cloudy water, eyes wide, filled with resignation, bubbles streaming up from her nose and mouth. He knew he couldn't hold his breath much longer, and so he grabbed her and hugged her to him, wondering if it were possible to make up for all those years of lost love in their last seconds together.

A hand grabbed him and pulled him roughly aside. He saw Bertrand's piercings and his nose stud and the grim set of his mouth. He had strapped on Samu's hard hat, and its lamp cut a sharp beam through the murk. The boy took the chain and, like Enzo, braced himself against the wall. Well-toned muscles, built during hours of patient exercise, bulged and strained. Enzo saw the veins stand out on his forehead. Still the ring did not move. Bertrand let go, then, and wound the chain around both elbows, bending his arms and placing his feet flat against the wall again. Enzo held on to Kirsty, air escaping now in great billowing bubbles from his lungs, and saw Bertrand strain every living fibre, jets of air exploding from his mouth and nostrils. He heard himself saying, *I don't want Sophie throwing her life away on a waster like you*, and felt a dreadful surge of guilt. And then, suddenly, the ring gave, in a cloud of brown rust, and they were free. Bertrand grabbed Enzo by the collar and pulled him back along the transversal. The limp form of Kirsty trailing along behind them.

As soon as they hit the ramp, Bertrand hauled them both clear of the water, and Enzo felt air tearing at his lungs, choking and wretching and gasping for breath. Charlotte and Samu helped drag them up into the tunnel.

428

Enzo got himself on to his knees, tears streaming from his eyes. Kirsty lay on the floor, eyes shut, mouth gaping. She was no longer breathing. He was too late. He had always been too late.

Samu pulled him away as Bertrand bent over the prostrate form of his daughter, pinching her nose, and putting his mouth to hers. He blew air into her lungs, and then placed his hands on her chest to pump it out again. Water spluttered and spurted from her mouth. He repeated the action. More water. A third attempt, and this time a cough, and then an involuntary gasp, followed by a fit of coughing and water bubbling from her lips and nostrils. Her eyes opened, full of fear and incomprehension.

II

Warm summer rain poured down on them out of the night as Bertrand slid aside the heavy IDC plaque. He pulled himself up on to the pavement, and then knelt to help Enzo out after him. Kirsty was still only semi-conscious. Enzo had insisted on carrying her, and now he laid her out on the hard wet paving stones, easing her down from an aching shoulder, before collapsing beside her, utterly exhausted. He saw neon lights in the window of the Brasserie Les Facultés. Traffic lights on the corner of the Rue Joseph Bara were at green, but there was no traffic. He rolled his head the other way and saw, at the far end of the street, the Faculté de Droit et Sciences Économiques d'Assas, from which the young Jacques Gaillard had graduated all those years before.

Hands helped him to sit up, and he turned to find himself looking into dark eyes full of concern, and something more. Something he couldn't quite define. Charlotte smiled and kissed him on the forehead. "No more secrets," she whispered.

Samu and Bertrand pulled him across the pavement so that he was propped up against the wall below a line of billboards. And then they leaned Kirsty against his chest, and she drew up her legs like a child in the womb. He put his arm around her shoulder and let his head fall back against the wall, and he found himself looking up at Bertrand. He held his gaze for several seconds, and then reached up a hand. When the young man gave him his, he held it tight. "Thank you," he whispered.

He was only vaguely aware, then, of Bertrand talking on a mobile, and had no idea how much time had passed before he heard a car draw up at the kerbside, and the sound of sirens in the distance. There seemed to be people and voices all around them. He saw Nicole's pale-faced concern drift in and out of his field of vision. He heard Raffin say something about the police. He looked up and saw a tearful Sophie looking down at them. "I promised you I'd come back," he said.

She nodded. "I still hate her, though."

Kirsty turned her head, something in the voice that dragged her back from the deep. That strange, whisky-sweet Scottish accent. "Who? Who does she hate?"

"You," Sophie said.

Kirsty looked at her father with eyes that she could barely keep open. "Who is she?"

Enzo smiled. "She's your sister, Kirsty. But she's only kidding. Aren't you, Sophie?"

Kirsty looked up at her again. Sophie smiled. "Sure I am." And she got down on her knees to put her arms around them both, and buried her face in her father's neck.

CHAPTER
TWENTY-SIX

Enzo stood in front of the Président's desk. Sunlight streamed in through the windows and lay in geometric patterns across the blue carpet. The Lycée Bellevue shimmered distantly in the August heat. Summer courses were drawing to a close. A fresh intake would soon be arriving, young minds exercised in the arts of science and technology. The Président's desk was as untidy as it always was. He came through from the outer office with his nose buried in an open folder. He wore a pair of frameless designer glasses perched lightly on the bridge of his nose.

He looked up and over the top of them at Enzo, and shook his hand. "Congratulations, Macleod. Damn fine job."

Enzo was surprised. After their last meeting he was half-expecting to be sacked. "Thank you, Monsieur le Président."

"Take a seat, take a seat." And he took his own advice, flopping into the captain's chair behind his desk and dropping his folder in front of him. He removed his glasses and let them swing gently from his thumb and forefinger. He rubbed his chin and regarded Enzo thoughtfully. Enzo pulled up a chair and sat down, and the Président picked up his folder again and held it out. "You'll have seen most of these, no doubt."

Enzo opened the folder to find it full of newspaper cuttings about the Jacques Gaillard case. He looked up. "Yes, Monsieur le Président."

The Président leaned forward on his elbows. "There's been a lot of interest, Macleod. We've had offers of funding." He waved a hand to indicate the paper blizzard on his desk. "A proposal to establish a Chair of Forensic Science. That would be quite a feather in our cap. Of course, I'd expect you to head up the department."

Enzo raised an eyebrow. "Interesting idea, Monsieur le Président."

"It'll take time, naturally, to set things in motion. So I've appointed a new head of biology, and I want you to take some time off. A sabbatical. Paid, of course. Come up with a concrete plan of implementation. A budget. Nothing too outrageous, mind."

"No, Monsieur le Président."

"And while you're at it, it wouldn't do any harm at all if you applied your very particular talents to unravelling a few more of those unsolved cases that Raggin's been collecting."

"Raffin."

"What?"

"Raffin. His name's Roger Raffin."

"That's what I said." The Président replaced his glasses carefully on the bridge of his nose and looked over them again at Enzo. "So what do you say?"

Enzo cocked his head and looked at him for a very long time. "Are those new glasses, Monsieur le Président?"

Acknowledgments

I would like to offer my grateful thanks to some "extraordinary people" who gave so generously of their time and expertise during my researches for this book. In particular, I'd like to express my gratitude to pathologist Steven C. Campman, M.D, Medical Examiner, San Diego, California; Mike Baxter, Head of Forensic Science Services at the Police Forensic Science Laboratory, Dundee, Scotland; Ariane Bataille and Gilbert Raffin, for the studio in St. Germain des Prés, their wonderful Paris apartment, the farmhouse in the Corrèze, their endless patience, and most of all their friendship; Laurène Castelli for her insights into the byzantine workings of the mind; Jean-Pierre and Jacqueline Lelong, for the use of their home in the "thirteenth"; Patricia and Jean Yves Bourbonne, for allowing me access to their apartment in the Avenue Georges Mandel; Charles-Henri Montin, ENA graduate, Promotion Michel de l'Hôpital, 1979, and civil administrator in the office of the French Prime Minister; Antoine Durrleman, Director of the École National d'Administration (ENA); Anne-Marie Steib, Chargée de la Communication, ENA; Alain Lynch, artiste extraordinaire, for his wonderful studio on the Île St. Louis; Delphine Cerf, author of *Les Catacombes de Paris*; and last, but certainly not least, my wife Janice Hally, against whose IQ of 167 I had to pit my wits to crack the clues she set me for the book.